Revenge of the Golden Dragon

By
Gig Goodloe

Llumina
Press

Requests for permission to make copies of any part of this work should be mailed to Permissions Department, Llumina Press, 7101 W. Commercial Blvd., Ste. 4E, Tamarac, FL 33319.

ISBN: 978-1-62550-373-2 (PB)

Dedicated to my loving wife Annette,
who saw something in me that no one else did.

In memory of my brother Dugan,
my big brother, my best friend.

Introduction

Avalon, a quaint seaside fishing and tourist village nestled in a picturesque cove on the leeward side of the enchanting island of Santa Catalina.

The immense circular peach stucco and red-tile-roofed casino of Moorish architectural style dominates the landscape of small clustered shops and restaurants and moderate bungalows that cling to the steep hillsides overlooking the pristine azure harbor.

While the boardwalk, adjacent to the harbor, and the entire city of Avalon, which encompasses all of six or seven square blocks, are teeming with typical resort and sportfishing activities, the surrounding island and the numerous serene coves are intimate sanctuaries of warm tropical Edens, small havens sheltered from the stormy seas of life.

Catalina is a comforting natural escape from which to cast off the daily routine, the humdrum, the ugliness of a gray, unchanging existence. A fantasy to enjoy upon the ascent from the ever-deepening rut one plows on repetitious schedule.

Inhibitions fade into the balmy evenings like the Latin and Caribbean rhythms that waft gently over the placid harbor. Passions of love and lust are revitalized upon the sun-bleached sands and within the pale ocean waters. Avalon is a rejuvenation, a celebration of life.

CATALINA ISLAND

Starlight Beach   East Starlight   Arrow Point

Emerald Bay

Land's End   Parson's Landing   Howland's Landing

Eagle Rock   Ship Rock

Cactus Bay   Cherry Cove

4th of July Cove

Isthmus Cove

Star Bay   Fisherman's Cove   Ripper's Cove

Paradise Cove

Iron Bound Bay   Blue Cavern Point   Lava Wall Beach

Empire Landing

Ribbon Rock

Whale Rock   Cabrillo Beach

Cape Cortez   Goat Harbor

Lobster Bay   Italian Gardens

Catalina   Long Point Beach

Harbor

Button Shell Beach

White's Landing

Moonstone Cove

Little Harbor   Willow Cove

Cottonwood   Toyon Bay

Canyon   Gallagher's Cove

Frog Rock Cove

Ben Weston   Hamilton Cove

Beach   Descanso Cove

Avalon Bay

Lover's Cove

Pebbly Beach

China Point   Silver Canyon

Salta Verde Point

Palisades

Seal Rocks

East End

Chapter One

I arrived on a bright sunny afternoon aboard the *Catalina Steamer*. I had returned to Avalon on several occasions last season to enjoy the fishing and absorb the sun, the rum, and the sand- bunnies. This was my first crossing this season, and I was looking forward to more of the same.

This sojourn, however, was not entirely of the "busman's holiday" category. There was a certain anticipation attached to this trip, a sense of unfinished business that needed to be attended. Perhaps a closure of sorts. A chance to put right one of those nagging little injustices that must fester in the back of your mind until the time is right, and the opportunity presents itself, for you to muster the personal armies of indignant mercenaries within, and march them out upon the fields of battle to once again engage the enemy of greed, corruption, and the perversion of power. And vice versa.

During my initial investigation into the disappearance of the Rigney family's heir apparent, Johnny the eldest of two sons, I allowed myself to get side-tracked into the search for the ill-fated lost treasure of the thirteenth century Mongolian Emperor Kubla Kahn. The 'Crown Jewel' of the cursed treasure is a ruby and emerald encrusted statuette of a "Golden Dragon." I would not make that mistake again. I would not allow myself to get side-tracked this time around.

As we approached the steamer pier, reaching majestically into the harbor adjacent to the Yacht Club, the excited tourists hurried to the ship's rail to toss coins down to the smiling island boys, who eagerly swam about and dived for the shiny coins as they splashed into the water and began their gentle zigzag descent toward the smooth sandy bottom.

I lingered aboard until the exuberant masses disembarked, gathered their overstuffed luggage, and dispersed down the pier to meld with the energetic hordes already swarming to and fro along the busy boardwalk. I emerged down the gangway onto the pier, collected my lone duffle, and continued down the pier, threading my way across the wide boardwalk that separated the harbor and beach area from the rest of the town. I went through the anonymous entrance and climbed the enclosed stairwell that led to the Edgewater Hotel.

The Edgewater was a nondescript shoe box perched atop the Sea Grotto restaurant and a cluster of souvenir boutiques and knickknack shops. The hotel consisted of eight average-sized rooms, separated four on either side of a long narrow hallway running the length of the building, with two additional adjoining suites at the front overlooking the harbor and the deep blue Pacific.

My room was number 8 at the end of the hall on the right. Just beyond, the hallway opened onto a small veranda enclosed around the sides by vine-covered lattice. A fire escape extended down the back of the building off the patio, and into the alley that ran parallel to the boardwalk behind the shops.

I'd stayed in several different lodgings on my previous trips, including Mrs. O'Malley's clapboard rooming house, the Whispering Waters Inn. During Prohibition Mrs. O'Malley ran the inn as a speakeasy and upstairs brothel. She was a grand and feisty little cherub-faced Irish lady who treated me like a son. I called her Moms.

Number 8 was of comfortable size, with two windows overlooking the patio, a private bath, and an alcove room furnished with trundle bed. The room itself had a soft double bed, a small two-seat dining set, a bureau and end tables, and hot and cold running room maids—all the necessary comforts.

The room was located toward the rear of the building and away from the congestion of the excited tourists and late-night barhopping inebriates. It was relatively quiet and sufficiently secluded, yet situated smack-dab in the middle of the "fun zone."

I dropped my duffle on the bed, removed the spit kit, and placed it on the bathroom sink. I slipped the room key in my pocket and locked the door behind me. I whistled down the hall, descended the stairs onto the boardwalk, and merged into the flow of camera-toting tourists shuffling along trundling armloads of kids, kids' bags, toys, trinkets, and baubles. Crisscrossing between the tourists were the fishermen and divers dragging little wooden wheeled carts brimming with the accoutrements of their endeavors.

The Fourth of July celebration was only a few days away, and this was as big a tourist week as they get here on the island. The Independence Day parade and the evening's elaborate fireworks display are richly enjoyed by all, and the preparations were being attended with excited anticipation. The mood was festive and highly contagious.

I emerged from the throng at the south end of the boardwalk and continued down the narrow road in the direction of Lover's Cove. I walked out to the private dock where Commodore Rigney, the island's patriarch, kept his yacht, the *Lucky Dutchman*. I was looking for an old friend.

Across the pier from the *Lucky Dutchman*, and tied forward of the boathouse where the Chris-Craft was kept, lay a sleek wooden seventy-footer vaguely resembling a British PT boat. She had been stripped of the traditional battleship gray and refinished to her original rich mahogany. The torpedo launchers were removed and the gunnels had been raised to a higher elevation above the deck.

As I approached, I could hear the sounds of tortured sea ditties, as the old salt emerged on deck. "Ahoy, Skipper," I called. "Permission to come aboard?"

"Ahoy, Polliwog," the old man chuckled through toothless grin. "Welcome aboard, the *Bad Penny*, son." I had to laugh; Captain Wally had remembered my drunken war stories from my first visit to the island. The *Bad Penny* was the name of the big beautiful Superfortress that I flew over every microscopic coral outcropping in the Pacific during the war. So christened, because, as the saying goes, "A bad penny always comes home." And that gorgeous silver bird did just that for sixty-four rivet-shattering missions.

I was glad to see the old dog. He was a cantankerous old fart, but beneath that barnacled exterior beat the heart of a sweet and gentle soul. He had seen the world from the deck of one kind of ship or another, and he had come to find his "Shangri-la" here on Catalina Island. He helped pluck my polliwog butt from the clutches of an angry sea during my maiden excursion to the island, and I owed him my life.

Captain Wally used to skipper a tugboat back and forth, barging granite boulders from the island's quarry to the mainland. The boulders were used to construct breakwaters and harbor jetties along the California coast. He sold his tug sometime ago and found this converted subchaser that he could charter to weekend sportfishermen. Easier life, more leisure time, no schedules to keep, less grind on man and machine. He seemed to enjoy plying the waters around the island for the easy *dinero* of the eager fat cats here to experience the "deepwater safari."

"So, Polliwog," he asked, "how do you like my new baby?"

"She looks like a fine craft, Captain. She should make a great sail-fishing boat," I responded.

"Yea, we do pretty well during the season. Gets a little slow in the winter. Gives me more time to pursue my other interests," he said, with a twinkle in his eye.

"Other interests?" I queried. He smiled, put his arms out, palms up, and looked skyward.

"Weather prognosticator," he said. He looked back at me with a wide grin. "I think it's going to martini," he announced. Then he slowly and deliberately withdrew his tarnished silver flask from his hip pocket.

"May there be wind in your sails and lead in your pencil," he toasted, and then downed a short slam. He then handed the flask to me.

"May your gunnels be filled with sailfish, and may there still be some sail in your sword," I responded and hammered her down. I ran to the rail and blew a widely dispersed high-pressure spray over the starboard side. I was semiprepared for the pirate rum to claw its way down my gullet, which the old crust normally packs around, but this was almost an actual martini. It was old and stale and had a strange metallic aftertaste. Pretty raunchy.

He snatched the flask back. "That's no way to treat a good martin-eye, ya damn Polliwog."

"What the hell is that?" I asked. "Tastes like dirty socks. What happened to that liquid sandpaper you used to promote as rum?"

"Oh that stuff began to churn my innards," he said. "I had to switch to a more sophisticated concoction. Look, if I do this"—he raised the flask to his lips once again, only this time, he extended his pinky finger—"I look pretty swave, don't I, Polliwog?" he cackled, mangling the language.

"Swave and deboner, Captain," I responded. "Swave and deboner!"

"Well how about a two-bit tour, Polliwog?" We proceeded down the main ladder into a spacious lounge, furnished surprisingly with handcrafted antique furniture, deep-pile carpet, and highly polished mahogany bulkheads. It looked more like a playboy party boat than a charter fishing vessel.

"I removed some of the fuel capacity to make room for more open living quarters," he said proudly.

"Well to be perfectly honest, Polliwog," he confessed, "I didn't order these renovations. This boat was another acquisition of P. K. Rigney's before his untimely disappearance near the East China Sea. I don't know how he managed it, but somehow he smuggled this boat away from the Samara Islands in the Philippines at the end of the war when all the PT boats were ordered to be destroyed. He brought it back to the Higgins shipyards, in Louisiana, and had her retrofitted to his custom specs. This is what's known as a British Elko boat. Built for sub patrol in the Pacific, and lightning strikes against Japanese cruisers and destroyers. The Japs called 'em devil boats. Seventy feet, step hull, powered by three twelve-cylinder, thirteen-hundred-horsepower Packards. This baby does sixty knots in calm seas burning alcohol aviation fuel, and she draws only five feet of draft. She's quite a boat, Polliwog."

"They used to call these plywood boats, didn't they?" I asked.

"Oh squid piss," he snorted. "Follow me."

We proceeded aft, through what was once crew sleeping quarters, now renovated for the comfort of charter clients and serviced by way of separate access to topside. The captain opened the hatch leading into the engine room. He removed a section of deck grate and pointed into the bilge area.

"See that, Polliwog? Laminated mahogany beams with inch-thick double-hull mahogany planks. Plywood boat my barnacled bottom!"

We continued the tour up the ladder, through the aft hatch, and out onto the stern deck. The gun base for the original forty-millimeter was still intact, as were the mounts for the two thirty-millimeters on either side amidships, as well as the twenty-millimeter mounted on the bow.

He was most proud of the new control panel and helm. Part of the retrofit at the Higgins yard included separate cockpit controls for each of the three engines and a custom marine transmission. Originally, a crewman in the engine room manually controlled the boat's transmission. But that could now be operated from the comfort of the cushioned pilot's chair, on which Captain Wally plopped himself. I joined him in the adjacent copilot's seat.

The overhead cover had been designed as mini–flying bridge and con tower equipped with the original radar, radio antennas, spotlight, and other electronics. The *Bad Penny* was a stealthy craft with a low silhouette and a wide beam. (I had a girlfriend like that once.) She sat squat upon the water and her fifty-ton displacement smoothed the ocean swells while at mooring, and when up to speed, the step hull lifted the forward half of the boat out of the water and created a stable ride plate in the stern at the point of propulsion and rudder control.

We sat content in our plush captain's chairs, slowly swiveling, enjoying the clear afternoon skies and warm gentle breeze. The old man mentioned that he had a charter for tomorrow but would be available the following day if I wanted to try my luck at the big fish. I happily agreed, so we made a reservation for the day after next.

"Have you seen Lara or Rita since you've been back?" he asked.

"No, I haven't seen either of them yet, but I plan on having dinner tonight at the ballroom. I suspect I'll see them both at that time."

"Yep, you'll no doubt see them there," he said. "Lara has pretty much taken over the ballroom entertainment and dining operation. Nicky Fallon is still running the casino, but I think Rita is taking on more of the day-to-day responsibilities . . . ya know, the business end of it."

I was somewhat surprised to hear that. Lara taking over the ballroom, booking entertainment and overseeing the dining arrangements, I could understand; she was a natural. But Rita moving into the business end of the casino operation seemed out of character for her. She was so free-spirited and feisty. The nine-to-five banality of the "suits" would seem too regimented and confining for her impulsive, spitfire, and impetuous lifestyle. However, the image of her in a short business skirt and translucent blouse of pastel, in contrast to her dark smooth skin and shine of silken hair cascading about her neck and shoulders was very exciting—a warm, alluring apparition.

"Ya know, Polliwog, it seems you've changed a bit since the last time I saw you. I don't rightly know what it is? More confidence, a little maturity, a few extra pounds? Maybe it's that deep saltwater tan?"

I explained to Captain Wally, over a few more agonizing belts of his metallic martini, that I had slowly changed my outlook in life and my style of living since my first visit to the island. I had come to the realization that either life could be short, crude, and brutish, or it could be an exciting and leisurely cruise through sunny harbors filled with good food, fine wines, and sandy-rump, deeply tanned fun bunnies. I had come to the conclusion that I would prefer the latter and was thoroughly enjoying the beginnings of the conversion.

I recounted how Precious Goodlay, my secretary extraordinaire, and I had pooled our savings and bought into a small percentage of her nephew's rapidly expanding personal and estate security business. The Hollywood movie and entertainment industry had grown by leaps and bounds after the war, and with it came legions of adoring, overzealous fans, squads of off-center, bloodsucking parasites, as well as platoons of curious, run-of-the-mill, well-wishing weirdos. The big movie and recording stars, producers, moguls, and the large Brentwood-style estates they inhabited needed protection from the well-meaning masses, as well as the hard-core deviants, kidnappers, and extortionists that stalk the seedy underbelly of LA's neon streets.

Precious Goodlay's nephew's had carved out a very profitable and ever-expanding niche within Tinseltown's entertainment industry. And from that came a comfortable income for Precious and myself, as well as some very lucrative contracts funneled toward Travis Dugan Private Investigations. The town was full of studios concerned about the off-camera behavior of their stars. Stars concerned with the poolside behavior of their spouses. Spouses concerned with cabana behavior of their consorts. If the town had a thousand tales to tell, it had ten thousand to suppress. Travis Dugan Private Investigations had become the discreet conduit through which Tinseltown funneled its private affairs and personal intrigues. We were the machine within which lotusland laundered its soiled undergarments or recovered its lost, stolen, or swindled treasures and/or reputations. We were the finders for the seekers, the hiders for the keepers, and the keepers of the well-kept.

"Aha!" the old man laughed. "Slick as hot shit through a tin horn, as you used to say, huh, Polliwog?"

"Olé, mi Capitán!" I toasted.

Chapter Two

I arrived at the casino just after dusk, elegant in my off-the-rack original Bill Blass dinner jacket of fleecy white. The mountain behind Avalon was a deep purple silhouette against the golden radiance of the setting sun. The mooring lights of the many boats in the harbor shimmered softly upon the silvery calm of the water. A warm Santa Ana blew gently across the channel and over the twinkling lights of Avalon.

The casino was bright and festive, and the Latin rhythms of Xavier Cugat drifted across the boardwalk from the ballroom. I entered the dazzling brilliance of the grand ballroom and was once again awestruck by the grandeur. The immense black walnut beams arching majestically from mirrored brilliance of mahogany dance floor, high above to radiant ceiling, from which hung enormous crystal chandeliers.

I casually strolled to the left along the hand-carved teak bar, the orchestra straight ahead and the gleaming dance floor to the right. Surrounding the perimeter of the dance floor were elegantly decorated dining tables filled with exuberant party patrons. All apparently having a wonderful time. The dance floor was awhirl with rumba, and "Cougy," directed his orchestra, while his current tango partner named Chu-Chu, or Chi-Chi, or Cha-Cha, rumba'd her way back and forth across the stage in eye-popping frantic shimmies of electric red Spanish frills.

"Hello, Travis, glad you could make it," came the familiar smokey-velvet voice from behind me. I turned and gazed upon a golden bronze goddess gently caressed by liquid copper poured smooth over her statuesque and softly rounded body. Lara Rigney was even more beautiful than I had remembered. Her long auburn hair flowed across her smoothly tanned shoulders and cascaded gently down the silkiness of her back. My pulse quickened and the hair on the back of my neck bristled. Just as it had the first time I saw her in the soft, foggy neon glow of the intermittent "bait" sign, little more than a year ago.

She put her arms around my neck, holding me close, and gently melted into my arms. She felt soft and warm, the scent of fresh carnations. Her breath was deep and longing, hot against the nape of my neck. She kissed me softly on the neck and the cheek, then firmly on the lips. She held me close and whispered in my ear, "I'm so glad that you came, Travis, I hoped that you would."

"Angel, you know that no matter where I am, or what I'm doing, I'll always come running. All you have to do is whistle. You do know how to whistle, don't you, Angel?" I asked with sly smile.

"Just like I said before, Travis, too many Bogart movies. You're a hopeless romantic . . . or maybe that's hapless?" she giggled.

She took me by the arm and gently guided me toward the bar. "Can I buy you a drink, sailor? Perhaps a vodka martini, shaken, not stirred?" she asked coyly.

"Yes, I meant to thank you for the tip, Angel," I responded.

"I had a feeling you might want to know when Blaine Pond returned to the island," she said. "He's been in here every night since his arrival some three days ago. He's upstairs in the casino as we speak."

"What has the dashing secret agent been up to since his return?" I asked.

"Well, so far, he's invited me to a candlelight dinner, and he's made an appointment at the tile foundry to purchase another bulk order for shipment to the East Asian Trading Company in Singapore."

"Has he shown any overt interest in Dr. Con's bat guano mining operation in Smuggler's Cove, as he did during his last visit?" I asked.

"No," she answered. "Nothing in particular, but I've only seen him here in the casino at night. I don't know where he's been otherwise. Dr. Con has been keeping a very low profile since the excitement of your last visit," she continued. "He has fortified the entry gates to his compound, and the confrontation with the Island Conservancy Committee regarding the suspected dredging of Smuggler's Cove has for now subsided. There has been no further evidence of sediment or other materials from Smuggler's Cove found in any other areas around the island. Dr. Con has been very low-key as of late."

"And have you seen anything of our omnipresent overstuffed quasi salvage consultant and artisan provocateur, Sir Arthur Sydney?" I asked.

"Yes, he was here at the beginning of the season to partake in carnival once again," she began. "He was quite excited about the art and treasure auction, as he was upon his first visit, and purchased a few trinkets and baubles once again, according to Sumner Renton, our curator. It's a shame you missed carnival this season, Travis. Everyone was asking about you, especially RJ."

"How is the good Commodore?" I asked.

"He speaks of you often, Travis," she said. "He thoroughly enjoyed your conversations and the time spent with you. He liked to share his Havanas and his brandy, reminiscing over good times and reliving the adventures of his youth. I know RJ genuinely likes you, Travis. He thinks you're one of a kind, something special . . . And I think I agree."

She took me gently by the hand and led me tentatively to the shimmering dance floor. Once again she melted into my arms as we effortlessly glided around the gleaming palace amid soft Latin rhythms, twinkling evening stars, and warm summer breeze. That familiar comforting warmth and, at the same time, overwhelming passion and allure gently engulfed us, as it did the first time I held her close on the dance floor. It was déjà vu all over again.

As the tune faded, we casually strolled arm in arm through the large glass doors out onto the promenade that surrounded the casino, and over to the seawall overlooking the serene harbor. We gazed silently up to the soft twinkle of the night's canopy for some time. Finally, quietly, gently, I pulled her close and kissed her long and passionately. She took me in with yearning breath, soft caress, smoldering desire. We melted into each other, drinking in all we could.

Finally, she softly whispered, "Oh Travis, you could be such a great lover. You certainly have the passion, the strength, the desire. You're obviously familiar with the territory. I could really fall for you, if you weren't such a womanizing dog."

"Dogs are loyal and trustworthy companions," I responded.

"Some perhaps," she said. "Most are just marauding mongrels."

"They can be trained," I said.

"Training has its limitations, most must be fenced," she retorted.

"Establishing boundaries is a good thing," I said.

"Yea, sure," she said. "Until they get a whiff of something on the wind, then before you know it, they jump the fence and you're left with nothing but a broken heart and a landscape littered with lingering piles of his crap."

"He could be tied up," I finally acquiesced.

She held me close and stared softly into my eyes. "Ooooh, now you're talkin' big boy. I like the way you think." She paused. She smiled that wicked little smile I'd come to know and love. Then she whispered, "Or there's always the threat of castration?"

"Hello, excuse me. Excuse me, Mrs. Rigney," the maître d' said as he popped his head out of the glass doors. "The airport just called. The chairman of the board is on his way."

"Oh yes, thank you. I almost lost track of time," she said as she reshuffled and prepared to return to the ballroom. "Would you like to come in and meet Frank?" she asked.

"Frank who?" I questioned.

"Old Blue Eyes, silly," she giggled.

"No, I've enjoyed about as much of that pleasure as I can stand before," I responded. "You go ahead and do your charming hostess thing. I think I'll go upstairs to the casino."

"Stop by later," she called as she opened the glass door to the ballroom. "I'll buy you dinner." She blew me a kiss, then she disappeared behind the glass reflection.

As I headed around to the entrance of the ballroom and up the ramp to the casino, I saw an imposing black limo pull to the curb, and from it emerged Old Blue Eyes and his ever-present entourage of sequined bubbleheaded blonde bimbos and a phalanx of no-neck Cro-Magnon knuckle draggers. They were fawningly shown to their tables, with the obligatory wave to Cougy and a kiss for Chu-Chu, Cha-Cha, Chi-Chi—whatever.

Before I began my ascent of the ramp leading to the casino entrance, two squad cars pulled abruptly to a stop alongside, and several stern gendarmes jumped out and persuasively hustled me around the side of the building and slammed me against the coarse stucco of the casino wall.

"Hands against the wall and spread 'em," came the all-too-familiar command from slick and shiny, always-perturbed Chief Constable Lafargé. One on either side held my hand to the wall, while a third kicked my feet apart with much aggression. I looked back over my right shoulder to where the inscrutable inspector stood, menacing in his newly added wardrobe accessories of English riding breeches, riding crop, leather gloves, and knee-high riding boots. When I'd see him next, he'd no doubt further accessorize with fancy sword and chrome cavalier helmet adorned atop with bushy rooster broom plumes. (I didn't know if he'd gone queer or was suffering Napoleon syndrome.)

"I can't spread 'em any farther, amigo," I finally said. "I don't know what you're looking for, but I can tell you that if one of you starts puttin' on a surgical glove, this examination is over."

"Still the funny man with the smart mouth," said Lafargé as his frisker removed the .38 snubby from under the left armpit of the friskee, then returned to the overly enthusiastic ensuing search.

"If this guy gets any more intimate with this vivacious expedition and adventurous probing going on back there, somebody's gonna have to buy me dinner," I said drolly.

Lafargé, apparently not amused, stepped forward and delivered a swift, short left-hook kidney punch that exploded just under my right rib cage. It almost buckled my knees. I wasn't prepared. The pain was sharp and penetrating. There was a prosthetic hardness to it. A roll of quarters within clenched fist. Or perhaps even brass knuckles. It was a cheap shot intended to separate rib from cartilage and bruise internal organs. The ramifications would be felt for weeks. If the gendarmes on either side weren't holding my hands firmly to the wall, I probably would have gone down. That little chickenshit knew it was going to cripple me for some time. I'd have a hitch in my get-along for the duration. That sumbitch would pay for that. I'm a firm believer in "What goes around comes around." I'd never taken any crap from anyone so far, and I was not about to start now.

"You dumb-ass arrogant cowboy!" Lafargé's French Algerian accent spit harshly through clenched teeth. "The last time you were here was an unmitigated disaster of epic proportions!" he continued with much articulation. "I had bodies stacked up in the morgue like cordwood. I had to call the mainland to ship a ton of ice over here because we ran out of available refrigerated space! You were warned at that time to keep your gun holstered and your nose in your own business! I was cautioned by LAPD that you were a loose cannon prone to destructive tendencies. Shoot from the hip, ask questions later. I knew you were a crude, clumsy, brutish clod. I should have shipped your ass back to the mainland as soon as you set foot on the island."

I slowly began to regain my breath and the stars began to clear from my head. I looked over my shoulder once again. "Then you would have had no one to solve all your cases for you, while you pranced about in your precious stretch pants, looking enchantingly like mincing queer bait, you savage bitch!" I said with as much lisp and eyelash flutter as I could muster.

I saw the rage build immediately. Clenched jaw, flushing about the neck and cheeks, bulging eyes. He stepped forward to deliver another kidney buster, only this time I quickly moved out of the way like dodging an inside pitch to the plate. His fist smacked into the stucco wall of the casino, crumbling a shallow hole the size of a softball. He followed up with a short left hook aimed at my head. I put my right foot against the wall and pushed away, pulling both of my guards with me, just in time for them to catch Lafargé's incoming hook, knocking both of their heads, stoogelike, into the wall. I freed my hands from the slumping Keystone Kops and stepped back to face Lafargé.

"I've only been defending myself so far, Frenchy," I said. "But don't think I won't kick the living shit out of you and your pantywaist girlfriends you brought to this party."

The two guards behind Lafargé quickly moved toward me as the other two began to rise and shake the cobwebs from their stucco'd brains. Lafargé raised his hand and brought his advancing mob to an abrupt halt. He said something in French and was handed my .38 and the cartridges they had removed.

"We have checked the serial numbers against the test-fired weapon that we took from you the last time, when we had you and Blaine Pond in custody. I see that you still carry the same primitive weapon as before."

I said nothing. Stared intently into his eyes. Something had changed. He seemed wound pretty tight and barely keeping the seams from separating. A few screws had loosened under that stern, controlled, spit-and-polish exterior. The mishmash of interior gears not quite synchronized.

He handed back my .38 and the loose shells. I holstered my snubby and dropped the cartridges in my pocket. With that bit of dramatics concluded, Lafargé and his band of merry mercenaries turned abruptly in unison and departed, leaving me standing like a roughed-up kid who just had his lunch money extorted by the school yard bully and his miscreant gang of grinning lackeys. I was pissed and wanted to extract some modicum of revenge. However, as my uncle Leo used to say, "Revenge is a dish best served cold."

I straightened my attire and dusted my shoes off on the back of my pant legs. I went back around the way I had been unceremoniously escorted and proceeded up the ramp to the casino entrance.

Upon entering the dazzling brilliance of the immense casino, I was once again struck by the glittering exuberance displayed by the excited gamers and their respective retinues of animated supporters and inebriated cheerleaders. The architecture of the casino was as breathtaking as the grand ballroom. Immense black walnut beams arched majestically to high ceiling from which hung huge ornate crystal chandeliers. The walls of the circular room were floor-to-ceiling sheets of thick plate glass which offered exquisite view of the pristine harbor and the surrounding quaintness of Avalon and the unspoiled natural beauty of Santa Catalina.

Similar to the ballroom downstairs, the casino had the hand-carved teak bar which curved around to the large gaming area on the right and a small mahogany dance floor beyond near the windows. A small dining area farther right of the dance floor completed the circular space back to the double-glass-door entrance.

I spotted the exotically beautiful, exceptionally erotic younger Rigney daughter, Rita, seated at the far end of the bar. Her long raven hair cascading in wild mane down the length of her smooth dark back and shoulders. Gorgeous brown legs exposed to silky thigh, 'neath slit of miniscule satin-smooth black slip dress. Her large almond-shaped ebony eyes gazed wantingly from under long lash and over sculptured Latina cheekbones. My pulse began to race and blood pumped freely. I remembered our rendezvous aboard the *Lucky Dutchman* during my initial sojourn to the island.

She smiled wide and bright from full pouty lips that seemed to whisper, "Come hither." I strolled to where she waited, my own grin widening as I got nearer. The hair on the back of my neck began to bristle, as did the restless manaconda stirring somewhere south of my morale equator.

We embraced and kissed passionately. That familiar sponginess of warm flesh, hot breath, groping caresses, the mesmerizing scent of fresh lilac. The rush of passion, wanting, craving, smoldering, insatiable. Yes, it all came rushing back in torrents of familiar all-consuming waves of passion not yet muted by the grays of time. The lustful joys of our own self-spun cocoon of gossamer bliss.

We held each other close for the longest time. She felt warm, exciting, and completely comfortable to be in my arms once again. Her breath alluring on my neck. One hand high up her thigh, under the silkiness of her black dress, the other at her side softly cradling the warmth of her firm breast.

She finally whispered softly in my ear, "Glad you could make it on such short notice, gumshoe, but you're really slipping, aren't you?"

"Oh, I don't know," I responded confidently. "I seem to have everything well in hand. A grasp of firm things, or I mean, a firm grasp of things, so to speak."

She leaned close and looked deeply into my eyes. "You have your back to the door, greenhorn. You have no idea who's coming or going, nor do you have any clue as to who may be behind you staring holes through you as we speak. Take a look around, rookie, I'm sure that peckerwood stuper you're currently wearing as an expression will give way to acute awareness shortly."

"A cute what?" I sophomorically asked.

"Get your perverted mind off the conquest of the sweet thing for a minute, dipstick. Turn around, Sherlock."

I paused, looked in her eyes. She was slightly glazed over from the alcohol but, curiously, uncharacteristically serious. She was dead-on right, of course. That particular proclivity had always plagued me. Getting laid always seemed to be the prerogative, the priority. Everything else seemed somehow secondary. I've found, however, that the perpetual pursuit of the pink folds tends to cloud peripheral vision and dull the other senses not neurologically connected to such passions. In the past I have screwed up a number of endeavors because of my shortsighted priority with regard to the purloined pubenia.

"Wake up, flatfoot," she finally said. "Take a look around, shamus, while I order you a drink. You're going to need it."

I slowly gazed around the glittering venue filled with vigorous players casting their fortunes to the wagering winds. Lots of gaiety and laughter, drinking and cajolery. Whirl of spinning wheels, pick-pock sound of bouncing ball upon swirl of black and red flashing blur. Tinkling of frozen cubes, clatter of cascading chips. All seemed sublime in "never-never land."

Then I came upon our host, the poster boy for tall, dark, and handsome, casino manager extraordinaire and self-anointed suitor of the aforementioned, Rita Rigney—Nicky Fallon. Nicky Fallon, nephew of underworld mob boss Dominick Licata, was staring laser beams (whatever those are) straight in my direction, while I still had my hand thigh high under his girlfriend's slinky black dress. He didn't seem real happy to see me. He never does.

It got worse. Seated in front of Nicky Fallon, at the blackjack table, was Uncle Dominick himself. The notorious Nick the Pick Licata, so named for the particularly grotesque manner in which he dispatched his intended victims when he was the executioner of choice for the then infamous LA crime boss Johnny Rosselli. An ice pick through the side of the head was his MO. By design did not kill immediately, but instead, prolonged the inevitable by way of torturous, painful, agonizing convulsions. It was a repulsive, unforgettable image to any who came upon the scene later. That of course was the intent.

The whisky shot arrived and I slammed 'er down. I placed the empty shot glass on the bar and ordered another. She was right, the atmosphere had changed dramatically. The wonderment, the magic, the luster seemed to have tarnished. It had turned sinister and evil. The world had all of a sudden become cold, cruel, and harsh. All innocents had corrupted and become cancerous. Light slowly faded, eclipsed by a shroud of doom and darkness.

The second shot arrived and I again slammed 'er down. I placed the shot glass back on the bar and looked over at Rita.

"Your prehensile appendage seems to have shrunk back a bit," she toyed.

"Are you kidding?" I asked rhetorically. "He sucked up so far that it's more like a terrified turtlehead peeking out my ass."

"Oh thanks, Travis. That's a real nice visual," she giggled exasperatedly.

"Maybe you should ask me to dance," she said. "You do remember how to dance, don't you, big boy? You just press your body close to mine and fffffllllllooooow." (Oh yeah, I remembered.)

We moved effortlessly about the dance floor for a short while, then made our way out onto the balcony that surrounded the gaming venue.

"What the hell happened around here?" I finally asked. "What's with all the pin-striped meatballs loitering around the place? Hasn't anyone noticed the change in atmosphere? The ambiance has become a little threatening. Not festive, carefree, and gay as before."

"Got a cigarette?" she asked. I lit one for each of us. She gazed over the quiet harbor and let the smoke drift away into the darkness. She finally turned away from the harbor and looked back inside the casino.

"It all occurred rather slowly," she finally said very softly. "In small increments. I think Nicky installed me in the business office as a front, or maybe a patsy. Someone from the family to legitimize the public perceptions of the gaming operation, while concealing the back room, behind closed-door collusion that I have begrudgingly come to suspect is occurring." She paused, took another drag from her cigarette, then let it drop to the pavement and crushed it out.

She looked back inside the casino. "You see those croupiers pushing the metal cart?" she asked.

I watched as two overstuffed meatballs made their rounds from one gaming table to another. They used a key to unlock and remove a small metal box from under each table and replace them with one from their cart. When they had finished switching the canisters, they rolled the cart to a set of elevator doors that were located at the end of the bar, out of sight of the gaming area, and just before the entry to the kitchen. The doors opened, they pushed the cart inside, and the doors closed.

"Where does the elevator go?" I asked.

"Down to the office mezzanine level directly into the counting room vault," she began. "When the elevator is up, the bottom of the elevator becomes the ceiling of the vault. Likewise, when the elevator is down, the top of the elevator then becomes the floor of the elevator alcove above."

"So let me get this straight," I said. "The croupiers periodically make their rounds and exchange the full-money boxes from under each table with empty ones from their cart. Then they take the cart brimming with full-money canisters to the elevator and down to the counting room vault."

"That's correct," she responded. "The croupiers will give the pit boss at each set of tables a chit with a number that corresponds with the number on the box they're delivering. Then they can correlate at the end of the evening whose table made how much during that night's session. It also functions as a checkpoint to see if anyone, dealer or croupier, et cetera, is palming or skimming at the table."

"What happens once the money boxes arrive in the vault?" I asked.

"Each box is emptied, counted, wrapped, and the numbered chit from the money box is then attached to the wrapped bundles and then locked in the safe," she explained. "Only Nicky Fallon and myself have the combination to the safe. One of us has to be here at all times while we're in operation. An armored Brink's truck picks up the bundles each morning and delivers them to the bank."

"Was the audit of the casino ever completed after my last trip?" I asked.

"No," she explained. "After your last adventure here, it took awhile to get things back to normal and we never actually completed the audit. It was originally Johnny's idea to order the audit," she continued. "He must have had a feeling something was amiss. Johnny always analyzed every move and their ramifications or consequences. He never made a decision without thorough research and a view from every angle. He must have thought something was up or he would not have ordered an audit from an outside third-party source."

"And therefore, that proposed audit may have provided the motive for Johnny's disappearance," I injected.

"From the way things look at this point in time, I'm afraid I can't argue with that theory," she said. "I'm sure Johnny would not like the way things have transpired as of late," she said softly, almost a whisper. Then she turned away from the casino, back toward the harbor, and fell silent.

After a while, we went back inside. I escorted her to her office in the mezzanine, where she collected her belongings, and then we made our way out to the boardwalk in front. We found Roscoe in his usual spot leaning on his cab. I asked him to drive Rita back to the mansion, then requested that he pick me up in front of the Edgewater at 9:00 a.m. tomorrow. He happily agreed; we exchanged short pleasantries and said good night until tomorrow. As the cab pulled away into the darkness, I couldn't help but wonder what kind of mess I had gotten myself into once again.

And once again, here on this island paradise, it never seemed to be just one mess, but a convolution of messes juxtaposed one upon another. I might have really stepped on my prehensile appendage this time.

Chapter Three

I reentered the grand ballroom amid the laughter and bumps of the bouncy serpentine conga line meandering its way around the room. Cougy was directing the orchestra and Chu-Chu, Cha-Cha, Chi-Chi, whatever, was still rumba-dancing her way back and forth across the stage. She was in good shape, I'd say that for her. Couldn't understand a word she was saying, but she was in good shape. Great legs, nice tits, pouty red lips.

The chairman of the board was still ensconced with his entourage of bimbos and bone crushers, all the while humbly accepting the endless accolades of fawning well-wishers with pushed-over noses and gravely voices. "Know what I'm talkin' 'bout? Forget 'bout it!"

I found Lara moving nimbly among the many spirited guests in attendance. I caught her attention and she waved me toward an empty table near the bar. I seated myself and a waiter arrived at once, took my cocktail order, and was promptly away. He soon returned drink in hand and prepared to take my dinner order. T-bone, medium rare, baked butter only, asparagus tips. And away!

As I sat quietly nurturing my glimmering martini, I noticed Nick Licata and his ever-present band of bulging knee crushers descend the gilded staircase from the casino above and confidently make their way to where Frank and his cronies played. When Frankie Boy noticed the godfather's imminent arrival, he leaped to his feet and rushed to greet him. Frankie was a good boy who showed gushing respect and knew full well on which side his bread was buttered—as he should.

Word around the backstreets of Hollywood was that when America's boy-next-door teen heartthrob wanted out of his singing contract with the Tommy Dorsey Orchestra so that he would be free to pursue a movie career with a costarring role in the upcoming production of *From Here to Eternity*, it was Uncle Dominick who convinced New York mob boss Vito Genovese to have a representative arrange a contract negotiation meeting with Dorsey. The meeting was short and negotiations were intense. The Genovese representatives placed a contract release form on the desk in front of Dorsey's face and a .45 automatic to the back of his head. They told him either his signature would be on the contract or his brains would be. Next thing you knew, Old Blue Eyes was an instant movie idol in a much-anticipated MGM production. Nice to have an uncle with connections. Hollywood is rife with nepotism.

I tried to look uninterested in the goings-on at Frank's table, though I noticed Uncle Nick glanced in my general direction on several occasions. I hoped that I didn't look familiar, as I had had a couple of run-ins with a few of his beef shanks in the past. One occasion did not turn out well for one of Nick's relatives. He might have a name associated with the mishap, but I was hoping he didn't have a face to put with the name. It was a long time ago, between the wars, when I worked for Nicolas "Pappa" Pappadopolis, recovering various weaponry throughout the world and selling it on the black market to fledgling South American rebels or in some cases through the underworld to organized crime.

On a dark moonless night long ago, one of Nick Licata's young nephews ate the big weenie while participating in an attempted hijacking of a truckload of tommy guns. I was riding shotgun and responsible for getting the cargo delivered on time and intact. It did, he didn't.

The steak arrived and I wasted no time in the process of consumption. I was famished. Eventually Lara found her way to my side and began picking over my meal, between giggles of excitement. She was almost giddy. Very uncharacteristic, but having a wonderful time. I wanted to discuss the apparent recent changes in ambiance, but wasn't going to. She was not in the mood, was not capable of required concentration, and besides I didn't want to piss on her parade my first night ashore. I moved to other things.

I asked if it might be possible to borrow a car for tomorrow. She said, between bites of my steak, to come up to the mansion in the morning and she would arrange something for me to drive. Her only condition was that I do my best to keep it on terra firma and not launch it into the ocean this time. Funny girl. Everyone on the island knew that Lara and I were run off the road, over a cliff, on my last visit, and wound up splashing her little red roadster into Lover's Cove. Only a select few knew, however, that the big black sedan that shoved us over the side also ended up in the ocean, after taking four shots from my .38 through the driver's-side windshield. That was the first day of my last visit to the island. It only got better from there.

Lara, unhesitant, pilfered a few more morsels from my plate, kissed me on the cheek, and was off to join the end of the conga line as it swept by. I finished my meal and ordered a brandy.

Nicky Fallon and Uncle Dominick's entourage said their adieus to Old Blue Eyes, and his bevy of bimbos, and made their way up the staircase to return to the casino. I lingered long enough to finish my brandy, then discreetly followed.

At the top of the stairs I moved along the bar to the far end, where I sat at the last stool against the alcove elevator wall and was able to observe new arrivals from the staircase or from the double-door glass entrance at the top of the ramp outside. I sat with my elbows on the bar, facing the mirrored back bar containing various glassware. In the mirrored reflection I could see Nicky and Uncle Dominick engaged in a low-key though apparently simmering conversation. As I watched, I recognized the other gentleman participating in the conversation as the stocky older Pisan that Nicky had unceremoniously tossed out of his office onto the pavement upon my first visit to the island. Crude, ethnic hand gestures spewed forth from the scuffed-up portly Pisan, as I recall.

After the stout gentleman had been bounced to the curb that night, Nicky Fallon frantically called a number in LA, which turned out to be Gazardi's nightclub on the Sunset Strip. Gazardi's was owned by Fat Frankie Fallontino. Fat Frankie, I found through impeccable, intuitive, and pugnacious detective investigation, was in fact Nicky Fallon's father and Dominick Licata's brother-in-law.

The conversation, I surreptitiously eavesdropped upon through Nicky's office door, was in Sicilian; but I managed to decipher a few words, like "heavy-handed" and something about more time, or longer time . . . something like that.

I wasn't sure, at the time, as to what that might pertain. However, from my present perspective, and the insidious encroachment upon casino operations by the connected ones, I'm left with no other conclusion except that Johnny Rigney's disappearance was a direct consequence of the ensuing coup d'état. Johnny realized there was a conspiracy occurring from within, and influenced from without. That's why he ordered the outsourced third-party audit of the casino books. Unfortunately, he was eliminated before anyone else noticed the approaching apocalypse.

As I sat and gazed through mirrored reflection, I watched another round of gaming-table money canister exchanges. Same routine as before, exchange of canisters and corresponding chit to pit boss, then back to the elevator and down to the counting room. Seemed to be an hourly pilgrimage.

It was getting along the shank of the evening when Uncle Dominick and his respective assemblage of Neanderthals, fashionably tailored "scar tissue," prepared to retire. An insipid round of handshakes, hugs, and kisses on both cheeks ensued as they made their way to the exit. Just before leaving, Uncle Dominick whispered something in Nicky Fallon's ear, and they both glanced briefly in my direction. A cold chill ran down my spine. That couldn't be a good thing.

I downed the last of my drink and tried unsuccessfully to quell my quivering kneecaps. I imagined the glassware on the shelves of the back bar tinkling as if in prophetic pronouncement of imminent earthquake or approaching tsunami . . . or perhaps an oncoming train wreck.

Nicky Fallon escorted Uncle Dominick et al. out the glass doors and down the ramp to the boardwalk in front. I took this opportunity to exit, stage right, out the rear doors, and out to the balcony that surrounded the second floor of the casino. I proceeded to the left, around to the less illuminated area of the building, and stood in the shadows as Uncle Dominick's sedan pulled from the curb and headed north down the narrow road that led to the Descanso Beach Hotel.

I crossed the boardwalk and entered the alley behind the Zane Grey Hotel. I continued up the alley, then turned south into another that ran parallel to the boardwalk behind the row of restaurants and souvenir shops. In the dim light of the alley behind the Edgewater, I reached up and pulled down the fire escape ladder, taking note of the rusting screech the rollers emitted with each revolution. I climbed the fire escape onto the patio and crossed to the hallway entrance that led to number 8. Once inside, I left the lights off and changed from fleecy white formal attire into my well-worn khakis, brown leather bomber jacket, and combat boots. I locked the door behind me and retraced my steps across the patio and down the fire escape. I went back down the alleys, the way I had come, and back across the boardwalk to the casino.

I waited in the shadows, concealed by tall shrubs, next to the building. I crouched in the darkness at the apex of the walkway leading from the mezzanine office doors to the boardwalk and the front entrance of the casino. I could observe the office exit, as well as the front entrance.

I waited in my darkened hiding place and lit a cigarette with as little glow of lighter as I could smother and took a quick look at my watch. Two thirty a.m. Casino was closed, and patrons had retired to their respective lodgings in town, or pricey yachts moored in the harbor. The casino employees began to exit the casino and head for home. It wouldn't be long now. I had to wait but a few brief moments.

I could see headlights approaching, and a black sedan pulled to a stop at the end of the walkway, directly in front of where I waited. In just a few moments the door from the office mezzanine opened and two thick meatballs came down the walk to the idling sedan. One of the pin-striped gunzels carried a medium-sized aluminum briefcase. They got in, and as the sedan pulled away, I took three steps from my darkened hiding place and climbed silently onto the rear bumper, holding on to the Continental kit as the sedan moved quietly down the narrow road toward Descanso Beach.

The car stopped at the beach that led through the grotto in the rock outcropping, at the water's edge, and onto Descanso Beach. The two Pisans got out and began to walk across the beach toward the cave. The sedan continued up the narrow dark road that would end at the parking lot farther up the hill behind the hotel. When the sedan slowed to turn into the parking lot, I quietly stepped off the back bumper and into the tall shrubs that lined the road. I scaled down an indigenous rock wall and into a darkened hiding place behind a tall hedge, up the pebbled walkway from where the two gunzels approached. As they got closer, I reached in my jacket pocket and removed my zap.

A zap is a stiff spring approximately ten inches long, filled with buckshot and wrapped in a thick black leather, including a wrist strap. It's a small springing club I used to bring down bail jumpers when I worked for an Orange County bail bondsman named Joey Barnum, former lightweight Golden Gloves champ.

I waited and held my breath as they passed. I quietly stepped out behind them, and with two quick whacks upside their thick melons, they went down hard, in unison, face-first with a distinct thud, onto the gravel walkway. I reached in their coats and removed their weapons, both ugly big .45 autos, cannons. I tossed them into the bushes and grabbed the handle of the shiny briefcase. I began to run when I was suddenly yanked off my feet and fell flat on my back to the ground, with my left arm under me. Damn, that smarts!

I had a sharp pain in my shoulder and sprained the fingers on my hand. I got to my knees, put the zap back in my pocket, and pulled out my Popeil pocket penlight. I shined the thin light onto the briefcase handle. "Damn!" I said under my breath. It was handcuffed to the big side of beef's wrist.

I placed the penlight in my mouth and reached in my pocket for my handy-dandy PI lock-picking paraphernalia. Within seconds I had removed the cuff from the briefcase handle and then snapped it shut around the other gunzel's ankle. If they came to before I had departed, they would have a hell of a time trying to pursue with one guy's wrist handcuffed to the other guy's ankle.

I got to my feet and was prepared to leave when one of the snoozing sack of potatoes began to groan his way back to consciousness. I gave him another whack with my zap across the bridge of his nose and sent him back to wise-guy woozy land.

I scaled the wall, crossed the narrow road, and made my way in the darkness back to the alley behind the Zane Grey. I retraced my steps once more through the alleys back to my hotel. I climbed the fire escape, crossed the patio into the hallway, and retreated into my room.

I grabbed my canvas duffle, threw in a change of clothes, my spit kit from the bathroom, and then forced the shiny briefcase into the duffle as well. I closed the door and locked it as I went out the way I had come. I crossed the dark patio, and just as I reached the fire escape, the ladder began to descend, with the corresponding rusty screech. I crouched down and retreated along the wall to a darkened corner and hid behind a large terra-cotta planter, from which a small sago palm sprouted and afforded only slightly more cover.

From my hiding place I could see down the length of the hallway to the top of the stairs that led to the boardwalk out front. Two imposing large dark figures emerged over the wall from the fire escape and dropped quietly onto the patio. They crouched along the opposite wall from where I hid, under the two windows of my room to the hallway entrance.

I watched as two other figures approached from the stairwell at the other end of the hall. They stayed close to the wall, keeping the floor squeaks to a minimum. They had apparently performed this operation a time or two in the past. All four converged simultaneously at my room, number 8. They tried the door . . . locked. One of the figures crouched down and jimmied the lock. Once again they turned the doorknob and slowly pushed the door open. One by one, they crouched down and entered the room, leaving the remaining hulk to guard the door and hallway approaches.

Quick streaks of penlight strafed the walls and reflected off mirrors. Muffled efficiency of thorough search ensued through drawers, closets, under beds, mattresses, and inside pillowcases. Within minutes the intruders emerged, and along with the lookout, all four retreated down the hallway and descended the stairs to the boardwalk and the moonlit paradise that is Avalon.

I waited in my darkened corner for a few brief moments, then descended the fire escape into the alley. I went directly uphill, away from the boardwalk and harbor. I stayed close to the buildings in the dark, like an escaped convict that had just slid down a rope of knotted sheets.

I continued uphill until I reached the junction at the "Burma trail." The Burma trail was an infamous three-foot-wide asphalt strip known only to the locals as a path by which to traverse across town without having to descend all the way back down to the boardwalk. So named because of its challengingly steep, seemingly endless incline to the top of a rugged hill and equally steep and challenging descent down the other side to the south end of town.

I eventually wheezed my way to the top of the hill, calves and hamstrings burning with fatigue, and crumpled upon a small wooden bench mercifully placed by some compassionate city council for the beaten and battered souls brave or naive enough to attempt this death march. I placed the duffle containing the shiny briefcase and my meager belongings on the bench beside me.

From here, on high, I could observe the entire town and harbor from Descanso Beach and the casino, all the way to the south past the shipping tarmac and Lover's Cove. I watched, in the starlit silence, as several dark sedans departed the Descanso hotel and dispersed through town in different directions. One went up the hill toward the airport. Another south to the shipping tarmac. Several cars converged on the casino from different directions, and within moments lights began to illuminate what had been a relatively dark office mezzanine area within the casino.

What was noticeably absent was an approaching police siren or any other official authority of any kind on scene. Curious . . . ? Perhaps not.

I sat in silence, contemplating my seemingly impulsive behavior. I wanted to shake things up and see what transpired, and how . . . the current theory being that hijacked skim money was not an injustice reported to authorities, and, ergo, a confirmation of my suspicion as to the motive for Johnny Rigney's disappearance and my original summoning to the island by Johnny's assumed widow, Lara. Question was, how would one go about proving aforementioned theory without getting one's head blown off in the process?

After a long wait, the excitement in town seemed to subside. The lights in the mezzanine went dark once again, and the sedans finally settled for the night. I grabbed my overstuffed duffle and began the long descent down the south side of the Burma trail.

As I made my way along the steep narrow strip of asphalt, twisting and turning its way down the rugged hillside, I began to wonder why the four hulking creepsters had descended upon my room almost immediately after my daring assault at Descanso Beach. Had they been dispatched beforehand? If so, what would they be looking for? The altercation had not yet occurred. Maybe they weren't looking for something, but someone. Me in particular. Why? They couldn't have figured me for the heist that quick. Maybe Uncle Nick finally put a face with the name, compliments of Nicky Fallon, and was seeking revenge for the demise of his nephew so long ago. Very perplexing, and likewise disconcerting. Like I needed this shit. I didn't have enough trouble already. Man, did I love this profession . . . or what?

I finally reached the end of the trail at Metropole Avenue and entered the alley that led south to the Pavilion Lodge. The Pavilion was a series of disconnected bungalows with a large tree-covered courtyard in the middle. I quietly crossed through the darkened courtyard and waited at the edge of the boardwalk in the shadows, across from the diver's pier. I quickly crossed the boardwalk and onto the pier. The diver's pier was lined down both sides with lobster traps, fishing nets, buoys, crates— all the accouterments required for a thriving commercial seafaring fleet. I finally came to the metal dive lockers at the end of the pier. I removed the small silver key, hanging from a chain around my neck like a dog tag, opened the locker, and placed the shiny attaché from my duffle inside. I locked the door, put the key back around my neck, and quickly made my way back down the pier to the boardwalk.

I walked briskly south down the narrow road that led to RJ's yacht, the *Lucky Dutchman*. Farther along the pier was the boathouse, where the ski boat was kept, and forward of that was Captain Wally's renovated PT, the *Bad Penny*.

I jimmied the lock on the cabin door of the *Lucky Dutchman* and stepped aboard. I locked the door behind me, threw my duffle on the chair, lay down on the plush, deep-pile carpet, and fell into an exhausted sleep.

Chapter Four

I awoke early in the morning to the sound of Captain Wally preparing for the day's "deepwater safari." As I tried to lift myself from the carpet, I was reminded of my not-so-friendly encounter with Lafargé and his men the night before. Sharp pain in my rib cage, strained shoulder and left arm, sprained fingers. I eventually struggled off the floor and managed to get myself showered, shaved, and dressed in the uniform of the day—Hawaiian print shirt, khaki trousers, canvas boat shoes.

I rolled up my old clothes and boots, placed them in my duffle, then stashed the duffle in the closet. I locked the cabin door behind me and hustled my way back toward town. There was an early-morning overcast that kept the temperatures cool, so I put on my bomber jacket and continued down Crescent Avenue to Sculley's Pancake House, the breakfast hangout of the fishermen and other seafarers. I had an hour or so to kill before Roscoe was to pick me up.

When I arrived, Captain Wally and Steve Canyon, the seaplane pilot that kamikaze'd his little red Grumman into the side of Dr. Con's runaway yacht at the conclusion of my last visit, were seated at the counter. Steve Canyon was a character right out of the *Terry and the Pirates* comic strip. Big strapping tanned brute, covered in a thick mat of sun-bleached blonde hair. He was energetic, over-the-top, push-the-envelope psychotic. But always a fun and entertaining lunatic.

"Hey, Polliwog, come join us for breakfast," greeted Captain Wally. "You remember your old flying buddy Steve?"

"I think we did more crashing than flying," I responded as I reached across the counter to shake hands.

"Mornin', Bombardier," Steve said. "Ready for another trip into the wild blue."

"What are you flying these days?" I asked.

"Catalina PBY baby!" was his response. "I have the twin plexiglass blisters on the sides, and a few other options I think you'll find very interesting. I've got some downtime tomorrow if you can arrange your schedule," he said.

"Captain Wally and I are going to try our luck with the big fish tomorrow," I responded.

"Great!" he said. "I'll catch up to you tomorrow out on the water."

Our waitress, Naomi, was your typical truck-stop waitress. Big eyelashes, simulated demolition-ball earrings, *I Love Lucy* red hair pulled tight into a braided ponytail tied with a big bow. Snapping gum, lots of bright red lipstick, and corresponding nails. Everybody was darlin' or sweetheart. She of course was also highly efficient, no wasted steps or unnecessary trips. Armloads of plates with each arrival to a table. She arrived to our counter location with a big smile and "good morning," delivered coffees, took our orders, and was off at a brisk pace, ponytail and demolition balls swaying to and fro with each quick step.

The interior of the café suddenly darkened as an imposing huge muscle-bulging knuckle cruncher squeezed through the seemingly inadequate doorway, blocking all meager beginnings of morning light. He was big and brutal, battle scarred rough with a deep saltwater tan. He was thick and raw, with ghostly pale gray eyes, a big bright smile, and a deeply tanned shaved head. He wore a khaki shirt with the sleeves cut off, exposing ginormous cannonlike arms, covered in thick reddish brown curly hair. The intimidating characterization was completed with khaki shorts and muscled calves squeezed into well-worn, bloodstained combat boots. He crossed behind us and sat down at the end of the counter next to Steve Canyon.

"Top of the morning, gentlemen," he said cheerfully as he motioned for the waitress.

"Polliwog," Captain Wally began, "I'd like you to meet Max von Jekyle. Max, this is Travis Dugan, an old friend of ours from LA."

We leaned across Captain Wally and Kamikaze Steve to shake hands. His rough, calloused ham hock engulfed my seemingly petite digit cluster; and though he tried momentarily to mercilessly fuse my knuckles, I was prepared for the alpha-dog demonstration of infantile behavior and was having none of it. He relinquished his vicelike grip with a reluctant, knowing smile.

Naomi returned with our entire order stacked precariously on one arm. She dealt off the top like a veteran blackjack dealer, then began off-loading various accouterments from her apron pocket, like Tabasco, ketchup, and something called salsa. Then, from nowhere, produced a fresh coffee pot and refilled our cups. She asked if she could do anything else to us, with a sensual lick of her ruby lips, a twinkle in her eye, and a mischievous smile. A big grin grew across each of our faces, but she was off before a cleverly inappropriate comeback could be formulated.

The "Captain's Mess" was a mishmash of hash browns, eggs, green peppers, sausage, mushrooms, something called salsa, and a few unrecognizable bits of stuff, all scrambled together, and topped off with a condensation-cloaked, scarlet red Bloody Mary.

Over the course of the breakfast, I learned that Max von Jekyle was a deep-sea diver with dubious connections to the world of sunken treasure hunters. *Great!* I thought to myself. Just what we need, another quasi salvage consultant. I wondered if Max von Jekyle and Sir Arthur had crossed paths as yet.

I finished breakfast, paid my tab, left an appreciative tip, bid adieu to my companions, blew Naomi a kiss goodbye, and was off down the boardwalk for my rendezvous with Roscoe. I had barely gotten out the door when Roscoe arrived. I jumped in, he engaged the meter, and we were headed up the road toward the Rigney estate. We exchanged pleasantries during the ride up the hill and got caught up on old news. I asked him about the sort of people that attend the Fourth of July celebration as compared to the ones that make the pilgrimage to the island during carnival at the beginning of the season. He explained, with his excited high-pitched gravely voice, that unlike the pampered, rich, and famous, old-money and nouveau riche top-drawer crowd that came for the grand ball, the art and treasure auction, the film festival, and the sailing regatta, the folks that arrived for the Fourth were more of your mainstream, day-to-day, working-class tourists here to enjoy a few brief days of vacation before returning to the dregs of daily toil within the grunge of mainland grind.

Finally, as we approached the well-manicured, tree-lined drive that wound its way up the hill to the mansion, I asked Roscoe if he had noticed any perceptible change in the atmosphere or ambiance around the casino. We pulled to a stop at the large iron gates at the entrance to the compound. Roscoe sat silent for a few moments. He finally turned to me with genuine concern on his face and said with hesitation in his voice, "You know, boss, I have noticed a change in the feeling of the place. It happened over a period of time. Slow but steady change from whimsical carnival to more like a traveling circus of sideshow freaks."

"That's an interesting way to put it," I responded. "Which reminds me to thank you for the phone call regarding the arrival of our own traveling circus geek, Sir Arthur, and his personal sideshow freak, Phangs Pa."

"Yes, sir boss. I knew that you would want to know ifin' them two returned. Sump'm strange 'bout them two. Bad mojo. I'll tell ya sump'm else too, boss. Seems to be some undercurrent of interest south of Descanso Beach in Hamilton Cove. I seen guys looking through spyglasses on tripods at other guys across the way holding tall measuring sticks. I don't rightly know what's goin' on, but sump'm goin' on that nobody else seems to know nuttin' 'bout."

Great, I thought to myself once again. Like I needed this shit.

Roscoe reached across and pushed the button on the intercom. Spaulding's familiar perturbed "yes" came over the speaker. Roscoe explained he was here to deliver yours truly to his scheduled appointment.

"Wonderful," was the response. The gates eventually opened, and we proceeded up the drive to the mansion. Roscoe pulled to a stop in the circular drive at the wide concrete steps that led to the huge thick wooden double doors that was the front entrance to the immense white mansion.

As I exited the cab, the manse doors opened, and lovely Rita breezed down the steps in a bright yellow sundress, matching purse, and open-toed pumps. Add a big summer hat, a brightly spinning parasol and a Mint Julip, and she would have looked as if she were attending the Kentucky Derby. She gave me a quick peck on the cheek, then leaned in the passenger window and asked Roscoe if he could give her a ride to work at the casino.

She jumped in, we all said our goodbyes, and the cab moved down the drive back toward town. The doors to the mansion opened once again and Spaulding emerged. "Mr. Rigney requests that you join him for coffee on the terrace," he said. "You may show yourself in."

"Nice to see you again too, Spaulding," I said and showed myself through the foyer and out to the terrace.

I found the Commodore in his usual spot on the terrace that overlooked Avalon and the entire harbor. He looked about the same as the last time I had seen him nearly a year ago. He was a weathered crusty with a quick whit, a warm smile, and a genuine paternalism toward the island and its inhabitants. For a dynamic man who led a life that I could only enviously imagine, he looked pretty good and seemed in good health. I considered him a great friend, and I was genuinely happy to see him.

The morning overcast began to clear, and the first shafts of warm sunlight bathed the terrace and surrounding gardens.

"Ah! Mr. Dugan, so good to see you again, my friend. Come, join me for breakfast," beamed the good Commodore.

"Thank you, Commodore. It's great to see you again as well," I responded.

I shook the old man's hand and pulled up a chair as Spaulding emerged from the manse and placed a set of car keys on the table in front of me. "Your chariot awaits in the drive, sir. Would you like me to bring breakfast for you as well, Mr. Dugan?"

"No thank you, Spaulding, I have already eaten in town. I could use a cup of coffee though, if you would," I asked.

"Bring the carafe and the brandy as well," the Commodore added with a chuckle and a wink. The old man seemed in very good spirits this morning.

"Tell me, Travis," the old man began with a twinkle in his eye, "how are you feeling on this bright sunny morning?"

"Well, let me tell you," I began reflectively. "Amidst the gossamer mist rising gently above the serene waters of the cove, in muted reflection of morning light . . . I must admit . . . I feel rather hobbitlike," I sighed, with a knowing glance.

"Aha! Aha! Yes indeed, you sly bastard," he laughed. "You remembered! Oh Travis, I can't believe you recall my geriatric-induced, fanciful diatribe from our first visit. Son, you have no idea how you've warmed an old man's heart, or eased the burden of solitary introspection. I do enjoy our conversations, son. You have no idea."

Spaulding once again appeared and placed the carafe of coffee and another with brandy on the table. He cleared the Commodore's breakfast plates and returned to his duties inside. I poured coffee for each of us and added a liberal splash of brandy to each as well. We settled into the serenity of the pristine morning and allowed the soothing warmth of our comforting brew to course our innards. To the old man's surprise and delight, I produced two fine Havanas from my jacket pocket.

With great relish he snipped off the tip and accepted the flame from my chrome service lighter. We surrendered with great pleasure to *beaux hue se*. Life was beautiful.

Life's beauty got notched up a couple of pulses when Lara emerged from the mansion and strolled across the patio, barefoot and with bewitching zigzag dance of perky nipples 'neath thin sheen of peach-colored silk robe. I stood as she approached and pulled out a chair for her. She placed a peck on the old man's cheek and one for me, then accepted the seat and poured coffee for herself.

"Good morning, boys," she beamed. "And how are my two favorite men this fine morning?"

The brandy is smooth, Havanas are sweet, the sun is shining, and we're in the company of the most beautiful and alluring woman on the entire island, I mused.

"I can't imagine life more heavenly."

"Wow!" she exclaimed. "You're in exceptionally cheery mood. Did you get lucky last night or what?"

The old man almost choked on his brandy, and I coughed up an immense smoke ring, which drifted across the terrace and dispersed over the surrounding gardens.

She giggled and excitedly began to divulge her itinerary for the day. This was the last night for Cougy and Chi-Chi, Cha-Cha, Chu-Chu, whatever, at the casino. Tomorrow night was the opening of Jimmy Durante (hot-cha-cha-cha) and Cyd Charisse with Les Brown and his Band of Renowned. Lara was excited and having a wonderful time running the dining and entertainment venues at the casino. She was a natural.

I downed the last of my coffee, snubbed out my Havana, and prepared to take my leave. I gave the old man a pat on the back and kissed Lara arrivederci. I grabbed the keys off the table and said I would have the car back tonight. I made my way through the mosaic-tile foyer and out the front door to the little red sports car in the drive.

I walked around the car a couple of times. I had to laugh. I couldn't believe it . . . it was a Muntz Mobile Jet.

Madman Muntz was an over-the-top energetic LA car dealer who desperately wanted to advertise on the newly introduced mass media entertainment phenomena that was television.

Automobile dealers had become the new movers and shakers of the postwar affluence that was just beginning to euphorically flourish across the "Levittown" suburban neighborhoods of an emerging, optimistic middle-class America. "A chicken in every pot, and a car in every garage" was the mantra of the new upwardly mobile, baby boom expansion of the "Golden Era of the '50s" and coincidentally the "Golden Age of Television." Ward and June and their growing "nuclear family," Wally and Beaver Cleaver, along with their neighbors Jim and Margaret Anderson's clan, and the Ricardos, were flush with newly minted GI Bills and VA loans, burning holes in their chinos and capri pants pockets.

Yeakel Brothers Wilshire Oldsmobile's *Rocket to Stardom* show, a prelude to Ted Mack's *The Old Amateur Hour*, and Chick Lambert and his dog Storm sponsored late-night movies, and Madman Muntz, who a decade later invented the eight-track stereo tape player, were all inspired by the advertising power of the miniscule-sized, argon gas tube, snowy, barely visible, enclosed picture screen sound box that was TV.

Earl "Madman" Muntz manufactured his own television sets so that he could advertise his own sports cars. The Muntz Mobile Jet was a two-seat convertible roadster, bright red.

I jumped in, fired her up, and was off down the road to the north across the hills. Avalon and the blue Pacific whipped by far down the steep hillside to the right. I was in search of an old friend.

Before I got completely out of town, I decided I would take a chance and do a little investigation. I downshifted and turned to the right, heading down a steep hill on Avalon Canyon road toward the harbor. I twisted around several tree-lined narrow roads until I eventually made my way to Descanso Beach Road. Then turned left in front of the casino, drove to the hotel parking lot in the back, and exited the north side of the parking lot, down a bumpy dirt path, and around a steep, rugged point to the windswept seclusion of Hamilton Cove.

Hamilton Cove was a wide expanse of exceedingly steep, rugged hillside that dropped precariously to a crescent-shaped rocky shore. I parked the little red jet next to an outcropping of granite boulders and got out. I walked farther down the road, shielding my eyes from the reflection of the morning sun. I followed a pair of shallow sporadic tire tracks in the rugged trail until they ceased. At that point there was evidence of disturbance in the terrain—loading and unloading, carrying back and forth, reversing course back the way they had come. Several vehicles . . . recently. I looked around until I came upon fresh footprints leading down the hill to a small plateau of scrub brush and prickly pear cactus. I searched the ground in that location and found the telltale three punctures into the earth of the surveyor's tripod. I removed my "cheating spouse" PI spyglass from my jacket pocket opposite the one containing my zap. (You don't want to mix up your pockets in the heat of battle). I peered through the tiny lens across the canyon until I finally came upon a short wooden stake with several strands of yellow ribbon tied at the top. Corner pegs . . . Property line markers . . . Surveyor stakes. I followed a visual line down the steep hillside to the bluff above the thrashing surf line. There I discovered another. Again, followed a visual line across the rugged shoreline to another. Then up the steep hillside to a fourth, partially hidden under an imposing cactus patch. The rudimentary beginnings of a surveyor's blueprint and grading plan. Roscoe was right. There was something going on over here . . . But what . . . ? And by whom?

I retraced my steps back to the little red jet and carefully backed her down the road to the parking lot of the Descanso Beach Hotel. I made my way back to the road that would take me north, through the interior of the island, to the isthmus on the far side of the narrow causeway at Two Harbors.

The jet cruised smoothly across the long plateau with the sun high in the noonday sky. The deep red of Manzanita and cactus terrain whipped by with occasional glimpse of bison, deer, or wild Russian boar. An occasional eagle soaring high overhead. I tried to clear my mind of the peripheral input that always seems to clutter one's focus on this quiet little island. Just as I found before, it was difficult to follow the proceedings without a program, and likewise hard to distinguish the participants without a playlist. It's always a riddle, wrapped in a mystery, surrounded by an enigma.

Chapter Five

The warm sun was still high overhead, and a tropical breeze began to wisp across the low gently sloping northern end of the island. I slowed the car at the approach to the narrow causeway separating a deep calm cove on either side, each the size of small harbors fringed with flat white beaches. Across the causeway, the land widened again for several miles, then dropped quickly to the sea at the rugged northern point—"Land's End."

Between the isthmus causeway and the end of the island, on a wide palm-covered plain, lay a neat track of white wood-framed bungalows, each with a smokestack through the roof and a cook pot hung over an open campfire in front.

"Cooley Town," once the billeting quarters for the navy and coast guard during the war, now inhabited by Chinese and Korean laborers who came to the island after completion of the railroad on the mainland, to work in the rock quarry or one of the mines on the island. Others plied the shallow coastal waters around the island for octopus, squid, eel, abalone, or other shellfish, like lobster and crab. As apparent by all the various fishing boats in the harbor, they did quite well.

As I slowly cruised through the palm grove, over what was merely two shallow ruts in the lush, sun-dappled grass at the water's edge, the pungent aroma of kimchee was in the air, bringing with it a recollection of the many days I spent in the Pacific during the war staring through a Norden bombsight and incinerating or pulverizing every papier-mâché hamlet between the Marianas and Tokyo aboard a B-29 Superfortress, and a few years later, in a B-26 over Korea. My aircrew and I spent a lot of time in the Philippines, and again in Korea, teaching the laundry girls to play volleyball. It was fun for the girls, and entertaining for the boys. In the summer the girls wore a long gauzy skirt that gathered as a bodice just under their breasts. Their top was a short bolero-type one-button vest that ended just below aforementioned breasts. The leaping about to spike a shot at the net or block a high serve was a wonderful sight to behold. We spent many joyous hours indulging in what has become one of my favorite coed sports. The laundry girls ate kimchee on a regular basis, and when they were ironing your uniform, they would spit on the fabric before applying the hot iron; thus, everything smelled of kimchee.

I rolled up next to one of the indistinguishable cabins that sat next to the harbor. A beautiful twenty-four-foot twin-screw skipjack sat at mooring in front. Ah Looey was the patriarch of the Chinese and Korean population in Cooley Town. Everyone referred to him as "Shifu," which means teacher or master in Chinese. He was revered as the wise one and served as the local apothecary and healer. Ah Looey loaned me his supercharged Chris-Craft to chase down a band of rampaging tong bandits upon my last visit to the island. Unfortunately, the beautiful mahogany boat was sacrificed during the high-speed pursuit and ultimately reduced to gleaming splinters of flotsam and jetsam scattered liberally across the surface of the ocean outside Dr. Con's compound on the other side of the island at Smuggler's Cove.

The old man emerged from the cabin dressed in traditional Chinese pajamas and a big wide smile. We bowed to each other, gave one another a big hug and enthusiastic pat on the back. We were genuinely happy to see each other. We had forged a bond of respect for one another. He was the wise master, "Shifu." I was the respectful and humble student. I was the "Polliwog."

"Polliwog, it is heartwarming to see you again, my son," the old man began. "I am honored that you would return to my humble home."

"It is I who is honored and humbled that you would accept me into your home, although I am naïve, crude, and unworthy," I respectfully responded.

"Aha! Aha!" the old man laughed. "Crude and unworthy may still yet to be determined," he said with a sly smile. "And both characteristics may be improved upon. However, naïveté, or innocence, I can assure you, Polliwog, are not traits for which you should concern yourself," he laughed. "That ship, Confucius says, has long ago sailed beyond the horizon."

"Aha!" I laughed myself. "Confucius my ass, old man. I may be uneducated in the writings of your revered master, but one imagines that you may be quoting confusion, rather than Confucius," I said with a grin.

"Perhaps I may just be choking your chicken?" he delivered with deadpan perfection of a straight man sidekick.

"No," I responded. "Now I know you're quoting confusion. I believe the phrase is, you're just pulling my leg. Maybe I'll explain later," I said with a friendly pat on the back.

"One wonders if that would be more information than one would require," he laughed.

"Come, Polliwog," the old man gestured. "Please be so kind to join me for afternoon tea."

We entered the small cabin and were instantly aware of the herbal aroma and incense that permeated the interior space. An extremely beautiful yet shy young Asian-mix girl, with long silky black hair tied in a ponytail that extended down her back past her petite and pouty derriere, emerged through the curtain from the adjoining room. She had large almond-shaped eyes that twinkled innocently beneath long curved lashes, and over exquisitely sculptured cheekbones. Wide, shy, childlike grin from full lustrous lips that, with some encouragement, sensually parted to reveal bright, luminous smile. Her perky young form was unmistakable 'neath the thin silky traditional jammies she wore. She was an innocent yet extremely gorgeous I guessed to be Chinese and Korean mix young beauty. She reminded me of Chin Lee. I sure missed that girl.

"This is my great-niece, Yung He," the old man said. "Yung He, I would like you to meet my friend, Mr. Travis Dugan."

She bowed sweetly. "I am humbly honored, Mr. Travis Dugan sir," she responded.

I believe I was correct in my assumption regarding her heritage. Yung He was indeed a Korean name.

The old man said something in Chinese to Yung He; she bowed, then returned to the adjoining room. He motioned me to a small table at the far end of the room where the large panoramic window offered a magnificent view of the harbor and glimmering Pacific beyond. We sat on large pillows cross-legged at the short round table. Yung He returned with a tray that contained a pipe, which was shaped like a baleros cup. The Mexican toy where you swing a small ball tethered to small bowl atop a short handle by way of a thin rubber band or a string and attempt to land the ball in the bowl. This bit of paraphernalia was not, however, a baleros cup. I recognized it as a chillum, or opium pipe.

He handed me the pipe, which I placed between my middle and ring finger, with half the handle and the bowl at the top protruding up, through loosely clenched fist, and the bottom half of the handle enclosed within my fist. The end within loosely clenched fist was wrapped in thin moist cloth. The old man cut a small cube from a yellowed chunk of what looked like amber, put a small flame to it for a short while, then placed the preheated cube in the bowl atop the pipe.

I placed my fist to my mouth as if to cover a cough, but instead the old man then put a flame to the cube at which time I drew in a large cool breath of soothing ambrosia magic. I handed the pipe back to the old man and slowly sank into the pillow, slumping helplessly against the wall. I was aware of the program. I had been through this procedure before. The opium was to soothe the queasy stomach that was to come upon the ingestion of the herbal tea, administered to extract the poisons within one's internal system and expel by way of profuse sweating, heavy breathing, and, in extremely caustic individuals . . . projectile vomiting. Sounds intriguing so far . . . no?

Once I had regained some sense of cognitive realization, Yung He returned and helped me to my feet and led me by the hand to the adjoining room through the beaded curtains. This room was dimly lit by small transom windows high on the walls, which allowed limited sunlight to filter through sweet clouds of incense and the rising steam of boiling herbs. She led me to a large galvanized metal bucket, or tub, at the end of a long table. The table was covered with a clean white cotton sheet. Ah Looey followed and instructed me to remove all clothing and stand in the metal bucket. I told him, through opiate haze, that I wasn't going to do that . . . so I was standing there naked in a metal bucket when Yung He arrived once again and carefully handed me a warm cup of tea. "Very hot," she said softly before returning through a maze of apothecary jars filled with bat wings, hummingbird beaks, eye of newt, and other nightmarish nauseating solutions floating in silhouette through shafts of transom light. Maybe I was hallucinating. I'd been through this torturous, though necessary, procedure before. Didn't mean I gotta like it.

I stood there dreading the next part of this. I delayed long enough for the "shrinkage factor" to begin to take effect, then reluctantly began to slowly drink down the herbal tea, which immediately brought on chills, profuse sweating, shivering, and shortness of breath. I felt weak, like I was about to puke, or pass out. I hated this part. Yung He appeared once again carrying a tray covered in a pile of some kind of succulent leaf. The smell of mint. She removed the teacup from my pitifully quivering hand, allowing me to hold on to the end of the table I was now leaning heavily against. She then began to softly, gently wipe the sweat pouring from my body with the mint leaves. Starting from my head and slowly working her way down, she gently swept away the impurities spewing from me and replaced them with a cool, refreshing, soothing tingle of minty rejuvenation. Slowly but surely I began to feel a revitalization begin to sweep over me. A stimulating arousal of the senses. By the time Yung He had gotten down to my most stimulated sense, she smiled up at me with a shy yet questioning expression. I knew I had not yet acquired "Big Bad Voodoo Daddy" status, but I wasn't exactly "Little Oscar Mayer's" wiener whistle either. Besides, I've seen plenty of Asian guys, and believe me, they're all packin' peanuts and raisinettes.

"She is intrigued by your meticulous personal grooming habits," the old man said. Yung He said something to the old man in Chinese and smiled, averting her eyes.

"She wonders if it is because of fetish or infestation?" the old man questioned, with wide grin.

"In Hollywood, it is referred to as 'adult film star grooming,'" I explained.

"Once again, Polliwog," the old man began, "perhaps more information than one would require."

Yung He began to giggle and flog me vigorously with the mint leaves. The old man began to giggle. We all giggled.

I lay facedown on the soft cotton sheet. There was a hole in the table at the location of one's face so that you could lie flat with your face staring at the floor through the hole in the table. Yung He began a soothing systematic massage starting again at the top of my head and slowly working her way down to the bottom of my feet. Very thorough. Extremely relaxing.

"Many old wounds," she said softly. "Many scars. Recent bruising as well. You have chosen a very dangerous path."

After the message, Ah Looey began to insert long thin needles into various locations of my body. Gently, meticulously spinning them in as he went. Starting at the bottom of my feet, and one by one working his way to the areas around my injured left shoulder and arm.

"There is evidence of a recent altercation," the old man said matter-of-factly. "Fresh bruising in area of right kidney and small cartilage at bottom of rib cage. Blunt force trauma. Acupuncture not help that," he said. "You will suffer pain from this injury for some time. Perhaps you should investigate raising koi fish for a living," he said with a laugh. "Few injuries suffered from koi fish farming."

After all the long thin needles were inserted from the bottom of my feet all the way up to the areas behind my ears, Yung He then began to systematically twist or spin all the needles one by one. Pain began to subside and a feeling of cleansing of joints and muscles and a resumption of flexibility and fluidity began to course through rejuvenated extremities. Youthful exuberance replaced old, fatigued, beaten, and battered.

When the treatment was over and all the needles had been removed, Shifu instructed me to dress, then meet him outside. Yung He helped me dress, then put her arms around my neck, and held me close. The fragrance of cherry blossoms filled my resensitized perceptions. She felt warm, soft, and innocently alluring. She finally kissed me gently on my neck and then looked softly into my eyes with her own beautiful large fawnlike eyes. "You will return soon?" she whispered.

"I will return as soon as I can, Yung He. I have an obligation to fulfill first. But I will be back as soon as I can."

"Please be careful on your journey, Travis. I will pray for your safe return," she said softly. She kissed me gently on the lips, then disappeared through the beaded curtain.

I found Ah Looey waiting outside, walking stick in hand. He took me by the arm and we began to walk along the waterfront under the palm-dappled sunlight toward Land's End.

"Polliwog," the old man began," I perceive a subtle change in your demeanor. Not merely a few years or a few pounds, but a certain measure of maturity. A perceptible calmness has slowly replaced the anticipation, uneasiness, and sense of anxiety that kept your inner self in turmoil, your eternal quest for adventure and the exhilaration of adrenaline rush."

I didn't bother relating the story of life change that I had revealed to Captain Wally aboard the *Bad Penny*. Shifu, the all-seeing, all-knowing soothsayer, the wise teacher, the master, was on a roll. Best to just let him scroll through his thoughts at his own pace, in his own rhythm.

"I mention this perception, Polliwog, only because the calmness and maturity you display, while comforting to those of us who are unfortunate enough to care for you, also becomes a detriment to your well-being, in that it tends to dull the senses on which you depend to be aware, and acute to your immediate situation, or surroundings. I hesitate to tell you this, Polliwog, however, I feel that I must tell you that I see trouble for you. The quest in which you currently find yourself is fraught with danger that comes from far away . . . and yet, disturbingly, from someone close. Someone you trust."

I asked the old man if he had noticed any perceptible change in the surroundings or unusual events or strange people around since my last visit. He said nothing for a few more steps; then as we approached a beautiful handcrafted bamboo bench, he led me over to the bench and sat facing the churning sea and rugged northern end of the island. I sat next to him in contemplative silence.

"It is interesting that you ask such a question," the old man began. He slowly removed a long-stemmed, intricately carved pipe from his pocket and struck a match to it. I waited patiently for him to continue. After a long pause and a few more tokes from his "Gandalf the wizard" pipe, the old man finally turned to me with concern etched across his wise and weathered face.

"As you may or may not know, Polliwog, most of the laborers in the mines, the longshoreman and stevedores on the shipping docks, and many of the food-service workers are residents of Cooley Town. There has been of late several attempts by unidentified union representatives to make contacts within these industries here on the island. Of course the workers are extremely suspicious of outsiders who are not of the same culture or heritage. Therefore, not much has thus far been gained with that regard. No one has been threatened or pressured as of yet, however, I fear that it is only a matter of time before such things occur. Thanks to you, my son, the first representatives sent here by the tong were vanquished in due haste and have not returned. But my fear is that a consortium will occur between the tong and the union representatives, and then my people will be in real peril. They fear the tong."

I thought for a brief moment then mentioned that the number of workers that could be unionized within either of these enterprises would not be of sufficient numbers to make such an endeavor monetarily worthwhile to union organizers, tong extortion, or anything else that I could think of. The number of workers on the island would not make it a worthwhile venture for anyone.

The old man nodded in agreement. "That is true, Polliwog, however, I feel that this would be but the opening gamut of a larger, more ambitious scheme. This is but one phase of a multifaceted plan. A serpent with many heads."

"You go on ahead, Polliwog," the old man said. "Pay your respects to Chin Lee. I will be waiting when you return." He reached in his pocket and then handed me a short thin stick of incense and a handful of shredded paper.

I continued along the narrow footpath to the rugged, windswept hillside that steeply sloped to the crashing surf that was Land's End. In the middle of the sloping terrain, halfway down from the jutting peak, was a gently sloping plateau covered in wisps of long grass and the unobtrusive small headstones of the island's Cooley Town Cemetery. I walked among the headstones until I came upon the one that said simply . . . "Chin Lee Beloved Island Daughter." I sat next to the grave, placed the incense in the small hole in the headstone, and placed the torn paper in the small impression just below the stick of incense. I put a flame to both and sat quietly gazing over the wide expanse of the ocean and sky merging into muted gray at the undistinguishable horizon.

Chin Lee was a young, beautiful, and innocent mixed-race Asian girl who had been dealt a tough hand in life and ultimately sacrificed that life trying to keep a secret for a beloved childhood friend. That beloved childhood friend was Johnny Rigney, heir apparent to the Rigney Candy fortune, and the mysterious disappearance of whom initiated my original invitation to the island from Johnny's presumed widow, Lara Rigney. I still carry heavy regret that I was unable to prevent Chin Lee's death. She was loyal and brave. With her dying breath she gave me the clue that allowed me to find her killers and dispatch them within raging firestorm of incineration. I quietly wept for her.

I eventually returned to where the old man waited upon a bamboo bench. I helped him to his feet and we walked the path back to his humble cabin in silence.

Chapter Six

Vicious Kittens

Lusty wench, leather boots, and riding crop,
for mortal men she's much too hot.
Latin blood to boil men's passions,
poured sexy chic in latest fashions.

Ebony eyes, cat looks that kill.
Boys to fondle and foot the bill.
Brown skin satin, smooth as silk,
supple firm, sweet taste of rapture's milk.

Dark feline purrs, on moonlit night,
then sleeks away by morning's light.
To come wild again with passion's bite.
These are vicious kittens.

As I approached the serene pastel bay called Little Harbor, where Lara Rigney and I enjoyed a leisure picnic lunch during my first visit, I noticed a magnificent black-and-white Indian pony casually grazing upon the clumps of wildflowers that grew upon the gentle white dunes encircling the bay.

I switched off the engine and let the little red jet roll to a stop on the beach. I sat gazing upon the beautiful creature lingering among the dunes. Then I noticed an equally beautiful creature calmly swimming in the clear bay.

She was a deep golden brown with a wild mane of shiny black hair that flowed around her on the surface of the water, reaching down her back just above the luxurious soft dimples and supple roundness of all-girl hips and spectacular ass.

She slowly, confidently swam about, scanning the bottom of the bay, snorkel protruding from the surface as she went. Occasionally, her smooth brown legs would rise in unison above the water; with precision and pointed toes, she would dive deep beneath the surface. Through crystalline waters I could clearly observe her shimmering form confidently descend to the bottom and retrieve the prize she had spotted from the surface. She would examine the object for a brief moment, while still on the bottom, then place it in a small net pouch tethered around her waist before majestically rising to the surface amid a sparkling cloud of glistening bubbles. It was enchanting. Resurgent pangs of familiar voyeurism emerged from somewhere deep within.

I climbed from the roadster and strolled across the beach to a small dune near where she had spread a towel covered with a variety of seashells. There were many small white elongated shells. The familiar spiral of the conch and the silvery turquoise rainbow of the abalone. I sat atop the dune, watching in silent fascination, as the young girl swam about, creating small ripples that drifted gently toward the pristine white beach.

She slowly swam toward the shore and emerged from the pale waters at a depth just above her firm, trim waist. She removed the diving mask and placed it atop her head. She was concentrating on the treasures within her net bag as she waded toward white sandy shore. She had not as yet noticed my presence.

A warm rush surged through me as I became aware of the soft, sweet voice and the somehow familiar song, as it gently drifted across the bay and over the sun-bleached dunes: "Underneath the mango tree, me honey, where we watch for the moon."

I remembered the wild mane of tousled blue black hair. The large, dark, captivating eyes with the peculiar upward tilt at the corners. I remembered the long silky lashes and the exotically sculptured high cheekbones. The warm, luxurious mouth that smiled wide and brilliant. I remembered the passionate nights of pagan ecstasy. The natural scent of wild lavender. Yes, I remembered . . . I remembered all too well.

She emerged from the water, her petite waist belying the supple movement of ample breasts or strength of robust thighs and calves. As I used to say, "She was built like a brick wickiup." She was wearing a bathing suit, of sorts, that consisted of a narrow band of translucent white silk stretched across stunningly firm breasts, and the same thin white silk tied like the most minimal of loincloths over wonderfully rounded feline derriere.

Her song ended abruptly when she spotted the Muntz mobile parked sprightly on the beach. She glanced at the car, then over to where I sat. She brought her hand up to shield her eyes from the sun. I could tell that she also remembered.

She dropped the shells from her hand and hurried up the beach, where I gathered her in entirely. The soft sponginess of smooth brown skin. The glistening rivulets of water coursing warm, lusty flesh. The scent of rain-washed lavender.

We held each other close without speaking. No words were necessary, nor would they be adequate. We kissed long and hard, devouring each other with impassioned gulps. We explored the smooth warmth of familiar curves. The embraces. The coming together of reawakened responses. The faraway dreams of oneness in the muted grays of long-ago twilights. Yes, we remembered.

She stroked my hair, then held my face gently in both of her hands. She looked deep into my eyes. "I knew you were coming," she said softly.

"Heck, I'm not even breathing hard yet," I sophomorically replied.

"Don't be nasty, Travlito. I meant that you came to me in a dream. I remember that I was very happy to see you. But there was a dark cloud that followed you, as before. Still the same old Dugan."

Yes, I remembered Raven Whitefeather. She was the original bohemian. She was the authentic American Indian of Cheyenne tribal heritage, before Native Americans became the ideological, iconoclastic symbol of wisdom and purity to the future generation of middle-class "love children." She was the prototypical seed from which the abundant harvest of future "flower children" would bloom a decade later, and follow merrily in the vortex of her incense trail. She was Peter Pan on peyote. Her conversations were soft, spiritual, cosmic, and herbal. Her thoughts were childlike, innocent, and naïve. Yet, she was exotically sensual, erotically feline, catlike, mysterious. Soft purr of temptation smoldering just beneath the surface, until the spark of passion would ignite within her a raging inferno of animal lust. She would become a screaming, biting, untamed wildcat. Primal, unrestrained, insatiable.

It was soon after I had received my "walking papers" from the 539th bomber group at Fairfield, north of Sacramento, that I eventually found myself meandering around the quiet little seaside hamlet of Seal Beach located just south of Long Beach on the white sandy shores of sunny Southern California. Palm trees, swimming pools, movie stars.

True to his word, Uncle Sam had signed me up for the duration, plus six months, and it had been almost six months to the day, after V-J Day, that I was cut loose with my duffle bag full of rarely worn class A's and a wad of faded khakis. All totaled I served three years, eight months, twelve days, fifteen hours, thirty-seven minutes. Give or take. But who's counting. Not to mention over twelve hundred combat flying hours. Thanks to those sixty-four rivet-shuddering missions and very little entertainment on Tinian in the Marianas, on which to spend my hard-earned government script, plus a couple of very lucrative crap games aboard the troop ship headed for home, I managed to squirrel away a tidy sum of wampum upon my discharge. I purchased a sharp little '40 Ford convertible in Sacramento and was taking my time cruising down the coast in the "Green Hornet" before coming upon the "Glider Inn" on Pacific Coast Highway in the sleepy little village of Seal Beach.

♦　♦　♦

The Glider Inn was a quaint little restaurant that had an army T-34 flight trainer perched atop a tall metal tower high above the restaurant roof. The interior was decorated with aviation motif, such as wooden propeller ceiling fans, parachute lamp shades, and replicas of virtually every fighting aircraft hung from the ceiling on clear fishing line. The partitions between the smooth leather booths were etched glass of milestones in aviation history: Wright brothers' first flight. Amelia Earhart, female aviator. Lindbergh's solo Atlantic flight. Biplanes to jets, and so on.

The waitress uniforms were short white pleated skirts, crisp white military-style blouse with billowed short sleeves and epaulets on the shoulders. Creased white campaign cap, dark stockings with seam up the back, and short black pumps with strap around the ankle. The waitresses at the Glider Inn looked like the Andrews Sisters on a USO tour. However, Patty, Maxene, and Laverne never looked as alluring as this exotic young Indian girl.

Raven Whitefeather was young, exotically beautiful, innocent, and built like a Betty Page pinup. Her dark features, smooth brown skin, and the shine of her blue black hair contrasted beautifully to her crisp white uniform. She worked the swing shift at the inn, and that was where I first met her. She was shy, soft-spoken, yet erotically alluring. Quietly sexy. Smoldering.

As it turned out, the Glider Inn was the hangout and watering hole of the local flyboys that frequented Meadowlark Field, a small one-strip public airport just off Warner Avenue, south of Seal Beach, and a couple of miles inland from the estuary wetland marshes adjacent to Coast Highway at Tin Can Beach and the hamlet of Surfside. They were all young aviators recently discharged just like yours truly. I was still wearing my faded khakis and brown leather bomber jacket, so I had no problem fitting in. It was like an NCO club anywhere in the world, the same camaraderie and shared experiences. A brotherhood. A fraternity of weary, war-torn veterans. A slightly shell-shocked motley crew of individuals who had sacrificed, and survived. We were now free to reap the fruits of our labor. Enjoy life, liberty, and the pursuit of happiness. The war was finally over; we could resume our lives that we had forsaken so many years and miles ago.

I spent numerous foggy evenings gulping endless cups of coffee, eating countless wedges of pie, and many hours over evening meals getting to know Raven. We gradually became friends, and on cold or rainy nights, she eventually trusted me to give her a ride home after her shift.

She lived south, down Coast Highway, toward Meadowlark Field, atop a small palm-covered bluff overlooking the wetland estuary, the wide white beach, and the deep blue Pacific beyond. We entered the property through an anonymous chain-link gate that led down a narrow driveway to a stand of tall palm trees. A neat, comfortable-size one-room cabin sat nestled among the serene palm grove. Across the drive was a one-car garage, and farther up the drive, against the mesa to the south, was what looked like a two-story barracks that had been converted to a barn and hayloft, where she kept her pinto pony, Dakota.

We spent many hours together becoming trusted friends, close companions, and eventually passionate lovers. We spent the remainder of the winter in the comfort of fur rug, in front of warm fire. We wiled away the glorious, breezy spring and warm days of summer fishing for herring, sea bass, and cod. Gigged for frogs, Dungeness crab, and crawdads. We hunted duck, dove, quail, jacks, and cottontail with handcrafted bow and arrow. We even hunted migrating grunion at the ebb and flow of the seasonal tide and lunar cycle. All were prepared scrumptiously over open campfire, and under the canopy of evening stars.

We rode her pony along the moonlit beach under the twinkle of the balmy night sky and gentle breeze. It was simple and enchanting. It was exactly where I needed to be. The perfect place to forget the recent past. A place to relax, regroup, enjoy, and begin to think about what the future might bring. No longer wondering how I survived when so many others didn't. But, instead, why I survived. What am I supposed to do now? Why am I still here?

As the waning days of that glorious summer began to fade, I felt that restlessness begin to stir within. I had acquired a deep saltwater tan over toned and rippled muscles. My hair was movie star sun-streaked, and my hands and feet were ruggedly calloused. I was probably in the best shape of my life, other than boot camp. I was refreshed, revitalized, reborn.

The nightmares that pursued the horrors of the war and haunted me continuously began to subside and become less frequent. I was ready to reenter the harshness of reality. The cruel, brutish banality of real life. But why? I dreaded the thought of leaving Raven and this palm-covered paradise. I wasn't sure I really wanted to leave. Why would I want to abandon this enchanting life in what was essentially a tranquil harbor in the stormy sea of daily grind? A virtual Garden of Eden in a warm sunny back bay on the shores of the beautiful blue Pacific. Why would I want to toil away stressing over work, bills, credit rating, vacation pay, overtime, mortgage payments, taking out the trash, mowing the yard, or keeping up with the Joneses? Why grind myself down to a stump in order to retire *if* I make it to a grizzled crusty and can afford to keel over in a place unlikely to be as idyllic as the one I already enjoy . . . and still am robust enough to relish the carnal pleasures and appreciate the natural beauty of it all, before I slip into senile bliss?

But above it all was the inner turmoil I felt about leaving Raven. How would I tell her? How would she take it? What would be her reaction? She was the most compassionate, understanding woman I had ever known. Her overwhelming passion, the fire and spirit within her that consumes you entirely. The exotically beautiful, erotically sexual, and uninhibited sensuality, given unquestioningly, vulnerably, and with unbridled primal desire was unimaginable before I met Raven. I was a fortunate man to have loved her. I must be a lunatic to contemplate leaving.

I was troubled, and as usual, she sensed my turmoil. She said nothing, let me have my space and time to work it out. At night she held me closer and made love with wanting emotion, deep yearning, craving, a desire even more passionate than we had ever shared before.

We spent the remainder of our time together in warm, comforting embrace. Enjoying each other, loving each other, and remembering each other. Etched the wonderful memories into a special place in our mind, and our hearts. We knew we may never see each other again. Why?

The soft light of summer began to fade, and the shadows of fall grew long across the silver serenity of the calm, pristine cove that was our paradise. And like the last act of a romantic American Western, the day finally came when I packed my saddlebags and rode silently off into the sunset. I walked away from a love that was unconditional and unrestrained. A love free of jealousy, judgment, or rejection. I somehow knew this would be a very special addition to my growing list of life's regrets.

I tried on several occasions to return, but somehow never made it. A few short years later, the fickled finger of fate pointed abruptly in my direction once again. In June of 1950, Communist North Korea crossed the 38th parallel, invading South Korea, and Uncle Sam recalled me to fight the good fight one more time.

I spent the next three years back in A-26s flying low-level, dark-of-night, train-and-convoy interdictions through the dark narrow canyons and valleys north of the 38th parallel. More gut-wrenching, terrifying, seat-of-your-pants, ground-hugging bombing and strafing runs through treacherous canyons in total darkness. Screaming, ear-shattering, high-speed dives into the black pit of hell. Then steep, full-throttle, butt-clenching climb out of the napalm incineration of Dante's inferno. All intensely loud, terrifying, ghastly, and unfortunately unforgettable . . .

And now, unbelievably, after all these many years, after all those horrifying campaigns, miles of open ocean, and memories of untold nightmares, here we were. Alive, together, holding each other close and never again wanting to let go.

♦ ♦ ♦

I dreamed of her often during those long, lonely nights in Korea so long ago. Dreams of Raven were the only things that kept me going and the only way to keep the nightmare wolves at bay. Now, I felt that I would never let her go. I wouldn't make that mistake again.

As the sun began to dip toward the horizon, we rolled Raven's assortment of shells and her diving gear into the towel and stowed it aboard the little red jet. She turned Dakota toward home, patted him on the rump, and sent him on his way up the beach. He knew the way; he would get there on his own.

Raven and I jumped into the roadster, fired 'er up, and were heading down the road away from the fading sun and toward the gray blue of twilight. Destination, China Point.

After a short drive south along the rugged windward side of the island, the road narrowed and began a steep climb up a cypress-and-eucalyptus-covered trail to a jagged peak, across Smuggler's Cove from China Point. We parked the jet in a lean-to shed attached to the end of the horse corral. We off-loaded her treasure trove of shells and her gear and walked along the corral to what looked like the edge of a steep cliff several yards ahead, with a large granite outcropping to the right and an amazing view of the windswept Pacific beyond.

Between the corral and edge of the precipitous cliff was a small mineral springs grotto nestled into the side of the granite hillside, energetically bubbling a mild sulfur steam cloud into the deepening blue sky to be whisked away high upon ocean breeze. We continued along the path until just before the ground dropped away into Smuggler's Cove far down the rugged slope; there was a small cabin porch built into the opening of a surprisingly large, accommodating cave within the boulder outcropping. The cabin porch merely provided a covered entry to the cave and allowed for a windowed enclosure and sturdy door to the wide cave entry. A means to block the intrusion of winter storms or interloping wildlife.

The interior of the cave was the size of a large cabin with a very high ceiling. The wall at the Pacific side of the room was a large rock fireplace built into the boulder wall of the cave. Raven had decorated sparsely with indigenous available necessities. The stone floor was covered with a thick woven grass mat. There was the heavy bear-skin rug in front of the fireplace that I remembered from long ago love nest within estuary palm grove. There was the familiar design of Indian blankets hung from the rock walls to create a warmer ambiance and less cavelike atmosphere, and blue lupines adorned the interior within abstracts of abalone shells and smooth, shiny driftwood sculptures. Across the room from the fireplace against the opposite wall was the food preparation area complete with a washtub sink serviced by pump-handle water fed from spring well.

I set about building a small fire in the fireplace, while Raven stored her shells and diving gear in a makeshift service porch in the rear of the kitchen area behind a beaded curtain. The last shafts of sunlight illuminated wisps of feathery clouds and made for a glorious magenta sunset. A cowbell clanked from the corral around the back, announcing the return of Raven's pinto pony, Dakota. "I'll go feed and water him," Raven said softly in my ear with a kiss before she went out onto the porch and around the back to the corral.

I stepped out onto the porch and lit a cigarette. From here I could see clearly down the mile or so of rugged slope to Smuggler's Cove and the entirety of Dr. Con's heavily guarded compound and harbor entrance. The immense entrance to the cave, from which the bat guano was extracted, was also visible to the left at the base of the mountain, adjacent to the wide, flat beach.

At sunset thousands of hungry bats fly from the cave in great, swarming black clouds. A continuous, undulating wave of sporadic, zigzag, spastic flight of nocturnal airborne rodents. It was like witnessing the endless exodus of flying monkeys, filling the sky of Oz, in desperate search for Dorothy and her ruby slippers . . . "and her little dog too"!

The heavily armed cadre of Chinese guards protecting Con's compound were not entirely unlike the Cossack-inspired guardians patrolling the Wicked Witch's castle. "Ho-ho hum . . . ! Ho-ho hum!"

When the resident bat population had departed for the night, the bat guano mining operation usually began to gear up for the evening's operations. Excavated bat droppings, rich in phosphates, nitrates, and other scarce, highly sought nutrients that can be used in industrial applications ranging from fertilizers and pharmaceuticals to the manufacture of explosives. A lucrative commodity, highly demanded, short in supply, and extremely difficult to recover in sufficient quantities to make such a difficult endeavor a profitable venture. Dr. Con's operation in Smuggler's Cove was one of the very few in the world easily accessible and near available shipping facilities. They transported the material from the cave by a railcar and deposited it in a huge dusty pile on the beach. A steam shovel then loaded it onto a flat barge, which was towed across the channel by a tugboat.

There seemed to be very little, if any, mining preparation going on this evening and a bit more excitement or anticipation in the compound than usual. A few more guards than normal and much scurrying about as if in preparation for the imminent arrival of dignitaries, diplomats, or other VIPs.

Raven returned with two lively catfish thrashing about within small net.

"Where did you snag those?" I asked, following her inside.

"There is a freshwater spring down in the cypress grove," she said, pointing out of the window above the kitchen sink. "I raise them in a pond that the spring feeds, to clean the parasites from the surface of the rocks."

She placed them on a makeshift washboard next to the sink. With a long, slender knife, she made a deep incision behind the head through the thick sharklike skin, slit completely around, then straight down the middle.

She then took a pair of pliers and grabbed a section of the skin at the incision and pulled the skin of the catfish off to the tail, exposing thick fillet slabs. She then gutted, cleaned, sprinkled with a potpourri of herbs and placed them in an iron skillet, which was then placed over the fire on an iron grate. She chopped a handful of onions, peppers, potatoes, and carrots and tossed them in the sizzling skillet as well. The whole place began to fill with the enticing aroma of frying onions and peppers.

When the mouthwatering concoction was ready, she served it with a measured shot of home-brewed agave juice, tequila. This stuff was a killer. Ingesting in small portions throughout a prolonged period of time was the prudent, and self-discovered, course of action. I remembered that even back on the mainland, so long ago, she always maintained a crop of agave cactus. Through a rigorous process of harvesting and shredding, which was done primarily with machete and drying, the thick, grainy, parchmentlike material would then be mixed like a mash into the homemade distillery to boil, ferment, and condense into a deceptively destructive perfection. With just the right amount, you could be invincible, indestructible; you could be Superman. Thus the motivation for the ceremonial peyote and agave induced delusion that a band of warriors armed with bow and arrow were capable of defeating a repeating rifle, and Gatling gun armed and endless wave of blue-coated cavalry during the destruction of the American Indian culture a century ago.

A tad too much and you would wake up in a pool of your own drool and be incapacitated for the remaining daylight of that particular dawn.

Raven was aware of my Irish and Cherokee Indian ancestry, and always monitored my intake diligently. She knew the "firewater" made the Irish in me belligerent and mean, and the Indian in me crazy. Mean and crazy. A recipe for disaster, and an experience to be avoided. A train wreck looking for some place to happen.

◆　◆　◆

We finished our catfish feast and took our agave juice onto the front porch, as the last glimmer of light faded to dusk. The lights around Dr. Con's compound came on as his shore boat approached the harbor entrance from the south.

I went inside and fetched my PI "cheating spouse" surveillance spyglass from my jacket. I returned to the porch, extended the eyepiece, and peered down into Smuggler's Cove. Dr. Con emerged from the bat cave with a small entourage of overly decorated Middle Eastern and Asian military types, and their well-dressed, studious, attaché toters. They walked along the beach to the boat docking facilities on the far side of the cove.

As they proceeded down the beach, I turned my spyglass toward the heavily guarded harbor entrance. To my surprise, I noticed upon the approach of the shore boat a newly installed set of antisubmarine nets began to open from the middle and slide toward either side. Controls assumed to be in one or both guard towers at the harbor entrance. Interesting. But why antisub nets? That very well could be the reason Dr. Con was allegedly dredging the bottom of Smuggler's Cove and creating a contentious issue with the island's conservancy committee upon my last visit to the island.

Raven emerged from the cabin and strolled across the porch carrying a mortar and pestle and a small leather pouch. She had changed into a thin cotton "wifebeater" man's sleeveless undershirt. The scent of wild lavender wafted gently on the summer breeze. Her large dark nipples danced unrestrained 'neath sheerness of inadequately thin white material. Length of miniscule garment not quite enough to conceal pouty mounds of sweetness nestled 'tween supple warmth of ample thighs. She sat close beside me and placed the mortar and pestle in her lap. She then removed a peyote button, also cultivated from her cactus crop, from her leather pouch and ground it to a course powder. She then sprinkled a pinch of the powder into each of our cups of agave juice.

The mescaline in the peyote cactus button, once again, when ingested in moderation, produces a spiritual introspective awareness. A cosmic journey within oneself, as well as a hallucinogenic appreciation of the natural world around us unseen or unrealized before. However, in excess, it makes you a raving lunatic capable of any impossible endeavor without thought of consequence. You think you are indestructible. A warm, soothing rush of tranquility began to engulf me. Enveloped me like a cocoon. I began to glaze over.

The shore boat arrived at the dock in the cove below, and Dr. Con's entourage was there to welcome its arrival. I peered through the spyglass once again and observed a tall sandy-haired Caucasian disembark with his own respective contingency of well-dressed, bespectacled briefcase humpers.

After the obligatory exchange of bows, handshakes, and compulsory kisses on the cheek, the entire congregation retraced Con's path back along the beach and disappeared within the entrance to the enormous bat cave.

I turned to Raven and asked, "Have you noticed any unusual activities in the compound recently?" She thought for a moment.

"I don't pay much attention to what happens down there," she began. "It seems to be the same operation all the time. Except for the strange lights under the water at night."

She took me by the hand and led me along the path in the dark to the mineral springs nestled within the grotto of granite boulders. We removed our clothing and slowly immersed ourselves into the comfort of warm, soothing bubbles. The mineral springs would help diminish the pain and enhance the healing of internal injuries to the ribs and kidney.

◆ ◆ ◆

That night, on the bear-skin rug, in front of the dwindling fire, Raven gently messaged the lingering awareness of internal damage. Her fingers slowly traced the long-ago healed-over scar tissue, as well as the more recent indications of primitive altercation. Fresh puncture wounds, various telltale train track of fresh stitches and discoloration of newly acquired bruising of soft tissues.

"Oh Travlito," she softly sighed, "I see that my dreams were correct. Nothing has changed. You still have that dark cloud that continues to follow you."

I tried to explain my inner turmoil. My inability to be content, no matter what the circumstance. I feebly tried to explain something that I didn't understand myself. I tried to explain why I was unable to fully commit to her so long ago.

She placed her finger over my mouth, silencing me. She squeezed a cool thick juice or gel from an aloe vera cactus leaf and began to gently message it into my skin. "As before, Travis, and as will always be," she said softly, "there are no conditions, no judgments, no rejections. You are who you are and I do not wish to change that. I place no shackles, no restrictions. No conditions, Travis."

She lavished her unrelenting passion upon me throughout the night. Each time more emotional than the last. Building to a savage, screaming, exhaustive crescendo. Climaxing into breathtaking sweaty shudders of rapturous ecstasy. Completely spent, collapsing into sublime contentment, until the feline purr of insatiable desire stirs inevitably within her once again.

Sometime late that night, I was awakened by the sound of a distant railcar slowly clip-clopping over rail ties. I unentwined myself from Raven's silken brown body. The fire had diminished to small clumps of fading embers. I got up, lit a cigarette, and walked out onto the porch.

Most of the lights around Con's compound below were off, except for a few at the entrances and exits, and atop the guard towers at the harbor entrance. All at once, a powerful explosion of light, as if a napalm charge ignited, burst from the cave, illuminating the entire harbor and night sky in a blinding flash. Following the initial blast was a loud, powerful, pulsating whooshing sound. The pulsating whoosh blasted an exhaust trail across the harbor like interconnected smoke rings, or knots in a rope of smoke. It was an immensely powerful series of calculated explosions.

Immediately afterward, the entire compound went completely dark. Total blackness that the meagerness of the new moon did little to enlighten. Total darkness. Total silence.

Raven came running to my side and held me close.

"What was that?" she frightenedly asked.

"It was some kind of explosion in the cave down in Smuggler's Cove," I answered. "Have you ever heard that before, or seen that knotted-rope smoke trail?" I asked.

"No," she said, still shivering and holding me tight. "I have never heard or seen anything like that before."

Just as suddenly as they had gone out, the lights around the compound began to come back on. Dr. Con, the tall sandy-haired stranger, and their respective entourages eventually emerged from the cave with much excitement and articulation. They proceeded back along the beach and went into one of the buildings adjacent to the boat dock.

"Did you mention earlier that you had seen strange lights under the water?" I asked.

"Yes," she said softly with a trembling voice. "They come and go from under the dock where the shore boat is now tied. They go out in the night, and return before dawn."

Chapter Seven

It was a bright, sunny July morning. The familiar morning haze had long ago given way to the warm gentle breeze and cheerful song of the meadowlark, the sharp report of the blue jay, and the gleeful chirp of sparrows and finches. The soft coo of a dove came gently from high in the cypress and eucalyptus grove.

Raven was tending to morning chores in the corral as I walked past and stowed my jacket in the car. She closed the gate and came to where I waited. I told her that I had an appointment with Captain Wally this morning, but I would return as soon as I could. She put her arms around my neck and kissed me softly, lovingly on the lips. She pressed against me firmly. She looked deeply into my eyes. "I will be here waiting for you anxiously, Travlito, as always."

I arrived in town from the south by way of Seal Cove, the rock quarry, and the moorings for the *Lucky Dutchman* and the *Bad Penny*. I drove down the alley and parked the red jet behind Sculley's. I entered through the rear door and continued through the kitchen. Sculley was busy with scullery detail and gave me a double take as I passed. I went through the café doors and entered the restaurant. Captain Wally, Steve Canyon, and Naomi were in a tight huddle at the far end of the breakfast counter, engaged in a hushed conspiracy. They all turned when I walked in and looked at me as if I had just clubbed a baby seal. Horrified astonishment swept over their faces as they came to me in unison and protectively escorted me to the last stool at the far end of the counter. They huddled around me as if to shield me from who or whatever might come through the front door.

"Where in hell you been, Polliwog?" was the first thing out of Captain Wally's mouth.

"We've been worried sick about you, Sunshine," was Naomi's concerned follow-up.

"I spent the night on the other side of the island," I answered quizzically.

"How did you get here this morning?" was the next question from Steve on our celebrity panel.

"I drove Lara Rigney's Muntz Mobile. It's parked in back," I answered a little more quizzically.

"Did anyone see you? Are you all right? Are you hurt?" The questions came in rapid-fire succession. I sat in silence, recognizing the genuine concern in their voices and in their eyes.

"What the hell is going on?" I asked calmly.

They all looked at one another. Finally, Captain Wally leaned close and spoke in a hushed, matter-of-fact tone. "Nicky Fallon was found murdered aboard the *Lucky Dutchman* early this morning. I noticed the cabin door open as I arrived back from the Marlin Club. I went inside and found Nicky hanging from the bulkhead. Impaled through the temple with a marlinspike."

I placed my elbow on the countertop and contemplatively stroked the scratch of my morning stubble. "No shit?" I quietly whispered rhetorically.

"That ain't the worst of it, Polliwog," the captain continued. "Constable Lafargé found your duffle in a dumpster at the end of the pier. It was stuffed with blood-soaked clothes."

"Son of a bitch!" I exclaimed and slammed my fist on the counter, startling everyone. The ruckus brought Sculley peering over partially opened café doors . . . meat cleaver at the ready.

"It's OK, Sculley," Naomi said nervously. "I'll explain later," she said, waving him back to his duties.

"Well that's just fan-freakin'-tastic," I began. "So now I'm Lafargé's prime suspect for the murder of Nicky Fallon."

"So far, you're being classified as a person of interest," said Canyon. "They're looking for you all over the island. They wrapped the crime scene and hauled the body away before dawn. The gendarmes don't want to schmuck up the upcoming Fourth of July celebrations, or scare off the tourists at the height of the season. The island news rag has agreed to keep a lid on for the time being."

"You do realize that an ice pick through the temple is Nick the Pick Licata's signature mob-hit calling card," I asked. "And a marlinspike is just a real big ice pick." They all looked at each other, puzzled.

"You know that Nicky Fallon is Dominick Licata's nephew?" Again, exchange of dull stares.

Captain Wally finally spoke, "Polliwog, we don't know what's going on. We're counting on you to find out what's going on. So is Lara and Rita Rigney. And the Commodore too. We know that you have the best interests of the Rigney family at heart. We trust you to do the right thing. If you tell us that you didn't kill Nicky Fallon, we believe you. Even if you did kill him, we know that you must have had a good reason. Right now our main concern is to keep you alive and well so that you're free to solve this murder and help the Commodore and the Rigney girls to regain control of the casino. We have seen the subtle changes that have occurred over time, and we don't like it . . . no, sir, we don't like it one bit."

I got up from the counter and paced to the door. I nervously looked up and down the boardwalk. I slowly walked back to the anxious crowd waiting at the end of the breakfast counter. I asked Kamikaze Steve if he could drive Mrs. Rigney's little red jet back to up the hill to the estate, then wait for Roscoe to retrieve him in his cab. He answered affirmative. I also asked if he could persuade Spaulding to supply a change of clothes from the guest quarters.

"Affirmative, Bombardier," was his response.

I asked Naomi if I could use the phone; I needed to call the mansion. Naomi produced the phone and set it on the counter. I spun the dial and waited for it to ratchet back the correct number of digits. After a short fuzzy pause, Spaulding answered with his usual curtness. I asked to speak with Lara. He didn't bother to ask who was calling, he recognized the voice.

"Oh my god, Travis, I'm so relieved to know that you're all right. You are all right, aren't you, Travis? Please tell me that you're OK!" she began, only slightly under control.

"I'm perfectly fine, Angel. I'm with Captain Wally and Kamikaze Steve. I wasn't anywhere near the *Lucky Dutchman* last night. This was the first I'd heard of it when I arrived in town this morning," I said.

I could hear her sniffling and holding back the tears, trying to regain her composure. She was a tough dame and a trooper, but it had been a rough night and it was starting to get to her. After a deep breath and long sigh, she began to sound more relaxed and more like the cool cunning babe I had come to know and love. Lara Rigney hooked me with a late-night phone call, not so long ago, with her smokey-velvet voice, that told me that she was someone to be reckoned with. She was streetwise and smart, but she was also soft, alluring, and a sensual majestic thoroughbred. She took another deep breath and began to calmly divulge the recent occurrences as she knew them. She had gone home last night before Nicky and was not aware of what happened to him until Constable Lafargé arrived at the mansion just before dawn.

"When the inspector told me that you were not in your hotel room and were nowhere to be found, I began to panic," she said softly. "Travis, I can't stand the thought of losing you. I can't lose another soul that I have come to love. I can't do this alone, Travis."

She broke down and began to cry. My heart was breaking for her. I wanted desperately to go to her and hold her . . . comfort her. Yet, we both knew that was not possible at this time. I was a "person of interest" in a notorious murder investigation, and the only way I was going to solve this case was to stay in the shadows and fly low under Lafargé's radar.

I tried to calm her down and get her to concentrate on more immediate concerns. I asked her if she had made any extra security arrangements for the mansion or the casino. She told me that she had indeed called my office early this morning and talked to a conscientious young woman named Precocious, who assured her that she would have a security team over on the first available flight. Lara told me that the young woman seemed quite concerned about my well-being, and that I should call her and alleviate her fears.

There was a distinct pause. She choked up. "Oh Travis, that's not the worst of it," she haltingly continued. "Rita hasn't come home. Nobody has seen or heard from her since last night at the casino. Travis, I'm really worried about her. I haven't told RJ about any of this. I don't know how I could at this time. Please find her before I have to tell the old man any more bad news. I can't endure the thought of laying even more tragedy at his feet."

She began to weep once more. That bit of info hit me like a ton of bricks. With Rita now missing, time was of the essence. I would have to expedite the process and find her before anything else.

"Angel, I need you to listen to me carefully," I began. "I'm counting on you to pull yourself together and be strong. I need you to be strong . . . the Commodore needs you to be strong . . . but most of all, Rita needs you to be strong. I can do this, Angel, don't you fret about that. I'll get Rita back, and I'll get whoever is responsible for Nicky's death. But I'm going to need you to be sharp and on top of your game. I'm gonna have to be rough and nasty, and I'm gonna have to do it in the dark. I'll need you to keep your eyes and ears open, and pay attention to what's going on around you. Be extremely careful. I'm going to contact Precocious and have her send a couple of personal bodyguards as well. Don't leave the mansion until they have arrived. Have Manuel close and lock the front gates, and don't open them to anyone until the security team is on the job."

"Yes, we've already locked the gates, and Constable Lafargé has posted a squad car and two uniformed officers out front," she responded. "I must go to the ballroom tonight, of course, as it is the opening night for Durante and Charisse, but I will wait until your security people arrive."

She sounded much better. She sounded confident and relieved that she was not in this alone. I assured her once again that we would get through this together and that I would keep in contact with her.

"I love you, Travis. Please be careful," she said softly.

"I love you too, Angel."

I put the phone back on the receiver and turned to the concerned assemblage. "Has anyone seen or heard from Rita since last night at the casino?" I asked.

"Oh no," gasped Naomi and put her hand over her mouth. She looked at the others, and they shook their heads in the negative. I asked Naomi if I could use the phone to call my office.

"You use whatever you need, darlin'. What can we do to help?"

"I need someone to see if they can flag down Roscoe," I asked.

Kamikaze Steve went to find him. Naomi went into the kitchen and began cooking eggs, bacon, and pouring pancake batter on the griddle. Captain Wally went to the front entrance and kept a lookout up and down the boardwalk.

I picked up the phone and stuck my finger in the zero hole. I spun the dial and waited for it to click back ten times. Mable, the island's switchboard operator, chimed in after the first ring. "Operator."

Mabel was literally "plugged in" to all the island gossip. During her infrequent off hours, she enjoyed the Filipino pachinko parlors at the pavilion on the isthmus.

I gave her the number on the mainland and waited, hoping she didn't recognize the voice or the number.

"Oh Travis," she exclaimed in a hushed tone. "The entire island is keeping the wires hot looking for you. Are you OK?"

"Well, I woke up this morning feeling great, but the shit has kinda hit the fan since then," I sarcastically responded. "Sorry, Mable. I appreciate your concern. I apologize for being a smart-ass," I said humbly.

"Not to worry, son," she said. "Mrs. O'Malley wanted me to tell you if I heard from you, that if you need a safe house, to come see her. Be careful, son. Hold while I connect you."

"Good morning, Travis Dugan Investigations," came the familiar sunny voice from my secretary-trainee, Precocious Goodlay—tall, blonde, gorgeous. Buxom movie-star looks, moves, big blue eyes, and a come-hither demeanor. A statuesque Swedish goddess that was but one half of an identical set of twins . . . (Yah! yikes! and begorn!). She could melt your hinky-dinky-donka in the middle of a frozen fjord. She was also the niece of my regular secretary extraordinaire, Precious Goodlay—also tall, blonde, and gorgeous. Also dinky-donka worthy. All their respective brothers, uncles, and cousins were associated with the FBI, OSS, CIA, Interpol, and numerous local law enforcement agencies and military defense contractors. Great connections, plenty of resources. These girls were worth their weight in drive-by-colonoscopy alimony payments, and I bent over forward to keep them happy.

"Good morning, my dove, notorious PI here," I began, keeping it light.

"Oh Travis, I'm so relieved to hear from you. Are you all right?"

"I'm fine, baby doll. No need to worry. Did you get the security team rounded up?" I asked.

"Yes, they're on their way, ETA Avalon within the hour. I sent a three-man security team with K-9 operative and three personal bodyguards. I figured you would want personal security for the Commodore and the girls," she said.

"Great work, baby doll, I appreciate your foresight," I responded. "If you need to get ahold of me, leave a message at the mansion. I'll do my best to keep in touch, but it may be a few days."

"OK, Travis. Be careful and take care of yourself. If you need anything, call me."

"Thanks, doll face. Do me a favor and have one or two of your cousins stay with you at all times. I don't want any problems at the office like we had the last time."

"Auntie Precious already thought of that and I have an entourage of big buff bruisers everywhere I go," she responded.

"OK good, I'll stay in touch. Aloha, baby."

Naomi set the breakfast she had prepared in front of me and poured a fresh cup of hot java. I thanked her as I gobbled it down. Who knew when I might get another.

Captain Wally returned to the counter as I finished breakfast and the last of the coffee. "Roscoe and Steve are coming down the road," he said.

I put a quarter in the vending machine, pulled the handle, and a pack of Chesterfield Kings slid into the tray. I gave Naomi a hug and a kiss, threw the keys to the jet to Kamikaze Steve, and followed Captain Wally to the front door. He got in the front, opening the back door as he passed, allowing me to climb in the back and hug the floorboard for our ride to the docks. Captain Wally informed Roscoe of the current situation during our ride through town. Roscoe pledged his help in any way he could.

We pulled to a stop at the entrance to the pier, momentarily scanning the vicinity for vigilant gendarmes, or knuckle-dragging gunzels. Eventually we drove down the pier and parked next to where the *Bad Penny* was tied. Captain Wally got out and went aboard. He opened the aft hatch and proceeded forward, below deck, emerging from the forward hatch. He returned across the gangway to the pier and opened the rear door of the cab while leaning in the front passenger window to pay the tab. I climbed from the rear floorboards, hustled across the gangway and down the aft hatch. Captain Wally untied the bow and stern lines, then clambered aboard. He fired up the Packards and within minutes was heading out of the harbor and into the open channel waters. Destination, unknown.

Once clear of the harbor jetty, I came from below deck and sat in the copilot seat next to Captain Wally. We turned south in the general direction of San Clemente Island, an off-limits military bombing and artillery range, some twenty miles away. The relatively calm four- to five-foot swells on the leeward side of the island increased to an aggressive eight to ten feet once out in open ocean. The steep swells came at us from the southwest, and about a boat's length apart at approximately two o'clock from our present heading. Under normal conditions, with your average ocean sport or fishing boat, you would laboriously climb at an angle to the top of the swell, then surf down the back side into the trough, hopefully without pearling the bow into the oncoming swell and swamping the boat. In contrast, the *Bad Penny*'s step hull, once up to speed, elevated the bow and most of the entire hull above the swells, leaving only the props and rudder in the water. Like a hydrofoil (whatever that is). It made for a perpetually swift and smooth ride.

The crazy old man pushed the throttles forward and the Packards began to sing. The wind whipped by with relentless force, which required you to keep your head ducked below the small windscreen, lest your jowls billow out like a parachute, dragging you off the stern. Or your eyelids blasted open and your eyeballs instantly freeze-dried (again, whatever that is; someone should be writing this stuff down).

He continued in a wide sweep to starboard until we were heading southwest with the rock quarry and Seal Cove quickly disappearing in our wake. The crazy old bastard glanced in my direction occasionally with a wide grin to see if I was butt-clenched to the seat or if I was enjoying the ride. He would laugh at my casual smile and thumbs-up. He knew full well that after what I'd been through in the recent past, it was gonna take a lot more than a fast boat ride with a maniac at the helm to agitate me.

We turned due west, keeping the rugged shore of Catalina a mile or two off our starboard side. As Smuggler's Cove appeared on the horizon, Captain Wally powered back on the throttles and brought the *Penny* to a comfortable cruising speed, the Packards quieted to a low rumble. The old man reached beside his seat and handed me an impressive set of powerful binoculars.

I focused to infinity and scanned the area outside Dr. Con's heavily guarded harbor entrance. All seemed quiet and normal in the immediate area of the compound. But as I scanned to the west, away from the harbor entrance, I noticed a dive boat bobbing in the swell several hundred yards away. They flew a "diver in the water" pennant, and I could see a diver on the transom in full scuba gear, speargun in hand, prepared to enter the water. As we got closer, I realized that yon aquatic was none other than my personal nemesis, Blaine Pond, the nauseatingly charming British Secret Service agent and self-anointed suitor of the island's beautiful bronze princess, Lara Rigney. We had an arm's-length agreement stemming from our brief incarceration together after our first not-so-arm's-length encounter at the casino entrance upon my last visit to the island. We gave each other a wide berth. (I'd like to give him a swift kick in his noble ancestry.) I wondered why he was out there. It sure wasn't for the fishing. I remembered Rita making that exact statement the last time we were here.

The old man spun the helm counterclockwise, and the *Penny* responded with a wide smooth sweep to port. He pushed the throttles forward and her turbos spooled with an impressive whine as we raced across the water at an ever-increasing speed. We headed southwest, straight into the oncoming swells, and toward the west end of San Clemente Island and the granite cliffs where Dr. Con's commandeered runaway yacht collided with a fuel-laden supertanker and was sent to the bottom in scattered bits of shiny confetti along with the golden dragon, upon the gripping, nail-biting, cliff-hanger conclusion of my last installment to this movie matinee serial mystery.

Eventually the old crusty throttled back to a comfortable cruising speed and began a wide turn to port with the immense sheer granite cliffs off our starboard side approximately five miles. He let her idle along, while pointing toward the island. I raised the binoculars once again a peered toward the towering cliff face.

About halfway between our location and the cliffs was another converted PT boat, with what appeared to be a rigging tower mounted on the original .30-caliber gun mounts on either side amidships. This boat was painted in a dull camouflage with no reflective or shiny surfaces. There was a dive flag visible on this boat as well and what appeared to be a deep-sea diver being hoisted onto the deck. I could see the big brass helmet and bulky pressurized suit with the air-line attachments. I lowered the binoculars and looked quizzically over to Captain Wally. He smiled and said, "That's Max von Jekyle's boat. Our newly arrived freelance salvage consultant with dubious ties to CIA, OSS, CID, or some such black-bag group of clandestine sumbitches. Why do you suppose that big hairy bastard is parked right over the remains of Con's destroyed boat? Do you suppose he's searching for the golden dragon? What else would he be looking for?"

What else indeed? Von Jekyle was a new player in this game. Another quasi salvage consultant. There seemed to be an abundance of quasi salvage consultants on the island. Not to mention a lot of war surplus. This could be a very dangerous place if someone were to ignite the wrong fuse.

And then there was the not-so-secret agent, Blaine Pond. A returning veteran of these intriguing summer games who still seemed fixated upon Dr. Con's enterprises. The last time I was out here, with Rita, Pond got excessively agitated that we were out here interfering with his business. As I recall, he got verbally abusive, accompanied by rude hand gestures. As I recall, I gesticulated in kind, to the humorous chagrin of my lovely boatswain's mate, Rita. That exotic dark vixen, who was smoldering and sensual, yet somehow innocent and playfully childlike. It was eating me up inside to think that someone was holding her against her will, or worse. I had to find her, and fast. But where would I begin?

We eventually arrived on the leeward side of San Clemente Island. The sun was now high overhead, and the sea was smooth, calm, and a pale turquoise that was crystal clear to the smooth sandy bottom at a depth of about fifty feet. We sat motionless and in contemplative silence for some time. Captain Wally got up and went below. He emerged from the aft hatch bearing two bottles of ice-cold Pabst Blue Ribbon beer and a shiny silver church key.

With the familiar accompanying *kachoo*, he adroitly removed the caps and handed me a beer that was covered in glistening condensation. And with the accompanying "Ahhhh," it went down cool and refreshing. The old salt produced a crinkled Viceroy for each of us, and I lit both with the familiar *ching* as the lid flew open on my chrome service lighter with a quick flick of the wrist. Funny how one remembers such familiar sounds and smells, tastes and feelings from the past that make you feel relieved, relaxed, comfortable, and safe. Like the fond remembrance from childhood of the smell of wet asphalt drying in the warm sun after a spring rain. Or the fragrance of new mown grass on a warm summer's day. The feeling of exhilaration as a young boy when you walk out onto the majestic green expanse of your first baseball field. (Funny how the mind works.)

The captain retrieved my empty along with his own and descended the aft hatch ladder. In a short while he returned with "a beer from the land of sky blue water" Hamm's . . . "That beer refreshment," Hamm's.

Funny how the mind works.

"Well, Polliwog? I showed you a few interesting things goin' on here and there. And I let you think about it for a while. So now what are you thinking? What's your first move?" he asked.

I took a long pull from my beer and stared into the bubbles rising back to the surface within bronze vessel.

"That's not a crystal ball, Polliwog," the old man said softly.

As was my usual modus operandi, I answered the question with one of my own. "What can you tell me about Von Jekyle? When did he first show up?"

"He first started comin' around at the beginning of the season," Captain Wally began. "He always seemed awfully friendly. Maybe too friendly. He hangs around the Marlin Club at night and has a great time. He's on the water during the day. He's been anchored over the golden dragon for the last few weeks. The scuttlebutt is that he was some kind of black-bag operative for the OSS during the war. Now he claims to be a salvage consultant, specializing in ordnance recovery."

"Deep-sea ordnance recovery?" I questioned. "Must be pretty important ordnance to require recovery. Doesn't make sense. He must be expanding his repertoire to include sunken treasure recovery as well."

"You know, Polliwog, you ought to ask Kamikaze Steve about Von Jekyle when he arrives. The two of them seem to get along pretty well. They play some kind of foolish strafing, bombing game out on the water. Steve will be able to tell you more about Von Jekyle."

I offered the old fart one of my Chesterfield Kings and lit both with the service lighter. I waited for him to settle, then asked where someone might keep Rita hostage here on the island.

"Oh hell, Polliwog," the old man began. "There's a thousand places to hide someone on or around the island. Boats, caves, ranch houses, bunkhouses, hillside bungalows . . . and as you well know, Cooley Town."

Yes, as I well knew. I was trying reluctantly not to think about Cooley Town, and the haunting death of Chin Lee. That sweet young innocent who gave her life at the hands of the vicious tong while keeping the secret of a childhood love. My inability to prevent Chin Lee's death relentlessly haunted me. I prayed that I wouldn't be haunted by Rita's.

"Well, speak of the devil," the old man said, pointing skyward. From out of the blue came Kamikaze Steve's Black Cat PBY Catalina. He made a shallow dive and a wave-top strafing run over our heads with a great roar of the Pratt-Whitney's as he passed.

"See, Polliwog!" the old man exclaimed. "That's the kind of foolish shit I was talkin' about. Him and that jackass Jekyle play that stupid simulated war game crap all the time. Stimulated dipsticks if you ask me."

The shiny black pigboat made a wide starboard sweep, then came in from the east, low and slow into the slight breeze and calm turquoise sea. He made a smooth landing and taxied within fifty yards of where the captain and I lounged aboard the *Penny*. Within minutes Kamikaze Steve had motored over in a small rubber Zodiac boat. He tied up at the stern and climbed aboard.

"Ahoy, mates!" he exclaimed. "Got a cold one?"

"Usual spot," the old man responded, pointing below. Steve descended the aft ladder and emerged moments later with a cool new domestic beer . . . Brew 102. Locally brewed off the 10 freeway in downtown LA. "It's the water."

"One of these days you're gonna pancake that dumbo into the drink, flying it like that!" the cantankerous old crust exclaimed.

"Oh shucks, Ma," Steve responded with a glint in his eye. "I didn't even bend the wings on that one."

He looked over to me with a wink. "Hey, Bombardier! You ready for a shakedown cruise? Maybe you can show this deck swabby how a proper attack dive should be done."

"I'm looking forward to it, Kamikaze. We can probably do a touch-and-go one-hopper right over the *Penny*," I laughed.

"Yeah," the old man shot back. "I saw how well that worked for you the last time you tried that. Hence, the nickname . . . Kamikaze!" We had to laugh at the old captain. He seemed to get a little bitchy with a couple of beers under his belt.

"You seem to be running a little late this morning," the captain said.

Steve took a big pull off his specimen bottle brew, then leaned back against the gunnels and smiled. "Ya, I was held on the tarmac this morning until one of Lafargé's men delivered an evidence bag for me to fly over to a representative of LAPD for analysis at their lab." He looked over to me with a smile. "Do you remember an Inspector Lugar?" he asked.

Of course I remembered Lugar. He was an old friend of mine, with good off-the-record information. I was sure Kamikaze Steve remembered him too. Inspector Lugar brought the coast guard, like the cavalry riding over the hill just in the nick of time, and plucked our sorry butts from the clutches of an angry sea upon the harrowing conclusion of our last installment to this serial (or surreal) saga. He arrived at the critical moment, and with the firepower required . . . and all on a hunch. I think it was Lugar who gave Steve his nickname, as I recall. Lugar picked us up just after we had kamikaze'd Steve's little red Grumman into the superstructure of Con's commandeered yacht. I felt somewhat relieved knowing Lugar was in the loop. He would watch my back, back on the mainland.

"So what was in the bag, fag?" the old crotchety piped up. Steve and I looked at the old man, then at each other. We began to laugh.

"Wow, extra pissy this morning, huh, old fart?" Steve asked while trying to prevent his beer from blowing back out of his nose.

"Maybe you should lay off the brew, and go back to that vicious concoction of metallic martini you used to pack around," I added with a wink.

"Ah, squid piss on the both of ya," was the old man's reply. "What's in the sack, Mac?"

"What I believe it to be was a bag of bloody clothes," Steve began. "I can't say for certain, but that would be the most logical guess. Lafargé doesn't have the facilities for such analysis. He must send it to the crime lab at LAPD."

"Did they send an escort?" I asked.

"No," he replied.

"Did you look inside?" the old man asked.

"No, they had it sealed up pretty well. Lots of thick packing tape," was Steve's reply.

"Hey, don't worry about it, Bombardier," Steve said with a sly smile. "Lay low for a couple of days. I'm sure things will turn out OK."

"Yea, the only thing is . . . Rita may not have a couple of days."

Steve downed the last of his carbonated brew, collected everyone's empties, and went below to stow them away. He came back on deck and prepared to shove off.

"Come on, Bombardier, let's go for your cherry ride. I added some accessories that I think you'll like."

I made arrangements with Captain Wally to rendezvous in this same vicinity before sundown. I thanked him for his help, gathered my jacket, and climbed into the Zodiac for the ride back to the Black Cat. We entered through the side hatch, stowed the Zodiac, and were strapped in within minutes. I sat in the copilot's seat and took a few minutes, while Steve fired up the twin twelve-hundred-horsepower Pratt-Whitneys, to familiarize myself with the instruments and controls. I looked out onto the starboard half of the 104 feet of wingspan and found myself somewhat ill at ease to discover there were no wing flaps. I was equally taken aback by the realization that the wings appeared to be skinned in a lacquered fabric of some kind . . . hmmm. Makes one ponder.

◆ ◆ ◆

He throttled forward as we turned into the wind and a slight chop coming from the west. Even with the engines at full throttle, the run-up to take off was nearly three miles of roaring, ear-shattering twin engines directly overhead, lumbering, bouncing, shuddering, dodo bird takeoff. This thing was a flatulent, laborious pig compared to what I had been flying, but he flew it like he was a Sabrejet pilot.

We eventually gained some comfortable altitude heading west with San Clemente Island disappearing off to our left and Santa Catalina slowly descending to our right. He rotated a handle in the overhead and the wing pods began to retract into the seemingly inadequate cloth wings. I banged my knuckle into the bulkhead next to my seat a couple of times.

Steve looked over with a knowing smile. "Sheet metal body with metal ribs and stays," he reassured as he began a long slow turn to port, in a big sweep around San Clemente Island. "The wings are cotton fabric with knotted seams, lacquered over metal wing spars. One-hundred-and-four foot wingspan that hold seventeen hundred fifty gallons of fuel. She burns one hundred gallons of fuel per hour at one hundred knots. She can stay aloft for seventeen hours and cover seventeen hundred miles. They built almost thirty-three hundred of the PBY-5 and the amphibious PBY-5A like this one, between 1936 and 1945, at Consolidated Aircraft just south of here in San Diego. Makes it convenient for parts and repairs. I added the plexiglass blisters on either side for the tourists' thrill. Great view on the way over and back. Exciting takeoffs and landings with the water splashing past. These boats were first built for search-and-rescue missions, but they made great sub patrol and recon planes as well. She can carry two five-hundred-pound bombs, depth charges, and torpedoes. During the war they had two .50-caliber waist guns, a .30-caliber tail gun, and a .50-caliber fixed gun in the nose . . . just like that one!" he exclaimed, pointing down into the plexiglass-nose section of the plane.

"Take the controls, Bombardier," he said as he climbed down into the nose and uncovered a pristine .50 caliber affixed with an ammo belt fed from a metal ammo box. (Yikes! This sumbitch is loony tunes . . . but I like it.)

He returned to the pilot seat as I continued the wide sweep around San Clemente and headed north over the channel between the mainland and Catalina Island.

"This baby is supposed to be able to perform an attack dive from about three thousand feet," he said with a glancing, wicked smile.

I grinned, pulled back on the yoke, and pushed forward on the throttles. She slowly climbed to the desired altitude and we began to search for a target. Far below in the middle of the channel sat what looked like a large supertanker, at anchor.

"That looks like the Global Explorer," he said just before I dropped the nose and began a screaming dive from three thousand feet.

As we gained speed, she began to shudder like a banshee. She bounced up and down and bucked like a bronco. She may have had attack dive capabilities, but it wasn't pretty. I looked over to my copilot, who was butt-clenched to his seat and mesmerized by the bow the laminated fabric wings had achieved. He looked at me with a nervous smile.

"Bombs away, Kamikaze! banzai!, banzai!" I yelled at the top of my lungs and pulled back hard on the controls.

She began to vibrate and shudder violently. We continued to dive on the tanker and the closing rate got increasingly uncomfortable.

"Yeeehaaa!" I screamed, as the flying pig slowly, laboriously, inch by inch began to level off with a great roar of the engines and sigh of relief from my now-agonized and recently soiled copilot. I made a shallow turn to port and we screamed by the starboard side of the ship, bow to stern, just above the tall drilling derricks that towered above the main deck. I continued to pull back until she finally groaned to a more comfortable altitude above the wide expanse of dark azure sea.

"You insane bastard!" he yelled with obvious hysteric relief. "I thought I was nuts, but you are a freakin' maniac . . . ! But I like it," he said with a wide grin.

I leveled off and throttled back to a comfortable cruising speed. She flew along effortlessly at such a slow airspeed; it felt like we were hovering. I set a course that would take us around the north end of Santa Catalina, with a slight tropical breeze and an early-afternoon sun dead ahead.

"What kind of ship is the Global Explorer?" I asked once we had settled in. "What are they drilling for with the derricks?"

"Well," he began, "the current scuttlebutt is that the Global Explorer is a top secret CIA project, built and financed surreptitiously by Howard Hughes. The cover story is that the Explorer was built to drill and recover usable resources from extreme ocean depths— petroleum products, oil, gas, whatever. Thus the drilling rigs, the huge spools of cable and decks piled high with pipe sections. The conspiracy buff theory is that the Explorer was built specifically to clandestinely recover a sunken Russian submarine."

"Are you saying there's a sunken Russian sub in the middle of the channel?"

"No, no. I don't think so," he said. "She's only been here a couple of days. Looks more like they're performing sea trials. Make sure she's seaworthy. Like a shakedown cruise."

I descended to about five hundred feet as the palm-covered isthmus came up on our port side. I could see the skipjack moored serenely in front of Ah Looey's cabin. I did not see Shifu or Yung He. We continued northwest over Arrow Point; then I turned due west, past Parson's Landing and Starlight Beach. When we reached the rugged windswept cliffs of Land's End, I banked hard left over the gentle grassy plateau where Chin Lee was buried. I made a couple of wing wags then throttled up and set a course southeast that would take us out past the point at Whale Rock, across Catalina Harbor and the serenity of Little Harbor, to converge once again with land at China Point.

Steve unbuckled and went to the rear of the plane. He came back with a gunnysack full of water balloons filled to the size of softballs. He began to load them into a makeshift aluminum tube, jerry-rigged to the bulkhead next to the pilot's seat. The tube extended downward and through the fuselage exiting next to the rudder controls to the outside. He closed the lid on the aluminum tube and looked at me with a sinister, wicked little grin.

"Locked and loaded for attack mode," he said. "Target Von Jekyle!"

Since he broached the subject, I felt obliged to take the opportunity to delve into Max von Jekyle's dubious affiliations. Steve told me that Von Jekyle had arrived at the beginning of the season. They met during drunken orientations at the Marlin Club. Von Jekyle told him that he was a private contractor. A deep-sea salvage consultant specializing in ordnance recovery. So far the same story I got from Captain Wally. He went on to say that when Von Jekyle wasn't under contract by various departments of the military, he indulged himself with the search for sunken treasure. Treasure that lay too deep for most to recover. "He's looking for the golden dragon down in Scripts Canyon."

When we reached China Point, I made a couple of circles around Raven's hilltop compound. I couldn't see much through the trees. The corral was empty. Down the cliff at Con's mining operation all was quiet, and outside the harbor Blaine Pond's boat was conspicuously absent.

We headed south across the channel between Catalina and the granite cliffs of San Clemente Island. Kamikaze Steve raised a set of binoculars and peered off into the distance. "There he is," he announced. "Dead ahead. Steady as she goes, Bombardier."

I looked at him quizzically. "Can you do another attack dive on his boat?" he asked. "But from a much lower altitude?"

"How about a skip-bomb run?" I asked.

"Sounds good to me," he said with a shrug. "What's the procedure?"

I descended to wave-top altitude. The dark sea whisked by as we skimmed the wave crests like a swift black pelican. We lined up on the target and came in low with plenty of speed and a high closing rate. I turned to Steve just before we reached Von Jekyle's boat. "When I yell bombs away, you push the button, or pull the cord, or whatever you do to release your payload. Ten-four, kemosabe?"

He gave me a tentative thumbs-up as we approached the target. Just before Von Jekyle's boat disappeared under our nose, I yelled bombs away and pulled back hard on the controls. We lurched skyward as Steve pulled the lanyard next to his seat and all the colorful water balloons deployed in a string and scored several skipped and direct hits, down the center beam, bow to stern. It was a lethal attack. Would have been terminal. Game over.

"Yahoo! Bull's-eye, Bombardier!" he exclaimed with clapping hands and a child's delight. "Oh that hairy sumbitch will never live that down. Great piece of flying, Travis. No shit, man, I'm impressed. You are the man!"

I pushed forward on the yoke, nosed her down, turned to starboard, and jammed down on the right rudder pedal. The right wing dipped, and as we came about, we gained increasing airspeed. I leveled her out and we began another run from the opposite direction. Steve scrambled to get his bomb load prepared as we quickly closed on Von Jekyle's camouflaged PT boat. As before, I yelled bombs away and pulled back on the controls. Steve yanked his lanyard and the multicolored bomblets deployed in a dazzling string and once again several found their target, dappling Von Jekyle and his deckhand with the swift sting of defeat. As the lumbering black pigboat groaned to gain altitude, a loud bang came from the bottom of the fuselage.

"Whoa!" Steve yelled. "We've been hit, Bombardier! That sumbitch scored a direct hit!"

"What was that?" I yelled. Didn't seem to affect the airworthiness. I still had control and the hydraulics were intact. The pressure gauges had not changed.

Steve turned to me with a big grin. "Potato mortar," he said.

"A potato mortar?" I questioned.

"Yea," he replied. "He uses compressed air and a metal tube to launch a nonlethal aerial potato barrage. Works like a grenade launcher. He's pretty accurate with that thing. I've got several dents in my bottom." (Sounds like a personal problem to me.)

Glad he didn't put one through one of our cloth wings, I thought to myself.

I made a wide turn to starboard and headed for our rendezvous with Captain Wally. When we reached the leeward side of San Clemente, we found the *Bad Penny* waiting. I turned the controls over to Steve and prepared for landing. There was a warm Santa Ana blowing across the channel from yonder mainland shore, uncharacteristically clear and bright due to aforementioned breeze clearing out a grunge of valley basin and whisking it westward to create vibrant magenta sunsets filtered through pollutant particulates.

He again reached overhead and began cranking the handle, lowering the wing pods. We came in excruciatingly slow and finally bounced from wave crest to wave crest until she finally settled with a tremendous whoosh. We taxied over to within a wingspan distance of the *Penny*. Steve helped me off-load the Zodiac, and I climbed aboard for the short trip to where Captain Wally waited. Steve tied a line to the rubber boat so it could be retrieved once I was aboard the *Penny*.

We gave each other a half-assed salute, and before I cast off, Kamikaze tossed a duffle into the boat. "Present from Spaulding!" he yelled. "He said he'd see you in the newspapers." (Spaulding, again that pompous little prick, tweaked my nose with a veiled reference to the front-page splash Lara and I created upon my last visit. I believe he sarcastically congratulated me for conducting such an indiscreet investigation at the time.)

Once I was aboard the *Penny*, Steve retrieved the rubber boat, fired up the Pratt-Whitneys, and was lumbering off into the wild blue yonder once again. As the Black Cat faded into the twilight of the eastern sky, Captain Wally and I were on our way north, destination, Avalon.

By the time we were approaching the pier at the Tuna Club, there was a deep purple shadow cast over the harbor from the setting sun silhouetting Mount Orizaba and the twinkling lights of Avalon where it met the Pacific. The Caribbean rhythms began to mingle with the soft warm breeze and drift romantically across the glistening calmness of the pristine harbor.

I gathered my duffle and climbed the short ladder to the pier. I waved to Captain Wally as he turned the *Penny* toward home and slowly disappeared into the dwindling twilight. I lit a cigarette and leaned on the rail, gazing across the festive seaside village. The bright pollutant-filtered yellow ball of a full moon began to rise above the dark, indistinguishable, unforgiving depths of the Pacific Ocean. I wondered if Rita could see the rising of the moon.

I took the last drag off my cigarette then flicked the butt into the darkness and watched the glow descend into its inevitable extinction. I retrieved the bag Spaulding had graciously provided, made my way down the pier, across the boardwalk and up the steep ascent of Whitley Avenue.

I walked across the familiar courtyard of the Whispering Waters Inn and knocked softly on the door. I heard the soft waddle of Mrs. O'Malley approach. The metal peephole in the door opened, and the cherub-faced Irish lady I called Moms peered from the soft light within.

"Oh Dugan, I'm so glad to see you," she chimed as she quickly unlocked the door. She opened the door and brought me in with a warm hug. "Thank the Lord, son, that you're all right. I prayed that he watch over you," she said.

She wasted no time and hustled me through the kitchen and service porch and across a small yard in the rear to a slightly dilapidated one-car garage, with a small apartment above. We climbed the outside stairs and entered a comfortable studio apartment complete with kitchenette and small bath. It was clean and well kept. A cozy little hideaway.

"You freshin' up, son. Get settled in. I'll be back shortly with a hot meal," she said as she closed the door behind her and clip-clopped her way back down the stairs.

I washed up and shuffled through the duffle Spaulding had supplied. I changed into a crisp pair of blue dungarees and denim shirt. There was a nice two-tone blue denim "Ricky Ricardo" jacket rolled neatly in the bag as well. I switched all the necessary accoutrement—zap, lock-picking tool, flashlight, and of course my old reliable .38 snubby—from my leather bomber jacket to my present wardrobe along with a pocketful of cartridges.

I heard Mrs. O'Malley making her way up the outside stairs and met her at the door. She came in carrying a serving tray steaming hot under a cloth napkin. She set the tray at the small dinette and removed the napkin, revealing a large bowl of Irish stew and piping hot slab of golden corn bread.

"Eat it all, son. You don't know when you'll get another," she said as she removed a bottle of scotch whisky and a shot glass from the pocket of her apron. "Here's a little dessert if you so desire," she said with a wink and a smile. She patted me on the cheek and told me that I was welcome as long as I wished. "Keep the shades down and the lights won't be noticed from the outside at night."

As she prepared to go, she stopped at the door and turned to me. "Oh by the by, son, my old Plymouth is in the garage below if you need it. Keys are in the ashtray. I don't drive much anymore. My hip can't push in the clutch pedal.

"Thanks, Moms," I said.

"You take care of yourself, son. Be careful. Be aware of your surroundings, Dugan."

Chapter Eight

The large pale yellow moon hung majestic in the clear star-speckled night sky and reflected upon the calm surface of the water. The immense casino, in silhouette against the moon, looked enchanting and at the same time ominous, like the castle of Oz. My view of the harbor, from the top of Whitley Avenue, was picture-postcard spectacular. Music and laughter were gently carried up the hill from town upon the warm Santa Ana. The atmosphere was festive, romantic, alluring, and yet somehow dark and surreal—like the mountains of Mordor. I did not feel so hobbit like at the moment. Maybe more like Gollum. "Ah, yes, my precious. Like Gollum he is."

When I reached the bottom of the hill, I pulled the fishing cap that I had grabbed as I went out the door, down tight on my head, and pulled the collar of my shirt up, jammed my hands into my pockets, and shuffled across the boardwalk to the casino. I went around the back, toward the mezzanine door, away from the bright lights of the main entrance.

Tonight was the opening of Jimmie Durante and Cyd Charisse. It would be all glitz and glamour, searchlights and flashbulbs, paparazzi, movie stars, and their respective entourages. Glittering, flittering socialites, globe-trotting aristocracy, jet-setting nymphets, and spanking, sparkling, giggly debutantes, all in exuberant inebriation of Fantasy Island.

I continued around the circular walk, to a location from where I could see through the huge glass doors to the interior of the ballroom. I lit a cigarette and leaned on the rail overlooking the harbor. Inside the ballroom the dinner show was already underway. Cyd Charisse had finished her opening act and was kibitzing with Durante onstage. The room was packed, but I caught a few brief glimpses of Lara, resplendent in white satin, fluttering from table to table, like a gentle butterfly, making sure all accommodations were satisfactory. The personal bodyguard was present but unobtrusive. The addition of a few Pinkerton uniformed guards in the area was a nice touch.

I went back the way I had come and climbed the outside ramp to the casino level of the promenade. Once again I went around the dark side of the building and took up a position at the harbor rail where I could see inside the gaming room, without easily being seen from within. I lingered nonchalantly, gazing over the festive harbor area, smoked a few more cigarettes, and scratched my ass a couple of times. I casually turned toward the casino and surreptitiously observed the goings-on within. After a couple of stiff pulls on the pocket flask of scotch whisky Moms had provided, I almost choked on the next one and had to turn away from the casino. I couldn't believe it. I hoped that I was hallucinating. Some terrifying flashback from my sordid past. What a nightmare.

The reflective twinkle of harbor lights obscured to unfocused haze as flashbacks, dimmed by time, once again raced uncontrolled through my mind. I tensed with fear, and a cold chill ran through my core as unedited recollections of past horrific events, once subdued, now scrolled across my overagitated neurological memory receptors and froze me in time . . . a time I had forgotten . . . until now.

Anthony Cornero Stralla, a good guinea from the north country, immigrated with his parents to the United States in the early nineteen hundreds. In the Roaring Twenties he was in the shrimp business supplying high-end clientele along the West Coast and such Hollywood iconic eateries as the Brown Derby, Chasen's, the Macambo, Ciro's, La Scala in Beverly Hills, and Villa Capri, one of the original Italian restaurants in LA, owned by Pasquale "Patsy" D'Amore.

Shrimp wasn't the only delicacy being supplied by Tony Cornero and his two brothers, Frank and Louis. Each fishing boat in the fleet could carry one thousand cases of high-quality booze smuggled down from Canada.

One of the many off-loading points along the coast was Smuggler's Cove, Catalina Island. That, of course, was where the original association between the bootleggers, sponsored by the fledgling LA mob run haphazardly by Jack Dragna, predecessor of Nick Licata, or his nemesis Mickey Cohen, and Commodore Rigney, likewise sponsored by Joe Kennedy and his clan, who brought scotch whisky from Europe through the Panama Canal with eventual destination, Catalina Island, was formed.

The deep cove and immense bat cave, now utilized by Dr. Con and his mining operation, was the ideal storage and distribution center of bootleg booze for the entire West Coast. The Cornero brothers made millions from that operation.

◆ ◆ ◆

In the 1930s the Cornero brothers imagined a dusty one-horse town they were keeping alive with their bootleg whisky could be transformed into the oasis in which to invest their ill-gotten gains, and at the same time lure not just the high rollers but the everyday man to an adult paradise in the desert where gambling had been legalized, and Boulder Dam provided twenty-four-hour electricity and an endless supply of water.

Tony Cornero saw the glittering possibilities of Las Vegas long before East Coast playboy mobster Benjamin "Bugsy" Siegel ever got his Florsheims dusty in the desert sand.

The Corneros first built the "Meadows" in Las Vegas and supplied it with bootleg whisky from their own five-thousand-gallon-a-day still in Culver City, California. Next, they acquired majority share in the Cal-Neva Lodge in Lake Tahoe. The Cornero brothers ran a smooth operation. They were known for good food, pretty good liquor, and a fine gaming room.

Everything ran fine for a while, until they started feeling the pressure from the Five Families that made up "the commission" of the East Coast La Cosa Nostra. The Bonanos, Genoveses, Gambinos, and other families were moving, although reluctantly, into Vegas in a big way. When the Meadows burned to the ground, the Cornero brothers moved back to the West Coast and set sail for the high seas.

In the 1940s Admiral Cornero commanded an armada of gambling ships. A neon flotilla that stretched across the outside of Santa Monica Bay, three miles past California's territorial limit, and an equally impressive fleet anchored twelve miles off Long Beach, beyond the federal territorial authority. Shore boats were crammed twenty four hours a day with adventurous gamers eager to arrive at the glittering party boats that beckoned from the golden horizon where sunset merged into sea.

It was at this point in time that I first became associated with Tony Cornero and his West Coast band of mafia thugs. After I left the estuary paradise I shared with Raven that summer after the end of Pacific War, I worked for a guy named Pappa Pappadopolis, a fun-loving Greek who owned the "Golden Bear" nightclub on Coast Highway in Huntington Beach.

I flew bootleg, nontaxed whisky from the Airport in the Sky on Catalina Island to Meadowlark airstrip, behind the estuary in Sunset Beach. Both strips were closed at night, and there were no runway lights or airport personnel. From Meadowlark Field the booze was transported by truck, through the oil fields to a concrete labyrinth of underground bunkers that were constructed in the uncertain days soon after the surprise attack on Pearl Harbor. The bunkers, some three stories deep in various locations, housed underground shore batteries and the required ammo, designed to defend the Seal Beach Weapons Depot, just north up the coast, from Japanese submarines that were suspected to be operating offshore. In those opening paranoid days of the war, the War Department and the military were terrified that an attack on the naval base in Long Beach, or the oil fields and storage facilities that stretched from Pacific Palisades to the wide expanse of vulnerable oil-producing derricks along the Huntington Beach mesa, near Tin Can Beach, would be such a catastrophic blow to the war effort that it must be avoided at all costs.

At the end of the war the military removed the weaponry and ordnance from the immense underground bunkers and abandoned the property above, surrounding it with chain link and razor wire. The only visible evidence of its existence was the palm grove and guard shack near the main entrance. The same palm grove and cabin I shared with Raven that magical summer, which now seemed so long ago.

The abandoned caverns made for ideal storage and distribution facilities for the major percentage of bootleg whisky moving inland from the coast. That was where the Corneros and I first crossed paths. Pappa Pappadopolis ran his own operation and supplied the Golden Bear nightclub and the quiet little gaming room in the basement with the booze I flew in from the island. The smuggled whisky was purchased from the Commodore or from one of the other cartels utilizing Smuggler's Cove. Once I had flown it to Meadowlark and off-loaded onto a truck, we would drive in the dark through the oil fields directly to the Golden Bear.

Pappa was under constant pressure from the Corneros and their connected associates within the disjointed LA mobsters to buy the smuggled liquor from them exclusively and/or cut them in on the gambling operation. The all-too-familiar cancerous infestation of an independent business that has been the hallmark of the mob's modus operandi since the days when the "Mustache Petes" began to shake down the pushcart venders of Sicily. And now, here we were once again. And once again, we prepared to "go to the mats." (I thought I was gonna need a bigger gun.)

♦ ♦ ♦

This was the big push I had feared. Nicky Fallon was the polite but firm foot in the door. Tony Cornero and Dominick Licata were the kicking down of the door and storming in. The hapless LA mob was totally shut out of Havana, Cuba, by the New York and New Orleans families, and their Vegas enterprises were being commandeered by the more powerful gangs from the East Coast and Chicago. When the authorities finally sank the gambling armada off Santa Monica and Long Beach, the West Coast contingent of pedestrian gangsters were running out of options. They had set their sights on the island of Santa Catalina. This was to be their Havana, Cuba, twenty-six miles off the Southern California coast. This was their destiny. To own their own island and transform it into Monte Carlo of the West, twelve miles beyond the federal territorial limits. This was to be their legacy. Their power base from which to build an empire that would rival the most influential East Coast or Midwest organizations.

I was reminded of the telephone conversation I overheard, through the door of Nicky Fallon's office, on my last visit to the island. It was entirely spoken in Sicilian, so I was only able to discern limited bits of the conversation. Something about being "heavy-handed" and something about "more time." I eavesdropped on this rather overheated phone call after witnessing Nicky unceremoniously toss a stocky older Pisan out of his office onto the street. The phone call, I found out later, was to Fat Frankie Fallontino at Gazardi's nightclub on the strip. Fat Frankie, as it turned out, was Nicky Fallon's father . . . and Nick Licata's brother-in-law. The stocky pepperoni Nicky had kicked to the curb I now recognized was Louis Cornero Stralla, Tony Cornero's elder brother. I should have put two and two together at that time, but I was sidetracked into the search for the golden dragon. I should have recognized the more immediate threat of the mob's initial efforts to take over the gambling operations within the casino. I should have realized the danger and been more effective in preventing the situation in the beginning. Now it might be too late.

I also began to get a real uneasy feeling that I might have brought this sudden turn of events on by my impulsive assault upon the two gunzel croupiers near the Descanso Beach Hotel. I was going to shake up the place and see what transpired. I had no idea this would be the result. Once again, I seemed to have outsmarted no one but myself. Once again I had stepped on my own prehensile appendage. I had a gut-wrenching feeling that I had inadvertently, amateurishly screwed up and made a monumental mistake that might have cost Rita her life. I needed a stiff drink, and I needed to get my shit together. (I was such a miserable douche bag that I could taste the bitter spittle of vinegar regurgitating within.) I retreated, quietly slinking away, Gollum-like, into the darkness.

The Marlin Club, as usual, was loud, bawdy, and uproarious. It was dark, smoky, and had an ambient odor of fresh chum. It was the local watering hole for the seafaring scalawags that frequented the island and plied the open ocean for their hard-fought existence. I sat at the last stool at the end of the bar, which jutted out into the room like the bow of a schooner. I ordered a straight shot from the enthusiastic young bartender, who looked somehow familiar. I realized when he returned with my drink that he was the young screenwriter wannabe who tended bar at the Blue Parrot upon my last sojourn to the island. He was working on a story about a doctor, wrongfully convicted for the murder of his wife, who escapes on his way to the big house and begins a feverish search for a one-armed man that he believes to be the real killer. All the while being pursued by a dogged federal marshal. I asked the bright-eyed young author how he was progressing.

He seemed surprised yet flattered that I had remembered. He smiled, then explained that he had literally written himself into the veritable corner. He had his hero trapped in a train tunnel with both ends of the tunnel blocked by federal marshals closing in on him. No escape.

At that moment a look of unadulterated fear filled the young tender's expression as his upward gaze seemed to eventually focus several feet over my head. A firm hand tapped me on the shoulder, and I too was forced to turn, facing belt buckle, and raise my sights toward the ceiling. The gigantic granite monument, somehow squeezed into an ill-fitting pin-striped suit, towered over me and menacingly gestured toward the beaded curtains of the corner alcove.

"Ah-ah," he mumbled and gestured toward the alcove once again. It was Phangs Pa, Sir Arthur Sidney's personal Chinese behemoth and ancestrally anointed bone crusher.

"Buzz off, odd job," I uttered while turning back to my bewildered young bartender and future film scribe.

"Sewer grate," I said to the puzzled youngster, as I was persuasively lifted off my bar stool by the scruff of my neck and dangled like a bobbing marionette, as I was unceremoniously escorted toward the beaded curtains of the corner alcove to which I had been so graciously invited.

The young bartender looked at me quizzically as if to ask, "Huh?"

"Sewer grate in the curb," I reiterated as I faded into the hazy darkness. "The curb opening into the sewer has always been a great escape route for me in the past. Give it a try. Underground sewers can go anywhere that you can imagine. Good luck, kid!"

I pierced the entry of multicolored beads face-first, toes barely touching the floor, and was lifted over the table and abruptly planted in the corner chair opposite my esteemed host, the obese one, Sir Arthur Sidney, in the abundant flesh. (What a flippin' pleasure this is gonna be.)

"Ah, Mr. Dugan, I'm so pleased that you accepted my invitation to join us for that fine bottle of cognac and lusty tales of adventure that we agreed upon at our last late-night orientation," began the rotund one with a hardy laugh.

"Well, Sir Arthur," I replied, "how could I not, with such a charming concierge possessing impeccable manners and persuasive demeanor to escort me to the party?"

"Ah-ah," came the boisterous reply from Godzilla with a ponytail, along with a beef-shank-sized hand over my entire face and a playful nudge that knocked me off my chair onto the floor. Sir Arthur howled with laughter as Phangs Pa leaned over the table and once again lifted me by the scruff of my neck and replaced me onto my chair.

"Bu-dah!" he exclaimed with a wide grin. "Bu-dah!"

"What the hell is with this big sumbitch?" I asked with a growl, trying to reshuffle myself.

"Oh calm yourself, my friend," replied Sir Arthur, still chuckling. "You're very lucky," he continued with a grin. "My esteemed colleague really likes you, Mr. Dugan. He likes very few individuals, but you, my friend, he genuinely likes. He's just playing with you."

"Well tell Fu Man Baby Huey here to go play with himself. I'm not in the mood," I grumbled, slumped in the corner.

"Oh come, come, my depressed comrade," said the jolly fat man as he gingerly poured from the crystal carafe into a delicate snifter for the guest of honor . . . *moi*. "Try a taste of that, my friend. Sniff the bouquet, then let the silky, warmth embrace you, soothe you, calm your soul, lighten your spirits, and make you positively warm and fuzzy inside," he toasted with a raised snifter, a wink, and a giggle. I swished. I swirled. I sniffed. I pounded her down. I didn't know about warm, but I was beginning to get a little fuzzy around the edges.

"There, there, my old friend," the fat man said soothingly. "We're just a couple of old friends having a drink. No need to get flustered." He proceeded to pour another round. The unimbibing gigantic Chinaman had hot tea.

"Tell me, my friend, what brings you back to this majestic and enchanting island?" asked Sir Arthur. I removed my cap, turned it around, and looked at the big swordfish embroidered on the front, then placed it on the table.

"I came for the fishing," I said matter-of-factly. "The only thing I caught so far is a case of crabs."

They both looked at each other and began to laugh. In the monolithic Neanderthal's case it was more of an "Ah-ah! Bu-da!"

"Now that's the Mr. Dugan I remember, indeed it is my friend," began the fat man with a hardy laugh. "Droll sense of humor and deadpan delivery. You are a card, Mr. Dugan. I truly enjoy your company."

"And what bizarre international intrigue brings our favorite 'artisan salvage consultant' back to our mysterious little oasis?" I asked through my increasing fuzziness. "Still searching for the golden dragon? Well get in line, Artie, you're not the only 'quasi salvage consultant' at the party."

"Ha-ha!" the fat one exclaimed. "Oh my friend, after the disastrous outcome of our last partnership, you'll understand my reluctance to confide in you with regard to my current adventure. No disrespect intended, Mr. Dugan, but you are rather brash and unpredictable. My perceived description of you upon our initial meeting proved to be, *dead-on*, I believe is the phrase. You, my friend, are the quintessential American cowboy. Ride into town, shoot from the hip, vanquish the bad guys, then pillage and defile the grateful town's delicate treasures. I actually had possession of the golden dragon and then lost it because of your interference. Now it may be beyond anyone's reach."

"Oh, I don't know about that," I responded. "There may be someone on the job as we speak. And besides, Artie, if you'll remember, you wouldn't have gotten near the damn dragon in the first place if it weren't for me."

"Yes, yes, of course, my brazen comrade," the fat man acquiesced. "Don't get defensive. I'm merely stating that my current endeavor may require more finesse, a more delicate approach. As with the search for the golden dragon, I have invested a tremendous amount of research, and the time and expense required to bring me to the present culmination of that effort. I venture to say that there is nothing that you could be of assistance to me in my present quest. There is nothing you could tell me, my inebriated friend, that I don't already know."

"So then, you therefore cannot have the slightest interest regarding the test firing that I witnessed recently, along with some very decorated dignitaries, that resulted in what I would describe as rope-knot exhaust trails," I responded with a slight grin. I was fishing, but I figured that might pique his interest. I waited for a reaction. Didn't have to wait long.

The obese one sat motionless for an instant, the look of bewildered astonishment, perhaps momentary disbelief, frozen on his rotund and ruddy facade. I watched his eyes intently as he attempted to regain outward composure. Game face restored, he cleared his throat and looked about the interior of the Marlin Club. Phangs Pa followed suit and gazed cautiously here and there throughout the room. They both looked intently at me. I then likewise looked conspiratorially about the small corner I found myself confined within as well.

The fat man leaned closer and spoke in hushed tones, "Mr. Dugan, do I understand that you were present at a test firing of a propulsion system that produced an exhaust trail that resembles an interconnected series of smoke rings?"

I paused, for dramatic effect, then slowly emptied the last drop of my snifter. "Yes, my friend, indeed I did," I finally responded. "Me and an exclusive group of highly decorated Middle Eastern and Asian dignitaries."

The fat man began to reach inside his jacket. I had my snubby out and on the table in an instant.

"Whoa! Whoa! Quick draw," he said, raising his free hand. "I merely want to show you a photograph, my friend. Relax."

He slowly, deliberately removed the photograph from his pocket and placed it on the table in front of me. I returned my .38 to the holster snugged under my left armpit. The picture was a fuzzy black and white, obviously taken from a long distance with a telephoto lens. The man in the photo was a tall Caucasian with curly blonde or reddish hair.

"Could this be one of the distinguished dignitaries present at the demonstration?" Sir Arthur asked in a more serious manner.

"Yes, I believe he was present," I replied. "He was accompanied by his own rather impressive bunch of four-eyed, pocket-protected, pencil-pushing, yes-men gopher geeks. They were shown a discernable amount of respect by their hosts and the other guests in attendance."

"Do you know the identity of the man in the photograph?" Sir Arthur asked.

"We were not formally introduced, and I don't recall his name at the moment," I responded.

"Could his name possibly be Gerald Bull?" asked the fat man, more intense.

Bingo! I knew I'd heard that name before, but I scrambled to come up with when or where. I couldn't remember . . . I stalled . . . coaxing my neurological receptors to retrieve the requested information from the farthest regions of my contextual repository. Eureka! With concerted effort the file was found. During my brief incarceration with dashing 00 secret agent Blaine Pond, the name Gerald Bull was mentioned by Inspector Lugar during a phone conversation. Pond overheard me repeat the name and told me in confidence that Gerald Bull had something to do with designing and producing long-range cannon technology. As I recall, Pond was on the trail of a shipment of clandestine cannon barrel sections surreptitiously destined for Catalina Island labeled as oil well casings.

"I do believe that very well might be the name I heard bantered about," I finally responded. "Some kind of brainiac regarding long-distance cannon trajectory."

Sir Arthur leaned back in his chair, and a wide grin began to form.

"Bravo, my friend. Bravo indeed. I must tell you that I am very impressed with your precognitive prowess. Very impressed, my friend. Perhaps we may very well have a basis for a continued relationship."

"Tell me, my friend," he began. "How is it that you, you'll excuse my surprise, were invited to such a demonstration? Why would the hosts of such an affair think that you would be of some benefit to them?"

I sat quietly, contemplating, staring into my empty snifter. Should I answer with obscure divisiveness? Or should I throw him a curveball?

"I didn't necessarily say that I was an invited guest. I believe I stated that I was merely in attendance," I answered with obscure neutrality.

"Ah yes," the rotund one began to giggle. "You are one in a million, my friend. Indeed you are. Never a straight answer from you. That is one of your characteristics that piques me to no end. Very well then, be that as it may. Let me go at this from another angle. Perhaps you won't be quite so defensive if you are truly aware of the consequences at hand. I know that you are a very cagey individual. I also know that you are much more cunning than you appear. That, ah sucks, mam, demeanor that you derive from your dime-store novels and your Western cowboy movies only camouflages the sly and discerning independent hard-core warrior that lies beneath. You are street-smart and explosively deadly. Both of those traits make you extremely useful in difficult circumstances and at the same time uncontrollable and dangerous. You are capable of being disarmingly charming, rakish, and have a smooth, cool air about you. You carry yourself with confident nonchalance, and yet you can be a loose cannon with scary consequences. All in all, you are a real piece of work, Mr. Dugan, but you somehow manage to get the job done. And besides, Phangs Pa thinks you're OK. That's good enough in my book. He's a very good judge of character. And as I've stated many times before . . . you are a character, Mr. Dugan. Quite a character indeed, my friend."

"Tell me, Mr. Dugan, how much do you know about Gerald Bull?" he finally asked.

"I don't know much more than I've already told you," I responded.

"Have you ever heard of an organization called HARP?" he asked.

"No."

"HARP is an acronym for High Altitude Research Program," he began. "According to Ganeway's Armor and Artillery, of which my family is associated as you know, and likewise *Jane's Defence Weekly*, Gerald Bull, while at McGille University in Quebec, was developing an artillery piece that theoretically was capable of firing a projectile into the upper atmosphere and perhaps even into space. The research was being secretly funded by the Canadian government under the code name 'Velvet Glove' and some believe more clandestinely funded by the CIA. Are you following me so far, Mr. Dugan?" he finally paused. He took a deep breath in preparation of his next long-winded diatribe and poured another round. (Seemed to me I had had this conversation before. The information sounded familiar. I couldn't remember who or when.)

"Mr. Bull fabricated two sections of a sixteen-inch artillery piece together and produced a barrel some one hundred and thirty feet long. That weapon fired a one-hundred-eighty-five-pound projectile, called a 'marlette,' approximately six hundred miles. By comparison, Mr. Dugan, the Paris Gun, manufactured by the Germans in World War I, fired a projectile about sixty miles. Big Bertha, produced by the Nazis, fired a shell over seventy-five miles. At the same time that the HARP project was developing, Gerald Bull's partner, a Mr. Rogers Gregory, was coincidentally beginning a program based out of Belgium called 'Space Research Corporation International,' which developed and manufactured weapons with the identical capabilities as the HARP program. These weapons, however, were being marketed throughout the Middle East, Southeast Asia, and China, through black market arms dealers like Sarks Saragarian, based in Brussels, and an American dealer out of Miami named Jack Frost. Those artillery pieces were code named 'the Babylon Gun.' Still with me, Mr. Dugan?" I nodded in the affirmative.

"That brings us to the present, my friend. My current quest is to find a clandestine shipment of flanged tube sections that were surreptitiously shipped from Austria, with ultimate destination believed to be Catalina Island. The manifest lists the cargo as oil drilling equipment."

Ah yes, I did remember a conversation that Blaine Pond and I had at the Blue Parrot shortly after our release from Constable Lafargé's custody during my first sojourn to the island. As I recall, the British government held the shipment briefly because of the precision of the manufacturing, and most notably, the real red flag was the rifling engineered within the tube sections. The British Secret Service released the cargo in order to follow it to its final destination. Unfortunately, according to Pond, they lost track of the cargo and were desperately attempting to relocate it. Ergo, the explanation for Pond's obsession with Dr. Con and his mining operation.

"Do you realize the ramifications if such a weapon is an actuality, Mr. Dugan?"

I paused, for dramatic effect, and slowly formed a confident smile across my face. "Yes, I believe I do," I confidently began. "You're talking about a big gun. A supergun with a bigger breech, a heavier payload, delivered from farther away. The ultimate goal in all weapons development programs." I paused once again for reaction. He seemed stunned. I continued.

"As I understand it, the problem with large, conventional, single-detonation cannons has always been size of detonation relative to weight and range of projectile. The finest deck guns on the biggest battleships afloat today can, at best, deliver a payload roughly the size of a small automobile approximately twenty to twenty-five miles. However, if an individual was capable of developing a propulsion system that produced a series of smaller simultaneous detonations as the projectile progressed through the barrel of the weapon, the distance or range of such a system would be far greater than a present-day single-detonation weapon could achieve. Likewise, the longer the barrel the projectile traverses, the more detonations can occur, thereby increasing velocity at the point of exit."

I sat back in my chair and raised my snifter as if toasting my uncanny ability to recover fascinating tidbits of useless trivial crap and regurgitate said trivial crap at the appropriate moment to either dazzle with brilliance or baffle with bullshit. I felt warm, fuzzy, and smug.

"Bu-dah!" the gargantuan Chinaman exclaimed, looking amusingly astonished at Sir Arthur. The obese one sat, aghast. Mouth agape, cigar fallen comically into his snifter perched atop his ponderous girth, and extinguished with a smoldering hiss.

"I am slicker than hot shit through a tin horn," I expounded with gleeful insolence. "We're talking about completely new and formidable technology," I continued. "If you'll allow me to postulate? Furthermore, with such weapons, any third-world camel jockey or turbaned despot could annihilate his hapless neighbor . . . or his neighbor's neighbor. Place a nerve gas or any number of biological warheads on the end of that projectile, and you've created a poor man's nuclear missile."

A wide grin began to form across Sir Arthur's round and ruddy face. He giggled uproariously and raised his snifter in a toast. "Ah, my friend, Mr. Dugan, you never cease to amaze me. Just as I had written you off as a bumbling, out-of-control wild man, you come along and astound me with your knowledge and intuitive perception of a very advanced technology. Not only that, but you also have apparently gained some inroads to the inner sanctum of clandestine conspirators. That is a feat that even I, with my list of numerous high-echelon connections, was not able to achieve. Bravo, my friend. Bravo indeed."

I raised my snifter in acknowledgement to Sir Arthur's backhanded compliment. "That's why this bumbling idiot gets the big money and the gorgeous babes, fat boy," I responded and pounded her down. (Whoa! I'd better easy off on the alcohol intake. I tend to get mean and belligerent.)

"Mr. Dugan, as you are aware, I have clients throughout the world that are willing to pay a king's ransom for access to such technology. They are also eager to pay a fortune for a completed operational system. If you are able to assist me in my quest, then, my friend, I am prepared to make you a very rich man. A very rich man indeed."

"Well, Sir Arthur, that is a very intriguing proposition. Very intriguing indeed. I have no immediate objection. However, I'm not sure how I would arrange such a request at this time. It would require a certain amount of finesse, of which you believe I am seriously lacking, and a time commitment that I may not have available."

"Mr. Dugan, I sincerely apologize for my inaccurate generalization. I have underestimated you on a number of occasions, and I have paid a heavy toll for my schoolboy immaturity and my adolescent ignorance. I stand before you humbled, and pledge my commitment to a well-earned admiration and respect of your wisdom, shrewdness, and abilities. Having said that . . . let me impress upon you the importance of preventing this technology from falling into the wrong hands. I must implore your sense of patriotism to ensure that this formidable weapon does not ultimately threaten the economic interests or sovereign security of our respective countries or their allies throughout the free world."

Interesting, on the one hand, the fat man was offering me a fortune so that he could sell this weapon to the highest bidder. Yet on the other, he impugned my patriotic duty to do the right thing. It was a riddle, hidden in a mystery, wrapped in an enigma. (Whatever that is.)

I rose to my feet with some difficulty and agreed to keep the rotund one in the proverbial loop. I mushed the fishing cap back on my head and shook hands with my two corpulent compatriots. Phangs Pa again lifted me over the table and placed me gently to the floor outside the confines of the beaded curtains. I turned, Chaplinesque, and sauntered, with some difficulty, through the smoke and haze, out of the Marlin Club and onto the foggy streets of Avalon.

I weaved my way down the street and merged with the other inebriated zots that ebbed to and fro along the boardwalk. Eventually I found my way back to the casino. I retraced my original path around the back and took up my position at the rail across from the glass doors of the ballroom. The show was over, the lights had dimmed, and the cleanup crew was in full swing. Lara gathered her belongings and, with her entourage of big, beefy, well-dressed, movie-star bodyguards, exited the ballroom to a waiting limo, and made haste back toward the estate. I felt relieved that Lara was safe in good hands, and the Rigney estate was secure.

I turned toward the harbor, lit a cigarette, and watched as the smoke drifted slowly away into the misty darkness. My head began to clear as I lingered, wondering how I got myself entangled in another convoluted web of intertwined conspiracies. (I hate when that happens.)

Suddenly a hand grabbed my shoulder. I turned instinctively and, with an open palm, caught Blaine Pond under the chin, knocking him flat on his back to the ground with a thud. He bounced to his feet and began a series of spinning back kicks intended to separate my head from my shoulders with much prejudice and enthusiasm. I ducked several and blocked one in order to deliver my own spinning back kick, which landed solidly on his chest, knocking him to the ground once again. He dragged himself off the pavement with some effort and a surprised smile on his face. He got to his feet, brushed back his golden locks, and complimented me on my recently acquired capabilities.

"I see you've taken a few karate lessons since we last met," he said, assuming the traditional fighting stance.

"There's only one way to find out, limey," I responded with a smile of my own.

We carried on a series of leaps, spinning back kicks, roundhouse front kicks, knees and elbows, punches and kicks, katas that would have made our "senseis" very proud. No serious damage was being inflicted, however, and we both began to fatigue. All we managed to accomplish was to attract the attention of a couple of the uniformed Pinkertons.

"Whew," exclaimed Pond, wiping the perspiration from his brow. "I could use a refreshment. Buy you a drink, mate?" He put his arm around my shoulder and gave me a couple of friendly pats on the back, as we briskly exited in the opposite direction from which the Pinkertons were casually approaching. We made our way around the casino and crossed the boardwalk unobstructed.

Luau Larry's was the tourist bar in town. Loud, boisterous, and bawdy. Drunken, sunburned, Hawaiian-shirted, and saronged revelers, each trying to yell over one another and the ear-shattering jukebox at the same time. Loud outbursts from one group followed by chants and cheers by another. It smelled of alcohol and cocoa butter.

I followed Pond through a never-ending sea of undulating boobs and butts to an empty table in the rear of the exuberant bar. A beautiful young Polynesian girl clad in a delicate sarong and several layers of flowered leis appeared through the ebb and flow of gyrating humanity to take our order with a soft wide smile. Pond ordered two vodka martinis, shaken, not stirred. (Of course, he's so vein; he probably thinks that song is about him). The Polynesian girl turned and was absorbed into the pulsating plasma of floral amoeba.

"Well, Mr. Dugan, we meet again," began a beaming Pond. "What, may I ask, brings you to this lovely island paradise once again?"

As before, with Sir Arthur, I removed my cap, stared at the embroidered sailfish, then placed it on the table. He began to laugh. I didn't even have to deliver the punch line. Nobody believes I came for the fishing.

"As I recall," he began, "the last time I saw you, you were on your way to intercept Con's stolen yacht and give Steve Canyon a 'crash course,' you'll excuse the pun, on the dynamics and intricacies of kamikaze dive-bombing techniques," he snickered.

"That shows how much you know, you smart-ass bastard. Oh sorry, I meant smart-ass bloody bastard," I retorted. "For your information, that was an advanced course demonstration of kamikaze 'skip bombing,' not dive-bombing."

"As I remember it," I continued," when I last saw you, Commander Pond, you were being fished out of the drink by Captain Wally, after you amateurishly allowed yourself to be broadsided by a bunch of half-pint, squinty-eyed landlubbers."

"Touché, my friend," said Pond. "I must admit that I was taken by surprise on that impromptu foxhunt. And I must also admit that I was somewhat surprised to see that you and Sir Arthur are still bosom buddies after the devastating consequences of that particular escapade."

"Smooth segue, Pond," I responded. "I was wondering how you were going to navigate your way to my world, and your continued obsession with the business of Sir Arthur, and for that matter, the not-so-covert investigation of Dr. Con's suspicious activities in Smuggler's Cove. For all your sophistication and suave affair, you're a pretty run-of-the-mill pedestrian street-bobby, aren't you?"

I could see the obvious consternation building within. He was pissed, but didn't quite know what to make of me. (That made two of us. I didn't know why I was being such an asshole. Maybe it was the booze.) You could tell that he really wanted to kick the shit out of me . . . but he also wanted something from me. He had to try and control himself and the situation in order to extract information he thought I possessed. That gave me plenty of leverage to abuse him and the situation. I wasn't sure I had the energy for it.

"You know, Dugan," he began somewhat haltingly, "I find you quite perplexing. You seem to me to be a stumbling, brutish clod, with a hot temper and a quick trigger finger. You thrive within the slimy underbelly, the back alleys of the neon city, and deliver justice, redemption, or revenge upon the miscreant predators of society's mean streets. Yet, you somehow manage to get to the core of any given situation, no matter how convoluted, and deal with it in a decisive and profound manner. You are, likewise, simultaneously capable of mingling with the most sophisticated and cultured individuals that inhabit the higher echelons of the social strata. I must admit, you are a unique individual. I don't see it, but Lara Rigney unexplainably finds you adorable and rakishly charming."

At that moment Constable Lafargé and a contingent of his uniformed gendarmes burst through the entry of Luau Larry's and began searching through the crowd of inebriated partygoers like Moses parting the Red Sea. I hurriedly excused myself and hustled down the crowded hallway to the men's room. I slid open the window and squeezed myself through, dropping the short distance to the pavement of the darkened alley that ran parallel to the boardwalk behind the various bars, restaurants, and souvenir shops that lined Crescent Avenue. To my surprise, Blaine Pond was hot on my heels as we hightailed it down the alley in the dark and eventually turned the corner at Sumner Avenue. Back among the maddening crowd on the boardwalk, we slowed to a brisk pace and climbed the stairs to the enclosed deck above the "Sea Grotto."

The Sea Grotto was a walk-in chili and beer joint that was open across the front, save for a few well-placed palms in large terra-cotta pots between several tables and chairs along the boardwalk entrance. The motif was rock waterfalls, ferns, and lots of tropical flora. The bar was along the back wall and boasted an impressive array of imported beers from around the world. The Mexican varieties seemed to be the brands of choice along with lip-puckering slices of lime squished into the top of the ice-cold open bottles. The outside stairs led to a large covered deck enclosed by sheets of thick glass that allowed for a wide view of the harbor area and the length and breadth of the boardwalk below. Pond and I grabbed a table in the front, next to the glass, with a bird's-eye view of the hustle and bustle along the boardwalk and of the entrance to the Sea Grotto.

A petite young Mexican girl in a skimpy mermaid-inspired costume appeared and lit the candle on our otherwise darkened corner table. She took our order and retreated from whence she came with a mesmerizing sway of ample curvaceous butt that commanded our attention until she had descended the stairs with a knowing last-minute backward glance and quick smile. She was a cutie. A real Mexican beauty. She would make a real nice brand-new tattoo.

"So, Dugan," Pond began with a grin, "judging by your reaction to Constable Lafargé's appearance at Luau Larry's, I presume that you have once again gotten yourself in a bind." That wasn't even a rhetorical question. It was more like a statement. I felt no need to reply.

The bubbly young Mexican girl returned with our Tecates and Coronas and the obligatory lime slices protruding from the open bottles. She placed a basket of tortilla chips and several small bowls of chili, salsa, and a mucky green paste called "guacamole" (whatever that is) on the table.

"If you wish anything further, please ask for me. My name is Lolita," she said with a soft smile and a twinkle in her eye (of course, Lolita).

After a couple of strong pulls from our cold brews and a few double dips of chili and chips, Pond got right to the point . . . finally.

"Mr. Dugan, your association with Sir Arthur quite frankly disturbs me. I'm not at all sure that you realize what a dangerous situation in which you may find yourself with such an affiliation. While I'm quite sure Sir Arthur presents himself as a jolly adventurer in the service of the Queen, I can assure you, Sir Arthur Sydney is a provocateur in the service to the highest bidder and the accumulation of his own offshore nontaxed Bahamian bank accounts. He may portray himself a nobleman with honorable intentions, but believe me, his intentions and his actions are contrary to the traditional benchmarks of honorable nobility."

"You know, Pond," I responded, "Sir Arthur claims that a good portion of the information you receive originates from his contacts with the underworld of provocateurs and black market musketeers. He claims that you wouldn't be here if it weren't for the tail that he put on Con and the oh-so-sought-after clandestine shipment of sectioned oil drilling casings with the peculiar rifling machined within."

Pond seemed a bit perturbed. "Of course he proclaims his importance and his irreplaceability to the crown, just as he unabashedly proclaims the authenticity of his title of nobility. It's all a very dangerous charade. It's a facade built from a house of cards. He is perched on a precarious platform of scaffolding constructed of lies and deceit that is on the verge of a catastrophic collapse. And for the record, Mr. Dugan, it was British Customs and the British Secret Service that first discovered the mysterious shipment of pipe sections. While Sir Sydney may provide a few tidbits of information on an occasional basis, I can assure you that such information is ultimately for his benefit, and he undoubtedly withholds the real gems of information for his own advantage. He may shroud himself within the union jack when required, however, his patriotism is measured in dollars, francs, and pounds. Do not be deceived, Mr. Dugan. The stakes are too high this time. We cannot afford to screw this up."

I began to realize the depth of Pond's concerns. His perceived severity of consequences. I likewise worried about his inclusion of *we* in his sharing of the responsibility should things go awry.

Another round of cold brews arrived from our Mexican beauty. How she got here I hadn't a clue.

"I'll level with you, Pond," I finally acquiesced. "I'm still trying to solve the mystery behind the disappearance of Johnny Rigney. Now Rita Rigney is also missing, and I'm the prime suspect for the murder of Nicky Fallon. I got sucked into the search for the golden dragon upon my last trip to the island thinking it might lead me to a motive for Johnny's disappearance. I don't want to get sidetracked this time around. You're dead-on, Pond. I can't afford to screw this up."

"Maybe we can help each other, Dugan. We made a pact the last time we were on the island that we would assist each other with pertinent information the other might use if we uncovered something. If you will recall, I questioned you about an individual whose name I overheard during your phone conversation with a police inspector that took place while we were in Lafargé's custody. Do you remember?"

I nodded in the affirmative. "Gerald Bull," I said matter-of-factly. Pond also seemed remotely surprised, as did his nemesis Sir Arthur previously, when I mentioned Bull's name.

He paused, smiled, and leaned back in his chair. "I underestimate you, Dugan. I imagine that occurs frequently?" Again a rhetorical question. I just smiled and sipped my brew.

"Dugan, British intelligence has tracked Gerald Bull to this island, and they believe that all the required components for the construction of the 'supergun' have also converged here on Catalina. We believe that Dr. Con, Gerald Bull, and a consortium of third-world despots and military dictators are very close to a demonstration of a prototype weapon. When I arrived to find that your rotund friend, Sir Arthur, was already on the island, then it became imperative that we find out what's going on, and make sure the weapon, nor the technology, ever leave the island. I don't know what Sir Arthur has told you, but I can assure you that we are sitting on a powder keg, and if it explodes, then you may very well find yourself back aboard a B-29 trying to bomb a weapon that is capable of blowing you out of the sky at thirty-five thousand feet. Do I make myself perfectly clear on the importance of this mission, Mr. Dugan?"

"I understand perfectly well the ramifications of such a weapon in the wrong hands," I responded. "Sir Arthur has likewise lectured endlessly upon various applications with which this weapon could inflict unspeakable abuses upon unsuspecting enemies or hapless neighbors. I have a layman's understanding of the propulsion system, and I have personally witnessed a test firing of said system that resulted in rope-knot exhaust trails."

Pond looked astonished. I half-expected a "Bu-dah!"

"Are you telling me that you were present at a test firing of the propulsion system for the supergun? How the hell did you manage that?"

"Again, you underestimate me, Mr. Pond."

Pond seemed to deflate slightly. He leaned heavily into his chair and stroked his chin, deep in contemplation . . . appeared more like constipation. He was torn. He stared at the floor. He sipped his brew. He gazed at the night sky and scratched his head. He finally took a deep breath and exhaled a big sigh. He leaned forward in his chair and stared directly into my eyes.

"Dugan, as you very well know, I have logged countless hours in the waters off Con's compound in an attempt to discover how and what he is up to. We have our suspicions, we have our theories, but I have yet to connect any of these to some concrete evidence that would allow me to call out the cavalry. You, on the other hand, seem to be able to travel within many circles, and apparently have cultivated an inside track. Reluctantly, I feel that I must impart some very top secret information to you so that I then can rely on your patriotism and sense of what's right, regardless of the monetary rewards your obese cohort may offer. First, let me ask you this, are you aware of any underwater activity in or around the compound at night?"

Once again I took a dramatic pause, sipped from my condensing lime-tainted bronze vessel of rising bubbles, and stared at Pond in deep constipation of my own. I decided to spill my guts and quit putzing around. Maybe he could divulge some pertinent info in the process. I was running out of time and anything might help at this point.

"I haven't personally seen anything stirring nocturnal underwater, but I have been told of such things as strange underwater lights around Con's operation at Smuggler's Cove, as well as reports of the same type sightings going to and from the main channel and the channel between Catalina and San Clemente Island. These sightings come from several different sources unrelated to one another. I consider them highly reliable and competent sources."

Pond listened intently and grew more concerned. He rubbed his eyes and stroked his stubble.

"Shit," he muttered. "Very well, Dugan," he began. "I must emphasize once again that this information is highly classified and should be kept in the strictest of confidence. The MI5 unit of British Military Intelligence has acquired information which indicates that your idiot friend Sir Arthur has unwittingly provided the Chinese tong, operating from Hong Kong, with several surplus two-man Japanese minisubs. We now suspect that at least two of those minisubs have been acquired by Dr. Con through his tong associates here on the West Coast. Do you have any idea as to why Con would want to acquire Jap minisubs?" he asked.

I spoke the first thought that came to mind. "He's searching for the golden dragon."

"No, Dugan, I'm afraid not," he answered with a hushed tone. "He's searching for nuclear bombs."

♦ ♦ ♦

I sat in ponderous silence for a brief moment. Collating, calculating, contemplating.

"Thus explains the presence of our newly arrived 'deepwater salvage consultant specializing in ordnance recovery' anchored off San Clemente Island," I finally stated.

"Very acute, my friend," responded Pond. "Yes," he continued, "the CIA and their various consultants are involved in a very big way."

"Does that also explain the presence of the Global Explorer conducting sea trials out in the main channel?" I asked.

Pond leaned back in his chair and laughed heartily. "Son of a bitch, Dugan," he exclaimed. "How the hell do you know about this shit? That goddamn boat is supposed to be top secret. She's only been afloat a few days. How the hell do you know so much about it?"

I smiled and responded, "I got juice, man. I got connections. I know stuff. I sleep my way to the top. I'm the boss with the hot sauce."

He laughed aloud once again. "Oh crap," he exclaimed. "I can't believe I'm about to divulge top secret, earth-shattering information to such a Yankee dildo. What a schmutz you are, old chap."

"Yea, keep it up, laughing boy, and I'll stuff my pip-pip up your cheerio, old chap," I responded.

He shook his head in consternation. He reached in his pocket and brought out a pack of Viceroys. Offered one to me and lit both.

"OK, Dugan, I'll cut to the chase. By all recent events it appears that Con and his associates are very close to completion and test firing of the supergun. That in itself is cause for extreme alarm throughout the free world. However, it has become quite clear that Dr. Con has also joined the search for the nuclear weapons that the CIA is currently so desperately trying to recover."

"That makes the 'big gun' a tad more than merely a poor-man's nuclear missile, doesn't it, old chap?" I asked. (Still being a Yankee dildo for some reason. Might be the DSB's; "Deadly sperm back-up.")

"And the sixty-four-thousand-dollar question, Mr. Pond, is, how did the bombs find their way to this picturesque little oasis? And, exactly how many bombs are we talking about?"

"Are you familiar with the Fairfield-Suisun Air Force Base near Sacramento, California, Dugan?" he began.

"Yes, I was discharged from there after doing my part in the defeat and subsequent surrender of Japan," I answered.

"Then you are also aware of the death of Brigadier General Robert Travis aboard a B-29 that crashed there on August 5, 1950?"

"I was flying A-26s in Korea at the time, but I'm relatively familiar with the incident," I responded. "As I recall, they crashed shortly after takeoff with a full complement of atomic bombs aboard, killing all twelve crew members and passengers. The high explosives in the detonator casings exploded during the ensuing fire, killing many people on the ground after the initial crash itself. It was a horrific disaster. Several years later they renamed the airfield Travis Air Force Base in his honor."

"Again, Mr. Dugan, I commend you on your precognitive prowess. That is precisely the approved story released for public consumption. They crashed shortly after takeoff with a full payload. All those on board perished as well as many more on the ground after several detonator explosions. All nuclear bombs were reported as recovered at the crash site. There was never a danger of nuclear detonation.

"However," he continued. "in actuality, they didn't develop engine problems until they were well down the intended flight path. They made a 180-degree turn over San Clemente Island, intending to release their nuclear payload and in the process gain enough altitude to initiate a return flight to Fairfield-Suisun. Unfortunately they were only able to release two bombs before they experienced a snagged bomb and were forced to abandon the procedure and limped back to the inevitable crash with the remaining bomb load still aboard.

"The first bomb settled into Scripts Hole, a deep trough in the seafloor that runs between Catalina and San Clemente Island. The second sank in what is known as the Redondo Trench, an extremely deep gorge in the seafloor that runs down the middle of the channel between Catalina Island and the mainland off Southern California. Dugan, we must prevent Con from recovering those bombs, and it is imperative that we not allow the supergun or its technology to leave the island."

At that moment Pond spotted Sir Arthur and his Chinese monolith making their way briskly through the crowd on the boardwalk below.

"If you'll excuse me, Mr. Dugan, I feel compelled to see where the obese one and his extra large Chinese crony are headed in such a hurry. I'll be in touch." With that he rose to his feet and made a hasty exit down the stairs to the boardwalk below.

I sat and stared at the pitiful reflection of myself in the glass. Suddenly, I was startled by the apparition that appeared behind my own reflection. At first I thought it was Chin Lee, as she had appeared before during my last trip to the island. Then I realized the beautiful young apparition now before me was that of Yung He. I turned to her. She had a look of concern upon her innocent face.

"My uncle has sent me to find you, Travis," she said softly.

Chapter Nine

In entertainment news, this year's Oscar-winning director of the Academy Award for Best Picture, On the Waterfront, Elia Kazan, announced the release of his latest motion picture, East of Eden, based on Steinbeck's novel. Starring Raymond Massey and Julie Harris, and introducing an exciting newcomer, James Dean as Cal, the tormented and troubled son, "bad seed" of a Salinas Valley lettuce farmer.

Kazan predicts a stellar career for the young Dean and thinks he has what it takes to become a cultural icon among the younger moviegoing audience. The West Coast premiere to be held at the Pantages Theatre in Hollywood, with the postmovie party at the Frolic Room next door. Date yet to be announced.

Spade Cooley, King of Western Swing, debuted his new hit single, "Shame on You," on his local TV show last night to rave reviews. According to this week's TV Guide, the popularity of The Spade Cooley Show makes Cooley LA's first bona fide television star.

CBS announced the debut of a new weekly Western series titled Gunsmoke, starring James Arness and newcomer Dennis Weaver. The dramatic saga of a U.S. marshal in the rough-and-tumble cattle town of Dodge City, Kansas.

And direct from the Aragon Ballroom, ABC's The Lawrence Welk Show, which debuted July 2, bubble machine and all, "was a wonderful, and a wonderful"!

For you, rock and rollers, Chess Records released the debut single 45 titled "Maybellene," by their new discovery, Mr. Chuck Berry.

Hey there! Hi there! Ho there! You're as welcome as can be! M-I-C-K-E-Y M-O-U-S-E! Attention, mousekateers of all ages, the grand opening of Disneyland theme park is scheduled for July 18 in Anaheim. Your hosts for dedication day will be none other than TV personality Art Linkletter, film and television star Bob Cummings, and motion picture star and current president of the Screen Actors Guild Ronald Reagan. Special guest appearances by Governor Edwin Knight and Los Angeles mayor Sam Yorty are also scheduled. Segments of opening day ceremonies will be broadcast on The Wonderful World of Disney.

And Jiminy Cricket wants to remind all you mousekateers that "when you wish upon a star, makes no difference who you are. When you wish upon a star, it might come true."

From the mountains, to the deserts, to the sea, to all of Southern California and beyond . . . this is Jerry Dunphy, for Ralph Story and Clete Roberts, wishing all Americans a happy birthday on this July 4, 1955.

We now return you to Dick Haynes at the Reins, on KNX, news, talk, and sports radio.

I fumbled around in a groggy haze, pushing buttons and turning knobs on the bedside radio, in a feeble attempt to cease the incessant ramblings of LA AM radio. A soothing señorita's voice finally wafted gently across the airwaves proudly announcing, "Xes eh' de elia, Tijuana, Mexico." Then came a startlingly loud, annoying, gravely male voice: "Wolfman Jack, baby! The boss with the hot sauce! Who loves you, baby? Owooooo! XERB, fifty thousand watts of clear-channel radio. *The Wolfman Jack Show*, baby!"

I managed to find the cord and yanked it out of the wall socket. Blissful silence permeated the room. Muted shafts of morning light shone through the window, and a cool breeze gently fluttered tattered curtains.

I turned and gazed across the short expanse of an empty bed. Yung He had gone in the early twilight of dawn. We spent the night together holding each other close. She had wrapped herself gently around me and I drifted away in memories of long-ago youth. The soft sponginess of fresh young girl parts. The smooth roundness of ample hip. The silky warmth of inner thigh. The supple firmness of perky breasts and taut, pouty butt. Long, flowing waves of shiny black hair cascading over us, embracing us in delicate sheets of silky satin. Large doelike eyes, trusting and innocent. Warm smile from soft, full lips. Delicate hands with gentle caress. She was comforting and compassionate, and I missed her already.

During our walk back from the Sea Grotto last night, Yung He informed me that her uncle, Ah Looey, had sent her to tell me that the intimidation of the local Chinese by the tong, that I had feared, was indeed now being forced upon the longshoremen and miners throughout the island. The tong had also taken over the Filipino pachinko parlors and bordellos in Cooley Town. The tong came for her uncle as well. They knew that the locals looked to him for guidance and wisdom. She and her uncle had gone into hiding in a secret location somewhere on the isthmus. She was afraid for her uncle's safety. Something had drastically changed within the last couple of days. I had a real bad feeling about this.

♦ ♦ ♦

The morning breeze brought with it, from the casino promenade below, the sounds of excited preparations for this morning's celebrations. The Catalina Cadillacs were cued up for the golf cart parade on the boardwalk along Avalon's palm-lined beachfront. They were festooned in their finest patriotic regalia of red, white, and blue. The *UCLA Bruins marching band* began to form up, as well as the bright, shiny chrome and brass of the U.S. Coast Guard Honor Guard. Human effigies representing Hitler, Mussolini, and Hirohito were chained together in a line to be dragged along the parade route and mockingly flogged, and periodically kicked in the pants by Uncle Sam as they proceeded. It would be a full day of celebration enthusiastically enjoyed by swarms of tourists and throngs of locals as well. The culmination of which boasts one of the most spectacular and bombastic fireworks displays anywhere in the world. Tonight's show featured a much-touted and highly anticipated, show-stopping, scaled-down simulation of an atomic bomb detonation on the end of the steamer pier.

Avalon's Fourth of July fireworks shows were world famous for their spectacular, high-altitude, wide-disbursement displays of multicolored intensity and variety, interspersed with low-altitude concussion bombs that rattled the windows of the shops in town, as well as those of the quaint bungalows that clung precariously to the surrounding hillsides. The harbor area, the beaches, and the entire town were inevitably packed with awestruck exuberant spectators. It was truly and extravaganza like no other.

I got cleaned up quickly, filled my pockets with the tricks of the trade, and made my way downstairs to the garage. I had the old gray Plymouth cruising down the narrow road high on the hillside behind Avalon, headed north. The desolate road to Cooley Town had become all too familiar. From the narrow, winding strip of asphalt etched precariously into the steep hillside above Avalon, to the long descent onto the windswept plateau in the interior of the island inhabited by indigenous wild boar, and deer, as well as prolific goat herds, originally introduced to the island by pirates of old. And of course, the Commodore's thriving herd of North American bison. At the isthmus the island narrowed to a short causeway between two harbors. Beyond the narrow causeway bridge the terrain widened to a large palm-covered plateau dotted with neat rows of clean white bungalows of the Chinese longshoreman, miners, and their families.

Fishermen's Cove and Parson's Landing at the north end of the isthmus plateau were small harbors filled with the Filipino, Chinese, and Korean fishing boats that plied the shallow waters around the island for squid, octopus, eel, and lobster. Across the isthmus on the windward side of the island were the Filipino pachinko parlors, bordellos, nightclubs, and the surrounding neighborhood of indiscriminate cabins and bungalows. No smoke visible from the chimney stacks. No pots of kimchee cooking over open campfires in front.

I slowly cruised by Ah Looey's cabin at the shoreline, and it too looked shuttered and abandoned. The skipjack was absent from its mooring out front in the harbor. The remaining moorings sat full of unattended fishing boats. There was an empty, desolate, ghost town atmosphere that permeated the entire area, like a plague-ravaged, apocalyptic twilight zone.

I continued down the dappled set of ruts that led to the Cooley Town Cemetery. I drove around the back side of the granite outcropping, at the top of the sloping hillside, where the caissons and pallbearers arrived and departed during burial ceremonies. I parked the car and walked across the gentle hillside, at the edge of the rugged cliffs and thrashing surf below, to Chin Lee's solemn resting place. While this windswept hillside was a somber and melancholy place, it also was familiar, comforting, and had a calming effect upon me. A place to sit in solitary silence, gaze over the endless expanse of deep blue Pacific, and contemplate one's purpose in life. A place to collect your thoughts and formulate a plan. Get your ducks in a row and calculate the logistics required in order to bring said plan to successful fruition.

I always seemed to be flying by the seat of my pants, making split-second, sperm-of-the-moment decisions. While they may be spontaneous, and exciting at the time, they often ended awkward, contentious, or catastrophic. Either way, I hate when that happens. My immediate priority was to find Rita and bring her safely home . . . provided I was not already too late. I must also find some way to stop the insidious takeover of the casino by the mob . . . Pretty tall order.

Then, of course, there was Pond and Sir Arthur's obsession with Dr. Con and his futuristic supergun. Another fine mess I'd gotten myself into, Ollie. Man, was I screwed. I seemed to have stepped on my prehensile appendage yet again. I hate when that happens too. Very discomforting and a big-time piss-off. As my old uncle Leo used to say, "The world is full of uncertainty. Get used to it . . . or get off."

Suddenly I felt the cold steel of a thick gun barrel against the back of my head. "Freeze, Dugan," came the command from a familiar south Brooklyn accent. "Turn around slowly," he said. "Keep your hands where I can see them."

I turned and faced my executioner. He smiled when he saw that I recognized him. It was none other than New York hit man Crazy Joe Gallo. He enjoyed torturing, maiming, and killing. He was in it for the pure perverted pleasure of it. He was a sick puppy . . . thus the nickname Crazy Joe.

"Well, well, Mr. Travis Dugan, famous, or is that infamous? LA PI to the Hollywood stars. We finally meet face-to-face. I'd ask for an autograph, but I don't think I have a pen," he said with a smirk while mockingly patting his pockets with his free hand.

"I think I might have one," I responded, reaching inside my jacket.

He pushed the barrel of the nasty big .45 auto against my forehead and thumbed back the hammer. I froze. I smiled. I looked directly into his eyes. He was twitching with anticipation.

"Always the comedian with the smart mouth," he said. "The boss wants his sixty grand, and the consensus is that you have it."

He kept the .45 firmly pressed against my forehead and reached inside my jacket with his free hand to remove my weapon. He unsnapped the strap and gently slid my old snubby from her holster.

"What kind of antiquated piece of shit is this?" he laughed, holding it at arm's length with his fingertips.

"It's got John Dillinger's initials carved into the grip," I responded matter-of-factly.

When his eyes momentarily darted to the snubby, I instantaneously grabbed the bottom of his gun barrel with my right hand and the top of his wrist with my left. Instantly, I yanked his wrist down and pushed the gun barrel up. His wrist snapped back and the gun fired with a tremendous explosion directly into his open mouth, blowing the top of his skull and most of his brain matter into a chunky spray that speckled the headstones of several grave sites behind him. I held his arm and allowed him to crumble to the ground on his back. I put his gun in my pocket, then quickly rifled through his. A set of car keys, a couple of full clips for his .45, and a couple of hundred in cash. No ID. I stuffed the cash, the keys, and the clips in my pocket.

I pulled the bottom of his coat up over his head, twisted it a couple of times, then dragged him down the hill to the cliff's edge. A firm nudge with my foot and he rolled off the edge and dropped like a lifeless mannequin, for the longest time before smashing into the cliff face, tumbling like a rag doll, and finally shredding into the thrashing surf below. There wasn't much left by the time he spattered into the churning surf.

I retrieved my trusty .38 and had the old Plymouth headed south back across the isthmus causeway and up the windward side of the island. So now I knew that the casino skim I had in the aluminum attaché case was an impressive sixty grand. No wonder they were pissed and scouring the island for their ill-gotten gains. I seemed to have shaken things up a bit more than I had anticipated. I was afraid that I might have caused them, or provided them, with the opportunity and impetus to expedite their ultimate plan and ramp up their schedule for the final takeover. So far, I'd outsmarted no one but myself. (Get your shit together, asshole. You're screwing this up. There are a lot of people depending on you to get this right. Get ahead of this situation, and get the hell on with it!)

I had almost reached Little Harbor, with its pristine white beach and crystal clear pale blue water, where I had come upon Raven diving for shells, but a few short days ago, when I realized that I had neglected to retrieve the spent shell casing from Crazy Joe's .45. An amateurish oversight that might come back later to bite me in the ass. That was one bit of ballistic forensics that I didn't have to worry about with my .38 revolver . . no spent casings lying about for evidence.

I continued down the road that eventually began to climb toward China Point. I drove up the tree-shaded drive and parked in the cypress grove next to the spring water pond. I got out and walked the short distance up to Raven's cabin. The corral was empty, as was the cabin. Most of her belongings were inside, but there hadn't been anyone there for some time. That worried me. I began to develop a bad feeling in the pit of my stomach. I hadn't seen or heard from Raven since my departure several days ago.

◆ ◆ ◆

The sun began to set into the endless horizon of blazing sea, and long shadows began to creep toward the east. Dusk would soon retreat before the clear night's canopy of twinkling stars settled over the serene island paradise.

I walked to the cliff edge in front of the cabin and gazed down upon Smuggler's Cove. Again, there seemed to be a growing activity within Dr. Con's secluded harbor and mining operation. Several impressive private boats were tied to the dock, along with Con's sleek, new seventy-foot Magnum Raptor megayacht. Several groups of military and civilian dignitaries loitered about. It looked like an encore presentation of Con's supergun propulsion system demonstration that I witnessed several nights ago. I felt compelled to get down there for a closer look.

I waited until darkness fell and the lights around Con's compound came on. I began my descent down the rugged cliff face grasping at shadows for hand- and footholds. I finally resorted to holding my "PI pocket penlight" in my mouth as I fumbled my way along in the dark. I came upon a small rock landing hidden from view behind a thick stand of prickly pear cactus where I could rest and still observe the activities in the cove below.

As I sat, midway down the cliff, in the relative comfort of my cactus blind, I noticed a faint light coming from within the bat cave below, and the other lights around the compound dimmed to the minimum required to negotiate the walkways. The booms and bangs signifying the start of the Fourth of July fireworks celebration began to be heard from the other side of the island, along with the accompanying brief glow far in the distance. There would follow approximately forty minutes of high-velocity pyrotechnics and low-altitude, window-shuddering concussion bombs.

Just then, I noticed the end of a long tube beginning to emerge from the cave entrance below, and the familiar clip-clop sound of railcars moving over railroad ties. As I watched, the enormously long sectioned barrel and the huge breech of Dr. Con's clandestine supercannon eventually cleared the cave entrance and sat, in all its majestic glory, and fully exposed upon the beach.

Once firmly blocked in place and secured to the tracks, the cannon crew mounted the railcar platform and began to manually crank the enormous cannon barrel off its cradle and raise it to the desired angle of trajectory. Likewise, another set of hand cranks pivoted the base on which the weapon was mounted, like a turret, in the specified direction. The big gun was pointed in the direction of San Clemente Island, the military bombing range, some twenty-six miles to the southwest.

The brilliant fireworks display continued over Avalon as the gathered dignitaries below began to take cover positions behind sandbag bunkers recently constructed along the beach at the base of the steep hillside. The gun crew loaded a shiny metal projectile into the breech, followed by three bags of Dr. Con's "specially formulated" secret propellant. They closed the breech and prepared to fire the immense weapon. Suddenly, a brilliant flash of blinding light filled the sky for a brief instant, turning night into day. At that precise moment the command to fire could be heard from below. Simultaneously, an ear-shattering boom from the simulated atomic bomb detonation came rumbling over the hill from Avalon, followed immediately by the tremendous boom of Con's supergun, and the successive spitting whooshes as the projectile streaked into the sky, leaving the now-familiar rope-knot exhaust trail.

An eerie silence fell over the island as a huge mushroom cloud rose ominously above the stunned populace of Avalon. I sat in stunned silence myself. Eyebrows singed from the heat blast of Con's propulsion system, my face scorched and damaged to my retinas, leaving me with cloudy spots in my vision.

I lingered for a short while gathering my wits. I spent the time extracting prickly pear cactus needles from my thighs and calves. The supergun's shock waves blew shards of cactus needles through my trousers and imbedded them into my lower extremities. Very painful and tedious task of extraction. It was a prickly situation. By the time I had completed the process, my head had cleared, as well as my vision. I prepared to resume my descent down the slippery dark cliff face.

I palmed the penlight in my right hand, shielding my location from the ever-vigilant guards in the compound below, while feeling my way along with my left, keeping my back close to the steep cliff. Progress was slow, tedious, and slippery. Each footstep and handhold first measured and tested for firmness. Each tentative step seemed to initiate a small landslide of rocks and small boulders that threatened to arouse the attention of the gathered masses below and expose my vulnerable position high on the cliff face. I clung precariously to the side of the steep cliff, like a neophyte Spider-Man suffering an acute case of acrophobia, or perhaps arachnophobia. Suddenly, the ground beneath my feet gave way, and I began an uncontrollable slide down the cliff face.

♦ ♦ ♦

I was in a free fall, engulfed within a developing rockslide. I tumbled down the cliff face within an accelerating landslide. I could see a dark shadow quickly approaching that appeared to be another large cactus patch. I prepared to be seriously impaled, skewered upon prickly pear shish kebab, I was overtaken by several large boulders that slammed me hard into the ground, then smashed into the dark patch ahead with a horrendous crash of sparks and thick clouds of dust.

I landed hard on the metal grate, which held momentarily, then gave way, and I began to slide down a metal pipe approximately four feet in diameter. I continued to slide down the steep pipe watching my Popeil pocket PI penlight fall before me, pinging sparks as it ricocheted off the pipe walls.

I tried to brace myself against the pipe walls in an attempt to slow my acceleration down the slick shaft. A slight bend in the pipe arrived with a crushing thud, then a virtual free fall straight down. I managed to get into an upright position just before crashing through yet another metal grate covering an exhaust fan at the opening of the air shaft. I slammed through the grate with a horrendous crash, then fell an additional twenty or thirty feet to a crushing thump on the cold hard floor in a dust cloud of bat guano. Fade to black.

Chapter Ten

I began to regain consciousness one sense at a time. First came an antiseptic aroma mixed with perfume and incense. Then came the sounds of rubber-soled shoes across the tile floor. Next came an internal inventory of assumed injuries. Extreme pain and soreness to back and rib cage. Minor scrapes, scratches, and contusions. I could wiggle my fingers and toes . . . always a good sign.

Finally I attempted to open my eyes. At first a fuzzy blur like bad reception on a Zenith eight-inch black and white. Gradually vision began to clear. I felt a hand touch my shoulder, and a soft shadow moved into my field of narrow and still-blurred vision. A familiar face slowly came into focus. I thought I was dreaming, or perhaps hallucinating. It couldn't be. I blinked my eyes. Sure enough, it was Rita. A smiling though concerned apparition. A feeling of joy and relief swept over me. I felt a tear roll down my cheek.

"Aloha, baby," I whispered.

She threw her arms around me and held me tight. "Oh Travis, I'm so glad you're all right. And I'm so glad you're here. You're here to take me home, aren't you? Please take me home, Travis." She began to cry.

"Don't worry, baby," I said comfortingly. "I'm here to take you home."

"Now, now, you two. Let's not raise those heart rates before I check a few vitals," came a soft Asian voice.

As Rita gradually regained her composure, a petite young Chinese girl appeared at my bedside. She was stunningly beautiful. She had silky black hair pulled back into a long ponytail. She wore a neat white nurse uniform and had a stethoscope draped around her lovely delicate neck.

"Good evening, Mr. Dugan, my name is Tang Poon-Song. I am very happy that you were able to join us. We were quite concerned that you may have injured yourself during your unfortunate fall," she said in a soft and soothing yet cheerful voice, while holding my wrist and staring at her watch. She leaned close, opened my eyelid wide, and moved a penlight back and forth across my field of vision. She had the fragrance of fresh cherry blossoms. She listened to my heart, then instructed me to take several deep breaths while she listened to my lungs. She sat me up on the side of the bed and had me wiggle my toes. She tapped both knees with a rubber mallet and performed that obligatory two-fingered thump search, up and down my back.

"Well, Mr. Dugan," she began, "I have examined you from head to toe, and I must say that I find you to be in very fine shape. Very fine shape indeed. I found much evidence of former injuries. You appear to lead a very dangerous existence. Many wounds . . . good thing you're built like a brick outhouse." She smiled contemplatively, tapping the end of her stethoscope on her fully pursed lips. She then moved off to the adjoining living quarters.

"You must hurry now," she said while showing Rita and myself the layout. She walked from room to room, opening doors and pointing out fully accommodated closets, fully stocked bars and other appointments that rivaled many of the finest hotel penthouse suites in the world. "Dr. Con is expecting you to join him for a small dinner party," she said, moving toward the exit door. "I hope you find the accommodations acceptable. However, should you require anything further, just ring the bell."

"I'll return shortly, to escort you to dinner," she said with a bright smile. She blew a kiss goodbye, removed a small perforated plastic card from her pocket, which she then inserted into a slot in the metal keypad next to the exit. The shiny metal doors parted like those of an elevator, then automatically closed again once she had departed.

We arrived at our dinner engagement immaculately attired in latest formal fashion, through a labyrinth of passageways apparently cut through the rocky outcropping of Smuggler's Cove. It was an impressive complex of clean, well-lit, with highly polished tile floor passageways interconnected by way of large shiny aluminum doors that opened quickly from the middle with a great whoosh.

Tang escorted Rita and me through the passageways to the final set of aluminum doors. "You two enjoy yourselves this evening," she said. "I will return to escort you back to your quarters after dinner." With that, she slid her card in the slot and the immense set of shiny doors parted. She blew another kiss and was off down the passage with perhaps a bit more sway to her stride and a quick look back over her shoulder.

I turned back to catch a raised eyebrow and slight look of bewilderment from Rita.

"I don't get her," I said hastily in my defense.

"Let's hope you keep that way," she responded. She turned smartly and strutted into the elaborately decorated dining hall like she owned the place. That was the Rita Rigney I'd come to love. The confident, self-assured princess. Not the frightened little girl I found upon my arrival.

◆ ◆ ◆

The dining hall was a huge open area carved out of the indigenous rock grotto. It had very high ceilings, from which hung ornate chandeliers. There was a long table in the middle of the room elaborately set for approximately twenty guests with the finest china, immaculate silverware, and sparkling crystal goblets and carafes. Across the room was an impressive view of the grotto's tide pools and the blue Pacific beyond. To the right was an equally impressive view of Smuggler's Cove, all through water-level thick sheets of floor-to-ceiling plate glass.

The room was filled with elegantly attired guests chatting with each other, appropriately poised with cocktails in hand. As I gazed around the room, I recognized several of the guests that were also attendees of the supergun demonstration. Many military types and of course the tall curly-haired Gerald Bull, sans his bespectacled geek squad. I was extremely surprised to see none other than the notorious Sir Arthur Sydney and his monolithic shadow Phangs Pa. Sir Arthur smiled and raised his glass in acknowledgement of our arrival. He seemed particularly pleased with himself. He was being accompanied by a tall gorgeous babe draped in long shimmering black hair and short shimmering red dress. The dress, what little there was of it, was poured over her like hot wax, the brightness of which matched full, pouty lips and exquisite manicure. Her "wow" factor was way off the charts. She looked like a sexy French cabaret dancer that could bitch-slap *you*, and drag *you* around the floor.

"Mr. Dugan, Ms. Rigney, I'm so pleased that you were able to join us this evening," came the calming voice of Dr. Con as he greeted us. "We were very concerned regarding your well-being. Especially you, Ms. Rigney. You were in very poor condition when one of our tugboat operators came upon you by happenstance only a few nights ago. He found you floating in a rubber life raft, in the middle of the channel, curiously, surrounded protectively by some very aggressive sea lions. Luckily he came upon you on his last trip from the mainland. The sea lions alerted him amidst the darkness with their incessant barking as he approached. When you arrived, you were extremely dehydrated and suffering from the effects of exposure. How are you feeling now, my dear?" he asked with concern.

"I'm feeling much better, thank you," she replied. "Have you notified my family as yet?" she asked.

"We only found out who you were this morning when you regained consciousness and were able to speak," he replied. "Unfortunately there has been a significant landslide that occurred sometime last night, blocking the road between here and the airport. The rockslide has apparently disrupted the telephone service as well. Unfortunately, because of the holiday, there is no tugboat operation occurring either. We are attempting ship-to-shore communication from my yacht at dockside, however, we have received no response as of yet. Rest assured, Ms. Rigney," he comforted, "we will continue to make all efforts to notify your family, who must be extremely worried, that you are well and will be returning home as soon as we are able to do so.

"For now, however, I invite you to relax and enjoy the evening. We will be serving dinner shortly. Until then, please have a drink at the bar and mingle with the other guests. You'll find some very intriguing people here tonight. If there is anything you wish, just ask one of the attendants."

At that moment, one of Con's associates approached and excused the interruption. He whispered in Con's ear, and the good doctor excused himself and accompanied his associate to an adjoining room.

Rita and I made our way to the ornately carved Oriental-design teak bar. I ordered a vodka martini, she ordered champagne. I barely got one soothing sip of my crystal refreshment down before we were joined by a beaming Sir Arthur and his stunningly doable escort, the intriguing lady in minimalist dress of brightest red.

"Ah, Mr. Dugan, so glad you could drop by," he said with a Cheshire cat grin. "Allow me to introduce you to my gracious sponsor, Ms. Voyent."

"Claire Voyent," she said as she stepped confidently forward and extended her well-manicured hand. When our hands touched, there was a quick spark. She was startled momentarily. Then, as we continued to hold hands, she exclaimed a soft "oh." Then a raised brow and a knowing smile.

"You'll forgive my curious expression," she began, "but I fancy myself to be rather psychic, and I feel that we are destined to become very special friends. I sense a very close relationship. It's a pleasure to finally meet you, Mr. Dugan. I've heard a lot about you."

"Very nice to meet you, Ms. Voyent," I responded, still grasping her hand. "Allow me to introduce you to my companion, Ms. Rigney."

"Very pleased to make your acquaintance, Ms. Rigney," said Claire. "Please allow me to compliment you and your family on such a wondrous paradise. The island is simply exquisite."

"Ms. Voyent," boasted the fat man, "is responsible for securing a last-minute invitation for me as her guest to this little soiree. She is a former systems analyst for the CIA. She assisted in the design and is the only woman qualified to fly the U2 Blackbird spy plane."

"I've never heard of the U2," I responded.

"No, I'm sure you haven't," he laughed. "And if all goes as planned, you never will."

A pleasant chime sounded, and all attendees began to gather at the long dining table in the middle of the room. Dr. Con was at the end of the table to my right with Ms. Voyent between us. Rita was on my left with Sir Arthur and Phangs Pa occupying settings intended for four guests directly across from us. When everyone had settled in their respective arrangements, Dr. Con chimed the side of his champagne flute with a caviar knife and rose to his feet for a toast.

"Welcome, friends, respected dignitaries, and invited guests," he began in the calm, comforting tone and impeccable pronunciation of a highly educated and socialite gentleman of the world. He had the air of a professorial background. "We are gathered here this evening for what I sincerely hope will be the first of many such events. I have invited all of you to not only witness the successful demonstration of the supergun, which I needn't remind you will place you in parity with any superpower on the face of the earth and secure the future of your respective countries, but also to begin a dialogue with regard to the future geopolitical realities that all of us will confront in the years to come.

"Among our distinguished guests this evening," he continued, "are several representatives including Señor Che Guevara from the Cuban People's Revolutionary Party, who are committed to the overthrow of the corrupt puppet dictatorship of Juan Bautista and rest control of their island nation from the clutches of American organized crime. We are also honored to have as our guest, Mr. Chou En-lai, representing the People's Republic of North Vietnam, currently engaged in a courageous and bitter struggle to liberate the southern half of their country from the colonial grasp of the French imperialists and reunite his people as one. Seated next to him is Chairman Arafat representing the Palestine Liberation Organization. As you all are no doubt aware, the chairman and his loyal followers are engaged in a heroic 'fatwa' to reclaim their most holy territories from the Zionist occupiers.

"Representatives from the Middles East, Asia, Central and South America, as well as the African Continent are here to discuss their respective sovereignty in the face of the immediate power vacuum through out the postwar world and their efforts to prevent the remaining superpowers and their opposing ideologies from circumventing or subverting the sovereignty of the fragile emerging governments and the inevitable exploitation of their natural resources. The result of which would of course be the ultimate devastation of your ancestral heritage and national culture.

"Ladies and gentlemen, I present to you the opportunity to take control of your own destiny. Together we can throw off the shackles of imperialist domination. Free your peoples of colonial enslavement and exploitation. Reclaim, rejoice, and revel in your ancestral heritage, your national culture and the promise of its future. As my Swahili friends are fond of saying, 'Bonja bula bonkai.' 'The promise of the day.'

"My distinguished guests, I invite you to step through the portal to the next century. Be the masters of the new millennium." Everyone raised their glass in tribute to our eloquent host and his inspiring speech.

An efficient cadre of beautiful young Chinese girls appeared and began serving. There was fowl aplenty: pheasant, duck, squab, Cornish gaming hens, and a variety of exotic species along with mounds of rice and steamed vegetables. It was an impressive and scrumptious feast.

The pleasant Chinese girls, each clad in dazzling white, served from large trays. When all had been properly served, the remaining portions were placed along the center of the table like a Chinese smorgasbord.

I've found pheasant to be a bit gamey. Duck too greasy. Squab is just a baby pigeon. So I opted for the Cornish hen. I realized, mid inhalation, that my ravenous behavior might be due to the fact that I hadn't eaten all day. I also began to realize, to my libidinous surprise, that Ms. Voyent's well-manicured hand had found its way to my slightly quivering thigh and was gently indulging in venturous quest. She eventually found her way to Thor, guardian of the family jewels, and with each caress brought a throb of appreciation. The transformation complete, Big Bad Voodoo Daddy was now in full attack mode, and with each caress came a corresponding thrust of enthusiasm each more robust than the last, until her knuckles eventually rapped the bottom of the table, gently rattling the fine china and silverware within the immediate vicinity.

A satisfied tap on the head and a contented smile signified confident pride in her abilities and accomplishments. It took all the willpower I could muster to keep my hands above the table and resist the temptation to respond in kind to the most gracious gesture, and explore what I imagined to be the smooth, firm regions of Ms. Voyent's inner thigh. I think I may have bent my fork in the process.

It took the remainder of the meal before my obvious enthusiasm had subsided to the point where I felt comfortable pushing back from the table a standing erect, so to speak, without risking embarrassment. A glance to my left and it became apparent that Rita had not eaten properly in several days either; her plate piled high in a skeletal aviary.

Cognac and cigars arrived punctually. Fine Havanas compliments of our Cuban guests at the other end of the table.

Rita and I excused ourselves and strolled together out onto the boat dock. We walked across the dock to the rail overlooking Smuggler's Cove. All was quiet save for the soft jazz now emanating from the dining hall behind us. A bright full moon began to rise over China Point and reflect serenely upon the calm surface of the water.

I noticed that Rita began to look very fatigued. She had not fully recovered from her ordeal, and this evening was probably a bit too much too soon. She began to wither. She came to me and put her arms around my neck.

"I want to go home, Travis," she said softly. "Do you really believe that they are going to let us go?" she asked in a barely audible whisper.

I held her close and spoke reassuringly, "Yes, I promise you. You will be home by tomorrow, one way or another."

"I'm going to see if there is some way we can get out of here tonight. I need you to be sharp because if I find a way out, we'll have to move quickly. I want you to go back to the room and get as much rest as you can. Don't accept any alcohol or medication. I'll join you as soon as I can."

At that moment our beautiful young Chinese hostess arrived. She smiled wide as she approached.

"I think that is as much excitement Ms. Rigney should experience at this time," she said. "She has not recovered sufficiently, poor dear. She requires more rest. I was happy to hear, however, that she ate very well. That is a good sign. Come with me now, dear, I will get you settled back in your suite."

She looked at me with a sly smile. "You will be joining us soon, Mr. Dugan?"

"Yes," I responded. "I'll be along shortly, Ms. . . . I'm sorry, I didn't get your name."

She smiled wide. "My name is Tang, Tang Poon-Song."

The moon had risen high in the night sky. I leaned on the rail, sipped from my snifter, and enjoyed my Havana. At this point it looked like a big turd hanging from my mouth. Out of the corner of my eye I noticed a reflection from a shiny surface below the deck boards. I looked around and found the ladder that led below the dock to a small landing at water level. Amazingly, tied to the landing end to end were two World War II Japanese midget subs. They appeared to be in pristine condition. Each had a peculiar metal strap apparatus that wrapped around the hull in two locations: one forward, one aft. Whatever these modifications were supporting, it was below water level and not visible from where I stood on the dark landing under the main boat dock.

My immediate thought was of the dredging operation Lara Rigney spoke of upon my first visit to the island. I could see why Dr. Con would need to dredge the cove to a sufficient depth to accommodate the midget subs and whatever they were supporting on the bottom of their hulls.

Suddenly the commanding baritone of Claire Voyent echoed throughout the dark covered landing. "Mr. Dugan, you are off-limits and out of bounds. You are in an unauthorized area."

"Oh, sorry," I responded innocently. "I was just admiring the vintage midget subs. They're in magnificent condition."

"I have something else for you to admire that's in magnificent condition," she whispered. "Come hither."

I walked back to where the ladder protruded through the deck above and looked up. She was straddling the ladder, and from my perspective it became intimately apparent why there were no visible panty lines on her skintight red dress. She was right. It indeed appeared to be in magnificent condition. However, I felt required a closer inspection to be sure. I climbed the ladder right up to the "promised land." I was in heaven, and my imagination and enthusiasm left no doubt in her mind and very little to her imagination. I was thoroughly indulgent, and judging by her soft sighs and small quivers, she seemed abundantly appreciative of my endeavors. With a subdued scream through bitten lip and the warm rush of satisfaction, she gently tapped me on the head and then stepped aside so that I could climb the remaining rungs of the ladder to the deck above. She took my hand and led me down the dock to Con's yacht. Once inside, she threw me down on the floor and proceeded to abuse me in the most wonderful manner. She was rough and tough. She rode me like she was busting a wild bronco complete with yips and yahoos. I heard the whirl of shiny spurs, the sharp crack and swift sting of the bullwhip. I was roped, hog-tied, and pounded into the floor with powerful relentless pile-driving thrusts, each more punishing than the last. I bucked and bumped and whinnied. I was rode hard and put away wet. She showed excellent form, perfect posture, and great balance. She stood high in the stirrups and rode tall in the saddle. She gave me the reins in the turns and let me develop my stride down the backstretch. She went to the whip down the homestretch and crossed the line a clear winner by several lengths, deserving of a photo finish and a standing "O".

She gently collapsed atop me, both of us completely spent. We lay in sublime silence bathed in sweet perspiration and muted moonlight.

"You see, Travis, I had a feeling we were destined to become special friends," she whispered softly.

"Yes, I recall that you mentioned earlier that you may be rather psychic . . . or was that psychedelic?" I toyed playfully.

"You bastard, it could be psychotic," she giggled.

"Everything I've heard about you, Travis, so far has been right on the money. You're rough and tough and a little worn around the edges, but you're also smart, cunning, and deadly. And I'm here to testify that no matter how tough the assignment, you get the job done with flying colors, I might add," she said with a wide smile. "Hallelujah, lover!" she exclaimed. "Let me hear an amen!"

"You seem to know a lot about me," I mentioned in passing while we showered.

She laughed. "I know everything about you, baby. I know you're one hell of a gutsy son of a bitch. You flew B-17s and 29s through sixty-four missions in the Pacific during World War II. Then came back and flew gut-wrenching, shit-your-pants dark-of-night, deep-canyon strafing and bombing interdiction flights in A-26s over Korea. You gotta have a mammoth set of cojones to come through that unscathed and as much a take-no-shit, ass-kickin' sumbitch as when you went in. I admire that. I admire your values, your fortitude, and your sense of duty. Yes, I know a lot about you. I even know about your enchanting summer with Raven between the wars."

"Raven?" I asked, genuinely surprised.

"Yes, monkey man," she teased. "I know all about your nature-boy, Tarzan-and-Jane summer of primitive exploits. In fact I know more about your exotic girlfriend than you do, I'll bet. How do you think she gained access to that estuarial paradise?" she asked. I shrugged.

"Her father was a 'wind talker' during the war. They broadcast military secret information in their native tribal language, so that our enemies could not understand or decipher the messages. Her father worked for the OSS during the war, and now continues to work for the CIA. I also know that Raven is here on the island, and she ain't here for the seashells."

We concluded our shower, dressed in the glow of soft moonlight, regroomed ourselves, and exited Con's enormous yacht, closing the cabin door behind us. We strolled together back across the dock to the dining hall. I finally asked her outright what was going on with Dr. Con and his supergun and how she was involved in the whole scenario.

We lingered at the doors to the dining hall. I lit a cigarette for each of us. She paused, took a drag from her cigarette, and watched the smoke drift into the darkness. She gave me a curious sideways glance and crooked smile.

"Sir Arthur sure had you pegged," she finally said. "He said you were a cut-to-the-chase, cutthroat kind of guy. No holds barred, take no prisoners, no pussyfootin', no bullshittin'. I believe the phrase he was so fond of was, he's slicker than hot shit through a tin horn," she giggled.

She stared at me for a few brief moments, then finally acquiesced. "Travis, I can't tell you what exactly I'm doing here, or for whom I'm doing it. I can tell you with complete confidence that if you knew the answers to those questions, then you would not ask me to divulge that information or compromise my situation in any way. You must trust me on that. I know your values and your sense of patriotism. Believe me when I tell you that I'm here on behalf of those same values and the people who have given their lives in defense of those values.

"What I can tell you is the premise upon which the individuals gathered here are presently functioning, the geopolitical theories to which they currently subscribe, and the motivations that will drive them and their decisions in the future.

"As a result of the recent conflagration throughout the world and numerous power vacuums or totally destroyed institutions of government that now exist, these remaining despots or aspiring dictators you see gathered here see the world divided into two opposing ideological camps. Capitalists and Communists. Each ideology championed by the only remaining superpowers on the planet. All of Europe, most of East Asia, the Middle East, and North Africa have all but been totally devastated. Their economies and infrastructure are in total ruins. They will be crippled and vulnerable for many years to come. North America has emerged as the world's only industrial superpower simply because of its very fortunate geographic location between two great oceans. Russia, with its vast size, enormous population, and its boundless natural resources, has managed to survive victorious, through tremendous civilian and military sacrifices. The Soviet Union is an extremely paranoid society, with good reason, and they have now found themselves atop of the remaining European rubbish heap. They are in an ideal position to subvert the fragile political institutions of their neighbors in order to create a defensive shield of satellite states to surround the 'motherland.'

"They can exploit the natural resources of their smaller, weaker neighbors and threaten their fledgling economies through external and internal political pressure, economic dependence, and sheer size and overwhelming brute force. Proof of which is clearly evident with the recent signing of the Warsaw Pact Defensive Treaty between the Soviet Union and seven of its neighboring puppet states.

"In the opposing ideological camp, the United States, its North American and European allies will exploit and manipulate its subordinate regimes under the guise of economic development, financial assistance, military defense, and promise of prosperity through capitalistic freedom. America and its NATO partners will pledge to protect their economic and democratic dependents from the evil expansionist Communist empire.

"The two opposing political ideologies have put all their eggs into one basket. We are in the beginnings of what is to become an unimaginable nuclear arms race. Eisenhower has already privately warned of the intrusive influence and the corruptive power building within the military industrial complex. The Russians are obsessively paranoid that they will be incapable of maintaining parity with the NATO forces at their borders. Both camps have staked their respective futures on a single defense strategy. ICBM's . . . MAD. Intercontinental ballistic missile systems . . . mutual assured destruction. There soon will be enough nuclear ordnance around to vaporize the entire population of both continents and contaminate the remainder of the world with atomic radiation.

"The two superpowers are engaged in an unrelenting competition to secure the political ideologies and, more importantly, the natural resources of the weaker emerging societies throughout the world. There will be a global tug-of-war that will utilize blatant, oppressive brute force to bring those who resist to pulverized submission.

"For the remainder of this century, Travis, for the next fifty years, all wars will be fought over oil. The world runs on oil. It's a limited, nonrenewable resource. There is a mad global scramble to secure as much oil as you can gobble up. Grab as much as you can, as fast as you can.

"The people gathered in that dining hall look at the future geopolitical realities and could convincingly argue the hypothesis that either of the superpowers, under guise of political stability, defense of freedom, or any number of thinly veiled excuses, would not hesitate to turn the sands of the Arabian Peninsula or anywhere else into an immense sheet of glass with the detonation of a thermal nuclear device, in order to harvest the petroleum resource beneath.

"That is what motivates the people you see gathered here tonight. The supergun gives them the perception of parity, and the capability to defend themselves against the nuclear aggressions they perceive to be ultimately inevitable.

"The United States along with Canada had the inside track on Professor Bull's technology, and they in fact sponsored the program and funded the prototype. Unfortunately, as I stated before, they had already decided to proceed with their ICBM programs and were underwhelmed, unimpressed, and could not comprehend the capabilities or the unlimited applications associated with the supergun and therefore dropped the project unilaterally. Very shortsighted on their part.

"That is why Bull's artillery technology, combined with Con's propulsion system, makes it an extremely attractive and relatively affordable offensive or defensive weapons system for most of the world's emerging military regimes. It also becomes a decisive tiebreaker in the hands of rebels, revolutionaries, political terrorists, South American drug cartels, or religious extremists.

"The world is going to be a very dangerous place to try and survive in the near future. It will be an extremely precarious existence. That is why me, and people like me, will depend on you and guys like you to help preserve our fragile existence against the dark and evil forces that conspire against us and our way of life.

"And there will be new enemies emerging. Not a military in defense of a nation-state. But a close-knit association of terrorist thugs and religious zealots, bound only by political or religious ideology. An unseen army that pledges allegiance to no one except other comrades of like purpose regardless of race or nationality. An invisible amoeba that moves silently across borders, unseen and unnoticed until convergence and chaos ensues. It will behave as a cancer that silently invades, then gradually destroys from within. It feeds upon the host organism, then moves on to its next inevitable victim. In other circles a similar scenario is described as 'the domino theory.' Dominos lined up on edge. Knock one over and all the rest follow in succession one by one." She took the last long drag from her cigarette, then let it fall to extinction in the dark waters below.

She finally looked over to me. I must have looked glazed over trying to process the overwhelming amount of information divulged. Separate fact from theory.

"What's the matter, Travis? Input overload? Did I complicate your perception of the world? Hope I didn't torpedo your relationship with Raven?"

Before I was able to formulate a response, she wrapped her arm in mine and led me toward the dining hall doors. "Travis, I need your help," she said in a hushed tone. "I need you to get Rita out of here tonight before all hell breaks loose. I think I've found a way for you to escape unnoticed. I'll check the route, then I'll come and get you both. Get as much rest as you can. You'll need to move fast when the time comes."

We reentered the great hall and approached the gathered masses. They were mingling around the long dining table that had been cleared of dinner accoutrements and now appeared to contain some sort of exhibit. We strolled to the table joining the others and observed an array of "Flash Gordon" gizmos of the future.

Dr. Con stepped to the head of the table. "Ladies and gentlemen, what you see before you are the latest development in weapons technology. These technologies will soon be available to you as well."

He picked up the first item on the table, which looked like a standard deer rifle scope. He asked for the lights to be dimmed in the hall and raised the scope to his eye. He pushed a button on the side of the scope and instantly a thin red laser beam shot out of the end of the scope and made a pinpoint red dot on an unsuspecting starfish clinging to a rock some fifty yards out in the grotto.

"There you see pinpoint accuracy with immediate application for sniper rifles," he began. "Just imagine, my friends, this technology in the near future can be applied to the supergun."

A hushed mumble swirled like a wave around the table.

The next item on the table resembled a large transistor radio with two sharp copper antennas protruding from one end and a single red button in the middle.

"Mr. Dugan, if I could request your assistance. Please stand where everyone can observe."

I obliged reluctantly, moving out to an open area of the room. I looked back at Claire, who had a knowing, wicked little smile on her gorgeous face. Perhaps a psychic precognition.

I was approximately ten feet away when he pressed the red button. Instantly, the two copper antennas shot out of the device and imbedded in my chest still attached to the radio by two thin copper wires. A jolting electric shock surged through my body, knocking me to the floor in uncontrollable convulsions as if I were suffering an epileptic seizure. It short-circuited my entire nervous system. I was writhing on the floor, biting my tongue in a convulsive fit. If my sphincter hadn't sucked up tighter than a frog's ass, I probably would have crapped my pants. All I could think about was kicking the living shit out of that slant-eyed little bastard, if I could ever get myself off this goddamn floor.

Eventually the effects of my laser treatment began to subside, and I was able to get to my feet with a little assistance from my now-giggling companion Claire Voyent.

"Nice way to treat your guests, you little prick," I said, struggling to regain my composure.

"Oh Mr. Dugan, please accept my utmost apology. I thought that you, of all the people here tonight, would appreciate the nonlethal effectiveness of such a device especially within the close quarters that you normally operate. You'll notice, Mr. Dugan, that there are no lasting side effects, other than surprise and embarrassment. That is why we call this device, the 'stun gun.'

"Now, ladies and gentlemen, if you'll follow me out to the grotto, Ms. Voyent will demonstrate our **pièce de résistance**."

Con slid the glass doors open to the grotto. Everyone filed out onto a small veranda that cantilevered over the tide pools. When everyone had assembled, Claire bent down and removed what appeared to be a bazooka with added accessories from a large metal ammo box.

Con shined a flashlight over to the guard towers at the entrance to the cove and motioned out to sea. The tower guards energized a large spotlight and pointed it out to sea beyond the grotto. The light illuminated a thirty-foot cabin cruiser anchored approximately one hundred yards from shore.

Claire assumed a wide stance, exposing gorgeous long legs that seemed to go all the way up to a stunning protrusion of perky ass. (But I digress.) She hoisted the bazooka onto her shoulder and looked through the telescopic site mounted to the side of the weapon.

Dr. Con stepped forward and proudly began to present the feature benefits of the weapon. "Ladies and gentlemen, with this weapon we can demonstrate the imagined integration of the technologies you have witnessed this evening."

He dramatically placed his hand on the telescopic site. "Here we have the laser targeting scope originally designed for the sniper rifle." He then placed his hand on the barrel of the weapon. "Here we have loaded the weapon with conventional explosives, however, we have added the perpetual propulsion component that you witnessed during the supergun demonstration." He then moved to the rear of the weapon where a large canister, like a film-reel canister, had been attached to the bottom and rested against the operator's shoulder blades. "And finally here, my friends, we have integrated a spool of optical cable similar to the one utilized in our stun gun demonstration.

"With that said, my friends, I'll turn the demonstration over to my esteemed colleague and the beautiful genius who helped design and performed the analysis for the systems technology integrated into this weapon, courtesy of the American CIA. Ms. Claire Voyent."

She placed a pair of goggles over her eyes and aimed the small cannon at the cabin cruiser illuminated offshore. She pushed the button on the side of the scope and the red laser beam made a pinpoint target on the side of the boat. She centered the beam amidships midway between the waterline and the top of the gunnels. Dr. Con turned to the assembled spectators and suggested they cover their ears.

She pulled the trigger and an enormous blast and huge fireball exploded from the rear of the weapon, followed immediately by tremendous whoosh as the projectile exited the barrel and gained velocity as it streaked across the grotto. The familiar rope-knot exhaust trail followed as did the copper wires attached to the projectile. The recoil of the weapon momentarily skewed the laser beam, but Claire was able to reconcile the target point just before the round impacted precisely on the red dot on the boat's hull. The cabin cruiser exploded with a tremendous blast, spewing bright fire and brimstone. It had been packed with fireworks so that upon impact the boat ignited into a glorious fireball with dozens of skyrockets streaking into the night sky and illuminating the grotto in a blinding succession of colorful explosions. The entire gathering of dignitaries broke into spontaneous applause and contagious laughter. It was an inspiring sales presentation.

I walked over to Claire as she set the modified bazooka on its metal case. The barrel of the weapon was glowing red. She removed her safety goggles and spat on the glowing barrel, which sizzled upon impact.

"There's a design flaw we had not fully anticipated," she said. "Con's propulsion system creates a tremendous amount of heat as the projectile progresses through the barrel. We will have to reformulate the compounds or modify the weapon with a thicker casing."

"The recoil seems to be a bit overwhelming as well," I mentioned.

"So you noticed that it almost put me on my stunningly perky ass," she laughed.

"Thank you, ladies and gentlemen," Con beamed. "If you will follow me back inside, we have dessert, and I also have a surprise that should be the icing on the cake, so to speak."

Everyone excitedly filed back inside the dining hall with hushed enthusiasm. Claire and I brought up the rear.

"What other surprise could the amazing Dr. Con have in store?" I asked.

"I don't have a clue," she answered. "This will be a surprise for me as well. I don't have a good feeling about this," she uttered with trepidation.

Sir Arthur reentered the room with a quick glance back to Claire and quizzically raised eyebrows. Her response was a barely noticeable shrug and the same raised eyebrow expression in return.

Once inside, everyone resumed their previous seating arrangements, cake and coffee already at each setting. Everyone chatted among their neighbors regarding the evening's events. The desserts gradually disappeared, and as the festivities began to wind down, Dr. Con once again rose to his feet and politely waited as the room fell silent with eager anticipation.

"Ladies and gentlemen, I have saved the best for last," he began. "This most recent acquisition has come to us courtesy of our ingenious friends in Great Britain's MI5 department." He bent down and retrieved the object from under his chair and proudly placed it on the table in front of him. Again, quick glances of concern between Sir Arthur and Claire Voyent.

The object resembled a jet fighter pilot's helmet. It was a dull OD green nonreflective color with a large very dark set of goggles or visor attached.

"Mr. Dugan, perhaps I could persuade you to demonstrate?" Con asked with a sly grin.

"Yea, right. Fuck you very much, but I'll pass," was my deadpan response. The gathered masses chuckled quietly.

Dr. Con handed the surprisingly heavy headgear to Sir Arthur and asked that the lights be dimmed once again. There was a soft glow of moonlight through the windows on either side of the enormous dining hall, which cast everyone in silhouette. Dr. Con moved to a darkened corner of the room and asked Sir Arthur to place the apparatus on his head and lower the visor. Sir Arthur attempted to do so, however, it would not fit over his enormous fat head. More giggling from the darkened masses.

Sir Arthur then handed the device to Phangs Pa, and more giggling ensued. Phangs Pa handed it to the metals-clad junta leader from Argentina who had recently orchestrated a military coup of the dictator Juan Peron. Everyone watched in exuberant anticipation as the junta leader placed the helmet on his head and lowered the visor.

"Oh, muy bien!" was his excited reaction.

One by one each guest placed the device on their head. Excited elation from each as Dr. Con moved back and forth across the dark corner. While everyone's attention was focused on the ongoing demonstration, Claire had moved around the end of the table and was engaged in a hushed discussion with Sir Arthur.

The helmet eventually made its way around the table to me. I placed it over my head and slid the visor into position. There was a ghostly green glow that followed Dr. Con as he moved about in the dark. A fuzzy flaring image that seemed to sense the heat emitting from his body.

"What do you think, Mr. Dugan?" Con asked as he returned to the table.

"It appears to utilize some sort of heat sensor," I responded, placing it back on the table, as the chandeliers once again warmly illuminated the great hall.

"Right you are, Mr. Dugan," chimed Dr. Con. "Very astute, my friend. I am sincerely impressed. Heat-sensing night vision goggles.

With a little work, the detail can be refined, and the contrast less distorted. As you can imagine, this device will give any nighttime offensive operation a tremendous advantage.

"Ladies and gentlemen, that concludes this evening's festivities. I sincerely hope that you all thoroughly enjoyed the occasion. We have valets waiting in the hallway to escort you to your respective rooms. We will arrange accommodations in the morning for your departure. For now, I wish you sweet dreams."

With that, the guests began to exit the dining hall via the swoosh of shiny elevator doors to the passageway outside. Claire appeared at my side and began to escort me to the doors along with the others.

"Travis, I'll be coming to get you just before dawn. You are to get Rita out of here safely and back to her family. I will have found an escape route by the time I return. For now, get as much rest as you can. We will need to move quickly when the time is right."

The bright aluminum doors parted, and Tang Poon-Song waited in white silk robe, slippers, and warm smile. Claire and I said good night as Tang wrapped her arm in mine and led me through the labyrinth of passageways back to my room.

When we arrived, I quickly checked on Rita, who was sleeping soundly. Tang took me by the hand and led me to the bath, where she slid aside a partition wall of etched glass, revealing an ornate therapy pool of steamy bubbles.

"You have one more therapy session scheduled," she said softly. She let her robe slide to the floor, revealing a delicate, porcelain China doll. She was fresh, petite, and unblemished. Tight and taut. She removed my clothes, then gently led me to the soothing comfort of the warm bubbling pool. She made love to me as if we were familiar lovers. Warm, deep-felt passion smothered in gentle kisses and labored breath. Again, I felt the reminiscent pangs of well-spent youth. The lusty excitement of new experiences and the wondrous feelings of discovery. She was sweet yet intensely passionate.

When the therapy session had wonderfully concluded, Tang dried us both with a thick terry cloth towel, then led me to an immense expanse of crisp bed. She massaged me gently, smoothly, softly, then made love to me again before we gently drifted into a deep sleep.

Chapter Eleven

I was rudely awakened being abruptly twisted into a pretzel. I felt like Freddie Blassie pinned to the mat in a full nelson, by that pencil-neck geek Gorgeous George, while Dick Lane yells, "Whoa, Nellie!" at TV ringside. Saturday-night wrestling and roller derby with Richie Valaderez and the LA Thunderbirds from the Olympic Auditorium.

In the harsh light of reality, it was Claire Voyent ensuring that I would not scream like a little girl or come out swinging when awakened.

"Get dressed as quickly as you can," she whispered. "I brought your clothes and your personal effects in the bag. Wake Rita and get her ready to go. Hurry. I'll watch out for the guards."

I gazed across the wide expanse of the empty bed. Tang had departed sometime during the night. (These Chinese babes seemed to come and go. I had yet to awaken with one still here in the morning.)

It felt good to be back in my own clothes. Khakis, combat boots, bomber jacket. I was also pleased to be reunited with my trusty .38 and my PI pocket paraphernalia. I got Rita up and dressed in a traditional black cotton Chinese pajama suit and sturdy rubber-soled canvas slippers.

When we were ready, we joined Claire at the passage doors. Claire slid a perforated card, like Tang's, into the key slot and the doors parted. We looked up and down the passageway then followed Claire at a brisk pace, staying close to the passage walls. We went a long distance before we stopped at another set of aluminum doors on the right. Claire once again slid her card into the slot and the doors opened. A guard in black ninja suit and carrying a Russian Kalashnikov assault rifle stood stoic in the doorway. Before he could get his weapon off his shoulder, Claire zapped him with a stun gun. A few sparks and several audible clicks later, he was convulsing spasmodically on the floor much like I had only a few hours earlier. I felt his pain. I felt his frustration and his anger. While he was still convulsing, I felt his door-slot card and his Kalashnikov. Having retrieved both, and as his spasms began to subside, I removed his ninja belt and hog-tied his hands and feet together behind his back. I took his hood and retied it around his mouth. I dragged him down the hall to a janitorial closet and locked him inside.

We proceeded down the long passageway to another set of shiny elevator doors. Rita and I stood to one side as Claire slid the card into the slot. She stood with her hands on her hips; the doors swooshed open. This Chinese guard was dressed in more traditional dark blue uniform with beret and Kalashnikov. He seemed momentarily startled, then pleasantly surprised to see such a gorgeous woman in skintight black leather jumpsuit appear magically before him. With a seductive come-hither, she stepped back and at the same time reached up and began to pull the jumpsuit zipper toward her navel, exposing most of her impressive sweater puppets. She crooked a finger for him to follow. As he cleared the doorway, I caught him under the chin with the butt of my rifle. He swapped ends and hit the floor hard. I removed the strap from his weapon and hog-tied him as I had done previously. I dragged him into a storage room and stuffed his beret into his mouth.

"I'm going to leave you on your own from here," Claire said. "If Con has that set of night vision goggles, then that means they have Blaine Pond as well. He was issued one of the few prototypes in existence. I must go another direction from here. At the end of this passage on the left, you should find the engineering and maintenance room. There is an exit to the outside through that room. Try not to fire that weapon unless absolutely necessary. Good luck." With that, she disappeared down the hallway into the darkness.

I looked at Rita, who now seemed vaguely apprehensive about the whole exercise.

"Are you ready?" I asked.

"Semper paratus, baby!" she replied with labored smile. (What a trooper.)

I took her by the hand and moved quickly down the passageway to the engineering room. I slid the card I had taken from the guard into the slot and the doors parted. I looked in quickly then pulled back. The immense room was full of operating generators, huge boilers, and air-conditioning units. There appeared to be no guards or maintenance personnel on duty.

We barely stepped inside when alarms began to sound. Sirens and bells blared from all areas of the compound. The overhead lights dimmed and the emergency exit lights came on.

Suddenly the doors across the immense room burst open and a squad of guards began charging into the room. I grabbed Rita and ran toward the corner behind twin boiler tanks.

The entire room erupted in automatic weapons fire. Round after round pinged and zinged off the machinery with ricocheted sparks. Bullets punctured the tanks and hot steaming water shot out under high pressure with a loud hiss as the steam began to fill the room.

I fired my weapon from behind the hissing boiler tanks to keep the hordes at bay. The room continued to fill with thick steamy fog. I fired sporadically as we crawled along the floor searching for an escape. Hugging the floor, I noticed a large drainpipe covered by a thin metal grate under each of the spewing boiler tanks. (The old escape through the storm-drain gambit. The tried-and-true suggestion I had given the young screenwriter at the Marlin Club.)

I scrambled around in the darkness searching for something with which to remove the drain grate. I came upon a mop bucket and wringer. I grabbed the wringer handle and crawled back to the boiler tanks amid continuous gunfire from the guards. I jammed the wringer handle through the grate opening and pried with all my strength and finally popped off several of the screw heads securing the grate to the floor. I repositioned the wringer handle and peeled back the grate like a sardine can. When the opening was large enough, I grabbed Rita and shoved her down the pipe feet first. She dropped down the pipe and out of sight, screaming like a banshee all the way. I got my feet into the opening, prepared to follow Rita, when a ricocheted round hit me right in the Kalashnikov, somersaulting me backward into the wall. It shattered the rifle stock and my left hand was stunned and stinging. I crawled back to the drainpipe and rammed myself through.

We slid down the pipe faster and faster, bumping and banging against the sides as we went. We hit a bend in the pipe with a hard jolt then continued our rapid descent albeit at more of an angle, less of a straight free fall. A faint light began to appear at the end of the tunnel as we plummeted at an ever-increasing speed toward it.

Finally, we were spit out the end of the pipe and fell for what seemed an eternity, before crashing hard into the churning surf that thrashed viciously against the rugged cliffs of China Point. It was a very long fall and an extremely hard hit. From that height the surface of the water was like hitting concrete. I was stunned. Not unconscious but confused, bewildered. I was limp and could only watch helplessly as the churning bubbles tossed me about like a rag doll in a washing machine. Over and over, I was tumbled beneath the crashing waves. Bashed and scraped against unseen obstacles that ripped and shredded as I was swept toward the jagged cliffs. I couldn't hold my breath any longer. This was it, I thought. After all the tough scrapes I'd gotten myself into, this was how it was going to end—mashed into fish bait, so much flotsam and jetsam. Merely an oily sheen upon the water to be disbursed with the outgoing tide.

My last thoughts were of Rita. She would surely perish in the relentless crashing surf. She would not survive this ordeal. Suddenly, an overwhelming sense of urgency swept through me. The instinct to survive took over. I could no longer allow the crashing waves to determine my destiny, nor Rita's. I frantically began churning my arms and legs toward the light that I hoped was the surface.

I breached the surface and gasped for a breath of air, just as the next set of towering waves barred down upon me. I dived beneath the immense wall of churning white water as it crashed overhead. Again and again I dived beneath the relentless swells only to be swept toward the rugged cliffs within the following wave surge. Each pulverizing wave swept me closer and closer to the jagged cliffs no matter how hard I swam away from them.

Suddenly, an immense backwash riptide swept me from the cliff face and carried me out beyond the surf line like the beginnings of an imminent tidal tsunami. I lay motionless, floating in a calm and suddenly immense deep blue sea.

I swam around frantically searching in all directions and calling Rita's name. I swam in circles, becoming more and more desperate. My combat boots and leather jacket were beginning to drag me below the surface of the water. I was exhausted and in danger of drowning. I began swallowing gasping breaths of abrasive salt water, while being dragged to the murky depths by my own bomber jacket. (I don't care who you are, that's some ironic bullshit right there, I thought to myself.)

Then, in the distance, I spotted her lifeless body loosely wedged between two huge rocks out beyond the crashing surf line. Each incoming swell would raise her motionless body floating upon the surface; then with the receding tide, she would be lowered back down into the tide pools between the two gigantic rocks.

I began swimming toward her as fast as I could. I reached her on an incoming swell and held her in my arms as we were lowered to the tide pools below upon the outgoing one. I picked her up and placed her over my shoulder in a fireman's carry. I began to claw my way up the barnacle-covered rocks, ripping and tearing large chunks of bloody flesh from my hands and knees as I scrambled. I could hear large volumes of seawater gushing from her, who was hanging upside down, as I scratched my way to the top of the jagged rocks.

When I reached the top and was out of the clutches of the relentless tide below, I stretched her out on her back and began to administer small breaths followed by several chest compressions. I continued the repetition until my arms were numb. Then continued some more. I was running out of gas and getting no response. Desperation began to sweep over me. I began to cry and scream at the same time. "Don't give up on me now, baby! We're too close to the finish line. I promised your family I'd bring you home safe! Fight, damn you! Fight!"

It was futile. I was losing her. I collapsed upon her and began to sob uncontrollably.

Then, like a miraculous mirage, I began to hear the unmistakable whine of an outboard motor. I turned and was amazed to see Yung He coming to our rescue aboard a rubber Zodiac boat.

"Travis," she called when she got near. "Climb aboard. I've got the skipjack anchored around the point."

Once again I hoisted Rita over my shoulder and began to clamber down the jagged rocks. Upon an incoming swell, Yung He maneuvered the Zodiac close to the rocks as I lowered Rita aboard, then climbed aboard after and pushed off the rocks with the receding surge. We were off at full speed around the other side of China Point.

I continued breath and chest compressions as we sped back to the boat. Yung He pulled alongside the skipjack and tied off the Zodiac. I carried Rita aboard and lay her on the deck. Yung He retrieved a scuba tank from below and placed the respirator in Rita's mouth. She gave her a couple of quick shots of oxygen as I continued to administer chest compressions. We repeated the procedure until Rita began to cough uncontrollably and convulse spasmodically, writhing around the deck. Yung He immediately jumped on top of Rita, pinning Rita's arms with her knees. Yung He began to slap Rita repeatedly across the face.

Suddenly, Rita's eyes snapped open and she took in her first big breath on her own. Her eyes were unfocussed and glazed. She had a faint look of bewilderment, but at least she was breathing, albeit labored, on her own. Yung He and I both let out a big sigh of relief.

Yung He looked at me with much concern. "She is suffering from the effects of shock," she began. "She has a laceration at the base of her skull and a deep contusion on her forehead. See?" Yung He pulled back a clump of bedraggled hair, exposing an ugly purple bump rising at Rita's hairline. "She is in need of immediate medical care. She must be taken to a doctor now."

"Can you take her to the hospital in Avalon, Yung He?" I asked. "I must return to Smuggler's Cove before Con and his cronies escape with the supergun technology. I must try to locate and help rescue Blaine Pond if I can."

"I will take care of her, Travis. I will take her to the hospital," Yung He replied. She then went forward to weigh anchor. I knelt close to Rita and told her that Yung He would take her home and that I would join her as soon as I could. I kissed her softly on the cheek.

Yung He powered up the skipjack and was prepared to get underway. She climbed down from the bridge and gave me a big hug and a long kiss.

"Take care of yourself, Travis," she said softly.

I climbed aboard the Zodiac and untied from the skipjack. I watched briefly as they disappeared over the southern swells. I yanked the cord and the outboard roared to life. I spun the Zodiac around and set course full throttle for Smuggler's Cove.

I couldn't go around the point without being seen from the guard towers on either side of the cove entrance. I would be forced to go ashore on the steep cliff side of the point. I would have to find a spot to land the Zodiac upon an incoming swell without smashing into the cliff face and being swept out to sea with the receding surge. (This could end badly.)

Suddenly, the deafening roar and swift shadow of Steve Canyon's PBY swept by mere feet over my head, followed instantly by the stinging impact of his water-balloon barrage. (Silly bastard.)

He made a wide turn and came in from the south. After several "gooney bird" bounces atop the following swells, he finally settled in and taxied over to where I waited. He had removed the plexiglass side blisters from either side of the aft fuselage, so I climbed aboard and pulled the Zodiac in after me. I stowed the rubber boat and clambered forward into the copilot's seat.

"Welcome aboard, Bombardier!" he yelled with a wide grin and a hardy handshake.

I buckled in and we were off. After several more clumsy bounces, we were airborne. The big black pigboat labored to gain altitude and eventually leveled off approximately fifty feet above the surface of the waves below.

We came around the rocky point and made a low-level pass across the cove entrance in front of the twin guard towers. He pulled back on the stick and pushed forward on the throttles. We slowly lumbered into a steep climb to the right up the cliff face; then he dipped the right wing and we screamed across the entire cove in a low rip-roaring, ear-shattering quasi-strafing run.

The tower guards were caught completely by surprise. They scrambled around, banging into each other like Buster Keaton and Hal Roach's Keystone Kops. They eventually coalesced and swung their .50 calibers into position.

The flotilla of small boats that had ferried the assemblage ashore in the days prior were now feverishly on-loading those same passengers and preparing to make a hasty departure. Their departure became even more hasty and the pace quickened chaotically following our surprise flyover.

In the midst of the confusion I spotted Blaine Pond and Claire Voyent being forced aboard Con's big black yacht. The impressively sleek and equally intimidating craft was powered up and spewing volumes of smoke from the stacks, straining at the cleats, ready to depart.

As we leveled off and made another pass across the guard towers, we began to draw some serious gunfire. Several .50-caliber rounds ripped through the fuselage amidships. Kamikaze Steve whipped around in his seat and gazed with amazement at the jagged holes along the starboard side of his lumbering pigboat.

"Those little pricks shot holes in my boat!" he yelled. "Oh, those little bastards are gonna pay for that!" he exclaimed. "We're gonna light those slant-eyed gooks up!" He looked at me with a wide grin and a crazed look that I recognized from the last time I flew with this psychotic sumbitch. (I didn't have a good feeling about this.)

"Here, take the controls," he said as he climbed below into the plexiglass nose and armed the .50 caliber.

"Fly her out past the point, then come around to starboard." He then clambered aft to the engineer's section and flipped several toggle switches, arming the considerable ordnance I was just beginning to realize he had aboard. There were three torpedoes under each wing and something really heavy in the bomb bay that made the flying pig even more cumbersome than I had remembered. He returned to the pilot's seat and took over the controls.

"Go behind the bulkhead and open the wooden crate lashed to the deck. I'm sure you'll know how to operate it," he said with a laugh. "Brace yourself in the starboard blister opening."

I climbed from my seat and went aft behind the cabin bulkhead. I pried open the crate. There, in pristine, like-new condition was a Thompson submachine gun, with a fifty-round ammo canister attached. There were several full canisters in the crate as well. I hadn't seen a brand-new tommy gun since the days when I smuggled them to the Golden Bear for Pappa Pappadopolis between the wars.

I took a position on the deck in front of the starboard blister hole and braced my feet on either side of the opening. We made a wide turn to starboard and climbed above the back side of China Point. Kamikaze brought her around and came sweeping in over Raven's cabin at treetop level. We came in hot, screaming down the cliff face with the .50 caliber in the nose ripping shells along the crowded dock, scattering the masses into frenzied chaos, like we had pissed on an anthill.

I opened up with my tommy gun on the twin guard towers, spitting a relentless barrage of hot rounds ripping through the roofs, shredding the towers and sending the guards diving for cover. We swept overhead with a tremendous roar and headed out to sea and out of range.

"Yeehaaa! Hot damn, Bombardier! Did we light those little yellow bastards up or what!" he exclaimed. "Air fives" all around. Kamikaze was pumped and ready for action.

We could see the flotilla of early departures making a mad dash for the commercial shipping lanes and the armada of mother ships in the distance waiting to whisk their respective benefactors to safety on the high seas. Kamikaze and I looked at each other . . . We smiled.

He pushed the throttles and the yoke simultaneously forward to the fire wall. The nose of the big clumsy dodo bird dipped, and we began a long, droning descent to wave-crest altitude. He lined up on the trailing boat, in a long line of boats desperately seeking escape. He pushed the button on the yoke and the .50 caliber in the nose spewed forth a hot burst, like a fire-breathing dragon, which followed its wake, then ripped through the small boat, stem to stern, straight down the center beam. The boat immediately turned hard to port and began to spin in concentric circles. We lined up on the next boat and began our approach. Once again, the .50 caliber ripped through the center of the fleeing boat. It came to an immediate halt and began to bob about at the mercy of the rising swells. As we roared overhead, wisps of smoke began to rise from the crippled vessel.

"Go aft of engineering and you'll find another crate lashed to the port-side bulkhead!" yelled Kamikaze, with a backward motion of his thumb.

On the side of the crate were stenciled the words PROJECTILE/ GRENADE LAUNCHER SERIES M-5. I grabbed an armload and brought them forward. We climbed to a higher altitude and prepared for a dive-bombing run.

As we approached our next target in line, a sleek thirty-five-footer, the nosed dropped and we began an ugly, shuddering, ear-shattering dive. As the closing rate increased, I yelled bombs away and slid two projectiles down the makeshift water-balloon chute. Kamikaze yanked back on the yoke and the flying pig creaked and groaned, shuddered and shook, but did eventually level out just above our intended target and barely ahead of our exploding payload. The first hit the stern, disabling the propulsion and rudder control. It was of little consequence because the second hit dead center. The entire boat exploded in a huge fireball, reducing it to fluttering bits of confetti.

We gained a bit more altitude and set our sights on the bigger boats farther out in the shipping lanes, the mother ships that were lowering davits over the side in preparation to bring the smaller boats aboard and make sail for the high seas.

Kamikaze made a slight course adjustment to the right and lined up on a small frigate flying a Cuban flag. Our approach brought us in on its starboard side. When we got within a hundred yards, Steve reached to the overhead panel and flipped two toggle switches. One torpedo dropped from each wing and began churning their way to the unsuspecting target. They hit her broadside one after the other. The first exploded just aft of the bow. The second impacted amidships. The frigate began to list to starboard and columns of black smoke began to pour from the holes ripped in the hull at the waterline. Within mere minutes, she listed over and capsized. We made a tight circle and watched as she sank beneath the waves.

We turned hard left and headed south toward San Clemente Island. We flew along in silence for a time. As we approached the northern end of the island, we could see Von Jekyle's boat parked in the same spot it had occupied for the last several days. We flew around the point and down the windward side of the island. We were amazed to see an armada of foreign naval vessels anchored in a long line along the western coast.

They appeared to have on-loaded their shore boats and passengers and were in final preparations for departure.

Canyon began an attack approach that would take us straight over the entire fleet, bow to stern. He leveled off and increased our speed and closing rate. They were ready for us, however. The forward antiaircraft guns began firing repeatedly and the shells began to explode all around us as we screamed toward them. Each explosion knocked the hell out of the lumbering albatross and shrapnel was peppering jagged holes in the fuselage the closer we got.

Kamikaze opened up with the nose gun, and when we got within range, he reached up and flipped all the remaining toggles. The big pig lurched into the air as all the remaining torpedoes dropped from the wings. We barely cleared the con tower of the first ship and continued strafing the line of boats as we went. I dropped all the remaining grenades down the balloon chute as fast as I could load them, then looked back to see them find their target as we roared overhead. They impacted sporadically along the deck and superstructure like so many colorful water balloons. They weren't causing a tremendous amount of damage to the armor plating of the well-seasoned frigate, but they wreaked a lot of havoc and created *mucho* chaos.

The torpedoes went down either side of the first boat, but scored glancing hits on the second and third boats in line. The explosions occurred near the bow of both boats. Not enough damage inflicted to sink either, but enough to keep the damage-control crews scurrying to close off and isolate the compartments taking on water. One torpedo hit the shore and the other went MIA.

As we screamed past the last boat in line, she opened up on us with her aft AAC-AAC gun. The shrapnel tore through the rudder and ripped jagged holes in the underside of both wings from which rivulets of fuel began to escape and stream down the surface of the wings.

We banked hard left and flew around the southern end of the island, out of harm's way. The old boat was sluggish, cumbersome, and extremely difficult to maneuver with half of the rudder trailing in the breeze like a fluttering kite tail.

The engines were intact and would continue to run as long as the fuel supply lasted. There was a slight vibration coming from the starboard engine, but we surmised it to be most likely a chip in the prop and would not affect the overall performance of the engine . . . in the short term.

As we came around the leeward side of the island, we could see an armada of vessels converging on the channel between San Clemente and Catalina from all directions along the mainland coast. I recognized the coast guard cutter *Ponchatrane* moving at full steam, followed by an array of coast guard harbor patrol boats, LA County sheriffs, and U.S. Customs. We had a good laugh when we came upon Captain Wally in his converted PT way out ahead of the converging cavalry brigade, leading the charge.

We passed low over the *Bad Penny* and performed a labored wing waggle. Captain Wally waved us on as we headed back to Smuggler's Cove. We passed Von Jekyle's boat once again in the distance off our port side. He was in the same spot, still flying a dive flag.

As we turned toward Smuggler's Cove, I spotted two shadows running in a line just beneath the surface. When we got closer, I could see the small V-shape wakes created by the sub's periscopes. They were Con's two midget subs running toward San Clemente Island.

I tapped Steve on the shoulder and pointed down to the subs. He smiled and made a course adjustment that would bring us around and up their rear, so to speak. I went to the grenade crate and brought forward the remaining six projectiles. I would have to score direct hits on the subs or the grenades would simply "porpoise" to the bottom.

We made one very, very slow pass over the subs. I slid each projectile down the balloon chute as quickly as I could. All six splashed into the water and abruptly nose-dived to the bottom. We didn't hit a thing. We were getting pretty cocky if we actually believed that we were going to drop a bunch of grenades from a low-flying, crippled-up albatross and hit a pair of midget subs barely making six knots. It was a long shot at best.

The only damage we inflicted was perhaps to our overinflated sense of bravado. We did, however, manage to draw the attention of the irrepressible Captain Wally, who came streaking in with depth charges rolling over the gunnels, as he made progressive figure 8 maneuvers.

We climbed to a higher altitude in an attempt to act as a spotter for the ongoing sea battle below. In doing so, however, we also detected the slightest sputter from the soon-to-be-fuel-starved engines. We made one circle, struggling to gain altitude. From all appearances, the insufferable Captain, for the most part, had successfully carpet bombed every square foot of the immediate vicinity. There were no signs of the subs or any visible debris floating on the surface.

What also was apparent was the obvious consternation the United States Coast Guard had with regard to bombing and strafing runs performed by a civilian aircraft upon foreign naval vessels, some thirty miles off the California coast. The *Ponchatrane* was coming full speed ahead with forward guns blazing. Rounds streaked across the *Bad Penny*'s bow as Captain Wally cranked up the Packards and scampered away from the pursuing cutter like a scared rabbit. He added insult to injury by releasing a small smoke screen of humiliation as he disappeared from view.

Kamikaze leveled off and began a long slow turn to a course that would take us straight back to Smuggler's Cove. He seemed to have a plan. He currently sported a wicked little grin. (I didn't have a good feeling about this.)

He unbuckled and went aft to engineering, leaving me at the controls. He reached into the bomb bay then flipped the last toggle on the overhead panel. He then went forward and reloaded the .50 caliber. He climbed back into his seat and cranked open a small escape hatch over his head. I looked over my head . . . no such escape hatch for moi.

He looked at me with that same stupid grin as we approached Smuggler's Cove. I recognized that grin.

"Oh no! Oh no, you sumbitch!" I exclaimed. "I've flown with you twice and you've crashed 50 percent of the time. This one will really screw up your crash-to-landing ratio. Your averages will go all to hell!"

The stupid grin grew wider. "So are you suggesting that I not use that particular statistic as a benefit feature selling point in my advertisement brochure?" he asked with a laugh. (Silly bastard.)

"Are you ready, Bombardier?" he asked with the same stupid though slightly more sadistic grin.

I cinched up my sphincter and my seat belt. "Semper paratus, baby . . . always ready."

We began a long slow descent from the western sky, with the sun behind us to obscure our approach. Kamikaze cut the sputtering engines and we began a dead-stick glide straight into hell.

"You go aft!" he yelled. "Same fire drill as last time. After the first bounce, you bail out of the side blister!"

I gave him a thumbs-up, patted him on the shoulder, and yelled, "Good luck!" as I unbuckled and headed aft.

It was a tornado in the rear. The wind whistling through the swiss cheese fuselage and the open side blisters and the occasional jolting shudder as the stealthy black pig came silently out of the sun. (Banzai!)

Kamikaze leveled off at guard-tower altitude. He opened up with the .50 caliber in the nose and lined up between the two towers, headed directly for the cave and the supergun on the beach.

The supergun fired a projectile that streaked over the fuselage between the engines, taking out the props and then the entire tail section with an impressive explosion. In the next instant we swept between the guard towers, blowing through them with our wingtips and extended wing pods. We hit the water hard in the middle of the cove, wings ablaze. As we bounced back into the air, I scrambled to the blister hole, dragging Yung He's rubber Zodiac with me. I pushed the boat through the hole and dived in after.(Geronimo!) The Zodiac flew like a kite for a short time then smacked into the water with a jolt. I looked up just in time to see Kamikaze pop out of his escape hatch and slide down the top of the fuselage between the two engines. He slid off the side into the water just forward of the port-side blister hole.

The plane hit the water once more then bounced directly into the supergun, impaling itself on the barrel, nose to tail, and pushing the gun back up the track into the cave entrance. In the next instant the five-hundred-pound bomb in the bomb bay exploded in an immense fireball, igniting the propulsion bags stored inside the cave. A tremendous explosion belched from the cave entrance and from the various vent shafts scattered throughout the steep cliff face above, like an earth-shattering volcanic eruption. The entire island seemed to shudder as explosion after explosion spewed flaming debris high into the sky.

I cranked up the Zodiac and raced across the harbor to where Kamikaze thrashed about dodging gunfire that we were beginning to draw from dockside. It was only then that I realized that Con's sleek Raptor craft was gone. He had escaped during the ensuing chaos. I pulled Kamikaze aboard then came about and headed for the harbor entrance as fast as I could get the rubber boat to go. We screamed past the now-destroyed guard towers, out of the harbor, bouncing hard from one wave crest to the next.

The Zodiac took a couple of hits before we got out of range and began to lose air. I turned north and headed up the coast, looking for some place to land the boat before we sank and became shark bait. The outboard began to sputter and finally quit. We were now bobbing helplessly at the mercy of the sea, which relentlessly pushed us toward the jagged cliffs and thrashing surf.

To the south we could see the *Ponchatrane* arriving on station at Smuggler's Cove, followed by the armada of smaller boats. It seemed as though the entire harbor was ablaze. Huge flames and dense clouds of black smoke billowed from the cave entrance and vent pipes. A vision of Armageddon.

We were losing air quickly and were going to sink before we could be carried ashore and thrashed against the jagged rocks. The weight of the outboard motor began to drag the stern beneath the waves.

Just then, like the cavalry riding to the rescue, Captain Wally came riding out of the setting sun. He pulled alongside and extricated our bedraggled butts from the jaws of an angry sea once again. Once we were aboard, he wasted no time in getting the *Penny* wound up and heading north toward Land's End, leaving the Zodiac to sink into the briny deep and the Coast Guard to deal with the calamity and collateral damage back at Smuggler's Cove.

Chapter Twelve

After a quick stop in Lobster Bay to harvest a trap that Captain Wally had baited early that morning, we spent the remainder of the evening making our way, under the cover of darkness, around Land's End at the north end of the island. During our brief stop, we consumed *mucho* cerveza and many lobsters that had bathed in boiling water and then drowned in melted butter.

We arrived at White's Landing around midnight and moored among the commercial fishing fleet, under a canopy of camouflaged netting. I spent a considerable amount of time nursing my cuts and abrasions. The adrenaline was still pumping and the testosterone levels were still high among my compatriots. We retold every aspect of our recent adventure, each time more heroing than the last. We finally quieted and eventually drifted off to sleep. I wondered what happened to Pond and Claire Voyent.

Before dawn, the fishing boat crews began to assemble aboard their respective rigs and prepare for today's deepwater adventure.

White's Landing was home port to the bigger fleets of commercial boats that ventured far out to sea in the quest for schools of tuna and albacore. The yellow tail season had just begun, and there was excited anticipation among the various crews. There was also a considerable amount of speculation regarding the volcanic eruptions they had witnessed from many miles out at sea. Questions began to arise regarding the converted PT boat under the camouflage net as well.

The harbor eventually cleared as the fleet took to sea, long before the first grays of dawn. We made preparations to depart while Captain Wally fired up the Packards and the hot java. We untied from the mooring and began to motor out of the harbor, under the cover of the fading darkness, when Yung He's skipjack came around the southern point and pulled alongside at the harbor entrance.

"You must follow me to a safe harbor," she called. "Many federal agents are on their way. They will be here before sunrise. My uncle has sent me to find you. You must come with me now, while the tide is still high. You are in great danger."

She came about and we followed her out of the harbor into the misty twilight, neither boat showing any running lights. We turned south following the shallow point of land off our starboard side. The two boats continued to follow the misty gray of the shoreline to the far side of Moonstone Cove.

At high tide, a narrow inlet allowed access through a rocky maze to a small cove surrounded by high cliffs and rugged outcroppings that shielded the gentle cove from view in all directions. At low tide, the inlet narrowed and was too shallow to navigate. The water's depth within the secluded cove would rise and fall with the tides, but otherwise was unaffected by the unpredictable sea beyond the rocky surroundings.

We lashed the two boats together and anchored in the middle of the aquatic sanctuary. The first golden shafts of morning light began to waft muted into the pale waters of the serene cove.

We were to linger in this secluded cove for the day and give Yung He's cousin, Long Hung Dong, a chance to survey the situation around the island. Then at 1800 hours, when the tide was at its highest and a clear signal could be established, he would relay current conditions throughout the island.

Until then, we would spend the day swimming in the calm lagoon, enjoying the warm sun, and exploring the wonders of our secluded grotto paradise. At around midday the tide was at its lowest point and the receding water exposed billions and billions of smooth, shiny pebbles within every crevice and on every surface—moonstones. Highly polished hues of jade, deep reds, and ebony covered all surfaces, including the bottom, through fifty feet of crystal clear water.

We fished, we ate, we drank, we laughed, and we enjoyed each other's company and the serenity of our little piece of paradise. A short respite from the chaos beyond our glistening sanctuary. A brief time-out to lick our wounds and contemplate our next move.

◆　◆　◆

The shadows of afternoon arrived early once the sun had drifted behind the tall cliffs of Moonstone Cove. I was anxious to hear about Rita's condition. Yung He had taken her to the diver's pier yesterday morning and was met by an ambulance that immediately rushed her to Avalon's hospital at the top to the hill near the botanical gardens. Yung He assured me that Rita was conscious when they loaded her into the ambulance and that she would recover within days with plenty of rest and rehydration with intravenous fluids.

Kamikaze and Captain Wally were busy with their endeavors to catch several calico bass that were stragglers, left stranded in the shallow cove when the tide receded. Yung He took me aside and told me that she wanted to show me something. She stripped down to the smallest of bathing suits, the bottom of which was a miniscule triangle of thin white silk, with a thin string at each corner that tied in the back just below the enchanting dimples of her flawless hips, and just above her tight, pouty ass. The top was a strip of the same thin silk stretched across her taut young breasts. I was still sporting my drab green government-issue BVDs, in which I now began to pitch a small pup tent.

She filled a thatched basket with fresh fish, some fruit, and a small bag of rice. She then placed the basket into a large wooden platter shaped like a miniature canoe. We climbed over the stern onto the transom. She lowered the small canoe into the water and we began to swim toward the rugged cliff face.

With the tide at its lowest point, a small covered grotto was revealed under the massive cliff face. We swam under the cliff and into the darkened back corner where a small crevasse split the cliff and created a narrow inlet. As we swam into the narrow canyon, the walls towered overhead to a thin slit of sunlight at the top. We were escorted on our journey by a small school of bright orange indigenous Garibaldi.

Eventually, the small inlet widened to another open grotto of smooth, shiny moonstones. The depth became shallow enough for us to wade the last several yards onto a dry pebble-covered beach. The beach went up to another sheltered area under the cliff face. At the far end of the open grotto was a tall waterfall that cascaded from the cliffs high above to a small freshwater pond at the cliff base. To my amazement, in front of the pond at the base of the waterfall, in a small patch of sunlight, sat Ah Looey. He sat quietly, legs crossed, deep in contemplation. The scene created a real-life apparition of the quintessential Buddha in a state of transcendental meditation. As I watched enchanted, a small rainbow magically appeared above the pond in the waterfall's silvery mist.

We emerged from the shallows and made our way up the beach to where Ah Looey, "Sensei," opened his eyes and smiled widely upon our approach.

"Ah, Polliwog, I am relieved and happy that Yung He was successful in finding you and bringing you back safely." He then held out his arm and opened his hand. In the center of his palm was a small ebony moonstone.

"Snatch the pebble from my hand, Polliwog," he said, with a mischievous wide grin.

No sooner had I glanced at the pebble than he quickly closed his hand and exclaimed, "Too late!" with a boisterous laugh. "You possess the reflexes of an arthritic tree sloth," he giggled. "My dead grandmother moves faster than you," he continued.

I looked puzzled to Yung He. She just shrugged her shoulders.

Looey finally laughed, "Just kidding, Polliwog. Just choking your chicken. I had a vision during meditation. Future American situation comedy. Chinese grand master martial artist, posing as passive Buddhist monk, comes to American Wild West to dispense Buddhist philosophy to bronco-busting cowboys, hard-drinking gamblers, gunslingers, and wayward barroom chorus girls. Chinese Clint Eastwood. Mark my words, Polliwog, Hollywood studio nitwits will no doubt cast Chinese monk with a tall skinny Caucasian. Tape his eyes back at the corners, give him a funny topknot, and have him speak in halting broken English. Hilarious! Coming to theaters near you, Polliwog!"

"What the hell are you rambling about, you over-opiated old crusty rice burner?" I finally asked, exasperated.

"I tell them like I see them, Polliwog. One cannot always control where one's thoughts will take one."

He sat in silence for a moment, gazing at the pebble in his hand.

"I must apologize to you, Polliwog," he finally said softly. "I should have foreseen the trouble that you first brought to my attention. I should have been more aware of the apparent danger. It was you, Polliwog, who foretold of the approaching storm. Now, my people and I implore you to help us. We depend on your experience and wisdom during these trying times. You are the only one that possesses the determination, the fortitude, and the instincts of a predator to vanquish this enemy and free my people. We are depending on you, Polliwog. We will forever be in your debt."

"Come, Polliwog," he said, rising from his place at the waterfall. We walked up the beach and under the overhang of the cliff face. "Allow me to show you my humble home away from home."

Far back in the shadows was a comfortable-size cave. It was warm and cozy and appeared to have all the comforts one would require.

There was a teapot boiling over an open fire that Yung He had started upon our arrival. The floor of the cave was covered in a woven grass mat. We sat upon large overstuffed pillows around a low table of bamboo. Yung He brought tea for each of us, and we sat in silence for a short while sipping our tea.

"Polliwog," he finally said softly, "the people of Cooley Town are very much afraid, and they are depending on you to bring about a solution to this problem. They are prepared to help in any way they are able, however, I'm afraid they are no match for the brutal forces of the tong. There exists a culture of fear. They know how vicious the tong can be. Many of them are former victims, and that is why many of them came to this island. To escape the corruptness and brutality. That is why they look to you, Polliwog. There seems to be nothing of which you are afraid."

"Well," I interrupted, "I must admit, I do have one phobia. It's known as 'angoraphobia,' the fear of fuzzy sweater puppets."

Yung He began to giggle and covered her blushing face with her hand.

Ah Looey looked puzzled, then smiled. "Once again, Polliwog, perhaps more information than one requires."

"Just choking your chicken, Sensei," I responded with a hardy laugh.

"I wanted you to know, Polliwog, that for the time being, Yung He and I are safe and well, here in our secluded sanctuary. We wish you to feel welcome at any time. However, I must caution you to keep its location a secret, or this place will not provide future sanctuary for either of us."

"I appreciate your confidence in my abilities, Sensei. I only hope that I can live up to your expectations. I can only promise that I will do the best that I can to stop the tong onslaught and return peace to your people."

"That is all that we can ask, Polliwog. My people will be eternally grateful."

"Come, you and Yung He must go now. The tide has begun to rise," he said, shaking my hand. "Via con Dios, Polliwog," he said with a wide grin.

"Many miles of happy motoring," I said in jest reply, giving the old man a hug as we departed.

Yung He and I swam back through the crevasse the way we had come, pushing the now-empty basket and canoe ahead of us. There was only a foot or two of headroom to the overhang in most places along the route. A claustrophobic feeling began to creep over me. It was a reminder of a traumatic experience from my youth.

I grew up on the beaches of Southern California. The Santa Ana River jetty separated the yacht harbor in Long Beach from the city of Seal Beach where I lived. On a dare, my friends and I would swim into the intake tunnels under the huge brick steam-generated electric plant located on the banks of the river jetty. The dark labyrinth of tunnels eventually led to the cooling towers and then pumped back out into the river jetty as warm exhaust water. After the first turn, the remainder of the journey was in complete darkness. There was approximately two feet of breathing space between the surface of the water and the ceiling of the concrete tunnel.

On the last occasion that we gathered enough cojones to venture into the tunnels, we no sooner swam around the first corner into complete darkness than we heard a strange grinding noise and saw the daylight narrowing behind us. The gates to the intake tunnel were closing. We would be trapped inside with the water level rising to the ceiling, leaving us no room to breathe. We were going to drown. We panicked. There was complete hysteria. We frantically began swimming back to the tunnel entrance before it was too late. As we rounded the corner, the last glint of light disappeared as the gate reached the water's surface and continued down to close off the intake channel. We swam, panic-stricken, in total darkness, until we hit the moving gate. We inhaled what could be our last precious breath and clawed our way underwater to the bottom of the gate. At the last second, we squeezed ourselves under the gate just before it slammed shut on the tunnel floor. We thrust ourselves off the bottom and breached the surface gasping for air and scared shitless. We dragged ourselves onto the jetty boulders and laughed hysterically uncontrollably. I still have occasional nightmares about that. It still scares the hell out of me. We came that close to eating the big one, as we used to say. I've almost eaten the big one on several occasions since then. You'd think I'd get over it.

♦ ♦ ♦

We emerged from the cliff overhang into the open grotto, again accompanied by our Garibaldi escorts. As we climbed aboard the skipjack, the incoming tide had finally risen to the bottom of the cliff overhang, sealing the entrance to Ah Louie's secret sanctuary once again.

Captain Wally and Kamikaze emerged on the deck of the *Penny* with their freshly cleaned catch of the day and began cooking duties, as Yung He and I got ourselves cleaned up and ready for a fish fry. We all gathered on the deck of the *Penny* and enjoyed a scrumptious meal of broiled sea bass over a bed of brown rice, laden with Captain Wally's "'Fire Brigade" chili, and a glistening bottle of Pabst Blue Ribbon.

At 1800 hours the tide had risen to its highest point. Yung He and I climbed over the gunnels to the skipjack and attempted to contact her cousin Long over the ship-to-shore radio. After several unanswered calls, he finally responded.

They spoke in a singsong Mandarin dialect. We had our own version of "wind talkers." She scribbled furiously in Chinese characters as they spoke. After several minutes, the transmission ended with the familiar "out" at both ends.

Yung He began translating from her notes. "My cousin says he has spoken to friends that work in the hospital, and they say missy Rita is suffering from exposure, dehydration, and hypothermia. She has a concussion, but no fractures of the skull. She also has several cracked or bruised ribs. Her prognosis is good and the doctors expect her to fully recover with rest and later perhaps some physical therapy. Long also says that missy Rita's room is guarded at all times by employees of your security agency.

"Long says that Mrs. Lara Rigney is at Rita's bedside most of the time. Mrs. Rigney asks that you contact the mansion as soon as possible. She says that it is very urgent. She asks that we pass along a request from your office to contact them as well.

"Long says that the airport is crowded with aircraft from several federal agencies—ATF, FBI, and unmarked military aircraft as well. He says Smuggler's Cove and Dr. Con's compound are swarming with CIA military types, being shuttled back and forth aboard coast guard boats, to a fleet of suspicious fishing trawlers anchored out near the commercial shipping lanes.

"He says the rock quarry and the mines have shut down because the tong have forced the workers off the job sites. The tong have warned them to stay home and away from the quarry and the mines. The tong has done the same on the shipping docks. They have intimidated and accosted the longshoreman and stevedores and have placed thugs and henchmen at the gates to scare away any laborers attempting to go to their jobs. The teamsters have replaced them with something my cousin calls lesions or scars?" she said with a puzzled look.

"Scabs," I responded. "Scoundrels and thugs who forcibly replace the normal workforce by way of intimidation, threats, and brutality. Usually associated with 'strikebreakers' and union muscle. The teamsters are well versed and well rehearsed for just such a crude and brutish strong-arm takeover."

We took her notes and returned to the *Penny*, apparently just at teatime. In this particular case, however, tea and crumpets were replaced with cognac and cigars. Captain Wally had acquired a modicum of sophistication heretofore unimagined and seldom, if ever, displayed. (Makes you go hmmm?)

We sat and discussed a variety of options and scenarios regarding where we go from here. Eventually, the consensus dictated a delicate, prudent approach for the time being. We decided that Yung He would deliver me back to Avalon at high tide under the cover of darkness, while Captain Wally and Kamikaze cooled their heels here in our secluded lagoon for a day or two. While ashore, I would attempt to determine if the feds wanted to talk to Kamikaze regarding the whys, wherefores, and hows his PBY wound up skewered upon the remnants of Con's supergun, or perhaps what prompted Captain Wally to roll live depth charges over the side of his converted PT boat. I was to conduct a recon mission and report back at high tide. We toasted each other good night and good luck. (We were going to need it.)

A canopy of bright twinkling stars filled the night sky, and the pale moon reflected throughout the cove of shiny stones and calm, crystal clear water. Yung He and I pulled a small rubber raft on deck and flipped it bottom side up. For the next several exhilarating hours she introduced me to an ancient East Asian erotic massage therapy called Kama Sutra. It was one of the most intensely erogenous pleasures one could imagine. It involved a liberal amount of warm oil, intimate message techniques, and unbeknownst pressure points of passion and pleasure. To my surprise, it also involved a string of something called "benjou beads" inserted into heretofore uncharted virginal territory, then methodically extracted at the precise moment, creating an extended orgasm that could best be described as a string of beads. Or in my particular case . . . "rope knots."

Yung He and I lay content on the raft and stared into the endless space of twinkling stars and reflective moonstones. There were no reference points. There was no up or down. No east or west. It was as if you were within a three-dimensional plasma of cosmic lights. It was the hallucinogenic cosmic journey through time and space that Professor Timothy Leary would postulate upon to the emerging flower children, baby boom generation. A legion that would grow like hothouse mushrooms within the next decade. (far-out).

Chapter Thirteen

Three a.m. came quickly. I gazed across the expanse of the empty rubber raft. No Yung He. I wasn't surprised. I sensed a developing trend. I heard her on the bridge firing up the skipjack. She then climbed down and went forward to weigh anchor in preparation of our hasty high-tide departure.

The stars still glistened in the predawn blue black sky as I rolled off the raft, climbed over the stern onto the transom, and dived into the brisk dark water. I was attempting to wash the pungent aroma of organic bohemian love child from my skin.

I dressed, then stowed the rubber raft, untied from the *Penny*, and brought the fenders aboard. Yung He climbed the ladder to the bridge, and we slowly felt our way through the dark rocky maze. I went to the bow and scanned ahead with a flashlight for any submerged obstacles. Yung He manned the controls and gently maneuvered the twin screws as we quietly, cautiously meandered through the narrow inlet.

We eventually cleared the secluded inlet out to the open waters of Moonstone Cove. We made our way south along the shoreline in the darkness. No running lights. We listened for the crashing surf off our starboard side to navigate back to Avalon.

We came alongside the pier adjacent to the Tuna Club at the north end of town. After an extended goodbye, I jumped to the pier and waved as she disappeared into the misty darkness.

I made my way back to Mrs. O'Malley's Whispering Waters Inn by way of the now-familiar back alleys of Avalon. I climbed the stairs and entered my second-floor garage studio, shed my shriveled and waterlogged clothes, and showered as quickly as I could.

I heard Mrs. O'Malley waddle her way up the stairs. I wrapped a towel around my waist and listened for her soft knock on the door.

"It's me, son," she whispered through the door, with her sweet Irish brogue.

I opened the door and she entered carrying a laundry basket of fresh clothing that she set on the dining table. She gave me a short, surprisingly solid jab to the shoulder and then a big hug.

"I wore my rosary beads down to a fine dust with worry, you big Irish lunkhead," she whispered with genuine concern. "I hadn't seen or heard from you for days, and after all the commotion in Smuggler's Cove, I figured you'd be instigating it . . . ya hotheaded Mick. I'm happy as a drunken leprechaun that you're all right, son."

"Oh good lord!" she exclaimed, spying the soiled and soaked pile of discarded wardrobe. "Oh my, that salt water is going to get crusty and ruin that leather jacket and those boots," she said, holding the wad of wrinkled duds at arm's length. "I have a friend who makes saddles, bridles, and such. He knows all about preserving damaged goods. I'll see what he can do."

"Where's your weapon?" was the next question from the sweet cherub-faced granny.

I reached behind the bathroom door and retrieved my aging snubby and its salt-encrusted leather holster that now reeked of wet cow and sea brine.

"Oh, I see," she said, holding the bedraggled, waterlogged accoutrement with her fingertips. "Well, I'll see if I can clean this up," she said. "It's a good thing I brought this," she said, removing the folded clothes from the basket. There, in the bottom of the basket was a shiny like-new .45 auto in a fine leather shoulder holster along with six fully loaded clips and a box of a hundred rounds. Moms removed the weapon from the basket and handed it to me.

"I want you to have this, son. It was Mr. O'Malley's during the war. That's all that came back. That, and an American flag, a Purple Heart, and a letter of condolence from the president. I know Mr. O'Malley would want you to have it. You're a good man, Dugan. He'd be proud if you put it to good use."

She patted me on the cheek, then placed the wet clothes and my snubby into the basket and went to the door.

"You can use the phone in the main house to call the mansion and your secretary at your office. I know they're anxious to hear from you. I'll have fresh coffee waiting."

She closed the door behind her and waddled her way down the stairs and back across the courtyard to the main house.

I dressed in the clean dungarees and shirt that I had worn only a few days ago. I also found the two-tone Ricky Ricardo dungaree jacket and matching ball cap. The .45 strapped snuggly to my armpit was noticeably heavier than my snubby, but suitably comfortable.

The pale gray of dawn had begun its silent approach by the time I hustled down the stairs and across the courtyard to the main house. The aroma of freshly brewed coffee greeted me upon my arrival. Moms poured a piping hot cup, stirred in enough sugar to create syrup, and topped it off with a liberal dollop of Irish whisky. (Breakfast of champions. Olympian Bob Richards would be turning over in his Wheaties box about now.)

I brought the coffee to the phone in the hall and lit a Lucky Strike, my first of the day. I dialed the number to the mansion, took a few sips of my coffee, a couple of hits off my tobacco-filled paper cylinder, and waited for the connection. Eventually, Mabel, the island operator, stuck the two ends of cable into the corresponding beehive of slots in her switchboard and the phone at the mansion began to ring.

It was still too early in the morning for Spaulding to be anything but caustic, callous, and contrite. Anything resembling courteousness or the implication of compassion or caring would not occur until shortly after the cocktail hour. Fortunately for me, Consuela, the cook, answered the phone.

"Hola, buenos dias, hacienda de Rigney." After a few awkward moments of labored spanglish, she eventually "comprendoed" and put the phone down and went to retrieve Señora Rigney. Lara came to the phone slightly out of breath. She sounded both excited and relieved.

"Oh Travis, it's so good to hear from you. I was so worried. Are you all right?"

"I'm fine, Angel. How's Rita doing?"

"She's doing better day by day. She doesn't remember much, except perhaps a bizarre dinner buffet she believes that she attended with you, where Dr. Con was the host and demonstrated some kind of futuristic weapons. She's still very confused. She's not sure if it was real or a dream. It all sounded rather disjointed. She was rambling and rather convoluted. It didn't matter. What mattered was that Rita was home safe. Travis, I can never thank you enough. I have all the confidence in the world in you, but I worry that something will happen to you. I could never forgive myself for getting you involved in the first place. But now, I don't know what I would do without you. I'm so grateful, Travis. I'm so glad I have you to lean on . . . to depend on." She broke down and began to cry. I let her cry it out. She needed the release. I was hoping it would be cleansing, cathartic. I wished that I could be there to comfort her.

Finally, once she had regained control, I spoke calmly and matter-of-factly. "Angel, I promised you that I would bring Rita home safe. I fulfilled that promise and managed to put the 'kibosh' on Dr. Con and his merry band of mercenaries' plans to provide advanced weaponry to a bunch of ragheads, camel jockeys, and third-world revolutionaries. The feds should be on him like a pack of wild dogs.

"I also promised, from the very beginning, that I would get to the bottom of Johnny's disappearance. I'm going to keep that promise as well, Angel. And I pledge to you now that I'm going to get Nick Licata and his gang of Neanderthal, unibrowed, knuckle-dragging cronies off the island and return control of the casino to the Rigney family."

"Oh Travis, for God's sake, please be careful. I'm so frightened. I've never been frightened like this before."

"Angel, I'm counting on you to be strong. I know you can do it, and you know you can do it. You're a tough broad. You're my kinda dame. Kick-ass and take no prisoners. We've got this covered, Angel. Don't buckle on me now. We're in revenge mode, baby!"

(That was quite a halftime locker-room pep talk. I was not sure she bought it, but I was thoroughly convinced.)

She seemed to calm down appreciably and began to tell me about the security team's plan to move Rita back to the mansion. It was spreading the security personnel too thin. They wanted to get everyone in one location, under one roof. She also informed me that Tony Cornero had requested a meeting with the Commodore. (That couldn't be good.) I told her not to respond until I had a chance to talk to the Commodore myself. I asked if he was aware of the recent events. Lara said that after Rita had returned safe, she finally did sit down and tell the old man what was happening. She said he seemed concerned but not particularly surprised. She said the old man was anxious to talk to me as well. I told her that I would arrange a meeting as soon as I could. We said our goodbyes and hung up.

Moms came down the hall with the coffee pot and refilled my cup. I spun the dial for the island operator. Mabel answered with her familiar nasal "Operator." I gave her the number to my secretary trainee's home, as it was too early for her to be at the office. When Mabel recognized my voice, she sounded both excited and relieved. She couldn't wait to tell me how the lines had been buzzing with rumors about the strange lights and explosions in Smuggler's Cove. I just said, "Hmmm." I didn't add fuel to the fire.

After the obligatory series of buzzes and clicks, the phone began to ring. The cheery voice of Precocious Goodlay, my tall, blonde, and gorgeous secretary trainee and niece of Precious Goodlay, my equally as tall, blonde, and gorgeous secretary extraordinaire, answered. She also seemed relieved to hear from me and wasted no time informing me about the invasion of my office by a rude bunch of dubiously affiliated federal marauders.

The security team kept them at bay for a considerable period of time, with a lot of pushing, shoving, and yelling, but they eventually gained entry and began trashing the place.

During the melee she managed to call Inspector Lugar, LAPD, and within minutes he arrived on scene with a squad of uniforms and manhandled the intruders out with blunt baton persuasion and a lot of heated discussions regarding jurisdiction, search warrants, etc.

She said Lugar told her there had been a lot of buzz about the occurrences on the island and he figured that I was probably the instigator. He was also anxious to talk to me. I asked her to call Lugar and inform him that I was alive and instigating. "Ask him to keep his ear to the ground because the shit is about to hit the fan." We said our goodbyes and hung up.

I returned my cup to the kitchen where Moms was preparing breakfast. She asked if I was hungry. I explained that I was in a hurry to get to Sculley's and that I would grab a bite there. I needed Roscoe to drive me to the other side of the island to retrieve the old Plymouth.

She went to the service porch and returned with a fishing pole and a beaten and battered tackle box. She placed a pair of cheap sunglasses on my face, patted me on the poopoo, and sent me on my way.

"Good luck, son. Give 'em hell."

I pulled my cap down tight and whistled out the door and down the block. I looked like a green pea tourist on his way to the deepwater safari.

When I reached the corner, I turned south on Crescent Avenue heading for the boardwalk and Sculley's in the middle of town. I was taking a chance walking around in the open, but at this hour of the morning fishermen and municipal workers were the only people on the streets. I looked like all the rest of the anglers on their way to the charter boats. It was yellow tail season, and the town was full of fishing schmucks.

Roscoe's cab was parked at the curb in front on Sculley's when I arrived. I walked in the door and stowed my pole and tackle box by the coat rack. There was a small group of tourist fishermen at a table in the corner excitedly anticipating their upcoming deep-sea adventure. I went to the far end of the breakfast counter and sat next to Roscoe. It wasn't until I removed my cheap shades that someone recognized me. Naomi whizzed by with an armload of breakfast plates for the congregation in the corner and did a double take on her way by. Roscoe looked up from his newspaper and a bright wide smile slowly grew across his animated face. Without a word, he leaned over and gave me a big bear hug. He was genuinely glad to see me. The feeling was mutual.

Naomi rushed over and threw her arms around me from behind. She kissed me on the neck then whispered in my ear, "Oh Travis, I'm so relieved that you're all right. You had us scared half to death. We hadn't heard from you for days." She came around and sat next to me. She held my face in both of her hands and looked deep into my eyes. She was searching for any perceived apprehension, fear, or weakness. Peering deep within me for any sign of lost confidence or conviction. I just smiled. That drew a big smile from her, and she gave me a big kiss. She patted me on the chest and asked if she could cook up some breakfast. She jumped off the stool and headed for the kitchen.

I asked Roscoe if he could drive me over to the other side of the island. He looked at me, slightly puzzled. "You don't want to go over there, boss. Lots of federales. You're pressing your luck being here."

I explained to him that I didn't want to go to Smuggler's Cove, but up the hill across from China Point, to retrieve the Plymouth. He seemed somewhat relieved and reluctantly agreed.

Naomi returned with a "Captain's Mess" and a hot cup of java. A Captain's Mess consisted of scrambled eggs, potatoes, bell peppers, sausage, and onions, all fried together in a hot skillet. A spritz of Tabasco and you got yourself a gift that kept on giving all day long. She took both my hands in hers and turned them over to reveal the deeply etched wounds across my palms and fingers.

"What's with this?" she asked. "Do you have a skiff on the beach with a swordfish skeleton lashed to the side?"

Roscoe almost choked on his breakfast; Naomi and I burst out laughing. She went to retrieve some kind of sauce.

Roscoe and I finished our breakfast and sucked down the last drop of coffee when Naomi returned with a small piece of aloe vera plant and began rubbing the squeezed juices gently over my sore and scabbed hands. These were not the hands of an accountant. More like a hod carrier.

I kissed Naomi goodbye and joined Roscoe out front in his cab. I stowed the tackle box and pole in the backseat, making sure the pole stuck out the window, flying the colors of an official tourist. We pulled from the curb and went around the corner going up the hill toward the 'Airport in the Sky' above Avalon. I asked Roscoe if we could go the long way around to China Point by way of the shipping docks and the rock quarry. Again, I got a puzzled look from my skeptical compatriot, but he reluctantly complied and turned south toward the requested locations. Roscoe and I went back a long way. He'd learned to be skeptically apprehensive.

♦　♦　♦

As we rolled through town, now beginning to bustle with shopkeepers preparing for the day's tourist onslaught, I asked Roscoe if he had noticed any discernable change in the mood or atmosphere around town. He told me how the islanders began to get very anxious when the docks were shut down for several days because of the striking longshoremen. He explained how virtually everything on the island was shipped across the channel from the mainland. The slightest disruption in delivery and inventories on hand were depleted rapidly. The postage-stamp-sized airport at the top of the hill was too small to accommodate large airfreight transport, and as of late had been crowded with military and other small unmarked aircraft.

We drove by the seaplane tarmac that was now stacked with backed-up cargo waiting for ground transportation to its final destination. The shipping docks were bustling with teamster scabs off-loading the freighters that had been anchored offshore during the brief takeover by union thugs masquerading as strikebreaking saviors. The entries were guarded by beefy tong toadies, and they did not project a warm, welcoming demeanor.

While we continued past the shipping docks and up the hill toward the rock quarry, I briefly explained the actual behind-the-scenes circumstances surrounding the surreptitious takeover of the docks by the teamsters. They were not the strikebreaking saviors here to rescue the captive islanders from the ungrateful and uppity Cooley extortionists, as they would have you believe. But instead, they were the frontline thugs and henchmen in an insidious invasion that employed intimidation, implied threats, and blatant brutality to invade and occupy. The teamsters would take over the shipping docks and eventually all ground transportation, in cahoots, and with the condolences of the West Coast mob, who simultaneously planned to take over the casino operation and eliminate any influence by the Rigney family. "It's the big push."

We reached the top of the hill and the entrance to the rock quarry. Once again the gates were shut and guarded by a scruffy contingent of menacing tattooed tong toadies. The area was quiet; there was no mining occurring today.

I asked Roscoe if he had noticed anything different or out of the ordinary around the casino, as we crested the south end of the island and began the long descent down the narrow road toward Seal Cove. He pushed his cap back, shook his head, and stared forward. He was silent for a time.

"Ya know, boss," he finally began, "it seemed to happen so fast that I scarcely noticed until it was too late. I can't help but feel partly responsible 'cause I didn't snap sooner. I should have realized what was happening and warned somebody. It's not good, boss. I have a bad feeling about this."

He then began to tell me how the whole place had been overrun by a bunch of paunchy, knuckle-dragging pin-striped pompadours, which reeked of pomade and patchouli oil. The casino had been taken over by a bunch of wiseguys, and the atmosphere had changed from gay and festive to artificial, dark, and sinister. He went on to say that, for the time being, the "pachucos" in pinstripes had for the most part left the dining venue and Ms. Lara to themselves. There had been no overt interest in that area up to now, but he felt that it would be just a matter of time before they took control of that enterprise as well. He was genuinely afraid that the carefree, picturesque paradise he had grown to love was about to morph into something cancerous, corrupt, and hideous. I tried to reassure him with a paraphrased version of the halftime pep talk I gave Lara this morning. (I was not sure he bought it either, and I seemed slightly less convinced than before. Must have lost some enthusiasm in the presentation.)

At China Point we stopped and got out. We walked to the edge of the steep cliffs and peered down into Smuggler's Cove. It was a beehive of activity on the beach and a continuous shuttle of shore boats to and from the suspicious-looking trawlers anchored out near the commercial shipping lanes. The coast guard had the cove and immediate area blockaded against all unwanted curiosity seekers. To my surprise, the Global Explorer had taken up station and anchored just outside the cove, to the southwest toward San Clemente Island.

I gave Roscoe a brief synopsis of the recent occurrences in Smuggler's Cove as we walked back to the cab and continued down the dirt-rut road to Raven's. I told him of my concerns regarding Blaine Pond and Claire Voyent's apparent kidnapping and disappearance aboard Con's Raptor megacraft. I asked if he had seen Sir Arthur or his monolithic sidekick Phangs Pa. I received a negative response. Not hide nor hair of either in several days.

We pulled into the cypress grove and stopped next to the old gray Plymouth resting in sweet repose right where I left her. I paid double what was on the meter and thanked Roscoe for the ride and the info. I removed my fishing props and waved goodbye as he returned down the road the way we had come.

I removed the right rear hub cab and retrieved the keys. I opened the door and stowed the pole and tackle box inside. I walked through the cypress grove to Raven's cabin. Dakota was back in the corral, but the gate was open, so that he could come and go as he pleased. I walked past the hot springs grotto and up to the cabin porch. I entered the cabin and took a quick look around. Someone had been here since I was here last, but didn't appear to stay very long. No hot coals in the fireplace.

No perishable foods in the kitchen area. No trash. Whoever was here, it appeared as though it was merely a pit stop. I was beginning to become quite concerned. There was no sign of Raven, and she hadn't been here for some time. It made me wonder before; now I was worried.

I went back to the car and pushed the starter on the floorboard. She fired up on the first push, and we were moving down the road at a brisk pace. Destination, Avalon Municipal Hospital.

Chapter Fourteen

I arrived at the hospital before noon. I drove around the area to see if all was secure. I recognized the security teams in several cars strategically located throughout the area. They weren't hard to recognize. It was the Samoan contingent. Huge burly hulks specializing in personal security. They looked mean, and when escorting their client on foot, they would surround their client within an imposing and impenetrable gauntlet, making them virtually invisible behind the human shield of menacing Samoan muscle. They were calm, quick, and brutal. They were quietly efficient and suitably intimidating for the job.

I parked in the back of the hospital parking lot and watched as several attendants brought someone on a gurney out of the emergency room doors and loaded them into a waiting ambulance. The ambulance pulled away and out of the hospital grounds, following one security car and being followed by another. I continued to watch from my vantage point as a Brink's armored truck drove up close to the emergency room entrance and again someone on a gurney was loaded into the armored truck. The Brink's truck pulled away from the building and drove around the parking lot to where I waited. I got out of the car and into the Brink's truck as it pulled alongside.

Rita smiled brightly and held out her arms to me. I knelt down and held her for a good while.

"I love you, Travis," she whispered softly.

"I love you too, baby," I whispered back. "Let's get you home."

"Welcome aboard, boss," came the familiar happy voice of Makato Mouusitopo . . . Kato. He and his massive brother took up most of the remaining space within the back of the armored truck. Equally massive cousins drove and rode shotgun up front.

We arrived at the front gates of the estate. After a brief discussion and quick look inside, we continued up the drive to the mansion. The front doors were open, and the Commodore's private doctor and nurse were already waiting at the curb. The armored truck pulled to a stop and the four Samoans calmly removed Rita's gurney and gently carried her up the steps and into the foyer surrounded by a phalanx of Samoan bodyguards.

When I entered the foyer, Lara was whispering softly to Rita and holding her hand as the contingent of escorts wheeled her across the highly polished marble floors to the foot of the stairs that led up to Rita's room. As the entourage began to ascend the now-crowded stairwell, Lara turned to me and rushed to throw her arms around my neck and kiss me long and hard. She had tears of relief and joy streaming down her smooth peach-hued cheeks.

"Oh Travis, I can never thank you enough," she softly cried. "I would be lost without you. I love you so much, Travis." I held her close and we gently meld to one another, just as we had the first night we met on the glittering dance floor of the casino's mystical ballroom. It was an enchanting evening.

I don't know what possessed me. Perhaps I was an impulsive hopeless romantic. (I recall Lara describing me as a "hapless" romantic somewhere in our sexual innuendoes past.) I carried her in my arms out to the terrace that overlooked Avalon and the pale azure harbor below. I continued to hold her in my arms and then I kissed her with burning passion and insatiable primal hunger. I slowly lowered her to her feet. Her smooth silken robe gently slid aside, willingly exposing pristine, wanting breasts. I softly kissed her nipples and gently explored the moist warmth of her silken thighs. We held each other close and gazed into each other's eyes for some time. We gave each other soft, intimate kisses. It was a magical moment in our lives that I was sure we both shall always fondly cherish. An insatiable thirst yet to be quenched. A sexual desire yet to be satisfied. (As I thought the first time I saw her, she was a thoroughbred of unimaginable grace and beauty . . . and way out of my league.)

We strolled together to the terrace railing overlooking the vast Pacific Ocean before us, giving me the opportunity to calm my growing enthusiasm and remove the lipstick from my kisser, and Lara the opportunity to close her robe and reapply luster to sumptuous pouty lips.

"Good morning," came the familiar and uncharacteristically strong greeting from Commodore Rigney. Spaulding wheeled him onto the terrace and over to the umbrella-covered table at the far end of the richly flowered hillside veranda, from where he gazed down upon his fiefdom paradise below that stretched to the horizon. The old man seemed in surprisingly good spirits. He was relaxed, sprightly, and anxious to talk to me. He looked relieved and genuinely happy to see me. The feeling was mutual.

Lara and I walked arm in arm across the veranda to the Commodore's table. Lara leaned in and kissed him on the cheek.

"You boys will excuse me while I check on Rita and then get dressed," she said with a smile and lilt in her voice. She fluttered back across the terrace and disappeared into the house.

"Please have a seat, Travis," the old man said, motioning to the chair across the table. He looked at me earnestly and smiled.

"I can't tell you how happy I am to see you again, son. And it is abundantly apparent that a huge weight has been lifted from Lara's shoulders as well. I haven't seen her this happy in quite some time. I thank you for that, my friend. I sincerely do."

Spaulding appeared on the terrace with a silver serving tray laden with the customary teatime hors d'oeuvres of tea, brandy, and cigars. I courteously passed on the tea and cigar, but accepted a liberal dollop of brandy with aplomb. I swished and swirled appropriately then threw her back. The old man watched me skeptically, while he enjoyed his spiked tea and sniffed the cigar smoke rising from the ashtray; he wasn't supposed to smoke them, but he could still enjoy the aroma of a fine Havana cigar. He too seemed to be searching internally for my present state of mind. The status of my stoic resolve. The steadfastness of my spine, my intestinal fortitude, and the load-bearing strength of my cold, calculating nerves of steel. I just smiled. It seemed to satisfy his curiosity. He smiled broadly and drew his index finger alongside his nose then pointed to me. The secret sign in recognition of "the sting."

Spaulding returned with the second course. A thin chicken broth and finger-food sandwiches. We ate in silence for a time, until the old man had his fill. He pushed his plate to the side, wiped his mouth with his linen napkin, and leaned forward to speak in matter-of-fact terms. The Commodore had his game face on.

"First of all, Travis," he began, "I have a pretty good grasp of the current situation. It's not my first trip around the block. I've had individuals attempt to intimidate and extort their way into my enterprises in the past. Furthermore, I believe that Johnny's disappearance was but the opening salvo of this particular gambit. It is my firm belief that they tried to subtly muscle their way in on Johnny, and he paid the ultimate price for his resistance. Johnny was not the type to roll over for anybody, and neither am I."

"This is the big push, Travis. We are in the midst of the final assault by the sadistic forces of darkness and evil. I shall ask no quarter, and I shall give none. I feel compelled to exact my ounce of vengeance, or by god I'll die trying. The future of this family and the entire island rests upon our success in repelling this invasion. We have nowhere to turn for help. We're in this alone. We're counting on you, Travis. You're the only guy I know that possesses the compassion to help, and the cojones and capabilities required to take on the mob. You're rough and tough and you got guts, son. Thank God 'cause you're going to need them." (Wasn't the most inspirational pep talk I've heard. Certainly didn't have the uplifting qualities that my particular version brought forth; however, he did impress me with his newfound spirit and vigor.)

This was going to be vicious, brutal, and ugly. And they got the right man for the job. I had a lot of pent-up vengeful aggression inside, just itching to burst forth and rip somebody to shreds. I wanted to rampage and kill. I wanted to be vicious, nasty, and crazed. It wouldn't be pretty. I seemed to thrive under these circumstances. There was no use denying the fact that I was an adrenaline junkie. I lived for the hunt. The thrill of the kill.

Dessert arrived, and with it came a candid discussion regarding the requested meeting between Nick Licata's representative and island underboss Tony Cornero and the Commodore. The old man felt strongly that a meeting should indeed be arranged to see what they had to say, if for no other reason than to try and determine what their modus operandi might be. Or what leverage they thought they possessed. Perhaps gain some insight as to their plan of attack. At any rate, he wanted to meet face-to-face with them and make it perfectly clear that there would be no deal, or percentage, or takeover. He was not going to roll over for anybody. The old man was stoked and ready to rumble. I was impressed with the newfound spunk of the crusty old fart. I recognized flashes of his former corporate dominance. It was apparent that in his prime, RJ Rigney would have been a cunning, resourceful "tour de force" to be reckoned with and respected.

I assured the old man that I would make the necessary arrangements for the meeting and keep him informed as best as I could. We shook hands and wished each other good luck. I excused myself and went to check in with Kato and the security team. It was the opening night of a three-night engagement starring "scat king" Louis Prima and featuring the stunning, dark, and beautiful Keely Smith. Lara, of course, insisted that she be "the hostess with the mostess," regardless of the perceived danger around the casino. She managed the dining and entertainment venue of the casino ballroom with confidence and dignity. She took her responsibilities seriously, and she wasn't about to leave such important events to a loyal staff. Kato and an entourage of big, beefy, well-quaffed, supersumo-sized Samoans would escort her to and from and keep a close eye on her and her surroundings while at the casino. Lara would be safe within her security cocoon.

The casino was abuzz with excitement. Searchlights crisscrossed the clear night sky, and the entrance to the elaborately decorated ballroom was packed with industry celebrities and Hollywood heavyweights. The Louis Prima and Keely Smith engagement drew the top-drawer entertainment personalities and, of course, the high-rolling, pin-striped Pisans and their bejeweled and bubbleheaded entourage of cheap bleach-blonde bimbos. The crowd was excited, dressed to the nines, and eagerly anticipating a rousing and raucous night of uproarious entertainment. I had no problem melding into the haute couture–coiffed crowd of swell-smelling highbrows. I was elegantly attired in my Bill Blass white dinner jacket and patent leather Florsheims.

I casually meandered through the gathered masses and eventually worked my way to the large glass windows through which I was able to see Lara and her contingent of Samoan escorts. She fluttered about from one table to another, like a social butterfly. She appeared to be having a wonderful time and looked spectacular in shimmering gold lamé.

All seemed under control in the ballroom, so I ascended the outside ramp to the promenade, overlooking the festive harbor, and the rear entrance to the casino. I leaned on the rail and lit a cigarette. From my darkened vantage point outside the gaming room I could observe all the various high-stakes wagering venues being enjoyed within the immense gaming lounge, adjacent fully staffed bar, and small bandstand and dance floor. I could also spot the wiseguy gunzels that mingled about not being unobtrusive. They had an unofficial costume apparently created by a B movie Hollywood wardrobe designer with a miniscule budget. They all wore dark suits and shirts with the obligatory white tie and spats. Overstuffed greaseballs in cheap suits, bawdy jewelry, slicked-back fenders to hair-sprayed ducktails, and Elvis Presley sideburns. (What a bunch of George Raft wannabe matinee goobers.) I also spotted Tony Cornero overseeing his ill-gotten, newly acquired enterprise from the comfort of his bar stool at the far end of the bar, near the front entrance and stair landing from the ballroom downstairs.

I waited patiently until Tony was briefly distracted by the arrival of several members of "the rat pack" as they were called among the industry insiders, then moved quickly to enter the casino and take the last stool at the bar opposite Cornero, and next to the elevator alcove and kitchen entry. The bartender arrived; I ordered a vodka martini, shaken, not stirred. (Very suave, ay?)

I sat and observed another round of canister changes from each table in the immense gambling venue, through the reflection in the huge mirror of the elaborate back bar. I also noticed that Tony Cornero had spotted me and seemed rather surprised. I watched as he arrived at Nick Licata's table to deliver the news. There was a brief discussion, which ended with Cornero shaking his head and shrugging his shoulders.

My martini arrived as the canister cart passed behind me on the way to the elevator and down to the counting room vault. I casually turned to observe the procession when I was momentarily startled to see that a stunningly beautiful and exotically sensual petite young Polynesian girl had suddenly appeared standing next to me.

"I am very sorry to have startled you, Travis," she said softly. "I was instructed to deliver these keys. Your automobile is in the parking lot." She handed me the keys to the Plymouth that I left at the hospital. I looked deep into her gorgeous dark brown eyes that sparkled beneath the longest lashes I had ever seen. She looked very familiar, from a long time ago it seemed.

"You don't remember me, do you, Travis?" she asked, looking slightly hurt. She stood shyly in front of me. She had long silky black hair that cascaded to smooth, dark, and toned shoulders and arms. She wore a slinky black silk slip dress and slingback opened-toed pumps. Her legs were tanned, toned, and seemed to go on forever. She had a stunning firm young butt and a spectacular set of proud and perky sweater puppies. (You'd sure as hell think that I would remember this gorgeous innocent young beauty. I was rampaging through my memory banks attempting to come up with a name. It was at the tip of my tongue, so to speak.)

"I'm Fia," she finally said, disgusted with my feeble cerebral masturbation. "I'm Kato's niece."

I finally snapped. "Fia, yes, I remember. You were just a cute little girl the last time I saw you, and now you've grown into a beautiful young woman. I've got to say, girl, you really clean up nice. You look spectacular, Fia. What are you doing here?" I asked.

"I was your decoy on the gurney for the ambulance ride from the hospital to the mansion. I am a member of the security team now. I am Mrs. Rigney's escort to places where the boys can't go."

"You seem so sweet and demure," I said with a twinkle in my eye.

"Looks can be deceiving, Travis. You should know not to judge a book by its cover, or it may come back to bite you in the ass," she said with a wicked little twinkle in her eye as well.

"I must go now," she said. "I should get back downstairs to the ballroom. Will I see you later?" she asked.

"I certainly hope so, Fia. I look forward to it," I responded. She leaned forward and kissed me softly on the lips, then turned and strutted out the glass doors onto the promenade and disappeared into the darkness. (Whew, what a pleasant surprise. And a surprisingly pleasant departure as well.)

My enchanting visual was rudely interrupted by the dark suit and white tie of Tony Cornero sliding into the space previously occupied by the young Polynesian apparition. The pressure of the cold steel in my back announced the arrival of Tony's hired muscle to our uncomfortably intimate newfound relationship.

"You've either got to have the biggest balls on the island, or you've got to be the dumbest bastard I've ever seen. Which is it, Dugan?" asked Cornero, with a condescending smirk and a look of feigned bewilderment on his face.

"Well, I definitely have the biggest balls, no doubt about it, I'm the fly-eyes champ," I responded with an equally condescending smirk. "But you don't have to call me Champ, you can call me Ilene."

Cornero looked at me, puzzled. "Ilene?" he asked.

"Yea," I responded. "I lean over like this, and you kiss my ass."

Tony's puzzled expression immediately turned to one of anger. His ears glowed red and his eyes bugged out. I got a quick jab in the back with the gun muzzle.

"However, this meathead, with the ass-breath behind me, is probably the dumbest bastard in the place," I continued to instigate. "He obviously doesn't realize that my hand is firmly grasping a big nasty .45 under my arm that is pointed right at his quickly shriveling nuts, and that one twitch from him and I'll blow his balls into tomorrow."

I looked back over my shoulder to the hulking gunzel holding the gun to my back, then looked back to Cornero.

"He's the ugliest motherfucker I ever saw too," I said with a wide, shit-eating grin. I heard the hammer click back into firing position on his piece. I clicked back the hammer on my .45. We stood there smiling at one another for a few uneasy brief moments . . . Mexican standoff.

"There you are, Dugan. I've been looking all over for you," came the comforting and familiar voice suddenly seated next to me. I turned and was pleasantly surprised, and especially relieved, to lay eyes on my old friend Inspector Lugar, LAPD. He leaned forward across the bar, allowing his coat to fall open, exposing the bright, shiny badge hooked to his inside coat pocket and the imposing Smith & Wesson .38 Police Special snugged into his holster. I felt the pressure in my back instantly disappear. I made polite introductions and casually mentioned the meeting Cornero had requested with the Commodore was scheduled for noon tomorrow. Cornero and his hired beef shank politely excused themselves and evaporated into the background posthaste.

I uncocked the hammer on my .45 and released my grasp. I shook hands with the good inspector; I was genuinely glad to see him.

"Boy, am I glad to see you," I said with a sigh.

"Wasn't that Anthony Cornero, former commander of the gambling flotilla anchored off Santa Monica?" he asked.

"Yep, that's him all right. Now he's trying to muscle his way into the Rigneys' casino operation with backing and auspices of Nick Licata and the LA mob," I responded.

Lugar just smiled knowingly and shook his head. "There's a lot of buzz over the airwaves regarding the conflagration in Smuggler's Cove, and when the feds tried to ransack your office, I knew you'd be in the middle of it. I just knew you probably stepped on your dick again," he said with a laugh. "I figured I'd take a few days off and make an unofficial visit to your lovely island paradise and see what kind of a mess you'd gotten yourself into this time. And then your buddy Steve Canyon delivers an evidence bag full of bloody clothes for crime lab analysis, I knew you were in trouble. The evidence was contaminated with fish chum, by the way. We sent it off to the FBI to see if they could extract any useful information from it. So far it's inconclusive."

At that moment I noticed Constable Lafargé in his finest regalia, along with a small contingent of gendarmes enter the casino. I motioned to Lugar and we made a hasty retreat out of the casino and onto the darkened promenade. We walked down the outside ramp to the ground-level front entrance to the ballroom. There was still an ebullient throng of onlookers lingering around the brightly lit entrance along with a squad car of vigilante gendarmes loitering about. We turned and walked around the back into the darkness and through the rear doors of the darkened ballroom. Louie and his gorgeous costar, Keely Smith, shimmering in white satin and in dramatic and arousing contrast to her stunning dark features, were zat-scatting their way back and forth across the stage bathed in bright hot spotlight. The band was rockin' and everyone in the audiences was thoroughly engrossed in this evening's entertainment extravaganza. The room was packed and everyone was having a wonderful time. Lara was no doubt glowing with pride in the success of the opening night turnout.

Lugar and I found a couple of unoccupied stools in the dark at the end of the bar. The bartender eventually realized the new arrivals and hustled down to our end of the bar. I ordered a vodka martini, agitated, not propelled. Lugar ordered bourbon and branch water. We sat in the darkness enjoying our refreshments and the rousing show onstage for a short while before Lara spotted us and appeared suddenly from the darkened crowd. She smiled widely and threw her arms around me.

"Oh Travis, I'm so happy you're here!" she exclaimed into my ear, over the sound of the band. "Stick around, I'll buy you dinner." She exuberantly kissed me quickly on the lips several times, then fluttered off into the darkness as magically as she had arrived, followed up closely by her unobtrusive security cocoon.

Lugar just smiled, shook his head, and took a short sip of his drink. "I don't get it. I don't get how a knuckled-up, womanizing dog like you always manages to score the finest, most gorgeous, out-of-your-league, classy, beautiful babes in the world. Some guys have all the luck," he whined, leaning heavily on the bar.

"Well, Lugar, as my uncle Leo used to say, the world is full of uncertainty. Some guys got it and some guys don't. What can I say? Chicks dig bad boys."

The pianist tickled the ivories a few notes into the familiar tune and the crowd responded enthusiastically as Louis and Keely began to weave that "old black magic spell of love." We finished our drinks and exited the way we had come, before the end of the set and the inevitable encore. Once out on the promenade, we turned left, around the dark side of the building and past the mezzanine entrance where I had intercepted the two dickwads with the aluminum attaché only a few nights prior. We found the Plymouth in the parking lot and drove down Casino Way to Crescent and parked near the Blue Parrot. We climbed the stairs and entered the dimly lit, relatively subdued, rapscallion watering hole and found a quiet booth in the back with a view of the bustling boardwalk below.

We settled into the comfortable, well-worn leather as our cute little pirate waitress arrived. She gave us menus and took our drink order— ditto on the earlier casino bar order. We perused the variety of exotic seafood entrées and decided on the obviously pedestrian New York steak and eight-ounce lobster tail. Medium rare, baked with sour cream and chives. The petite buccaneer arrived sprightly with our drinks, efficiently transcribed our food order, and was away with a flirtatious "Ahoy, mateys!"

Once we had enjoyed a few sips of our refreshments and observed an appropriate pause for reflection, I quickly spewed forth all the events that had occurred since my arrival. I was like a desperate car salesman on the last day of a losing month. I had a lot to say and a short time to get there. He sat quietly, sipping his B&B, occasionally nodding his head, rolling his eyes, or raising a brow.

Our bubbly, vivacious little swashbuckler returned with a big tray and a stand on which to set it. She disseminated the steaming hot contents from the tray, tied a big bib on each of us, and was off once again. There was very little discussion for some time. We were ravenous and it was obvious.

When it was over, nothing remained but hollowed-out exoskeletons. Another round of drinks arrived, and we settled into our warm leather pouches and observed the hustle and bustle of the boardwalk below and the festive harbor beyond.

Lugar took a long pull from his drink, then fished around and found a crinkled pack of Chesterfield Kings in his coat pocket and offered me one. He clicked open his service lighter with a flick of the wrist and lit both. He took a satisfying drag and exhaled the smoke up into the swirling bamboo fan overhead.

"Dugan, I'd like to help, but there's only so much I can do. We're beyond the three-mile territorial limit and far beyond my jurisdiction. I have no official powers out here. All I can do is utilize my contacts through my office at city hall to collect information normally unavailable to you. I can get on the horn and try to get a line on Con and his yacht. I can see if anyone has picked up Sir Arthur and his Chinese sidekick, and I can put out my feelers regarding Nick Licata and Tony Cornero's plans. I'll be your backup as long as I'm here, and if you need a wingman anytime, just call. I'll do what I can, Dugan. But my powers are limited, and the knuckle draggers know it. I can make life in LA a bitch for them, but I can only push so far."

"I know, Lugar, and I appreciate everything you're doing," I responded. "You've always been a square guy, a straight shooter, and guys in my profession don't receive a lotta respect from you boys with the badges. You've always helped in the past if you were able, and I need your help now.

"What I need to find out right now is how hot are Captain Wally and Steve Canyon. I need to know if the feds are on the lookout for them. If you could pull some strings through the coast guard, perhaps we could determine just how much trouble or danger they are in. They're in limbo right now, but we need to determine their status. If there's any way possible, Lugar, I sure would like to find out if anyone is looking for Blaine Pond or Claire Voyent also."

We paid our tab and left a generous gratuity for our exuberant and vivacious buccaneer. We descended the stairs and found our way back to the car. I dropped Lugar at the Hotel Catalina on Whitley at the bottom of the hill on the way up to my second-floor walk-up at Mom's. I drove around the block several times looking for suspicious cars, loiterers, or tails. I made abrupt course changes through alleyways and impromptu U-turns. Having satisfied my instinctive paranoia, I pulled up to the garage, got out, and opened the door. I got back in and pulled the car into the garage, turned off the headlights, and shut off the car.

Suddenly, out of the darkness came a quick reflection in the rearview mirror as he came up from the backseat and swung a piano wire over my head and around my neck. Before he could yank it tight, I managed to get my right hand up and prevent the wire from slicing into my neck. The wire cut into my fingers as we struggled. I couldn't reach my gun with my left hand and the punches I threw backward over my head were having no effect. My head was being slowly dragged over the back of the seat. He was pulling with all his might and was going to snap my neck if I didn't do something. I placed both feet on the dash and pushed off as hard as I could, somersaulting backward into the rear seat. He rolled with me and held his death grip on the wire. We struggled furiously within the confines of the rear seat until I grabbed the door handle and we tumbled out onto the garage floor. We wrestled around the floor between the car and the garage wall. I struggled to my feet and attempted to throw him over my shoulder and slam him to the ground. We stumbled out of the garage and fell hard to the driveway. With the wire shredding my fingers and ripping into my neck, I reached deep within, struggled to my feet once again, and with him gripped tightly on my back, I leaped up and fell backward on the picket fence lining the drive. It was an ugly sound, like the splintering of a tree branch under the weight of a heavy snowfall. The tension on the wire eased, and I quickly yanked my head out from his grip. I stepped back and pulled my gun. He lay impaled on the fence. Horizontally crucified, arms outstretched, mouth open wide in grotesque silent scream, dull eyes staring wide from a lifeless mask of disbelief. He convulsed, as if to raise himself off the fence, then slowly went limp. I crumpled to the ground gasping for air.

Eventually, I regained by breath and my composure. I got up and walked over to the limp corpse impaled on the fence. I got my penlight and shined it on the grotesque death mask staring dull and lifeless into the night sky. (*I'll be damned,* I said to myself.) It was Frankie Carbo, another imported East Coast mob executioner.

I opened the trunk of the Plymouth, found an old tarp in the garage, and spread it in the trunk. I went back to Carbo and with some difficulty lifted him off the fence. I threw the dead weight over my shoulder and carried him over and dumped him into the trunk. I rolled him over and pried several broken fence pickets out of him that were imbedded deep into his back. I went through his pockets and, as before, came up with a couple hundred in cash, a motel key, and a .38 affixed with a long screw-on silencer. I was lucky that Frankie was a psycho and liked to get up close and personal with his intended victims; otherwise he could have blasted my brains all over the interior of the car. He was a sick puppy that just got euthanized.

I drove to the Descanso Beach Hotel parking lot and cruised around with the lights off until I found the sedan that I had stowed away on for the trip from the casino to the hotel a few nights ago. I jimmied the lock on the sedan and popped open the trunk. I retrieved Carbo's lifeless corpse from the Plymouth and dumped him into the sedan trunk and closed it. I drove a few blocks to the nearest set of phone booths and called the cops. I told them that I had just witnessed somebody put a body in the trunk of a sedan in the hotel parking lot. I gave them the license number and hung up the phone. I returned to Mom's, parked in the garage, and climbed the stairs to my apartment and watched through the window as several squad cars arrived at the hotel parking lot. Several minutes later, lights began to come on throughout the hotel and the parking lot was bustling with cops and bathed in red and blue flashing lights. That should put a kink in Cornero's "get along."

Chapter Fifteen

Cornero's sedan arrived at the front gates of the estate a few minutes after noon. He and one consigliere were allowed through the gates and then thoroughly searched. The sedan and its remaining occupants were directed down the drive back to the entrance to wait with the squad car Lafargé had posted several days ago. Cornero and his counselor were loaded into the security car blocking the entrance behind the gates and driven up to the mansion.

They seemed surprised to be greeted at the door by Inspector Lugar, LAPD, who proceeded to have them reluctantly assume the position and once again submit to a thorough body search. Once Lugar was satisfied that our unwelcome guests were without weapons, annoyingly humbled, and sufficiently humiliated, he escorted them across the goddess Pomona's mosaic-tile foyer and out onto the terrace.

I met Cornero and his associate at the entrance to the terrace, and once again, Tony Cornero was obviously surprised to see me. His highly paid imported East Coast assassins were having a tough time out here in paradise. Crazy Joe Gallo disappeared off the face of the earth, and now the infamous Frankie Carbo turned up in the trunk of a car registered to Cornero's brother Louis. Coincidentally, Louis, as I recall, was the stout little guinea that I witnessed Nicky Fallon toss out of his office onto the sidewalk during my first sojourn to the island. According to Lugar, Louis and his driver were presently in the custody of Constable Lafargé, attempting to explain how Frankie Carbo's corpse happened to wind up in the trunk of his car.

I escorted the two well-dressed wiseguys over to where Commodore Rigney waited, stoic and commanding. They introduced themselves, the consigliere being Stefano Parola, and shook hands with the Commodore, who motioned for them to take a seat. Spaulding arrived abruptly with coffee, brandy, and small biscuits or crumpets, then just as abruptly departed.

"Gentlemen, and I use the term liberally," began the Commodore, "I suggest we dispense with the customary courtesies and gratuitous indulgences and get to the reason for your request of this meeting."

The old man seemed to have acquired a newfound gusto. He was alert and had a steely glint in his eye. His voice had dominating strength, intimidating and commanding tone, and an aura or persona of an ironfisted "godfather." He demanded respect, and I for one was very much inclined to give it to him. I was surprisingly impressed. The old man was on his game and bristling for the fray.

"Mr. Rigney," Cornero began, "the purpose of this meeting is to discuss a business proposition." He began to unroll the set of blueprints that he brought. He stood and stretched the plans across the table in front of the Commodore. He used the brandy carafe and the pot of coffee to hold down the edges. The title page read "Hamilton Cove Casino Resort and Spa."

As he flipped through the pages of the blueprints, he delivered a well-rehearsed sales presentation describing the details of each phase of the project in glowing, wonderful terms befitting a snake oil huckster or a seminar flimflam man offering the "inside deal of a lifetime" on Florida swampland.

The plans represented an elaborate and ostentatious casino on the beach and terraced condominiums (whatever those are) rising like an immense pyramid against the crescent-shaped hillside behind. The tentative grading plans and the exterior elevations as represented on the blueprints were what I saw generally depicted by the surveyor's stakes in Hamilton Cove only a few days ago.

The Commodore sat quietly studying the plans as Cornero concluded his presentation. He poured himself a brandy and one for each of his guests. He sipped his brandy and gazed over Avalon harbor below.

"What resources have you available to finance such an elaborate project?" the old man finally asked.

"We have an unlimited line of credit approved through the Teamsters Union Pension Fund," Cornero responded confidently.

"I see," the old man said. "The same source of financing utilized to build Vegas. Let's hope you don't suffer a similar fate as your predecessor Mr. Siegel, the ramrod who ran roughshod on that calamity of errors."

The old man stared deep into Cornero's eyes. The old man's steely glint was like a laser beam into your soul. He studied Cornero for a flinch, a twitch, a telltale bead of sweat, the slightest change of hue or palpitation of breath. It was a rhetorical question, and Cornero chose not to respond. He remained composed. He didn't allow the old man's subtle jabs to rattle him. He was a cool customer.

"Well then, Mr. Cornero, that brings us to the sixty-four-thousand-dollar question, doesn't it? The eight-hundred-pound gorilla in the room would like to know, what's in it for me, Mr. Cornero?"

♦ ♦ ♦

The clean-cut young rookie consigliere, who had been "on deck" until now, straightened his tie, cleared his throat, knocked the clay from his cleats with his bat, spat a wad of chew, pulled at his groin, and stepped up to the plate. Stefano Parola was a tall, lanky kid of about twenty-five, who no doubt made his mother proud.

He removed a neatly folded stack of paper from his inside coat pocket. (He was not allowed to bring his very impressive leather attaché with the combo locks and gold-plated appointments. No doubt his cum laude graduation present.)

"Mr. Rigney," he began, while placing a pair of black horn-rimmed glasses on his nose, "we are prepared to pay the current appraised value of aforementioned property, as well as a very generous percentage of the revenues generated upon the completion of the entire project. Furthermore, once the project is up and operational, we envision a tremendous opportunity for continuous employment for a major portion of the island's indigenous population. We anticipate approximately eighteen months for general construction of the casino itself, with an additional six to eight months for interior decoration and gaming venue installation—slots, roulette, etc.

"The second phase of the project would begin immediately upon the grand opening and operational revenue generation of the first. The rather intense terraced grading of the steep hillside behind the casino will take approximately six to eight months to complete, with an additional eighteen months to construct the Mediterranean-inspired oceanfront villas."

At this point the novice young orator took a moment to catch his breath and a sip of brandy to wet his whistle and steady his nerves. Cornero studied the Commodore for reaction. The old man simply glanced briefly in my direction, then back to the articulate Ivy League counselor, who seemed prepared to continue.

"Phase 3," he began, "will commence upon the completion and initial occupancy of phase 2. Phase 3 encompasses the championship tennis courts, Olympic-size heated pool, a conference center, and luxurious day spa. We envision an eighteen-hole championship golf course in the future, with the acquisition of adjacent parcels."

The young man seemed very impressed with the scope of the project and equally impressed with his presentation thus far. He looked across the table to the Commodore for some sense of acknowledgement or adulation, perhaps an attaboy. The Commodore simply glanced nonchalantly in my direction, then briefly to Cornero, and back to the kid. The old man casually kibitzed, futzing with the reignition of his aromatic cigar, a snippet of crumpet, and a smidgen of brandy. (He was a pretty cool sumbitch himself.)

"With all due respect, Mr. Rigney," the brash young barrister continued, "you must of course recognize the enormous possibilities for future revenue a project this vast can create. A project of this scope will attract the most prominent individuals from throughout the civilized world. Hamilton Cove will transform Avalon into the Monte Carlo of the Pacific. Santa Catalina will rival the finest, most elegant locals anywhere in the world."

"First of all, Mr. Parola," the Commodore began, "your vast and expansive plans rely on an enormous amount of erroneous assumptions. The least of which is the fact that one cannot purchase land outright on Catalina. There are of course long-term lease options and arrangements that may be negotiated, but typical land purchase in the traditional sense is not possible. Your second problem will no doubt be trying to fly your set of blueprints by the Avalon Planning and Building Department, which, by the way, hasn't granted a new building permit in quite some time. Their interests lie in preservation, rather than new construction. The Catalina Conservation Committee will not be receptive to your exotic and ecologically disruptive tentative grading elevations either. The Conservation Committee is a staunch and hardheaded bunch. You'll have your Ivy League hands full with that group. They will put your spit-and-polish, wing-tipped higher education to the real-world litmus test. You better cram for this exam, frat boy, or they'll cram it right up your tight, privileged, pansy little ass."

The frat boy was taken aback. He sat aghast.

"Mr. Rigney," Cornero interjected, "please be assured that we have anticipated those concerns and have contingency options available to address those obstacles and alleviate any unnecessary interference."

"Yes, Mr. Cornero," the Commodore responded aggressively, "I'm well aware of your various contingency options and persuasive methods of eliminating annoying interference." He paused for dramatic effect. "Let me make something perfectly clear to you, fuckin', sausage-suckin' dickwads . . . This is my island, and I'll rip off your head and shit down your neck before I would allow some asshole, ignorant, immigrant guinea and his band of greaseball garlic heads to take it over."

"Mr. Rigney, please calm yourself," Cornero pleaded. "I can assure you that we mean no harm to your lovely island or its inhabitants. To the contrary, we envision an enchanting paradise even more spectacular than the famously quaint and charming island oasis you have already created. We simply wish to bring Avalon to prominence among the world's most desirable and fascinating locales. Mr. Rigney, I implore you to look beyond the immediate horizon. You must have envisioned in your wildest dreams that someday Santa Catalina would be the ultimate destination for the world's most intriguing and fascinating people. The movers and shakers of the world would beat a path to a luxurious, breathtaking Monaco-inspired island of glittering opulence shimmering brightly in the warm blue Pacific. An enchanting wonderland of temptation, an alluring mirage upon the horizon, enticingly visible from LA and the entire Southern California coast. Can't you just imagine it, Mr. Rigney? The opportunity is here, Mr. Rigney. We have the resources and the organization to make this dream a reality. There may never be a better time than now."

Cornero paused for dramatic effect. He leaned forward, sipped his brandy, and spoke as if in confidence. "Mr. Rigney, let me be perfectly honest. The organization leadership has come to a realization, through its affiliation in Las Vegas, that the time has come to establish legitimate business ventures. They have experienced an epiphany, if you will, again by way of Vegas, that enormous amounts of revenue can be generated from legitimate enterprises, without the obvious pitfalls associated with criminally orchestrated activities. The 'Rio' of the Pacific they envision would rival the most festive and opulent playgrounds throughout the civilized world. The life of crime and corruption is a thing of the past. This is their future, their opportunity to legitimize the organizational skills and business expertise they have developed in the past and create a legitimate foundation from which to build upon into the future. They have gazed beyond the distant horizon, and they have seen the promised land."

Spaulding arrived carrying a serving tray and began to distribute its contents upon the round, glass-top patio table. Today's menu, in honor of our ethnic guests, linguini and clam sauce, a light vinaigrette salad, warm garlic bread, and a robust red wine. Our guests seemed pleased and dined indulgently.

When all were comfortably satiated, Spaulding cleared the table and returned promptly with coffee and cigars. Once everyone had sipped, snipped, applied flame to Tiparillo, and settled, the Commodore finally leaned forward and prepared to speak.

"Mr. Cornero, I commend your oratory skills and your inspiring and grandiose vision of the future. Very persuasive. I can see how you managed to finagle the local authorities and keep your gambling fleet afloat off Santa Monica and Long Beach for so long before the feds finally torpedoed the *Rex* and the rest of your armada. I must admit that I was suspicious of your intentions, apprehensive as to your motives, and repulsed by your methods." Once again he paused for dramatic effect. Tony Cornero and his legal beagle protégé in training anticipated the "however" continuance to the Commodore's statement. They never got one. The old man let the observation stand. He left their participles dangling.

"At any rate, gentlemen," the Commodore began in conclusion, "I believe we have a basis on which we may continue further discussions. I would request that you leave the blueprints for further study of project feasibility and comprehensive calculations regarding the tentative grading plans, by myself and my architectural and engineering staff. I would also request upon our next meeting that you are accompanied by your accountant and are prepared to produce a complete cost analysis and financial prospectus for this rather elaborate and what at first glance appears to be an amateurishly optimistic and overly ambitious view of this project.

"Until our next meeting, gentlemen, I bid you good day."

Tony Cornero and consigliere Stefano Parola rose to their feet and shook hands with the Commodore. They thanked him for his indulgence and looked forward to their next meeting.

I escorted our guests through the foyer to the entrance where Lugar had already summoned the car and security personnel, who waited at the drive to return them to the front gates. I bid them "many miles of happy motoring" and closed the door upon their departure. Together, Lugar and I rejoined the Commodore on the terrace. He was speaking to Spaulding, who excused himself and was off to retrieve something the old man had requested.

The Commodore invited us to join him for a spot of brandy. We took a seat at the table and sipped from our snifter as Spaulding returned from his appointed quest to deliver the cardboard tube that the Commodore had requested. Lugar and I glanced at the tube then at the old man and each other, puzzled.

The old man opened one end of the cardboard tube and extracted another set of blueprints. He stretched them across the table. The cover page read "Hamilton Cove Casino Resort and Spa."

♦　♦　♦

I stood and examined the two sets of blueprints, one atop the other. The title page contained identical dates, document numbers, and architectural and engineering firm located in LA. I compared each page of the blueprints one by one. They were duplicate copies of an original set of plans.

I spun the plans around so that Lugar could get his first look at what all the hubbub was about. I returned to my seat and downed the remainder of my brandy. Lugar noted the architectural firm that produced the documents, then examined each page individually. I took the liberty of pouring each of us another round from the dwindling carafe of brandy and waited for Lugar to conclude his perusal of the documents.

He sat and took a long pull from his snifter. He fished around in his pockets and came up with a severely crumpled pack of Viceroy nonfilters. (Hard-core throat harshness). He offered one to me, which I promptly rolled back and forth on the table, attempting to make it appear a properly manufactured product, rather than twist the ends, thereby making it resemble a "frajo" one would acquire through "dubious" connections within the south central mean-street barrios of LA.

"I'm no building contractor," Lugar finally remarked, after igniting each of our poorly manufactured tobacco-filled paper cylinders, "but that appears to be a very ambitious proposal. The immense casino alone will run into the millions of dollars to construct, not to mention the opulent interior appointments. And the Mediterranean villas terraced into the hillside will be an engineering, grading, and compaction nightmare. I doubt that Avalon's planning and building department has the expertise required to plan-check the engineering involved, nor the on-site inspections required for grading and compaction tests that would be critical to such an ostentatious project."

The old man laughed out loud and clapped his hands together. "Bravo, Inspector. Bravo indeed. Very astute, my upstanding public servant. You not only protect and serve, but you are extremely intuitive as well."

Lugar sat, looking slightly embarrassed. He wasn't sure if the old man was being sarcastic or sincere. The Commodore, realizing his perceived faux pas, smiled widely and reached across the table and patted Lugar's hand affectionately.

"Seriously, my dear Inspector Lugar," the old man began, "your observations and protracted conclusions mirror my own initial concerns as well. Furthermore, a point upon which no one thus far has addressed is if projected farther along the timeline, one could postulate convincingly that the logistics involved to supply the enormous quantities of materials required for such an ambitious undertaking would quickly overwhelm the facilities presently available at Avalon's shipping docks, and therefore would facilitate the construction of a shipping pier in Hamilton Cove and mode of transportation of materials to and from the building site. You are totally accurate, Inspector, this is a very ambitious proposal, and I fear a very dangerous one as well."

"Commodore," I interjected, "If you don't mind my asking, how and when did you acquire that set of duplicate blueprints?"

"Ah yes," the old man laughed and made that same recognition of "the sting" maneuver, or perhaps it was parlor game charades indicator of on-the-nose response. He laughed and looked over to Lugar. "That's why Dugan gets the big money," the old man exclaimed. "Cut to the chase, stay focused on the prize."

Lugar leaned back on his chair and laughed out loud. "Just the facts, mam. Just the facts," he mimicked in his finest Jack Webb's *Dragnet*'s Sergeant Joe Friday deadpan delivery.

"Book 'em, Danno!" I responded. (Whatever that means. Someone should be writing this stuff down.)

"We came upon that set of blueprints soon after my son Johnny's disappearance. We utilized the safe-cracking skills of our local locksmith to obtain access to the contents of a rather formidable, fireproof vault my son had installed in his living quarters here in the mansion. At the time I didn't give them much thought. I assumed they were commissioned by Johnny, perhaps as 'plans for the future.' I was consumed with grief and searching for any clues that may have led us to his whereabouts or any perceived threats against him that could have been uncovered. We were desperately grasping at straws." The old man's voice quietly trailed off, and he welled up with tears. He turned and silently gazed over the beauty of the calm blue Pacific Ocean.

Once the Commodore had regained his composure, he threw back a brandy shot and then clasped his hands in front of him. "Gentlemen," he began in clear and concise tone, "as I stated to Mr. Dugan upon our first meeting sometime ago, I do not expect to find my son's remains or experience the solace of closure in a burial ceremony. But let me make this perfectly clear, I still intend to find out what happened to Johnny, and who is responsible."

Spaulding appeared once again and prepared to take the old man for his afternoon nap. I told the Commodore that I was extremely impressed by his commanding performance in the face of a dangerous and intimidating adversary. He stood his ground with bravado and had them back on their heels on several occasions. Especially the brash young barrister who gained some insight and respect for the rough-and-tumble big time of real-world corporate America. The Commodore took command of that meeting and officiated the proceedings with efficiency and authority. I was sure Cornero and his humbled protégé left the meeting with newfound respect for RJ Rigney's grasp of the situation and his aggressive instincts when confronted with intimidation or perceived threat.

"Great job, Commodore," I said. "You had those pantywaists on the defense the entire time and sent them packing, licking their wounds with their tails between their legs."

Lugar and I lifted our snifters in a toast of honor. "Commodore, we salute your *machismo*, your bravado, and your *mucho grande* cojones."

All three of us slammed back the last of our brandy and the Commodore exclaimed, "Olé! Muchachos! Let's take these meatballs to the mats, boys. Reek some vengeance on those bastards. And if you should stumble across whoever is responsible for my son's death . . . make that motherfucker suffer greatly before you kill him." (Whoa! Perhaps a bit too much brandy for the candymeister. Got a flash fire combusting in the confectioner's boiler chamber.) He gave us an enthusiastic thumbs-up as Spaulding wheeled him away.

Kato arrived on the terrace carrying a long wooden box in one hand and a familiar drab green ammo box in the other. He set both boxes down and flipped the latches on the long wooden box, then opened the lid.

"Precocious sent this over with the replacement personnel. She asked that we deliver it to you ASAP."

Lugar curiously attempted to peer into the box, as I reached in and pulled out a big, nasty, modern-day version of a Gatling gun. It was a Browning automatic rifle. A BAR. It fired .30-caliber shells from a twenty-round box magazine, and literally shredded whatever it hit.

"Jesus Christ!" Lugar exclaimed, taken aback. "Who the hell do you think you are? Audie Murphy? Captain America? Flash Gordon?"

"No problemo, dickwad," I responded in cosmic Nazi deadpan persona. "They call me the Polliwoginator. Hasta la vista, baby!" I exclaimed, hoisting the butt of the rifle onto my hip and firing a short burst into the air with one hand.

The startling, ear-shattering repetition of explosions shot fire from the barrel like cannon rounds from a dragon's mouth. It echoed repeatedly off the canyon walls, setting off security alarms and barking dogs throughout the immediate vicinity. It sent Kato and Lugar diving for cover as well.

Lugar peered from under the ridiculously inadequate protection of the glass-top patio table and in exasperation asked loudly, "You freaking lunatic! What, are you nuts? You'll knock a satellite out of orbit with that damn thing!" (Whatever those are.) Kato just laughed. He already thought I was coo-coo for cocoa puffs, bra. (Cocoa puffs? Samoan sativa, wrapped in dried coca leaf, rolled into gigantic Rastafarian ganja reefers, and smoked . . . ergo, "cocoa puffs." Yea, and they think I'm nuts.)

Chapter Sixteen

I entered the casino ballroom, dressed in my off-the-rack Bill Blass original, through the rear entrance and found Inspector Lugar, likewise impeccably coifed and enjoying a refreshment at the bar. The encore presentation of the Louis Prima–Keely Smith musical revue had not yet begun, and I hoped to indulge in a hearty feast of New York steak before the entertainment ensued.

Lara floated across the floor and appeared at our side, stunning in silver sequined, strapless floor-length gown and eye-popping brilliant diamond necklace and matching earrings. She wore her hair up and wrapped into an intricately braided French roll in the back. As always, she was devastatingly breathtaking.

She ordered another B&B for the good inspector and the usual for yours truly. She requested that the drinks be brought to the table, and then led Lugar and me to a small dimly lit table off to the side in a private alcove normally reserved for entertainment industry VIPs that would create a distraction among the audience out on the main floor.

Lara slid into the booth next to me and snuggled close. She was in a festive mood, and her effervescence was bubbling over and surprisingly contagious.

"You left me twisting in the wind last night again, you big prick," she teased. Lugar simply looked over at me and shook his head. "I was under the impression that you were going to stick around and have dinner with me after the show."

The drinks arrived and Lara pilfered a quick sampling of my crystalline elixir. She smacked her lush, sumptuous lips, kissed me on the cheek, and absconded with my swizzle-skewered, pimento-stuffed olive.

"Order dinner. It's on the house. Whatever you want," she exclaimed as she flew out of sight. "Merry Christmas to all, and to all a good night!"

Lugar's gaze lingered as the shimmering silver apparition disappeared into the darkness. "I still don't understand how such a ravishing, intelligent beauty with such elegant grace could possibly be attracted to a punch-drunk, womanizing whoremonger like you."

"It's all part of the charm, my friend," I said with a rakish smile. "I'm a dashing, ruggedly handsome bon vivant in the eyes of the social elite. I'm the dangerous and mysterious lover who comes in the night and satisfies all their naughty, pent-up fantasies that their uptight, button-down, preppy boyfriends or husbands are too inexperienced or inhibited to perform with any skill or expertise."

"Yea, aha," Lugar exasperated. "And you can call me Ilene."

"Perhaps a token demonstration of my prescient reputation will better illustrate my point." I turned to him and proceeded to stick out my tongue and place the end atop my nose, then up one of my nostrils.

"Oh yuck!" he exclaimed. "There goes my appetite, you gross bastard."

"Want to see me stroke my eyebrows with it?" I asked playfully.

"No, no, that's OK," he responded, throwing back a hefty gulp of his drink. "You've made your point nauseatingly obvious. I'm dually impressed, nauseously convinced, and at the same time uncomfortably intimidated."

I continued to demonstrate dexterity by twisting it into a corkscrew and wiggling the tip with come-hither poignancy and agility.

"OK, OK, enough already!" he exclaimed. "You've thoroughly satisfied my curiosity, you can put that thing away now."

"If I had a nickel for every time I've heard that." I laughed out loud. Lugar held it in as long as he could, but he eventually had to reluctantly burst out laughing as well.

Mercifully, the cummerbund-adorned waiter arrived, transcribed our dinner request, and was off with aplomb. Lugar waited until our server had departed before initiating a change of subject.

"I placed a call this afternoon, to the architectural and engineering firm listed on that set of blueprints," he began. "I asked them who had originally initiated the preparation of the documents, and who had actually signed the contracts approving the commencement of preliminary engineering and structural calculations." He paused for dramatic effect. "You'll never guess who signed those contracts."

"Bozo the Clown. Sky King and his niece Penny. Howdy Doody, " I responded facetiously. He just stared in consternation and shook his head, while downing the last of his drink.

"Freaking twerp," he sighed, exasperated. "You can be such a dildo sometimes, I swear. No, you twat. It was none of those characters you so immaturely mentioned, you jerk-off! It was none other than Jack Dragna, Nick Licata's boss and LA's mafioso crime czar." (Well, that sobered me right up.)

"I thought that might spin your propeller," Lugar teased. "Do you feel as though you have stepped on your prehensile appendage again?" he continued to provoke playfully.

"I also spoke to a friend of mine in the coast guard. Commander J. F. Angelico, commanding officer of the Eleventh District headquarters based on Terminal Island in San Pedro. He in turn had been in communication with a Captain McCrory aboard the cutter *Ponchatrane*, stationed off Smuggler's Point. They would indeed like very much to speak with Airman Steven Canyon and Ship Captain Wallace W. Brennan with regard to the ongoing investigation into the alleged detonation of illegally obtained black market military ordnance and the circumstances prior to and resulting in the impalement of Canyon's PBY upon the immense barrel of Con's supergun. They may have additional questions regarding the apparent sinking of a commandeered World War II Japanese midget sub that has some kind of deep-sea retrieval davits attached to its hull.

"According to Commander Angelico, there are also reports of an ensuing sea battle ongoing around the Channel Islands off Santa Barbara. His resources are stretched pretty thin at this time because of the logistics being rendered to the feds in Smuggler's Cove and the armada of unmarked trawlers anchored near the commercial shipping lanes. He has dispatched search-and-rescue aircraft to the area, but has not received any contact confirmation as of yet. Sounds like it could be your boy, Con. Who do you suppose is in pursuit?"

Before I could venture a guess, Lugar peered through the beaded alcove entrance, then nodded his head for me to check it out. I scooted to the end of the booth and moved aside the strands of beads to see Tony Cornero personally escorting several members of the rat pack to a table where Nick Licata and an assortment of unibrowed, harelip mental gimps were finishing their meal and waiting for the show to begin.

Joey Heatherton, the sexy little blonde pixie who wowed the audience six nights a week in Vegas with her elaborate stage-show revue, and Angie Dickinson, Hollywood actress and resident, rat pack party girl, were accompanied by Peter Lawford and Joey Bishop. That party would have been likely candidates for the alcove Lugar and I occupied, if they were able to squeeze them all in here.

Our waiter returned and distributed the sizzling, inch-thick, tender, and juicy center cuts smothered under a mountain of mushrooms sautéed in garlic butter. He replenished our drinks and was off once again. We were ravenous and prepared to indulge in major grubbing. As we ate, we casually observed the comings and goings around the Licata/rat pack table. There seemed to be an unusual amount of shuttled messages being whispered to Nick the Pick from his sideline flunkies, followed by elbow nudges and more whispered secrets to an associate, who would promptly excuse himself and make a hasty exit. (Curious behavior. Made me nervous watching, for some reason. My gut feeling was to get the hell out of there.)

At the conclusion of our meal, the opening-act floor show had just begun. Mob favorite comedian Norm Crosby was onstage telling amusing anecdotes while mercilessly butchering the English language in the process. The opening-act warm-up costar for the evening was the staccato machine gun delivery of comedian and impersonator Jackie Mason. A Jewish comedian from Brooklyn that had them rolling in the aisles with his whirling dervish impersonation of television impresario Ed Sullivan. ("Right here on our stage, a really big shoe." Spin, spin, point to the wrong side of the stage.)

It was about this time that I noticed Constable Lafargé, regaled in his finest French Foreign Legion–inspired uniform, entered the ballroom accompanied by a carload of gendarmes and began to disperse around the perimeters of the room to cover the exits unobtrusively searching for someone.

Not wanting to get ensnared in his pompous, self-indulgent, narcissistic, drama queen bullshit, I motioned to Lugar to head for the backstage exit before Lafargé's parade-ready, band camp brigade secured that set of doors to the outside as well.

We arrived on the boardwalk and found Roscoe leaning on his cab in the usual spot. He drove us down Casino Way to Crescent Avenue, then turned right at Sumner and went up the hill to the Chi-Chi Club.

Before we parted ways, I introduced Roscoe and Lugar and asked if he had any information for me. Roscoe said that he was working on some information but wouldn't know anything until later tonight. He would locate me in the morning and tell me what he had come up with, if anything.

We climbed the enclosed stairwell from the sidewalk and entered the Chi-Chi Club at the top to the stairs. It was loud, close, and smoky. It was awash with spinning strobe lights and a twirling crush of perspiring dancers on the crowded floor. The drinks were tall, tropic, and colorful. And so were the glistening women gyrating provocatively within the mesmerizing swirl of sweaty party participants.

Lugar and I found our way to a dimly lit table in the corner just off the dance floor from where we could observe the entrance at the top to the stairs and still make a hasty retreat if necessary. An odd bohemian waitress eventually squeezed through the undulating amoeba of glandular excretions that was the dance floor and arrived at our table for our drink orders. She was a thin pale beatnik with jet-black spiked hair that resembled a kinetic coal mine explosion in mid burst, from the top of her head. She had tats on her fingers, bells on her toes, and a ring in her nose ho-ho! (She was "Ahab the Arab, king of the burning sands.") She enhanced the chic ensemble in a body stocking of black leotard, unbridled adolescent minibreasts with pubescent nipples that danced the zigzag dance of youth as they protruded provocatively through thinly stretched translucent material and what I imagined was ungroomed "earth-girl" legs and armpits. The pungent aroma of patchouli oil enhanced the experience and reminded me of a roach-infested club located in a urine-soaked dark alley on Lido Isle in Newport Beach called Cosmo's Blue Moon Bistro and Expresso Bar. The entertainment at Cosmo's was an eclectic assemblage of chain-smoking bongo players in cheap sunglasses and an open-mike, never-ending lineup of doomsaying, impromptu, esoteric poet-reading geeks that wore hush puppy Birkenstocks and leather patches sown on the elbows of their crocheted turtleneck sweaters. (I was originally introduced to Cosmo's by my dear and unpredictable grandma Ireland, on a particularly raucous and rowdy night of drunken Irish mayhem, where she eventually closed the bar, onstage punching out the ill-prepared, anemic bohemian nightclub "bouncer." But that's another story.)

"If you can communicate with Captain Wally and Kamikaze Steve, I would advise them to stay put for the moment, until the smoke clears!" Lugar yelled over the pulsating rhythm of incessant primitive drumbeat.

"I can, with some difficulty," I responded at the top of my lungs. "But I'll need a ship-to-shore radio and a tide chart!" I yelled once again, not realizing the music had stopped momentarily, thereby announcing my odd requirements to the now-staring and puzzled assemblage of sweaty onlookers.

The avant-garde, minihumped, camel-toed leotard returned with our drinks at that precise moment, out of nowhere.

"Yea, boys! Sounds tre kinky, baby!" she exclaimed upon the distribution of our refreshments. "Call me if your plan comes to fruition, I'll bring the snorkel and the aqua lube." She gave us an over-the-shoulder wink and a wicked little spank on her proud and pouty butt as she departed with a smile.

I smiled widely at the good inspector. "There you go, my friend. 'Bohemian Rhapsody' with ménage à troi in A minor," I laughed out loud, once again during a momentary electrorepetitive, techno-music respite. (Awkward-a-mundo.)

Lugar shook his head in utter chagrin once again. "You know, Dugan, I left the seedy underbelly of LA to get away from the assorted predators, parasites, and perverts, just to come over here and wind up finding the sickest puppy of them all."

"Hey, wait a minute," I interrupted. "I think I resemble that remark."

He laughed. "No, no, don't miss-come-screw- me," he mimicked in his finest Norm Crosby imitation. "I think I like it," he finally confessed with a silly drunken grin.

At that moment our spanking-hot auditioning porn princess reappeared, who, by the way, was looking even more alluring through ever-foggier beer goggles, just in time for me to excuse myself to visit the downstairs watering trough. I got up from the table, kissed our exuberant future film star on her tattooed neck, and slid her into the booth next to the salaciously intoxicated inspector, then navigated through the pulsating amoeba of the inner sanctum and down the stairs to the men's room.

I had just gotten bellied up to the bar when the door burst open and three burly knuckle draggers rushed in and caught me in a compromising and vulnerable position. I barely had time to get my affairs in order before a swift kick to the groin was delivered with great prejudice. Luckily, I already had my hands in a defensive position, anticipating such a chickenshit maneuver, and managed to block the main thrust of the blow. The second blow arrived and I wasn't so lucky. It slammed my head into the wall, cracking the ceramic tile and momentarily disconnecting my neurological receptors and nearly buckling my knees. I managed to stay off the floor and kept thinking what my daddy used tell me: "Stay on your feet and keep punching. If you get knocked down, come up swinging. No matter what, never give up!" He told me that bit of sage advice right after I had come home from the fifth grade dejected because I had just gotten beaten up by the sixth-grade school bully. His name was Butch, and he looked exactly like the redheaded freckled bully in *The Little Rascals*, *Our Gang* film comedies.

I made a promise to myself at that time that I would never get my ass kicked again. And never had, to this point. I suddenly realized that I might be in danger of breaking that promise, and several bones in the process as well.

I managed to stay on my feet and keep my head down while jackhammering a barrage of punches. With three big hulking "guidos" in the confined space, there wasn't much room in which to maneuver. I was taking some vicious shots and getting steadily pushed into a corner. One blinding punch caught me square in the face and smashed the back of my head into the metal towel dispenser, knocking it off the wall. I slid down the wall and hit the tile floor hard with my ass. As one of them reached down to yank me off the floor by my throat, I grabbed the towel dispenser on the floor beside me and bashed him upside his head with it. He face-planted into the porcelain sink, then thumped to the floor with his *cabeza*, making the "splattering" sound of a dropped watermelon.

I jumped to my feet and, with a backhand swing, slammed the metal dispenser into the face of the oncoming gunzel swinging the zap. It took him out and he went down hard. The remaining throbbing side of beef, however, pulverized my midsection, rib cage, and sternum with a series of powerful, crushing body blows. Each punishing jab delivered with the intensity and effectiveness of a professional boxer.

He was Joe Palooka in a pinstripe suit. Once I was pinned into a corner, the incredible hulk delivered the knockout uppercut, which seemed to come from the floor and blasted me right in the jaw. It lifted me off the ground, slamming me into the corner and scattering my brain cells, like the break shot in a pool-parlor eight-ball game.

Everything went silent and into slow motion. I could see the tile floor coming at me, but I couldn't seem to do anything about it. There were cerebral supernovas exploding within the cranial universe. Then the swirling descent into the imploding, all-consuming abyss of the black hole. (Whatever . . . that . . . means.)

I was tied at the wrists to a cane-back barroom chair. The rural aroma of fresh, new-mown hay, and even-fresher aroma, of recently mucked horse manure, created an ambiance I imaged to be "turn of the century" Midwestern woodpecker and worm-holed barn wood with penthouse hayloft and stables adjacent.

I hung limp against my restraints, listening for familiar voices or uninvited strangers. I kept my head down and my eyes closed. I performed an internal audit to determine if all my inventory was still on premises and intact. I was having difficulty breathing, and each labored inhalation brought with it familiar and excruciating pain, symptoms normally associated with injuries like cracked ribs and separated cartilage. I was aware of a small stream of warm seepage emanating from the back of my head, running behind my ear and down my neck. There was a steady stream of blood trickling from my nose and mouth, and I could taste blood and the grainy mix of chipped teeth. The jagged edges and painful lacerations of tongue and cheek confirmed the origin of the granular syrup seeping from my lips.

I moved my feet, ever so slightly, and determined that they were not tied to the chair legs—critical oversight. My hands were tied at the wrist behind me, but again, not secured to the chair.

Once I had determined, though bashed and bruised, that I was still relatively in one piece, I assumed that the beatings would soon begin. I couldn't take much more abuse without being severely damaged and put out of action. Whatever I was going to do, it would have to be before the damage was inflicted, while I was alert and before they realized that I was not sufficiently secured to the chair.

They were your typical knuckle-dragging knee crushers normally utilized to collect gambling debts or persuade some intimidated shopkeeper or business owner to pay tribute or purchase inventory from the syndicate under threat of brutal violence. They were not known for subtlety or compassion.

I opened my eyes, just enough to see where and how many beef-shank gunzels I had to deal with. There were two at the far end of the barn, chatting and smoking cigarettes. I hoped that the third participant had eaten enough porcelain sink to warrant a trip to the hospital. At any rate, I didn't see him and I didn't hear him.

I slowly gazed around my immediate vicinity searching for weapons and escape routes. The two ham hocks either realized that I was conscious or had finished their smokes and were ready to clock in and punch my time card. It would be systematic and brutal. They would pummel my innards until I talked or hemorrhaged internally. Either way, they wouldn't kill me until I spilled my guts, one way or another.

I heard the squeak of the pump handle and the water splash into to the metal pail. They walked over to where I sat and, with great gusto, threw the bucket of water hard into my face, sending water up my nose, causing me to choke and cough up blood. I pretended to be in worse shape than I actually was. I continued to hang limp against my restraints.

The big Neanderthal who punched my lights out in the Chi-Chi Club bathroom picked my head up in his giant beefy hand, leaned in, and looked into my eyes. He looked like Slappsy Maxey Rosenbloom, former heavyweight punching bag turned B-movie gangster gunzel. The flattened nose, cauliflower ears, and layers of eyebrow scar tissue only added to the Cro-Magnon mystique. The gravely voice and Bronx vocabulary littered with *des*, *does*, and *yous guys* were the figurative topping on the stereotypical wiseguy pizza pie.

His ancestral primate sidekick leaned in to take a look. I restrained my immediate impulse to laugh out loud. He had the appearance of a rabid raccoon who had stuck his head down a badger hole. In this case, the two rapidly immerging shiners and the numerous lacerations across his face were the result of him eating my backhand, towel dispenser sandwich for lunch. He was itching to extract his ounce of revenge.

Slappsy Maxey grabbed a handful of my collar and slapped me across the face a couple of times. He shook me back and forth and gave me a few more smacks across the kisser. I opened my eyes slowly, dazed and purposely staring, unfocused. I exhibited labored breathing, and I was wobbly and apparently only semiconscious.

"Hey, Dugan. Where's the money, Dugan? Do yourself a favor, tough guy. Just tell me where the money is."

Maxey leaned in close and began to poke me in the forehead repeatedly with his polish sausage-sized finger.

"Come on, gumshoe, wake up so we can kick the crap out of you," chimed in Raccoon Boy.

Slappsy Maxey took a firm grip on my collar with his left hand and stepped back to deliver the opening salvo of punishing, straight-right cannonball shots to my previously damaged and vulnerable torso. Before the pulverization process commenced, he stepped on my right foot, pinning it to the floor and keeping the chair upright during the ensuing beating. It also minimized my opportunity for retaliation. (This was not his first fire drill. He had been around this block before.)

"I'll ask you one more time, Dugan. Where's the money? Show me the money!"

"At Bob's," I whispered. Maxey leaned in close.

"Bob? Bob who?" he asked.

I looked him straight in the eye and with a wide grin replied, "Bob over here and kiss my ass."

He exploded with anger. With rage burning in his eyes, he pulled back, cocked his bulging fist, and prepared to sledgehammer my rib cage into pulverized bone fragments. As he pulled the trigger and the battering ram began to move forward, I yelled at the top of my lungs and kicked up with my left foot, planting it with a vengeance deep into his groin. I somersaulted backward, absorbing the punch as we toppled over, crushing the chair into splinters. I rolled over backward once more and pulled my shackled wrists under my feet and in front of me as I rolled to a standing position. I grabbed a hay hook hanging from a nail on the barn wall and swung it down, burying it into Maxey's left hand, impaling it to the floor as he lay on his back screaming with pain and trying in vain to remove the hay hook.

I grabbed a leather bridle draped over a stall gate and smacked a startled Raccoon Boy across the head with it, then wrapped it around his neck and cinched it tight. We struggled around the open barn, banging into the walls and stall gates. As we stumbled around in circles, I glimpsed out of the corner of my eye that Slappsy Maxey, nailed to the floor, had retrieved his gun and was about to blast away. I quickly spun Raccoon Boy around to face the barrage of incoming point-blank gunfire. Maxey emptied the entire clip in rapid-fire succession. Raccoon Boy ate all ten rounds. I dropped him to the floor like a gunnysack full of rancid fish guts.

Before the dust had settled, Maxey had managed to yank the hay hook out of the floor, freeing his impaled hand. He began to swing the bloody hook furiously back and forth like a wounded scorpion. I ducked and blocked each vicious swipe, getting bounced off the walls and floors. He finally caught me with a backhand, the round part of the hook hitting me in the ear and knocking me to the floor up against the wall. As I lay there trying to reconnect my arcing circuits, Cro-Magnon Maxey smiled, reached down, and retrieved a shiny chrome .38 snubby from a holster strapped to his calf under his pant leg.

He calmly aimed directly between my eyes, cocked the hammer back, and smiled. "You got one more shot at the right answer, funny boy. Show me the money."

Suddenly, five shiny spikes shot through his chest in a precise line from his collarbone down to his belly button. He looked down in utter disbelief. One of the spikes had clearly penetrated through his heart and a pulsating stream of blood squirted from the puncture wound with each dwindling heartbeat.

He looked up at me with astonishment etched upon his ashen face. In the next instant he was hit hard from behind, flew through the air, and was impaled to the barn wall. Crucified by pitchfork.

It was Yung He. She had skewered Slappsy Maxey with a pitchfork, then impaled him to the wall with a surprisingly powerful sliding side kick. She was thy savior, who crucified thy enemies. She was Vlad the Impaler. She seemed to be my guardian angel. Whichever, I was really glad to see her.

She helped me to my feet and retrieved my weapon and personal belongings from my unfortunate former captors and would-be torturous assassins. We stumbled to the black sedan parked outside, and I crumpled into the rear seat. Yung He drove across the hills behind Avalon and down the long, narrow road, descending onto the wide plateau, north to the isthmus causeway and the relative safety of Cooley Town.

Chapter Seventeen

The gentle morning tide softly caressed the smooth sloping sands that surround the pristine, crystalline harbor. The familiar repertoire of the meadowlark floated upon the warm ocean breeze, like a butterfly upon delicate, gossamer wings. The harsh call of a seagull soaring high over the calm, clear waters in the distance. The familiar intimacy of a mild summer sea breeze.

I slowly opened my eyes and gazed around a small room bathed in muted early-morning sunlight. There were transom windows high up on the cinder block walls near the ceiling. It appeared to be a subterranean basement or storm cellar. I was lying on what seemed like a large floating bed encompassed within a heavy wooden frame.

I became aware of the sound of a gentle waterfall. I turned, and at the far end of the room, engulfed within delicate shafts of golden sunlight, was Yung He under the soft curtain of water gently falling from a makeshift shower. Her lustrous long mane of jet-black hair softly cascading down the length of the pristine porcelain body of my beautiful young China doll. She was an innocent and enchanting vision.

My initial attempt to raise myself off the bed was abruptly aborted with wincing pain and an audible groan, as I slumped back into bed, creating a small tidal tsunami in the process. Yung He, hearing my discomfort, stepped from the open shower, wrapped her hair in a towel, and came gently to my bedside.

She looked deep into my eyes and smiled softly. She sat on the side of the bed, her naked body glistening in the muted light. An aura surrounded her, like an angelic vision in a fantasy fairy-tale dream.

Yung He quietly slid into bed next to me and pulled the sheet over us both. She gently snuggled close, and together we calmly drifted off to sleep.

When I came to, it was late afternoon. The interior of my basement sanctuary was bathed in soft candlelight. Yung He quietly fluttered about the room in thin black silk Oriental robe, emblazoned all over with bright Mandarin red fire-breathing dragon. She softly hummed the familiar song of the "Mango Tree."

I watched as she brushed her long mane of shiny black hair. There is nothing more intimate and sexy than a beautiful woman softly brushing her hair. When she was done, she went to the hot plate in the corner where she was preparing a steaming broth that had the aroma of ginseng root, eye of newt, freeze-dried bat wings, and those other crusty slings of supporting athletic things. My initial diagnosis may be too Dr. Suess—I'm verging on plagiarism and legal abuse. I may be this, and I may be that, but I'm certainly not some schmuck in striped hat. I'm not the Grinch that stole Christmas and left the who's with a loss, but I am still the boss, with the spicy-hot sauce. I may be delusional. I may be delirious. I'm certainly delightful and simply delicious! (Whoa, whatever she was feeding me, perhaps we should slack off a tad. Lighten up a smidgen. Slightly harsh my mellow. Totally bum my trip. That reminds me, do you know what a snake and a limp dick have in common . . . ? You don't screw with 'em.)

Mercifully, Yung He arrived to interrupt my hallucinogenic ramblings, carrying a tray with a bowl of hot broth. She set the tray on the bed stand, tied a bib around my neck, then gently helped me up to a sitting position. There was great rib cage pain associated with the maneuver, but not the worst I'd endured.

She patiently spoon-fed the warm broth, wiping my chin as necessary, like I was a stroke victim in a nursing home. The soothing concoction tasted slightly better than it smelled while being prepared, and Yung He made it a bit more palatable for my taste, with a liberal splash of Tabasco and a pinch of pepper. Whatever it was, it seemed to do the job as advertised. I felt more alert, my thoughts less scrambled and rambling, and the dull, throbbing pain from within the cranial orb and chest cavity seemed to subside appreciably.

"How are Captain Wally and Kamikaze Steve holding up?" I asked as Yung He removed my bib and set the empty bowl on the bed stand tray. "Have they gone stir-crazy yet?"

"That is why I came looking for you, Travis," she replied softly. "Night before last, I stayed with my uncle in the secret grotto. When I returned to the skipjack the next morning, the *Penny* was gone. They left a note. It said that they were monitoring shortwave and ham radio transmissions at high tide and they had received information regarding a sea battle near the Channel Islands. Captain Wally and Kamikaze Steve are on the hunt for Dr. Con and his Magnum Raptor mega yacht."

"I have also spoken to my cousin, Long," she continued, allowing me only momentary contemplation of the previous distressing information. "Tonight the local Cooley Town fishing fleet will begin to blockade the harbor outside the shipping docks, in an attempt to stop or inhibit the delivery of the island's imported requirements of daily necessities, food supplies, and commercial goods. Their hope is to bring pressure upon Avalon's town council to address the situation at the docks and find a solution to the strong-arm takeover by the tong, in conjunction with criminal elements of the Teamsters Union. It may be very dangerous. Many people may be injured. We have few options at our disposal at this time. We feel that we must somehow force the issue, before it is too late."

She removed the tray and soup bowl from the bed stand and took it over to a pump-handle washbasin and rinsed them off. A few minutes later she returned with a small basket filled with some kind of steaming mint leaves. She carefully wrapped the warm leaves around my chest and rib cage. She removed the bloody bandage from my head, applied a cool ointment on both my wounds, and then carefully changed the dressing with fresh gauze bandages.

"You have suffered a mild concussion," she said softly. "Apparently not your first. That is why you are experiencing disconnected delusional thoughts and rambling, incoherent speech patterns. You also have received undetermined internal injuries. I am closely monitoring you for any developing distension of your abdominal area or bruising around your kidneys. This could be a sign of internal bleeding."

"Thank you, Yung He," I whispered. "You are indeed my savior, and my guardian angel."

She leaned in and softly kissed me. She looked deep into my eyes. "I must do whatever is necessary to keep you healthy and strong. My people are counting on you. The Rigney family is counting on you as well." She smiled brightly. "I think you will recover quickly. You have been down this road many times before. One would imagine that perhaps you may one day become weary of such a journey and desire an alternate path that may lead in a different direction. You may benefit from the diversion."

Yung He fed and bathed me for the next two days. She never left my side. Her cousin Long had taken the skipjack to resupply the boats participating in the blockade of the shipping port and to go to Moonstone Cove and check on Ah Looey. We were isolated in our underground bunker and were unaware of the events unfolding in the outside world.

In the last few days, while my thoughts were random and dispersed, I kept thinking of Raven. I hadn't seen or heard from her in a long while, and I was beginning to worry that something had happened to her. My mind raced from one implausible scenario to another. I was unable to focus on any of the scenarios for any duration, and it was creating anxiety within. That feeling I got when something was out of sync in my universe. Something was not right, and I felt compelled to mount up and ride out to check the perimeters.

I also had a real bad feeling about the situation at the casino and what Nick Licata and Tony Cornero were going to do when they discovered their two hatchet men had been turned into swiss cheese, and/or crucified by a pitchfork, impaled to the old barn wall. Crucifixions seemed to be a trend.

Lugar must be wondering what happened to me. I hoped nothing happened to him. I gotta get outta here. The whole world could be going to hell while I sat here wrapped in steaming mint leaves and sipping ginseng root and gym-socks tea.

The sun had set, and Yung He was busy lighting the candles within our cozy "hobbit hole." I pulled myself, with some difficulty, to the side of my "aqua bed" and climbed over the side to the floor. I was somewhat wobbly at first, but soon got my land legs under me. Yung He watched me from afar, while preparing the coffee she knew I would soon be requesting.

I navigated successfully around my tidal enclosure and found a pack of Old Golds crumpled in the trash can. I dug around in my pants pocket hanging over a chair and found my trusty service lighter.

I skillfully clicked her open and thumbed the flint to a blue and gold flame with which I ignited my first smoke in two or three days.

I climbed the short set of stairs and opened the storm doors. I stepped out into the warm night and gazed up to the star-filled sky. The moon was on the far side of the mountain, and the sky was dark over Cooley Town, except for the myriad of dazzling stars blazing throughout the night's canopy.

Yung He came to me with the cup of coffee she had prepared. She held me close, saying nothing for a while. Together, we gazed into the night, silently wondering what the future might bring.

Yung He held me close and softly whispered into my ear. "I fear you are leaving soon?" she asked.

"Yes, Yung He," I answered. "It's time to roll."

She held me close and we kissed long and hard. I wished we could stay together in our underground hideaway, but we both knew that there was unfinished business at hand, and until we resolved this conflict, there would be no time for unrestrained romance.

We went back inside and I began to get dressed. Yung He brought the .45 that Moms O'Malley had given me and the Browning automatic rifle that Precocious had the Samoans deliver.

"Where did you get that?" I asked.

"A beautiful young Polynesian girl brought it night before last," Yung He replied. "She said her name was Fia. She was accompanied by two big Samoan boys. She seemed genuinely concerned about your condition, and spent a long time by your side."

"How did they know where to find me?" I asked.

"Lara Rigney called Joe at the boat rental on the tourist pier and asked him to speak to my cousin Long about your whereabouts and condition. Mrs. Rigney was also very concerned for your well-being. I told Long that they could send someone down to Cooley Town, and they would be stopped at the causeway, where we now have guards and a barricade. The guards would then direct them to your location within Cooley Town. They also brought a metal box full of ammunition and a duffle bag with a change of clothes."

"Where is the sedan that we came in?" I asked, inspecting the contents of the ammo box and the duffle.

"It's down the road in an empty shed. I'll show you," she replied.

Before she went to change, she came to me and kissed me with great passion, open robe, open mouth, and probing tongue. She was young, innocent, and wanting. I held her close, our breath heavy with emotion. I kissed her neck and relished the enchantment of her fresh, cherry blossom scent. She was smooth, taut, and flawless. My China doll.

She turned and disappeared into the shadows, fluttering the candles as she passed. Yung He was a very special young girl. Wise beyond her years and showing compassion that far exceeded expectations. The kindness and insight she possesses belied her young years and life experiences. While she changed, I inspected the BAR, loaded a full clip, and injected the first round into the chamber. I set the safety and adjusted the strap, then slung the formidable personal Gatling gun and weapon of choice for the infamous marauder of the thirties, Clyde Barrow, over my shoulder. I picked up the duffle and ammo box and headed for the storm doors. Yung He met me at the stairs and opened the doors into the dark night. We walked along the beach for a short while, then turned away from the shore and went between two bungalows back to the narrow rut of a road.

As we began to cross the road, we heard a loud commotion, yelling and gunfire, coming from the causeway barricade. Automatic weapons fire erupted, shattering the tranquility of the dark starry night. Three black sedans roared up the narrow road throwing huge clouds of dust into the air. They came to a rampaging, dust-swirling stop in a semicircle surrounding Ah Looey's cabin and the basement shelter we had just abandoned. Several dark figures approached the cabin, while four or five more took offensive cover behind the sedans across the road.

Suddenly, the sound of shattering glass and a huge fireball exploded within the small cabin. The figures who had thrown the Molotov cocktail retreated to the shelter of the sedans across the road, and the others began firing sporadically into the burning cabin with tommy guns.

"Oh no, Travis!" Yung He exclaimed in great anguish. "They are burning down my uncle's house!"

"Stay here, Yung He," I whispered. "Try to find better cover."

I crouched down and maneuvered around the corner of the shed and quietly moved to a position behind their left flank, taking cover behind a brick incinerator. In the midst of their murderous gunfire, I opened up with a continuous ear-shattering burst from my fire-breathing BAR. Each round ripped through sedan metal and gunzel flesh like lightning bolts from Thor, the god of thunder and lightning. The hapless marauders scattered under and over the cars to take cover on the other side, leaving their wounded comrades in the open and vulnerable. I continued to lay down a spray of automatic gunfire that shattered windshields and tore through metal, blasting white-hot shrapnel in all directions, like a grenade exploding in a bucketful of nails.

I ejected the spent clip and injected a fresh one, cocked back the hammer, and loaded one into the chamber. I continued to lay down a barrage of cover fire while moving to my left, back toward the road and closer to the front of the lead sedan. I dived behind a stand of palm trees next to the narrow road that separated Ah Looey's burning cabin on the left and the three sedans on the right.

There was a melee of chaotic yelling and scrambling around in the dirt. They were in full retreat, hugging the ground, scratching their way to the farthest car in line, desperately attempting escape without getting blasted like rabid jackals in the process.

I ran out to the middle of the road and opened up on the retreating stragglers, ripping a continues burst of gunfire along the line of bullet-riddled sedans and filling the blazing night sky with ricocheted rounds, exploding shrapnel, and acrid blue smoke.

I ejected another spent clip and jammed in a full one. The remaining four or five marauders piled into the last car and were moving down the road at high speed, in reverse. I ran down the road after them and emptied another full clip in the direction of the fleeing sedan, which had pulled a 180 degree end-swap and was headed down the road toward the isthmus causeway.

I stood in the midst of an acrid, chocking blue cloud of spent gun powder. It was eerily silent, except for the continuous high-pitched ringing in my ears. The barrel of my "fire-breather" glowed red-hot as I sank to my knees in the middle of the dark dusty road.

The remaining inhabitants of Cooley Town began to tentatively arrive and quickly organized a bucket brigade that efficiently delivered water, hand over hand from the shore, across the beach to the blazing cabin. They were not going to be successful in saving the structure, but it was a heroic effort and they would prevent the fire from spreading from one cabin to another.

There were five dead or dying gunzels lying in various grotesque poses alongside the two remaining destroyed sedan heaps. They lay in the dirt and pools of their own blood. I pulled out my .45 and put two of the moaning miscreants out of their misery with a point-blank shot to the head.

I turned and walked back up the road to where I had left Yung He and where a crowd now began to gather. I began to panic. I ran, desperate, into the crowd and fell at Yung He's side. She was lying next to the shed on her back, breathing heavily and bleeding profusely from her left shoulder. Her eyes were wide open and she was obviously in shock. I tore open her blouse and inspected her wound. A ricocheted round had torn through the corner of the shed and ripped through her shoulder just below the collarbone, passing completely through and leaving a jagged exit wound between her shoulder blades.

The crowd parted and an elderly Filipino woman, in colorful moo-moo, arrived on scene with a hand full of cloth diapers and a roll of gauze bandages. She knelt beside Yung He and began to administer first aid. She removed two bottle corks from her pocket and jammed one in each of Yung He's entry and exit wounds, instantly blocking the flow of blood. She efficiently applied the diapers to the plugged wounds and wrapped the bandage around her shoulder and across her chest.

"I am Yung He's auntie Lola. I'm Long's mother. I will take care of Yung He. Do not worry, she will be all right. It is a clean wound, there is no bullet to remove, just a few wood splinters. I will sterilize the wound and prevent infection. You go. Do not worry about Yung He, I will take good care of her."

She quickly organized a litter party and gently lifted Yung He and began to carry her down the road to Lola's cabin.

I opened the shed doors and loaded the ammo box and duffle into the back and brought the BAR into the front seat of the sedan with me. I turned the key and stomped the starter pedal. The gunzel's sedan roared to life. I backed out of the shed and headed down the road in pursuit of the fleeing sedan.

I passed through the now-smoldering rubble of the barricade and over the causeway bridge. I had the sedan in high gear and screaming down the road toward Avalon and the faint taillights quickly disappearing ahead in the distance.

I cursed myself for allowing Yung He to be injured and at the same time prayed that she would be all right. I could never forgive myself if I got that innocent young girl killed. I cursed the bastards and punched my fist into the dash repeatedly. I was hell-bent on revenge and dying to kill somebody. Kill somebody in a real vicious, ugly way. There would be no prisoners. There would be no mercy. There would only be death. Dark, nasty death. I was the Grim Reaper. I would wield my scythe with vengeance and cleave the guts from the evil ones!

I roared down the road through the darkness, faster and faster. My mind raced in all directions, adrenaline pumping furiously through my veins, hands gripped tight to the wheel, sawing back and forth, barely keeping the rampaging sedan on the pavement. Tires squealing and dust flying, the sedan screamed across the countryside in a blinding flash. Road signs, mile markers, and phone poles whizzed by in the blink of an eye.

I careened through the darkness in a blind rage. It was an impulsively bad move, which always inevitably turned out bad. But always, inevitably, I went off half-cocked anyway. I was an enraged bull in a china shop. The destruction was always complete devastation. There were no survivors.

I raced across the flat plateau and up the long ascent into the hills leading to Avalon. As I crested the top of the first hill where the narrow road was cut between two rocky outcroppings, the headlights illuminated a large stake-bed truck parked across the road. There was no way to avoid it and not enough time to stop. It was an ambush, and I was rushing headlong right into it. I steered straight at it, mashed the gas pedal to the floor, and dived under the dashboard.

The sound of a grinding train wreck exploded over my head as the sedan broadsided the stake bed at full speed and ripped the top off the car, like a sardine can, as it careened under the truck amid a firestorm of flames and shattered glass. The sedan blew out from under the flaming hulk at high speed, skidded to the right, and began a series of spectacular, bouncing, twisting barrel rolls along the road, finally coming to a crushing stop, a smoldering, demolished heap of shredded metal fragments.

I lay, like a rag doll, alongside the road in a cloud of dust and with a mouthful of grit and shattered glass. It was deathly silent, save for the escaping hiss of radiator water and the faint clink and clank of severed car parts scattering their way down the hillside.

The searing pain of severe asphalt-road rash and scorched raggedy flesh began to engulf my senses. I tried to realign my hopefully still-attached appendages into their correct order and facing in the same direction. I managed to raise myself up on all fours, spitting a mash of grit and glass, a couple teeth, and a mouthful of blood.

I became aware of running feet and lots of yelling. "You better hope that stupid bastard didn't kill himself. The boss wants him alive."

Running feet stopped in my vicinity. A pair of wing-tipped cordovan Florsheims appeared in my limited field of vision, staring at the dirt. "Here he is."

"Is he alive?"

"Yea, he's over here coughing up his cookies."

I wanted to reach for my .45, but I just couldn't seem to do it. It was all I could do to just sit here and breathe. I didn't want to lose consciousness.

More running feet to where I was puking pavement grit and periodontal particles into the dirt in front of me.

"Get him on his feet and let's get out of here."

They hoisted me up, stripped me of my .45, and dragged me over to a waiting sedan. I was tossed into the backseat, and two hulking meatballs sandwiched me from either side. Two others piled into the front, and we were off down the road with another carload of gunzels following.

We drove along the hills behind Avalon as the sun began to rise over the distant mainland to the east and the beautiful blue Pacific below. We turned toward the harbor on Clarissa Avenue, on the south side of Avalon, and around to Pebbly Beach Road that led past Lover's Cove and the shipping tarmac. We began the climb up the road to the southern end of the island, then turned into the entrance to the rock quarry.

The two sedans drove up the dust-choked road to a ramshackle wooden complex of foreman's quarters, maintenance shacks, and equipment sheds. We pulled to a stop at one of the large equipment sheds. I was yanked out of the car and shoved through a pair of wide barn doors. Once inside, I was roughly pushed to the dusty wood floor with a thud. I lay on my face with my hands cuffed behind me. I heard the rattle of chain as an overhead wench was maneuvered into place, and the ratcheting clank as the chain was released and hit the floor. They dragged me to the chain and placed a hook in the links between my cuffs. The pulley handle cranked around and the chain hooked between my cuffs ratcheted tight and pulled me off the ground. I hung about a foot off the floor, with my arms pulled backward at the shoulder.

Before the burly beef shanks departed, one of them gave me a crushing punch into my midsection, knocking all the wind out of me, but allowing me to pull my legs up to my chest and at the same time hook my fingers through my belt behind me. That subtle maneuver allowed me to take the increasing pressure off my shoulders and transfer that pressure to a more evenly balanced fulcrum point at my waist, with my wrists and fingers. I wasn't going to be able to endure this way for very long, but at least I wasn't going to eventually dislocate my shoulders. I didn't need that punch to the belly. I was having trouble regaining my breath.

They sadistically chuckled to themselves, eagerly anticipating their early-morning brass-knuckle workout. They eventually retreated to their ongoing poker game, under the glaring droplight in the corner, and inspecting my Browning automatic and the ammo they retrieved from the scene of the accident. They seemed to be killing time waiting for somebody's arrival.

♦ ♦ ♦

I swung back and forth, casually assessing my immediate situation. The prognosis didn't look promising from my current vantage point. Curiously, the aforementioned vantage point hearkened me back to my glorious youth as a letterman on the high school gymnastics team, specializing in parallel bars, high bar, and rings. (Funny how the mind works.) I prided myself, or perhaps deluded myself, into believing that I was still capable of performing most of the more challenging maneuvers demonstrated during my competitive adolescent career. I had better convince myself in a hurry, because I was only going to get one shot at this, and it had to be a flawless routine.

I slowly began to swing back and forth until I got the top of the arch ten or twelve feet off the floor before the assemblage of underachievers in the corner realized that I had become a human pendulum.

"Who the hell does that crazy bastard think he is, Peter Pan?"

They rose in unison from their corner table and slowly wandered over to where I swung back and forth. I hung lifeless from my pendulous industrial trapeze. They gathered about in wonderment as to how I got swinging while hanging semiconscious, without their noticing. There were three of them. They looked at each other and shrugged their shoulders in bewilderment. One of them still carrying my BAR they had been admiring earlier.

The first palooka stepped into the path of my forward trajectory. "Look!" he joked. "He's a swinging punching bag. A moving target." He took a boxing stance, ready to deliver a punishing blow, when I reached the bottom of my forward swing. At the last second, just before the two opposing forces collided, I rose up in my shackles and delivered a blinding scissor kick that caught the unsuspecting dimwit under the chin, swapping his ends and slamming him to the floor hard. He was out cold.

At the top of the front swing, I brought my knees up to my chest and somersaulted forward, pulling my feet inside my handcuffs so that my hands weren't tied behind me any longer. I kicked out and began a backswing, like a circus trapeze artist. I was a flying Wallenda.

It momentarily stunned the remaining knuckle draggers. They couldn't believe it. As I completed the returning backswing and began forward once again, the on-deck batter, warming up with my Browning autographed edition, Louisville Slugger, stepped up to the plate and prepared to swing for the cheap seats.

As the point of impact quickly approached, I kicked up into a handstand as the phantom pitch crossed the plate. The rookie in the batter's box swung through the pitch, like a second-string benchwarmer swatting at an off-speed slider. He did a spinning off-balance pirouette, like a sandlot tee ball munchkin. He turned around just in time to catch both my feet hard into his face on my return backswing. It knocked the shit out of him and stopped my swing cold. I did a backflip dismount, freeing my handcuffs from the hook in the process, and stuck the landing like an Olympic champion. Before the last Mohican knew what hit him, I grabbed my Louisville Slugger off the floor and proceeded to beat the living shit out of him with it.

He made an attempt to grab his gun, but one swift blow from my improvised bat and a broken wrist was all that he extracted, along with a loud yelp of pulverizing pain. I pulped him up good with repeated vicious blows before I finally began to fatigue. I wanted to punish him for the beating I took earlier in the boy's room. I crushed his knees and his elbows with some wicked cracks of my bat. He screamed in agony and winced with excruciating pain, until I delivered the final fatal blow to the bridge of his nose, crushing his skull and caving in his face. I stumbled away, dropped my bloody metal club, and crumbled to the floor in complete exhaustion, heaving breath, and overwhelming pain.

I lay there gasping for air for what seemed an eternity. I slowly pulled myself off the floor and began searching through the pockets of my unconscious assailants for the keys to my handcuffs and all their concealed weaponry. I eventually found the keys and released my handcuffs. I rolled the *gumba* with the caved-in cranium on his stomach and handcuffed his pulverized wrists behind him, then replaced the key into the pocket of one of his buddies.

The first palooka that ate my perfectly timed scissor kick began to groan his way back to consciousness. I took the rookie batter's .44 Magnum and fired one round into the groaning gunzel's chest, with an explosion that shook the rafters and scattered the pigeons aloft. I then took his gun and put one through his friend in the handcuffs, and likewise with his weapon fired into the third guy. I replaced all their weapons into their respective owners' hands and placed their fingers on the triggers, including the dipshit with his hands tied behind his back. That ought to confuse the hell out of the investigating officer. "They all shot each other."

♦   ♦   ♦

Suddenly, I heard the sound of a car roaring up the road. I grabbed my Browning off the floor and ran for cover in the corner behind the overturned poker table. I reached up and turned off the overhead light, then put a fresh magazine into my gun. I had two or three full clips left in the ammo box, and my duffle bag was stuffed in there as well.

The sedan pulled to a stop outside the shed entrance. All four doors slammed shut, followed by a muffled conversation. The large barn door slowly opened just a crack. Cautiously, one by one, three hulking figures, guns drawn, entered the shadows of the building and quietly slinked along the wall until they came upon the first hapless victim. More muffled conversation. They eventually found all three.

"Vinny! What the hell is going on in there?" came a voice from the outside.

I recognized that voice. It was none other than the don, Dominick Licata himself.

"Don't come in, boss. They're all dead."

The three dark figures spread out across the room and began to advance toward my position in coordinated unison. They took cover behind crates, machinery, and stanchion posts as they moved slowly toward me. I couldn't figure out how they knew where I was. I looked over my head and found my answer. In my haste, I left the droplight swinging when I hurriedly switched it off. Oh well, shit happens. Now it was about to hit the fan. Let the fun begin.

I took three deep breaths and gathered my cojones. I leaped up from behind my overturned poker-table bastion of safety and opened fire with a continuous ear-shattering blast of fiery explosions that I sprayed across the room, shredding everything in its path with vengeance of Browning and brimstone wrath.

I emptied the clip then ducked down behind my impromptu and inadequate barricade to reload. My sufficiently overwhelmed adversaries made a hasty and chaotic stampede toward the exit, like the place was on fire. Amid a lot of yelling and screaming, they piled into the sedan and made a harried retreat back down the road in a cloud of dust toward the quarry entrance. I grabbed the ammo box and ran in pursuit through the thick cloud of acrid blue smoke that filled the room.

I jumped into the sedan in which I had unceremoniously arrived and had her racing down the road close behind Licata and his band of henchmen. Before they left the compound, I fired a burst through the passenger-side windshield of my car and rammed the barrel of my Browning out through the newly created gun slot, supporting it on the dash. I could pivot the barrel back and forth like a gun turret out the front of a marauding tank.

I chased them down the road firing sporadic bursts, puncturing their sedan repeatedly with volleys of metal-shredding rounds that tore through their car with white-hot shrapnel and sparks of ricocheted bullet fragments, like Chinese skyrockets on the Fourth of July.

They drove out of the quarry entrance and made a tire-screeching hard left out onto the main road headed back toward Avalon. I followed through the clouds of dust and out onto the road, firing blindly, taking out the hood ornament and several coats of paint off the front of my pursuing sedan.

I ejected the spent clip and inserted a fresh one, while careening off the hillside on my left and the indigenous rock pilings intermittently dispersed along the road on my right. I grabbed the remaining magazines from the ammo box and stuffed them into my pocket. I took my duffle from the ammo box and placed it on the seat beside me, then shoved the box through the passenger-side window to tumble down the rugged cliff and into the thrashing surf below. (I had a momentary flashback of the terrifying runaway train wreck of a bobsled ride that Lara Rigney and I experienced at the conclusion of my initial island tour during my maiden voyage, which now seemed not so long ago. As I so vividly recall, we flew off a tall cliff, in a small roadster, at high speed, and crashed into a cold, hard, deep blue ocean. The sea was angry that day, my friend.)

After a series of sharp switchback curves, we came to a relative straightaway etched precariously into the rugged cliff face. I fired several short bursts from my makeshift battle tank as the fleeing sedan disappeared around the next corner to the left. I heard the sharp bang as the sedan sideswiped the hillside just out of view.

When I rounded the corner, I could see that I had punctured the left rear tire of the sedan and it had begun to fishtail back and forth across the steep, narrow road as we careened, out of control, toward the unsuspecting quaint little hamlet that was Avalon.

Suddenly, at the bottom of the hill, the fleeing sedan swerved hard to the right in a wide broadside slide, verging on a high-speed rollover. It careened downed the road and through the open gates of the shipping tarmac. I yanked the wheel to the right, which began a wide, sweeping slide, where the back end of the car almost caught up to the front end, on my left side.

I turned to the left and stomped the gas pedal. Amid the roar of the engine and the belching clouds of screaming rubber, the sedan slowly drifted back to the right, into a straight line, and roared headlong toward the tong hatchet men, now scrambling to close the gates before my imminent, unexpected arrival.

Incoming rounds began to puncture the radiator, ricochet off the top, and shatter the remaining half of the windshield, as I raced toward the tall chain-link gates. I sprayed a continuous burst of gunfire back and forth across the entrance, scattering the ragtag assemblage of miscreant riffraff, like bilge rats abandoning a burning ship.

I smashed through the gates and drove full speed toward the abandoned warehouse at the far end of the now-vacant tarmac, where the bullet-riddled sedan was parked. The fishing-fleet blockade of the harbor had brought the shipping docks to a standstill.

The sedan smashed through the warehouse doors and continued across the immense interior at full speed. I grabbed my duffle and the Browning, opened the door, and stepped out onto the running board. I jumped off as the sedan roared by an abandoned pile of cargo nets and shipping tarps. I performed a couple of inadvertent cartwheels then plowed into the stack of tarps and nets with a sudden thud. The sedan careened across the warehouse and smashed through the doors on the other side. It seemed to lose very little steam as it roared across the shipping dock and launched into the air, crashing down into an armada of boats tied together at dockside with a horrendous fiery explosion. The sky immediately filled with dense billowing clouds of black smoke and roaring flames leaped furiously from boat to boat in a raging conflagration. Small explosions erupted from beneath the decks, and detonating small arms rounds crackled within the ensuing inferno, like Mexican firecrackers at a wedding fiesta.

Incoming rounds began to ricochet off the concrete floor and impact into the pile of nets and tarps behind which I currently took refuge. Licata and three of his henchmen where making a hasty retreat to a set of offices at the far end of the open building. I returned fire sporadically until they had disappeared behind the office facade. I could hear them barricading the door with filing cabinets and desks. They climbed up on their makeshift barricade and began firing through the transom window over the door. They were going to the mats and made a stand from within their fortified bunker. It was going to be a "shootout at the OK Corral."

I put a fresh clip in my Browning—the last one—and took a quick inventory of available options. Thunderous, fiery explosions continued to erupt along dockside, as the ordnance aboard the assembled armada detonated with earth-shattering hellfire explosions that sent raging flames of brimstone high into the fiercely billowing clouds of choking black smoke rising high over the harbor. Blaring sirens began to converge on the shipping tarmac from all areas of the island. The conflagration continued unabated, furiously consuming the entire fleet assembled at dockside. Horrendous explosion after explosion kept the fire brigade at bay and subjugated to fighting the collateral fires that began to spread to the docks and adjoining warehouses and storage buildings.

I retreated, under continuing fire from the fortified bunker at the end of the building, to an abandoned forklift sitting idle next to a stack of wooden pallets. I climbed aboard and fired her up. This particular forklift was not equipped with the standard forks, designed to lift and transport shipping pallets, but rather one single long stinger, like a big steel javelin, which was designed to be inserted into immense rolls of carpet or any cargo that shipped in large rolls: sailcloth, iron, clay, and concrete pipe, fabricated copper tubing, rolled-steel drill casings, etc.

I took a brief moment to familiarize myself with the controls. I elevated the long metal stinger and the thick metal plate that attached it to the lift so that it served as a steel shield for the driver, and with the stinger about four feet off the floor.

I propped my Browning on the lift, to the right of the metal shield in front of me, and looked through a small slot in the thick metal plate in order to navigate without mishap. I grabbed a handful of steering wheel with one hand and a firm grip on my Browning with the other. I mashed down the go pedal and slipped my foot off the clutch, slamming her into forward with a lurch and a squeal of tires on the concrete floor. I sprayed a continuous blast of thunderous gunfire as the forklift raced across the warehouse, gaining speed, hurtling toward the barricaded fortress.

Just before impact, I tossed the Browning to the side and braced for the impending train wreck. The metal stinger punctured the office wall twelve feet ahead of the runaway forklift, like a SWAT team battering ram smashing through a crack house door. (Whatever that is.)

My personalized minitank plowed through the wall with an explosion of splintered desks and the shrapnel of shredded filing cabinets, amid a snowstorm of fluttering documents. The stinger caught one of Licata's thugs square in the chest, driving him backward into the cinder block wall at the end of the room, impaling him to the wall and continuing through him until the forklift came to a jolting stop when it hit the wall, smashing the unwitting gunzel in between, pushing his guts out both ends and bulging his eyeballs.

I leaped from my smoldering battering ram and fired a couple of rounds from my O'Malley .45. The muzzle blasts belched thunder and lightning like close-quarter cannon fire. I hit one of Licata's boys in the chest, lifting him off the ground and slamming him to the floor, spraying most of his innards across the far wall. The third gunzel was scrambling for an exit, like he was trampling old ladies and kids in the middle of a fire drill.

I left the relative security of my minitank to dash across a short distance of the open floor, firing several cover rounds in Licata's direction in the corner as I ran. I followed the gunzel in hasty retreat through the gaping hole that my mechanical rendition of a medieval armored horse and jousting javelin had created. I ran after him firing in rapid succession as I went. He got within steps of the ragged opening that once was large barn doors, through which I drove the sedan upon my unannounced arrival, before a couple of rounds found their mark, and he went down hard sprawling across the floor like a tattered rag doll. I ran up to him and quickly put two more into him before the clip emptied. I ejected the spent magazine and replaced it with a full one—my last.

The building began to fill with smoke from the rampaging fire that relentlessly swept over the helpless fleet at dockside. The immense flames began to reach toward the building itself and it too began to burn. The fire spread quickly throughout the old wood structure.

I ran back through the smoke into the nearly destroyed office, looking for Nick Licata. I had a score to settle, once and for all. I stuck my head quickly through the ragged hole in the wall, then pulled it back just as quickly. Instantly, a well-thrown ice pick hit the wall, not one inch from my eye, and imbedded itself almost to the hilt, with a sharp *chunk* sound. I yanked the ice pick out of the wall and moved into the room behind several blasts from my O'Malley hand cannon.

LA mob boss, respected organized crime czar, and infamous hit man Nick the Pick Licata stood against the wall with his hands up, screaming hysterically, "Don't shoot! Don't shoot! We've got to get out of here, the place is on fire!"

I took maybe two steps forward and threw the ice pick as hard as I could. It hissed through the air, impacting the middle of his right palm, impaling it to the wall with a harsh thud. He screamed in agony, grabbing his right wrist with his free hand and trying in vain to pull his hand off the wall.

I mercilessly bitch-slapped him across the face with much persuasion.

"Shut the fuck up!" I screamed directly into his face and slammed him upside his head with Mom's .45. I bashed him in the head once more for good measure. I was "maxihyped" and chomping at the bit to jack this bastard up.

Flames began to lick through the roof and creep down the walls overhead. It wouldn't be long before the structure collapsed upon us in an immense funeral pyre. I jammed the muzzle of the big .45 hard into the mouth of the terrified mob boss.

"I want to know what happened to Johnny Rigney," I growled into his face, eye to eye.

"I had nothing to do with that," he pleaded. "That was a final extortion attempt ordered by the commission, the Five Families. It was an extortion attempt gone wrong."

"Keep talking, Nick, or I'll leave you here to burn," I threatened.

"I don't know anything else. Something went wrong and Johnny was killed. That's all I know, I swear!" he yelled, grimacing with pain.

I unleashed a ferocious barrage of punches and kicks to his body, like he was a gym punching bag. The last was a flying side kick that crushed his kneecap and left him hanging from his impaled hand and screaming in agony.

"It was Tony Cornero!" he screamed, while struggling with his good leg to stay upright and relieve the pressure from his hand. "It was Tony and his brothers Frank and Louis. They hijacked Johnny at sea and tried to persuade him to sign over the rights to the gaming venues at the casino. Johnny resisted, there was a scuffle, and he was accidentally killed. It wasn't supposed to happen like that. Nicky Fallon was our inside man. The takeover of the casino was to be handled with finesse and subtle persuasion. But Nicky didn't have the balls it took to get the job done in a reasonable period of time, and the Five Families were losing their patience. They had been down that road before in Vegas, with Bugsy Siegel. They weren't going to make that mistake again. When the casino skim got ripped off, that was the last straw."

"They killed Nicky Fallon and tried to frame you for it. Kill two birds with one stone is how they figured it."

"Freeze, Dugan! Drop the gun," came the command from a familiar voice behind me.

I let the .45 drop from my hand and thump to the floor. I slowly turned around to face Tony Cornero himself. He had an equally intimidating .45 auto trained on me. I was a dead man.

"Well, Dugan, now that Dominick has spilled his guts, I guess you know the whole story. He's right. It wasn't supposed to go like that. It should have been a smooth transition, but Nicky Fallon got too close to the Rigney family and couldn't muster the cojones it took to get the job done. Nicky was well educated in the finest traditions of 'high societies,' Ivy League cultural elite, but he was an ineffectual novice when it came to street smarts. He let personal loyalties get in the way of business.

"We tried to negotiate an equitable agreement with Johnny Rigney, but he was just too hardheaded. He stubbornly resisted our final offer. A scuffle ensued and he was accidentally shot. At that point there was nothing we could do but kill the deckhand and scuttle the boat.

"With pressure mounting from the Five Families, we made one final attempt to negotiate directly with the Commodore. It became obvious that you were going to be the obstructionist in our negotiations, and that Mr. Rigney was just as obstinate and hardheaded as his son Johnny.

"So here we are, Dugan. You've fucked up the whole program, and it's about to burn down around you."

It was an extremely literal observation. He wasn't exaggerating. The entire building was engulfed in massive raging flames and huge billowing clouds of thick black smoke. Large sections of the roof and walls began to cave in all around us. Immense funeral pyres crumpled to the floor as the entire building began to collapse in flaming heaps.

Nick Licata screamed hysterically and futilely tried to yank out the ice pick impaling his hand to the now-disintegrating wall of scorching flames.

Tony Cornero took a few steps forward. "Nothing personal, Nick, it's just business. You're not the boss anymore. How ironic, hey, Nicky Boy. You're passing the torch, so to speak. Trial by fire, as it were." He smirked, leveled the .45 at Licata, and pulled the trigger.

The explosion scorched my face and hands with red-hot powder burns and shattered my eardrums. The bullet passed through Nick Licata's left hand, upraised in defensive posture, and hit him in the left temple, blasting out the opposite side of his head, along with a sizable chunk of smoldering wall.

In one quick move I leaped onto the wall, like Spider-Man, pinning Licata's wrist with my right foot and grabbing the handle of the ice pick with my right hand. I lunged off the wall, dived toward Cornero, and threw the ice pick with deadly accuracy. It hissed through the air and struck him right between the eyes with a thud, penetrating to the hilt. (Bull's-eye.)

I lay upon the smoldering floor and watched as Cornero gazed at me with astonishment etched upon his ashen face. He reached up and grasped the handle protruding from his forehead. He calmly extracted the thin chrome shaft from his cranial lobe and held it out, as if it were a classroom presentation of show-and-tell. He looked at me and smiled. There was no blood. None on the ice pick or from the neat symmetrical wound in his forehead. He slowly raised his .45 until I was staring down the business end of it. It was ugly from this angle.

Suddenly, a thin stream of blood began pulsating from the hole in his forehead. His eyes dulled into a lifeless stare, and the remaining color drained from his already-ashen face. His arm went limp and the gun dropped to the floor. Then, his eyes rolled back and he simply keeled over backward, hitting flat on the floor with a deadweight thud, amid a cloud of smoke and dust.

The wall behind me collapsed, pinning me to the floor under a pile of flaming debris. I lay helpless under the flames, gasping for air, my lungs filling with searing black smoke, and unable to move. Fade to black.

Chapter Eighteen

The melodic song of meadowlark. The enchanting aroma of morning glory. The warm glow of early light. I must be in heaven. I thought I was dead. I was not scared, but I was afraid to open my eyes. I wondered if I even had eyes. I wondered if I had arms and legs.

I began to concentrate on trying to move my fingers and toes. I wondered if I even had fingers and toes. The familiar voices of the Andrews Sisters and their swing wartime rendition of "Boogie Woogie Bugle Boy from Company B" began to filter into my consciousness from somewhere afar. I thought that I was actually wiggling my fingers and toes. I felt myself breathing. I felt someone caressing me. I felt a soft hand on my cheek. Maybe I was not dead. Oh god, I hoped I was not all burned up. I hoped I was not all screwed up. I hoped I could still communicate to them to "pull the plug." I was not aware of any pain.

"Travis? Travis, can you hear me?" came the soft whisper. "Travis, please try to open your eyes. Please come back to us, Travis."

I slowly opened my eyes. The beautiful, soft vision of Yung He's gorgeous ebony eyes and her warm, comforting smile slowly came into focus.

"Aloha, baby," I whispered.

Her eyes welled up with tears. She held me close and began to softly cry.

"Where am I?" I asked.

"You are safe and well in Avalon hospital. We are all safe and well, thanks to you, Travis. It is all over. You have liberated my people from their oppressors, and at the same time you have freed the Rigney family from the grips of their plundering invaders as well. Oh Travis, my people are so grateful and joyous. You have made them so happy. Your courage saved many of my people from injury or death. The armada of boats that you destroyed at the shipping docks were laden with many weapons and explosives. They were preparing to attack the Cooley Town boats blockading the shipping harbor that night. You have rescued the hopes and dreams of the local inhabitants and prevented their suffering much pain and loss, and we will always be in your debt. I am so grateful, Travis. I love you so much."

She lay gently upon me, held me close, and softly wept. Catharsis.

I let her cry it out. It felt wonderful to hold her. I finally asked about her injury. She slowly sat up with a soft smile beginning to form on her beautiful, innocent face. She wiped away a wisp of dark hair and a tear from her cheek.

"You are very sweet to be concerned about my insignificant wound, Travis. It is who you are, however, a rough, tough exterior that allows no one to approach, and yet, a warm, compassionate heart and virtuous soul within. You are a lamb in wolves' clothing."

She pulled aside the top of her blouse to show me the small gauze dressing on either side of her shoulder.

"It gives me little discomfort, and I have full range of motion."

"Why am I here?" I finally asked. "What's wrong with me?"

A wide smile brightened her face. She pulled back the sheet and the hospital gown, exposing various patches of scabbing road rash from my head to my toes. Rainbows of discolored old and newly developing bruises, along with a matching set of raw, scraped, and crusting knuckles.

"You live a charmed existence," she said with a wide smile. "I don't know how you managed it, but you have no broken bones and no internal injuries. The doctor was amazed that you have no serious injuries, especially the way in which you initially appeared when you first arrived. He says that you may be discharged as soon as you feel able."

"How did I get here?" I asked.

"Your friend, Inspector Lugar, pulled you from the burning rubble of the collapsed warehouse," she responded. "You are very lucky that he was able to find you. The shipping docks and the warehouses along the tarmac were completely destroyed, along with the armada preparing to attack the blockade of Cooley boats."

I gingerly raised myself and sat on the side of the bed. At that moment Inspector Lugar entered the room.

"Well, well, tough guy, I guess you're going to survive another episode in your continuing saga of self-destructive escapades, hey?" he said with a wide grin. "How are you feeling, Dugan?"

"I'm feeling fine, Lugar. Thanks for saving my life . . . again."

"That's what I'm here for, Polliwog. To drag your sorry ass out from under the smoldering ruins of your own destruction.

"Come on, Dugan, tie the back of that gown closed and shuffle your scabby butt out onto the terrace, I have something I think you're going to want to see," he said, opening the double french doors that led outside.

◆　◆　◆

We went out onto the terrace and over to the brass telescope by the rail overlooking Avalon harbor, far below down the hill. Lugar pointed at the scope then gestured for me to look into it, toward the harbor entrance. I peered into the eyepiece and adjusted the focus.

I had to smile. There, coming into the harbor and being greeted by Avalon's fireboat, spraying a huge plume of water into the air celebrating their arrival, was Captain Wally and Kamikaze Steve aboard the *Bad Penny*, with Dr. Con's Magnum Raptor superyacht in tow. They were escorted into the harbor by the Cooley Town fishing fleet, and the entire population of Avalon lined the piers and beachfront to cheer their arrival and welcome their return. They were hometown heroes, and deservedly so.

Aboard Con's yacht, gathered on the fantail, was the dashing British secret agent Blaine Pond and his equally stunning CIA contemporary Claire Voyent, popping the cork on one of Con's premium champagnes. Joining them for a commemorative toast were none other than the infamous, aristocratic rotund one himself, Sir Arthur Sydney, provocateur and privateer extraordinaire, and his monolithic Chinese sidekick Phangs Pa.

At the rear of the convoy, the U.S. Coast Guard cutter *Ponchatrane* escorted the flotilla into the harbor, flying full colors, with Captain McCrory and crew on deck, resplendent in crisp white class A uniforms. The glorious blasts of ships' horns throughout the area rose festively up the hill from the jubilant celebration occurring below. It was party time in Avalon. (Seemed like the perfect opportunity to initiate an annual carnival celebration.)

Lugar and I leaned on the terrace railing, enjoying the observation of the ensuing celebration below. He offered up one of his Raleigh Filter Kings, took one for himself, and lit both. Yung He kissed me on the cheek, then returned inside to retrieve my clothes and gather my belongings.

"Captain Wally and Kamikaze have already staked claim upon Con's yacht based upon the Abandoned Vessel Salvage Provisions recognized under established international maritime law," he laughed. "Their tentative plan is to convert it to a high-speed hydrofoil superliner, transporting boatloads of ebullient tourists and gamblers to their instant gratification, vacation destination." We both laughed.

"What about Con?" I asked.

"He has apparently disappeared," Lugar responded. "He either escaped or was lost at sea during the melee. Sir Arthur and Phangs Pa initiated the original chase of Con's yacht toward the Channel Islands. They somehow commandeered a boat during Con's hasty escape and utilized Con's own hijacked weaponry against him. They used one of those laser-guided shoulder-launched missiles. Sir Arthur's boat ran out of fuel during the chase, but they were picked up by Captain Wally and Kamikaze and resumed the fight aboard the *Penny*. Con's yacht was eventually disabled out beyond the Channel Islands. Pond and the CIA broad were rescued once the battle was over and the motley crew from the *Penny* had control of Con's yacht. A davit was extended over the side, and one of the rubber Zodiac boats was missing from the deck. There was no crew and no Con aboard. It's a mystery, wrapped in an enigma, surrounded by a riddle."

At that moment Fia and her Samoan brotherhood arrived to expedite my discharge from the hospital and escort me back to the mansion. She ran across the terrace and threw her arms around me.

"Oh Travis, you big dummy. You almost got yourself killed. You scared me to death. You deserve a good spanking when I get you home," she said with wicked little grin.

"With fishnet stockings and stiletto heels?" I queried.

"See, you do remember me," she giggled as she went back inside to supervise. Lugar just smiled and shook his head.

Yung He helped me get dressed, while Fia and the boys arranged my discharge and brought the car around. Lugar went to see Constable Lafargé regarding the logistics required in order to transfer Frank Cornero to Los Angeles to stand trial for the murder of the individual found in the trunk of his car.

Yung He came to me and held me close.

"I must go to meet my cousin Long. We will go to Moonstone Cove and bring my uncle Ah Looey back to Cooley Town. He can stay with Auntie Lola until we are able to arrange more suitable accommodations. I know that my uncle will be anxious to speak with you, and I hope that you are able to see him. It would be my wish to spend some time with you as well."

We looked deep into each other's eyes, then kissed, lingering and passionately. She whispered, "Goodbye," then turned, blew a kiss as she departed, and disappeared out the door.

♦ ♦ ♦

On the way to the mansion, Fia informed me that they were going to begin sending members of the security detail back to the mainland in pairs. They would reduce the "boots on the ground" gradually, as the perceived level of danger subsided.

She said that there was a sizable contingent accompanying Lara and Rita Rigney to the casino this morning to inventory the contents of the vault and inspect for any damage. They were also meeting with the local locksmith to change all entry door locks. They planned to rendezvous with me back at the mansion. She said that they were anxious to see me and practically giddy with excitement.

We drove up the tree-lined drive through the gates and on up the mansion entrance. Spaulding met us in the foyer, and even he seemed relaxed and had a certain lilt in his loafers. He appeared genuinely happy to see me. An expression rarely seen from him as of late.

"If you will follow me out to the terrace, Mr. Dugan, the Commodore is eagerly anticipating your arrival." Spaulding stopped short, as he was prone to do, just before we went out onto the terrace. "Mr. Dugan," he began, "if you will allow me to congratulate you on the success of your assignment, and sincerely thank you for bringing some happiness to this family and particularly Mr. Rigney. I must admit that I had my doubts regarding your conviction and abilities to bring about a satisfactory conclusion to this intricate, perplexing, seemingly impossible situation. To be honest, Mr. Dugan, I didn't believe you to posses the intellect required for such complex intrigues. I perceived you to be just another inept gumshoe that would cut and run as soon as things got rough. I was sure that you were in over your head from the beginning. I apologize for my preconceived prejudices. You are indeed a smart and cunning individual, shrewd enough to take advantage of your adversaries underestimating your abilities to their own detriment."

"So what you are so eloquently trying to say is that I'm not as dumb as I look," I responded with a laugh. Spaulding actually smiled, then turned and proceeded out onto the terrace.

The Commodore rose to his feet upon my arrival and snapped a crisp salute. He appeared as chipper as I had ever seen him. I clicked my heels together and returned the sharpest salute I could muster. He smiled widely, shook my hand with a newfound robustness, and gave me a bear hug that pert near squished my tender stuffing.

"Dugan, I can't begin to tell you how grateful I am that you had the drive and determination to hang in there and see this situation through to a successful conclusion. Just remarkable, son. My family and the people of this beautiful island owe you a tremendous debt of gratitude. Our entire future is once again within our own domain and our hopes and dreams may be pursued as we determine.

"Without your steely nerves, intestinal fortitude, and that stubborn, hardheaded, Irish barroom brawler that prowls the dark spaces of your inner sanctum, our quaint and peaceful sanctuary, our island paradise, would have been transformed into a wicked and sinister nightmare. We were vulnerable and helpless. We were hopeless without you. I owe you my life and the future of my children. I could never repay you for rescuing our hopes and our dreams, son. But you can name your own ticket from here, Dugan. I trust you, I love you, and I regard you as if you were my own son."

He raised his glass in tribute.

"Thank you, Commodore, I appreciate your confidence. I must admit that I was a little concerned about my abilities to unravel such a convoluted convergence of intrigues, mysteries, and conspiracies, with enough rogues' gallery of suspicious characters to fill an Agatha Christie novel. The plot was confusing and you couldn't tell the players without a program. I guess it just exemplifies the old adage, persistence triumphs over resistance every time."

"Oh Dugan, your persistence triumphed in so many ways that I'm sure you don't even realize as of yet."

I looked at him quizzically.

"I've had some very interesting visitors within the last couple of days, not the least of which was my old buddy, J. F. Angelico, commander of the U.S. Coast Guard's Eleventh District headquartered in San Pedro.

"Commander Angelico paid a visit the other day and stayed to have lunch. He was anxious to relay some rather classified information. It seems that they have successfully recovered the two nuclear bombs that were lost during the tragic events leading to General Travis's untimely death in the plane crash at Fairfield several years ago. That is why the Global Explorer has been 'on station' over near San Clemente Island, and just outside Smuggler's Cove. Likewise, the reason for the area to be swarming with federal agents representing every acronym in the alphabet. Security as watertight as a frog's ass, and classified to the hilt."

"Apparently," the Commodore continued, "either the torpedoes that you and Kamikaze dropped from your lumbering dive-bomber or the depth charges Captain Wally dropped over the side of the *Bad Penny* found their target and sent the two midget subs to the bottom. They still had the nuclear bombs attached to their hulls, by way of some sort of cable and pulley apparatus that had been fabricated for just such a deepwater retrieval operation. Quite an ingenious piece of engineering, really. Basically the same engineering techniques utilized to design and build the Global Explorer, according to other visitors I've entertained recently from the CIA and British MI5. I can tell you, Dugan, there seemed to be a collective sigh of relief from everyone to whom I've spoken. They don't 'officially' care 'how' you did it. They're just 'unofficially' damn glad you did. Of course, they are anxious to debrief you for the investigative record, but they are likewise willing to overlook the unorthodox and legally questionable methods you employed to execute the operation to a satisfactory conclusion. In this case, the ends justify the means."

The Commodore leaned back in his chair and laughed hardily. It was the best laugh I'd heard from the old man since I'd known him. It was deeply gratifying to see the old man in such good spirits. There seemed to be a great weight lifted from his shoulders. He was of great spirit and looked and acted ten years younger. There was a sparkle in his eyes and a song in his heart.

The girls arrived on the terrace amid bright smiles and giggly exuberance. They ran to me and smothered me with group hugs and a shower of jubilant kisses. They were bubbling over with excitement and joy, like effervescent schoolgirls at their freshman "sock hop." They were bebopping bobby-soxers in fuzzy sweaters, poodle skirts, and saddle shoes. Their exuberance was infectious and heartwarming. I felt a warm fuzziness inside. (Maybe it was the brandy hors d'oeuvre?)

The girls excitedly reported simultaneously what they had found upon entering the casino. Apparently, in their haste to abandon ship and desert the island, Cornero's henchmen and Licata's gunzels left everything, for the most part, intact. Their impromptu departure left them little time to loot the vault, or ransack the casino. It would take very little to reopen and continue operations as before. Lara and Rita were obviously relieved, and the Commodore was likewise happy and content with the ultimate outcome.

Spaulding arrived with brunch, and we casually enjoyed the warm sunshine, delicious spread, and friendly banter. Lara and Rita were excited to get a financial audit completed so that the casino would be able to reopen with a clean slate, restocked, refreshed, and ready for the scheduled appearance of Spade Cooley and his Western swing band and the opening act of Bob Wills and the Texas Playboys, due to debut their new hit "Tumbling Tumbleweeds" within the next few days. The girls were anxious to get their affairs in order and get back to their former lives. They wanted to conclude this troubled chapter in their lives and move on.

Upon the conclusion of our meal, the girls were off to their respective appointments. Lara was to attend an emergency meeting of the Avalon town council to discuss immediate options available to logistically resupply the island's exhausted necessities, utilizing the steamer pier and the piers located at the Tuna Club and the Yacht Club. The town council was also to address the rebuilding of the shipping docks and the storage warehouses adjacent to the tarmac, which were destroyed in the fire. There was also an immediate need to salvage the destroyed and sunken blockade-busting armada and remove the debris from the harbor.

Rita was off to the casino to arrange for an independent audit of the casino's books and to begin an inventory audit in order to expedite the resupply and reopening of the casino and the ballroom on schedule. They were going to have their hands full and be very busy girls in the next few days. And they were loving it.

I sat with the Commodore for a while, enjoying a short brandy and a long Havana. The sun was high in the clear, bright afternoon sky. I began to realize an uneasy feeling creeping up on me. (I hate when that happens.) I felt antsy. An uncomfortable wave of anxiety swept over me. A sudden attack of attention deficit disorder . . . (Whatever that is.)

It was that familiar nagging feeling in the pit of my stomach. That knot in my gut that told me that there was something not right in my universe. Something out of whack in my world. Time to mount up, ride out, and scout the perimeters.

But there was something different about this. Something different that I hadn't felt in a very long time. I hoped that I was wrong. It was a feeling that I had buried long ago. A memory that I had suppressed. Denial, I didn't want to remember this feeling. But, I remembered . . . I remembered all too well. (I had a real bad feeling about this.)

Chapter Nineteen

I borrowed the little red Muntz Mobile and had it heading up the road toward the airport, after stopping briefly in town to purchase a bouquet of wildflowers. It was an Avalon Chamber of Commerce picture-postcard day. The sun was still high overhead in a clear blue afternoon sky, with wisps of puffy white "cotton ball" clouds that slowly drifted along with the gentle ocean breeze.

Try as I might, I could not ignore the overwhelming feeling of melancholy that swept over me and the growing knot in the pit of my stomach. But this was different. This wasn't the normal gut feeling I got when something was askew in my world. This was an agonizing, gut-wrenching pain that had to do with affairs of the heart. A persistent ache that left you hollow and empty inside. It was a feeling that I had locked away and tried to forget a long time ago. But yes, I did remember . . . I remembered all too well.

We had been together a long time. What began as a high school infatuation soon grew into a blossoming romance and eventually a deep and passionate love affair. We were always together and we knew each other's most intimate needs and desires. When anyone spoke of us, it was always us, together. We began as high school sweethearts, and we had grown into enduring and compassionate lovers, deeply committed to one another, preparing to build our life together . . . forever.

Then came the war, the call to serve, and my first tour of duty in the Pacific. At first, the letters from home were upbeat, enthusiastic, and filled with warmth and eager anticipation of my return. Then, over time, the letters became more infrequent and the tone had changed.

They became distant, melancholy, and remorseful. Something had changed. It was unsaid, but I knew. There was someone else in her life. My whole world was falling apart back at home, and I was half a world away, helpless, and unable to do anything about it. I never felt so lonely. Eventually, I stopped writing home altogether. I was alone. I didn't care if I lived, or died.

Oh, she was there to greet me at dockside when the troop ship returned to Long Beach after my first tour, but something was different. The sparkle in her eyes, when we were together, had been replaced with torment, sadness, and regret. Her warm, loving smile was now drawn and superficial. Her tender caress became empty and shallow. Things had changed, and it brought tears to our eyes. We knew it would never be the same.

We tried to make it work for a while, but we both knew it was sadly coming to an end. Finally, one evening on our way home, I asked, "We aren't going to make it, are we?"

Her reply to me was, "You're sort of in the way now."

I was crushed. I felt like my guts had been kicked in and my heart had been ripped out. I was left with a jagged, gaping wound that would never heal. An empty, hollow void. A void around which I built an impenetrable wall. An impregnable barrier surrounding my innermost feelings and my broken heart that I would never again allow anyone to approach. I was never going to be vulnerable or allow myself to be hurt again.

Sadly, I never saw that girl again. I think of her often, and still miss her terribly. Such a shame. I often wonder what could have been? What would have been? What should have been? After all these years, I still have an emptiness in my heart for her. After all these years, I still love her. I suppose I always will. I guess it must have something to do with one's first love. (Funny how life goes.)

♦ ♦ ♦

I crested the top of the hill and passed by the nearly vacant postage-stamp-sized 'Airport in the Sky.' All the dubiously affiliated, questionably registered, and anonymously painted aircraft that had clogged the limited space on the gravel plateau, perched precariously atop a steep hill, sandwiched between a series of taller jagged and ominous peaks, had collected their particular piece of the Smuggler's Cove pie and flew off to various undisclosed secret locations.

Farther down the road I passed the entrance to Smuggler's Cove. There was still a contingent of uniformed guards at the gates and several military vehicles parked just inside. As I drove along the ridge overlooking the cove, I could see that the authorities on duty were in the beginning stages of the cleanup operation. Con's supergun had already been dismantled and hauled away, as I assumed had been the case with the two midget subs they had recovered, as the Global Explorer had weighed anchor and put to sea. There were hazardous material personnel in bulky rubber suits loading fifty-five-gallon drums onto pallets, then craning them onto a barge towed by a tugboat. A flotilla of small boats continued to ferry back and forth from the remaining trawlers anchored out near the commercial shipping lanes.

I continued down the narrow road descending toward China Point, all the while becoming more and more aware of the constricting knot growing in my gut. I glanced at the bouquet of flowers on the seat next to me; they seemed to have wilted appreciably during the ride up the hill.

I turned off the main road, such as it was, and drove along the rutted trail across the hillside, which eventually led to the cypress grove and the freshwater pond. I switched off the engine and let the little red roadster coast to a stop in the shade of the towering cypress trees.

It seemed eerily quiet. There was no gentle coo of the dove high up in the canopy or the melodic song of the meadowlark in the bright yellow hills carpeted in mustard weed. No buzz of the honeybee amongst the scattered clumps of bright orange poppies, or ratchet of the grasshopper within the deep red and bright green of the Manzanita.

I walked up the hill through the cypress and eucalyptus grove, to the corral. Dakota was happily munching on fresh fruit and a bucketful of oats. He gave me a slight nod of recognition as I passed, a swish of his long tail, then back to his equine smorgasbord. I continued past the bubbling grotto and up to the cabin entrance. There was no one inside, but someone was around. There were smoldering embers in the fireplace, and the familiar fur rug on the floor next to the hearth. Two goblets with remnants of the dreaded agave juice in the bottom and the intricately designed peyote pipe on the table. The hardening knot in my stomach had grown as big as my fist, and the pain emanating from it was becoming debilitating.

I walked back out onto the porch, then to the right around the corner of the cabin toward the edge of the cliff face that dropped precipitously to a small cove and secluded beach far below. As I began to descend the narrow path precariously etched into the cliff face, I noticed Max von Jekyle's camouflaged PT boat anchored in the shallow cove. The knot in my gut twisted one notch tighter. I thought to myself, *Why go down there? What I don't know won't hurt me. But as always, I'm foolishly going anyway..*

I proceeded down the narrow path toward the intimate white-sand beach. I didn't get far before I heard the familiar screams of ecstasy and cries of passion, like a foreboding ill wind sweeping up the cliff face.

Her wild mane of jet-black hair cascaded down the arching beauty of her dark glistening back. Facing skyward, mouth wide, gasping for air with each powerful thrust, until the final primal conquest. She slowly melted down upon him, exhausted and spent. Von Jekyle rolled her over and began to aggressively pile-drive her into the sand. He pounded her into the beach relentlessly with powerful thrusts that brought corresponding squeals of satisfaction from Raven, writhing wildly beneath him.

I turned and began to retrace my steps up the narrow path back toward the cabin, as the last climactic shrieks of rapture raced up the jagged cliff and tore through my insides like a barrage of an assassin's daggers. I stumbled across the porch and continued down the hill, away from the compound, unable to breathe, my knees threatening to buckle and my guts hollowed and empty.

I stopped to lean against an outcropping of granite boulders, some twenty yards beyond the cabin. I felt like I was going to puke. I felt "clammy" and began to sweat profusely. My mind was numb. I just stood there in the shade of the big rocks.

I heard them laughing as they came up the path and onto the porch. The song of the "Mango Tree" abruptly ceased when they noticed me standing down the hill. She said something to Von Jekyle, and he continued around the cabin toward the grotto. He gave me a curious smirk as he turned toward the grotto and disappeared around the corner into the bubbling water and sulfur steam.

Grasped firmly in the bastard's meaty, gnarled fist was the golden dragon. That son of a bitch had recovered the golden dragon. If there were any scurvy, syphilis-infested pirates in the centuries of sorted history related to that cursed jewel-encrusted deity that were least deserving of this treasure, it would be Max von Jekyle. While the rest of us were trying desperately to save the island from annihilation, this asshole was busy diving for sunken treasure.

Raven walked cautiously toward me. The look in her eyes told me that she was not happy to see me. Something inside told me that "I was sort of in the way now." She walked toward me and raised her index finger, as if to scold. "Remember, Travis, no strings . . . no conditions." She simply turned and walked away, disappearing into the grotto mist. She never looked back. She just walked away.

I stood and stared at the ground in front of me for a few moments. It was like déjà vu all over again. The same hollow emptiness inside. The pain of ripping open an old wound. The same feeling of life draining from you. The familiar loneliness. The impenetrable wall had been breached, exposing the inner darkness and despair. There was nothing left.

I walked back down the hill through the cypress grove to the roadster. Just then I heard a car coming up the road and stop at the cabin. I hurried back up the hill toward the compound. As I reached the edge of the grove, I could see a police squad car parked near the grotto. Suddenly, two quick gunshots rang out from inside the grotto. I ran toward the grotto just as Constable Lafargé came running out, holding the golden dragon. He was astonished to see me and swung the statue with a vengeance, striking me in the shoulder as I ducked away, sending me to the ground hard. He jammed the dragon into his prosthetic hand and reached for his gun. I lay on the ground and quickly scissor-kicked, sweeping his feet from under him and slamming him to the ground flat on his back with a thud. I leaped upon him as he cleared the holster with his gun. We wrestled around on the ground for the gun, while he slammed me in the head repeatedly with the golden statuette. I finally wrestled the dragon out of his prosthetic grip and began to smash him in the face with it over and over again. I pummeled him with the golden statuette until his face was a pulping mush, and I couldn't swing the golden hammer anymore.

I slowly got to my feet and stumbled to the grotto entrance. In the bubbling mist, Raven and Von Jekyle stared, eyes vacant, each with a small hole in the middle of their foreheads. As had been with all the others who had possessed the gold and jewel-encrusted deity, they had come to a scurrilous demise and never realized the spoils of their cursed and evil treasure. They had all been vanquished by the ghosts of its ancestral past.

I found myself driving north, down the windward side of the island in the direction of the isthmus causeway and Cooley Town beyond. It was a long descent down a lonely narrow road. A familiar route that I had traveled many times before. I passed Little Harbor on the left, where Lara Rigney and I had enjoyed a casual, intimate picnic on the pristine white sands, during my first sojourn to this island paradise. The same pale blue crystalline waters from which Raven emerged, like a beautiful, haunting apparition from my past. I was numb. I felt nothing. Just that familiar hollow emptiness inside. I didn't know where I was going, or why. I didn't know what I was going to do when I got there. I didn't care. I didn't give a shit about anything anymore.

I eventually crossed the isthmus causeway bridge and entered Cooley Town. I took the left fork in the road that would take me by the Filipino pachinko parlors on the windward side of the isthmus, then to Land's End and the Cooley Town Cemetery.

I drove up the caisson trail and parked at the end, near the edge of the treacherous steep cliffs that fell to the crashing surf far below. I glanced down on the seat at the bloodstained golden dragon and the bouquet of flowers that now had become a shriveled pile of shattered memories.

I carried the dragon and the dead flowers across the gently sloping grassy hillside to Chin Lee's grave. I placed the golden statuette at the base of her simple granite headstone and crumbled the fragile bouquet into the offering bowl. I struck a match to the crackling pyre and sat back against her tombstone, staring out to the never-ending expanse of deep blue ocean that stretched to a distant unseen horizon.

I gazed into a clear sky, now in the beginning throws of a glorious scarlet sunset, speckled with the early twinkle of evening stars. I felt the soft breeze against my face. I felt the cool steel of the muzzle in the roof of my mouth. I cocked back the hammer. My name is Dugan. Travis Dugan . . .

THE END

Epilogue

Well, Precocious, I suppose it's become all too obvious that the initial indications suggesting of my untimely demise were slightly exaggerated, factually inaccurate, and hopefully somewhat premature.

I know you won't believe what happened. I scarcely believe it myself. I can't explain it, but I had a vision. At the last moment, just before I pulled the plug on this episodic saga of adventure, I was overwhelmed, consumed by a warm, comforting apparition. It was Chin Lee. She appeared before me swathed within a gossamer mist. A gauzy silhouette, softly nebulous, cast against an aura of muted sunset. She whispered softly, "Your journey is not yet complete. The path that leads to your destiny still lies ahead. You have far to travel before your journey reaches its conclusion. Your future holds dreams and obligations yet to be fulfilled. Go with confidence, Travis, and let faith in yourself be your guide."

Somehow, Yung He was able to find me. She said that she was mysteriously compelled to venture into the night and bring me home. Equally mysterious, the golden dragon has vanished. Perhaps Chin Lee has mercifully returned it to the cold, dark depths from whence it came. Ultimately, it only brought death to those who possessed it. Death to those it ultimately possessed.

The Avalon town council has apparently approved preliminary building plans to replace Ah Looey's fire-ravaged seaside cabin with a two-story structure that will serve as a medical clinic and apothecary shop on the ground floor and residence for Ah Looey and Yung He on the top floor. Together they plan to provide health and medical care for the Cooley Town residents.

Here's a bit of ironic, idiotic insider island trivia for you, Precocious. Apparently, the aristocratic rotund one, Sir Arthur Sydney, and his monolithic Chinese sidekick, Phangs Pa, have submitted a proposal to the Catalina Steamship Company to lease the *Catalina Steamer* and convert it to a day-cruise ship touring the island, providing luxurious adventure, first-class entertainment, and the finest international cuisine to the world's high-end, elite, top-drawer vacationers. Since Captain Wally and Kamikaze plan to retrofit Con's commandeered megayacht into the sleek and swift *Avalon Express*, a high-speed superliner transporting eager island revelers to and from the mainland on a daily schedule, then it makes some kind of convoluted sense that Sir Arthur's proposal would provide an alternate and viable solution for the future of the venerable and beloved steamship.

On another unimaginable, unforeseen twist of fate, it seems that our own intrepid Inspector Lugar has been offered the job previously occupied and recently vacated by the infamous Constable Lafargé. Lugar previously stated that he was eager to escape the relentless scourge of perverts and predators that stalk the slimy underbelly and back alleys of LA's neon streets, and this may be the perfect opportunity for him to realize the pleasures one might enjoy within island paradise, lush with tropical breezes, exotic refreshments, and friendly natives. He's already sporting the latest fashion in floral-print Hawaiian shirts and the cool comfort of casual footwear. "He's an island boy, bra!" I see dreadlocks in his future, mon! (Whatever those are.)

In another related note, it seems as though your auntie Precious was spot-on regarding one Chief Constable Fontaine Lafargé when she performed a background check on him at my request during my first visit to the island. She stated at the time that he either was running from or had begun a quest for something that took him from French Algiers to Morocco, then to Martinique in the Caribbean. From there he traveled to Havana, then on to Miami. Precious found it intriguing yet disturbing that Lafargé's nearly two-year odyssey would eventually bring him to the island of Santa Catalina. A bit too much of an absurd coincidence according to her. She was right, he was another unfortunate soul, in a centuries-long history of unfortunate souls, in search of the golden dragon, who paid the ultimate price to possess the bedeviled antiquity, but for a brief period of time. Another scurrilous victim doomed by the vengeance of the golden dragon.

British secret agent Blaine Pond and his CIA counterpart Claire Voyent have departed the island and are hot on Dr. Con's trail, reported to be joining forces with the tong in San Francisco's Chinatown. Initial information indicates their involvement in a conspiracy to monopolize a fledgling industry having to do with computers, microchips, and something called silicon. (Whatever that is.)

I'm happy to report that RJ Rigney, the Commodore, has acquired a new lease on life. It seems as though a huge weight has been lifted from his shoulders and he has a newfound "spring in his step." He appears bright, chipper, and anxious to resume the responsibilities as the island's patriarch, as well as embarking on new projects and endeavors. The scuttlebutt on the island is that he has decided to indeed, after all, build the pyramid-shaped, terraced condominiums at Hamilton Cove. The old man is full of surprises. We'll see what comes of the new high-rise casino included in the original plans.

And then, there are the Rigney women. Lara and Rita, the stunningly beautiful island goddesses. Real-life fairy-tale princesses, strong, resilient, and committed to their station in life. Content within their surroundings and confident in their abilities to continue in the spirit and vitality that the Commodore had originally envisioned and had boldly and festively begun.

They also seemed to have had a great weight lifted from them as well. They were now able to conclude a dark and distressing chapter in their lives. I promised the Rigney family some measure of closure from the beginning, and I'm happy that I was able to fulfill my promise to them. They can put this suffering behind them now and move on with their lives, with hope for the future and excitement in the quest for the fulfillment of their dreams. As with all fairy-tale endings, I believe they all will live happily ever after.

And that, Precocious, brings us to yours truly. The befuddled and hapless womanizing whoremonger that at various times has been so eloquently described as reluctant, unambitious, and a decidedly middle-class flatfoot gumshoe. A bewildered slothlike dimwit, totally unprepared and incapable of comprehending the intricacies and entwining complexities hidden within prismatic theories of conspiracy and murder. (Hey, wait just a darn minute. I think I resemble that remark.)

Well, I guess we fooled them again, hey, Precocious? They wouldn't be the first to underestimate my abilities based on my outward appearance of deepwater, tanned, and toned physique, sun-streaked tousle of windswept hair, and my cool, casual, and suave demeanor. Are you buying this line of bull, Precocious? I thought not.

At any rate, I have another bizarre twist of absurdity for you. Hold on to your hat, it could be another Mr. Toad's wild and bumpy ride. But, believe it or not, I have been offered the position of casino manager, working alongside the lovely and vivacious Rita Rigney. How's that for a bolt of lightning out of the blue?

As I mentioned to your auntie Precious upon the conclusion of my last Catalina adventure, "This could be the beginning of a beautiful relationship."

Aloha, baby . . . Sweet dreams.

Writers Guild of America, West, Inc.
7000 West Third Street
Los Angeles, California, 90048-4329
Telephone: 323-782-4500
Fax: 323-782-4803

Documentation of Registration

The Writers Guild of America, West, Inc. issues this certificate to:

GREGORY G. GOODLOE

for the material entitled:

REVENGE OF THE GOLDEN DRAGON

by the following:

GREGORY G. GOODLOE - Writer

Registration #:
Material Type: 1498955
Registered By: MANUSCRIPT
GREGORY G. GOODLOE

Effective Date: 04/07/11
Expiration Date: 04/07/16

0000000049.2011040710434705.0000000012

www.ingramcontent.com/pod-product-compliance
Lightning Source LLC
Chambersburg PA
CBHW020728210626
46807CB00016B/470

www.ingramcontent.com/pod-product-compliance
Lightning Source LLC
Chambersburg PA
CBHW020728210626
46807CB00016B/470